IMMORTALS

When You Thought You Had Forever

PAM FLOYD

First edition January 2024
Editing by:
Astrid Vogel Johnsson
Breanna Floyd
Crab Editing

ASIN (e-book): B0CP33XX47

Disclaimers:

I wish to stress that this book in no way endorses a belief in the occult.

All characters and events in this book are fictitious. Any similarity to any
events or persons (alive or dead) are entirely coincidental.

I touch on the topic about 911 and the Pentagon because my husband worked
there at the time of the accident. It is only in homage to my husband.

Thank you.   .

A NOTE ON THE CONTENT

Please be informed this book includes content that may be difficult for sensitive readers. There is mention of smoking, suicide, death, death of a child, and disappearances. Furthermore, there is mention of the 911 attacks and some inspiration drawn from occult practices.

Immortality is something countless people have sought but the answers are simple...leave your mark.

Will you be immortal because you cure a disease like cancer or be a positive presence on the silver screen? People leave their mark because of great deeds.

My in-laws were indeed great but never had a platform to leave their mark. They did it by having two extraordinary sons. Mom was one of the kindest and greatest people I have ever known.

This is how I love and Immortalize
Ken & Helen Floyd

CONTENTS

CHAPTER 1

T he wet sound of hard slapping was all that could be heard against the soaked pavement. Chris ran until their feet hurt, but they could still hear something close behind. When they hit the mud, they should have worried more about expensive clothes, but the fear of being caught overruled it.

Chris snapped awake. Chris had that dream many times in the past, but never fell asleep in public with it.

Now embarrassed, Chris Shepherd sat up straighter, hoping nobody would recognize them. There was an upper crust crowd in the small port cafe Chris had dozed off in, but everyone seemed too preoccupied to have noticed. The water had seeped into Chris Shepherd's dream, though Chris had not actually been startled awake by the splash of the port.

Chris looked around, worried that strangers would be staring, judging. Everyone seemed engaged with their conversations, but Chris' stomach still twisted in knots as they felt the stares of imagined onlookers. With every step, Chris felt more and more on display, a curiosity that transcended the barriers of gender.

Chris took the mug from the table in front of them and sat up straighter, trying to center themselves again after the torment of the nightmare. True that Chris used to be haunted by the dream.

Their mother had always maintained Chris's dream was about goals because it never specified a location or a purpose for the chase.

That was from when Chris was still poor. Scratch that, when Chris's parents were still poor. Mom and Dad came from very limited means and Chris learned quickly the value of a dollar. Bills meant fear. "Turn off Tuesday" was a term they used to refer to the due date for the water bill. If not, water was off relentlessly by the first Tuesday of each month. When they returned from running errands, they knew to check the porch light, and if it was out, they knew the electricity had been shut off once more. They skipped the extras of cable and phones until they were required to have them for employment and school.

It was this inspiration that led Chris to bring brilliant ideas to life, quite simply – apps. Chris was born with more creativity than anybody else they knew.

Chris developed an app, which a well-known game company eventually purchased. Following this, Chris quickly came to value it in the millions, but their inventiveness continued. They continued to produce new mobile games. From physical fitness, mental sharpness, mindless games, and other activities, the games gave people the idea they had more control in their life or they were smarter than they were. Customers would pay Chris to keep upgrading or to introduce anything that would make it simpler.

Chris felt flustered having slipped off to sleep in the middle of the day. Chris' mother used to say that it appeared that Chris experienced those dreams prior to their revelations.

Chris thought it was a cool detail, but was concerned someone might have seen their lapses.

It was a balmy day in the harbor and Chris found it amusing how many people still donned sweaters. No, it wasn't because they didn't know how to dress; rather, it was because they were ignorant of Baltimore's weather. The expression goes, "you can experience all four seasons in Baltimore in just one week." You see, when these visitors left their hotels it was probably cold, so they dressed warmly, but now it was 85 and climbing. A 30 degree difference isn't something to sneeze at, but something to prepare for. New Baltimoreans quickly learned the need of dressing casually with layers they could doff quickly. Tees over tanks, hoodies beneath coats, or all of the above were acceptable outfit combinations, but dressing for the weather was essential.

Now, these people were stuck in their sweaters, sweat-shirts, and big shoes, whereas Chris was comfortable wearing shorts, a t-shirt, a lightweight sweater, and slides. Chris was still very amused as they sat in the outdoor cafe drinking coffee.

One individual, though, stuck out like a circus clown at a coronation. The man leaned so far back in his chair that it looked as though he would fall if the breeze blew just right. However, it was not the only thing to make him stand out from the crowd. He was dressed beautifully with a vintage top hat. He wore well-fitting dress slacks and a scarlet vest that, in some lights, appeared to be black. Chris could scarcely stop staring at his shoes since these were unlike anything they had ever seen up close. They were covered in white splats and shone like mirrors. To complete his ensemble, the strange man wore a coat with tails that clung to his waist like a second vest.

While he held his coffee cup in one hand, his other hand played with a black cane that had a shining top. His thin mustache appeared to be something a villain might twirl, and the brim of his hat appeared to cast a shadow over his eyes.

Evil?

He didn't appear evil, no. Quite the contrary, he exuded charisma and sexuality. It might be the fact that the vest he was wearing was so low cut you could almost see his abs because he had no dress shirt beneath it. It might have been his penetrating gaze or the intensity of his eyes that drew you in. No, it was confidence and Chris understood confidence was key.

The man had a level of nonchalance and assurance that made him incredibly attractive. In only a few weeks, Chris was sure everyone would be trying to emulate his style. So it went when one was a leader in a flock of sheep. Chris even considered wearing the same outfit to the club on Friday.

Chris hadn't realized how much they stared until that man smiled at them. That man's smile made Chris aware of how long they had been looking at them. Chris felt self-conscious and deliberately turned to look at the harbor. The tables were so close to the docks that you could occasionally feel a mist from the water, and the only sound louder than the gulls' cries were mindless children shouting "mine" at the oblivious birds.

"Can I get you anything else, sir?" Chris overheard a waitress asking someone a question, but Chris was preoccupied watching an approaching boat.

"Ça va," a silver voice with a heavy drawling accent replied.

Chris's eyes furrowed as they closely observed the waitress and the man with the top hat as they spoke.

"Excuse me?" She said from over her pad and paper.

"Ah said ah'm good, *ma chère*," he spoke slowly and languished over his words. People around him seemed to be bewitched by this man and his heavy accent and gave casual glances as he spoke.

She began to move away but he held up a single finger and she stopped. "Yes?"

"Ah want crawfish, si vous plaît?" He smiled at what seemed to be his own joke.

"Crawfish?" She maintained her expression of confusion. Taking a moment to reflect and tapping her pen lightly on her notepad, she never lost sight of the charismatic man in front of her. She added, shifting her weight from foot to foot and hanging on every word. "We don't carry seafood here, sir."

"You got pastries, non?" Seeing her nod, he grinned at her. "Beignets then..." He smiled while taking a sip of coffee. She looked clueless and he sighed. "Dey like fried powdered pastries..."

"Bin-yay?" She asked, touching her pen to her mouth almost obscenely.

He scoffed, "Dat how you gone murder French language?"

She giggled before he dismissed her with a sweep of his hand, at which point she moaned and walked away.

Chris took out their phone to make a note after getting yet another ground-breaking idea. Chris kept peering over at the man who talked on the phone and they wondered what type of French the stranger spoke.

Chris furrowed their brow upon hearing the man's faint chuckle, feeling as though the stranger was daring them to look back. Instead, Chris felt the stranger's gaze intensely scrutinizing them.

The man's sharp, steely eyes appear to pierce right through the soul. Chris and he both appeared reluctant to withdraw as they locked eyes.

"Didn't yo'r momma tell you it ain't polite to stare?" He drawled at Chris but neither of them turned their heads. The man snatched up his coffee and stood in one smooth motion. He took long strides towards the table and Chris realized that this man interpreted the stare as an invitation to a confrontation.

As he got closer, it became apparent how thin this man really was and how every serpent must have learned how to move from him. He placed his coffee beside Chris' without a sound and was so close now Chris could smell smoke mixed with a heavy cologne.

Given that he hadn't been invited, Chris tried to be polite and looked at him. "My stare is equal to your own, sir."

The man slipped into the seat next to Chris and let out a chuckle that was as light as air, "Yo' curious and been staring since yo' notice me." He took a swirling sip from the cup and then gulped it down quickly.

Chris scoffed, feeling robbed of their "me" time, and tapped the phone screen in an attempt to chase the man away. Since they had arrived at the cafe, there had been no emails for Chris to be distracted by, and no texts to respond to. An app where you matched blocks as the lines disappeared and more appeared was Chris's go-to activity. If they combined enough, they would have a bomb that would blast everything, sending them directly to the next level.

Chris could usually skip ahead and make bombs to finish levels, but not right now. The man leaned languidly on his cane, smirking as he did so. Their gazes converged. The arrogant guy turned up the side of his mouth as Chris arched an eyebrow in mock challenge.

The uncomfortable silence was broken by a cry from a nearby table. "He's choking!" Everyone turned to see a woman leap to her feet next to a big male. She stood there with her mouth open, pulling at a huge hat covering her head.

The man kept his mouth open without making a sound while he touched his chest. It wasn't as dramatic as in movies when you hear the victim scream for aid or gasp for air. He wasn't tugging at his throat or attempting to dislodge it by force.

The man on the other hand appeared powerless, and Chris had the impression he looked resigned to his fate. Chris had never seen anything like the forlorn look in the man's eyes. The man touched his chest as though he wanted it to rise. The woman with him continued crying as she called 911 on her mobile phone.

Chris noticed the crowd moving to and fro. The people around Chris were doing whatever they could to get closer to the scene, but there was little they could do. Some were calling emergency services while others pointed their phones and documented the incident in front of them. Meanwhile Chris sat there watching helplessly as many others moved closer to him. They were all so preoccupied with the suffering man that, at first, no one realized he was receiving assistance. Suddenly there was a stranger with hands balled up to squish under his breast bone. Nothing.

Another thrust was so powerful that the choking man lurched forward, still gasping, but his skin tone had become much paler. After another thrust, something emerged. The choking man heaved a loud gasp and seemed not to just breathe but swallowed air like water.

Nobody cheered. In a movie people would have been slapping the rescuer's back or cheering him on. No, this was real life and instead people just sat there. There was a moment of stillness as the man was let loose from the other man's life-saving hold and then everyone rushed over to check on the man who'd choked. Finally, the woman started crying out of gratitude and threw her arms around her portly companion.

The crowd applauded the hero, although their applause was short and hesitant. The coughing man was filled with gratitude but also carried a sense of embarrassment as he stayed seated.

They then became aware of the hero: the janitor. He was nearly half the size of the other man. He murmured something about volunteering as an EMT in his free time.

Chris absentmindedly took their seat without registering the act of standing. The oddly dressed man still remained in his chair, calmly puffing away on a cigarette. He was the only other person in the room who wasn't standing, and he seemed disinterested with his environment. Chris glanced over at him curiously., "You see this sort of thing often?"

"Ah see it all de time." He flicked the ashes from his cigarette into the dainty ashtray.

Chris scoffed, scooting the chair up. "How's that?"

Leaning back in the chair as he had done at his own table, the man muttered, "Ain't his time to be sainted yet, mon cher."

Chris's eyes widened as they stared at the person in front of them and after a few moments of silence, they finally spoke in a quiet voice, "Really?"

The other man grinned cockily with his mouth turned up.

"Call me Deacon," he said with a smile while offering a lazy hand to shake.

Chris's eyes widened at the name that sent chills up their spine. The simple moniker of this striking man sounded like the tolling of a bell, and they struggled not to display a shudder.

Chris took the man's hand and was amazed to feel how smooth his skin was and how thin his fingers were. They were like knobbly pieces of wood, but what was worse was how warm his skin appeared to be, almost burning. "I'm…"

"Ah know who you are." He pulled his hand back, amused.

Chris rolled eyes waiting for him to get to the point. "How do you know me? Is this a set up? Are you out for money?"

He chuckled, "Yo'r face ain't exactly anonymous."

Chris shook off his nervousness and nodded. "So why didn't that shake you?" Chris made a faint gesture toward the spot where the person who had been choking was currently drinking his coffee. "Do you work in a hospital?"

"Like ah said, it ain't his time."

"You're psychic?" Chris sipped the rapidly cooling coffee.

Deacon grinned, leaned closer, and said, "Ah just know. He gestured for Chris to do the same. "There's things in this world we all know exist, but people can't prove, so dey ignore it."

"Ah!" Chris snapped and pulled out some cash for a tip. The entire situation felt odd, and this strangely dressed gentleman appeared to be acting or to be completely callous after witnessing a near death experience while the other patrons buzzed around and doted on the man nearby. Chris nodded at him before gathering their belongings to leave, without offering further conversation.

"I scare you? "Deacon's voice was a challenge.

Being no coward, Chris took their seat again. "No, but I can't say it's not strange that a man choking didn't bother you."

He tossed his head up indicating something. "Ah know things." He pointed to the janitor that everyone was watching. "He's 'bout to brush death."

Chris scoffed aloud, but just then, sure enough, the man stepped into a puddle and slid towards the street. But just as he was about to stumble into incoming traffic, someone grabbed his hand. Everyone nearby heaved a breath of relief. After helping that man, someone murmured that he lived a charmed life.

"Cool, but coincidence." Chris shrugged.

A strong odor of cigar smoke mixed with a putrid tang came off of Deacon's breath as he drew closer. Could the scent be ashes? No, not quite. It was more akin to brimstone or burned wood.

Chris chuckled wondering what it was Deacon had been vaping. "I'd say where's the vampires and zombies too?"

Deacon gave Chris a sickening smile. "You're gone believe in dat, but not premonition?"

"Yeah, I was joking," Chris responded dryly. Impatience coursed through Chris as they let out a deep, frustrated sigh. All Chris could think about was getting home in time for dinner as an uneasy feeling crept over them. They felt like there was some kind of joke being played and didn't want to stick around to find out. Despite their growing impatience, they remained rooted to the spot, waiting to see what would happen next.

CHAPTER 2

"Deacon?"

A cheerful voice called and they both turned to see a stylish woman approach. Chris thought she looked familiar. Her larger frame and broad smile were familiar, almost hallmark. Chris knew her quickly from her barrage of films.

None other than Susan Click swooped in and sat down, completely ignoring Chris as she gushed over Deacon. Chris frowned, feeling invisible but could only stare at the starlet and hope she noticed they were there.

Deacon looked bored with her but was polite. "Who dat?" He tipped his hat and gave her a nod, "Where y'at?" Deacon took a breath when she furrowed her brow at his words, "How yo' doing, Susan?"

She beamed her brilliant smile and tapped his hand with her well manicured fingers. "I'm great thanks to you!" She sighed happily. "Your advice was a life saver." She winked at him.

Chris was certain now when she spoke. She was the same woman from one of their favorite LGBTQ films. "You're that actress?" Chris was awestruck. They started looking for something for her to sign.

She put her sunglasses on and sighed. "Aren't you that... you made that website that sold for all that money?" She replied politely.

"Yeah, I did. You just married that actor Tom Cav... something. He's Canadian." Chris grinned wryly at her.

"Yes. Tom and I got married last weekend!" She smiled meaningfully at Deacon. "Thanks to Deacon, I'm fine."

Deacon chuckled, "Ah heard dat Tom saved your life." He offered her a cigarette.

"Thanks to you!" She smiled and waved away the offer. "He pulled me out of the way of that bus!" Then she looked back at Chris.

Deacon chuckled, "Chérie, Ah was explaining to our internet friend here dat Ah have a gift."

Susan released a slow breath and fixed Chris with an unwavering gaze. "Yes, he does, and it saved my life!" She laughed and waved a hand.

"Technically, Tom did the saving, but I knew he would!" Her phone began to play a jaunty French tune that Chris had only heard in movies. She sighed looking at the phone. "If Deacon is helping you, then you're in good hands!" She stood up. "I have to meet my manager." She flashed Deacon a dazzling smile, showcasing her perfect teeth and crinkling up the corners of her eyes. Taking a deep breath, she straightened herself and prepared to deliver her next line."Let's have lunch next week!"

Deacon stayed sitting and relaxed. "Oui, you best relax, Susan, or you gone drive Tom crazy." He gave her a grin but she nodded as if dismissed. She waved at them and clicked her phone as she walked away.

"I know her! She played a gay Australian woman in that romcom!"

Deacon laughed. "She's just a client, but she was like you once. She didn't believe this at first."

"Wait, is she part of a joke? You saved her life?"

"Non." Deacon lit the cigarette. "She said Ah did, but all Ah told her was where, when, and how she gone die. Susan made sure dat Tom was dere to save her. Ah told her dat was risky but she made dat work." Deacon smiled wide as the smoke poured from between his lips, "And now Tom's her husband."

"So, you're like a prophet of death?" Chris's eyes darted around in search of the starlet.

"Oui!" Deacon said loudly. "She over dere, mon ami."

Like a flash Chris was on their feet with a pen and paper. "I'll be right back. I want her autograph."

Deacon used his fingernail to flick ashes from his cigarette. "Sure you do," A low chuckle escaped his lips as he tapped the end of his cigarette into the disposable, tin, ashtray. The gray ashes cascaded down, and he watched, mesmerized, as the embers slowly dissipated.

Chris made their way through a group of people, seeing as the starlet had been recognized by her fans. They cleared their throat to get Susan's attention.

"Are you signing autographs too?" She gave Chris the same smile she wore for the photographers. Slowly it reminded Chris she was working and Chris felt sheepish for the intrusion.

"I'm nobody," Chris smiled. "I actually wanted your autograph if you don't mind."

She reached for a packet she held with her professional pictures and pulled open a silver sharpie. "Anything for a friend of Deacon!" She scribbled 'With love, Susan Click' and Chris smiled.

"Could I ask you something about him?" Chris inquired with a nod in Deacon's direction.

She looked up. "Sure but..." she gestured for Chris to move off to the side with her. "It's not for everybody to hear."

"What's his deal?" Chris asked quickly.

"You mean his premonition?" She exhaled hard and looked far away. "He can do it!" She sighed again, still looking away slightly. "For a price. He doesn't help anybody without deep enough pockets, but it saved my life!" She seemed to glance around nervously before she continued. "At first I thought he was as crazy as a soup sandwich but then I found out my friend Jack had had the same deal from back in the day. Jack proved he's been Deacon's client a long time. So I didn't run from a good deal."

"So, he tells you when, where, and how and it's right...but there's a fee?"

She rolled her eyes. "It was a lot for me to take in too." She lowered her voice. "Did you read the papers? If I hadn't listened to him, I would be gone today."

Still holding the Sharpie, she gently touched Chris's arm. "I heard others he helped in Hollywood and they vouched for him. If he deems you worthy, you'd better move on it." She lowered her voice as fans moved closer and added, "He has an exclusive client list." She seemed to be happy to talk about this, even if in low tones.

Chris laughed as a thought struck them. "I guess Elvis wasn't on it!"

She shook her head. "Maybe he couldn't afford Deacon." She gave a wink.

"He saved your life, and other A-listers?"

Susan nodded and exclaimed, "Yes!" She laughed nervously.

"Incredible but true." The flash from the photographers kept going off in her face and she leaned into Chris to get a picture.

"Getting my pic with the internet tycoon?" She laughed as the flashes came faster and she moved away slowly. She turned back and whispered, "Let me know if you need to chat." Her words were spoken so close to Chris's ear it felt like a kiss. Then she raised her voice as she was pulled away slowly, "Good luck!"

Chris stepped away and the crowd surged forward, shouting.

"Susan, how did you survive?"

"What's it like to be married to your savior?"

"Did the bus really almost hit you?"

People all around her clamored for Susan's attention and Chris walked away, not interested in seeing how she got out of the throng.

CHAPTER 3

W hen Chris got back to the table, they held out the autographed photo for Deacon to see, but Deacon didn't say anything and merely blew a lazy smoke ring.

"She tell you Ah saved her life? Or about dat new husband?" He inhaled deeply from the cigarette, allowing the plumes of smoke to wrap around his head like a halo.

"Actually, she did." Chris turned as the press shifted their attention to them.

Deacon was already on his feet, "Let's go, mon ami. No peace here soon." He offered his hand for Chris to stand as if the perfect gentleman. "We got business to discuss."

Chris eyed the hand and felt that it had a deeper significance. Chris stood on their own without Deacon's help. As Chris followed the man, he managed to dodge the photographers or prying eyes, and it appeared that Deacon seemed to be an expert at avoiding the media.

"What's your rush?"

"Ah don't like dem cameras," He tipped his tophat forward, revealing his intense eyes. It rolled down his arm until he caught it with the same hand and flipped it back up with one elegant motion, setting it just right on his head to take its perfect perch.

"Why? You're a good looking guy."

"Ah been better and Ah don't like how de cameras catch me." He was clearly trying to play it cool, but he almost looked anxious as his gaze settled onto the cameras of the paparazzi.

"I think we've all had a bad pic or two..." Chris cocked an eyebrow at him, curious about why grabbing a bit of press would be bad.

Deacon looked back at the starlet and the corner of his mouth turned up. "What she tell you?" Deacon inched closer, his gaze like a weapon ready to fire. His demeanor suggested that he wanted to share something secret.

"Not much." Chris tensed as they felt Deacon's searing glance linger on them. They shifted and took a small step back, wary of the possibility that Deacon was going to try and make a move. "What was she supposed to tell me?"

"How de deals work." His lip curled upwards slightly, exposing his teeth as he peered through the top hat's brim. Deacon gestured towards another, tiny, much less crowded cafe. He sat down at a table and pulled an old piece of paper from the inside of his coat. "Seems to me... Ah am always saving people," he chuckled. "Saving lives."

Chris was taken aback by Deacon's greasy smile when they took the delicate paper, which felt as if it would crumble to pieces in their hand. To read, they narrowed sensitive brown eyes from the harsh light, and sighed. Chris wrinkled their nose slightly looking for a sum and exhaling audibly when none was present.

"So basically you'll tell me where and when I'm going to die and I just know to avoid it," Chris said.

"You see how many de rock stars die from accidents or

drugs?" He nodded to the signed photo Mary had autographed. "Same with stars and the famous. Some clean up right fast after I lay de deal down." In an attempt to make a point, he slapped the table and grinned.

The action drew the attention of the waitress instead. She ignored Chris but looked at Deacon with a slippery grin. "Can I get you anything?"

"You gonna catch me some crawfish?" Deacon chuckled to himself.

She lowered her pad and pencil and gave Deacon a stupefied look. "What?"

"Just water." He waved her away lazily, with just his fingers.

She hurried off, hardly looking upset over his dismissal. Instead, she stepped away as if it was her privilege to have been given leave by another celebrity.

Chris sighed, mulling over the idea. "Say I take the deal? How much is it?"

Deacon chuckled and gave a long languishing stretch. He nodded at the waitress bringing their water and grinned crookedly. Chris shivered at the predatory look in his eyes.

Chris accepted the plain glass of water with a polite nod. They had originally thought of asking for coffee, but didn't want to be rude now as they accepted the water. "Thank you."

Deacon cocked an eyebrow. "Bring them some coffee too."

Chris cocked their head when Deacon not only ordered the coveted coffee but also referred to them with the correct pronoun.

The waitress looked at Chris expectantly. "Coffee?"

"Please." Chris turned up the sides of their mouth and watched her hurry off. Their attention was back to Deacon with narrowed eyes. "Why did you order for me?"

"You wanted it," Deacon chuckled as he pulled a cigarette from his coat and lit it. "Dat's ya problem. You shy." He seemed to bubble in pure amusement at the thought and he laughed, "Humble!" His pleasure came from mocking Chris for being polite.

"I'm just not pushy," Chris countered fast and began to measure their temper with this man. "Why did you think I wanted coffee?"

"You was thinking it!" Deacon said tapping his temple and meeting Chris's eye as if for them to deny it.

The waitress stole Chris's words with her sudden appearance and placed a mug on the table. She beamed at them. "Let me know if I can get you anything else."

Chris's face contorted in embarrassment as a blush crept up their cheeks. They briefly looked into her eyes, but quickly averted their gaze and focused on Deacon. "You read my thoughts?"

"It's easy to know what a person thinking if you listen." Deacon exhaled a puff of smoke that hung in the air, swirling and twirling like a ghostly figure. The smoke seemed to have a life of its own as it danced around before effortlessly dissipating into nothingness.

Deacon seemed oblivious to the puff of smoke when he nodded to the paper. "You wanna deal, mon ami?"

"You never said what the price is."

Deacon nodded to the paper he'd given Chris. "Read it."

Chris looked at the crinkly old paper and turned it over again. Suddenly a very large sum was scrawled on it. "Funny... I could have sworn it was blank." Chris smirked at Deacon. "You're a magician and this is a joke?"

Deacon sighed and tapped out his cigarette. "Den don't take de deal. Ah don't think you believe it's a trick, cause it don't explain Susan none." He watched the indecisiveness and chuckled, "That's not so much for you. You got it coming in all the time and think of this as investing."

Chris nodded. "Do I have to decide now? Or do I have time to think it over?"

Deacon grinned. "Ah give all my clients one day."

"Could I get your number?" Chris pulled their fancy phone out and waited, but Deacon shook his head.

"All mah deals are face to face." Deacon tapped the table. "Tomorrow 'bout dis time."

Chris nodded, "Do I show even if the answer's no?"

"Oui! We all need to." He tilted his head giving a ghost of a grin, and as he rose from the chair, he said quietly, "Dey all like closure, non?" He started to whistle a song as flawlessly as if it were being sung by a professional.

Chris flipped the paper with the figure printed on it and sighed. They hadn't spent this much money since they bought their house. To make this deal a reality, they would have to ensure the funds were available. When Chris looked up, they could still hear Deacon's whistling, but he was nowhere to be seen.

As they glanced around for any sign of Deacon, Chris noticed someone else giving them a sidelong glance. The man had care-worn clothing with holes, and his hair was disheveled. He had a hoodie draped over his head like he was trying to hide from the authorities, and he fixed Chris with an intense gaze. It didn't bother Chris that he was staring, but Chris was sure they'd seen this man someplace before. Chris nodded at the man, sure they were a forgotten friend of the family.

The man got up quickly and nodded to the empty chair. "Do you mind?"

"Sure, go ahead."

The man sat slowly. "That Deacon dude creeps me out."

"You know him?"

The man sighed. "All too well." He met Chris's eye. "He cut me a deal." The man before Chris looked like he was cut from the same cloth as the Greek Gods. He had a chiseled face, his jawline was defined, the shadows of a beard adding contrast to his features. His sandy blond hair, though unkempt, stood in perfect tufts and flighty waves, like an angel who wandered from the heavens. His skin seemed to glow with a bronze foundation, a golden radiance that could have been a remnant of the sun. His eyes were dark and deep, giving a sense of foreboding and humility, like he had seen the dark and knew that it held no secrets from him.

The voice tickled Chris's memory. At last they recalled where they knew this man from. His voice crooned all too often from Chris's mother's vintage record collection.

Eyes widening in shock, Chris understood who the disheveled person standing in front of them was – or had been once, long ago. Nick Dallas, the rockstar, had barely aged since his days on vinyl album covers. His face looked almost exactly as it had back in the '80s.

Chris was overcome with excitement and stammered out, "You're that rock star."

"I was. Yeah."

"Nick Dallas?" Chris looked at the man in disbelief and tried not to be starstruck at the realization that they were sitting across from a rock and roll icon. "Aren't you in the Rock 'n Roll Hall of Fame?"

Nick Dallas had been a trail blazer and an icon. He had his handprints in cement and was inducted into halls of fame. Now he sat at this cafe looking like a vagabond. He pulled a cigarette from the pack, and a vintage metal lighter from his pocket. He shrugged and held up the lighter Chris stared at.

He gave a slight cough. "You like it? I've had it since the '80s. It's the only thing I have from back then." He spoke with such modesty it was hard to believe he was once a celebrated musician.

"Are you hiding from the public?" Chris tried not to make it too obvious they were studying Nick's outfit and youthful looks.

Nick scoffed. "No, I'm not really that guy now." He looked down at the mug.

Chris heaved a sigh, watching Nick carefully, "What happened? Did you get tired of the celebrity's life?" Chris couldn't help but notice the stark contrast between Nick's past rockstar status and his present unkempt look. Chris quickly averted their gaze, so as not to make him feel uncomfortable.

Nick met Chris's squarely. "The deal."

"With that guy? Deacon? What's he have to do with it?"

Nick tossed back a hard swallow of his coffee and took a deep breath. "Deacon was there after a gig. I found him in my dressing room acting as if he owned everything." Chris looked at him directly now. Nick returned Chris's hard stare and lit his cig. "He told me he knew for a fact when and where I would die, and if I wanted his help, I could avoid it."

"So he helped you?"

"He cursed me." Nick corrected sharply. "At first I didn't believe Deacon, but after he offered the deal I stumbled on celebrities he had helped. So, I agreed thinking my music would keep the money coming in. He let me know that I would die from a drug overdose if I didn't stop. He specified my death date, and I immediately got my life in order. Half a year later, the day came and went, and I was free from any dependency issues."

Nick shrugged. "I enjoyed a new life without alcohol or drugs. Everything was new again to me. Food tasted better, the air smelled cleaner, and seeing the sun was my reason to wake up."

"That sounds great. Why do you call it a curse?"

"I lived," he muttered. "After I got clean, my music was

different too. The rest of the band still kept to the fun life while I didn't join the parties." Nick sighed and took a swig of his coffee.

"We grew apart fast. We still toured, but I was in bed after the shows while they partied."

Nick leaned back in his chair and stared and Chris considered that they really had no clue what the intensity of the spotlight meant. "The lead guitarist and I did all the songs together. We put the music out, and the rest of the band only offered some feedback here and there. I had a new outlook on life, and we couldn't see eye to eye anymore. We wrote a few good songs, but they wanted me out."

The ex-rockstar shifted in his seat. Chris thought he looked upset. "When I changed my lifestyle, there was no way for us to be on the same page, let alone write like we used to. We no longer agreed on anything, and the music suffered. It was never the same."

"If you were still working and writing songs, then why vote you out?"

"You don't get it?" Nick scoffed. "The new songs took forever to write because we fought the entire time. I woke up and they were just getting to bed. They were drunk and I was sober. It got hard to find time when we were all sober to work. We ended up doing covers of our old material and that got boring fast." He puffed his cig, "I didn't belong after the deal."

"So you all only wrote when you were sober?" Chris asked quietly. It was obvious to Chris that Nick didn't belong, just like Chris. Although, Nick had been marginalized long before they were. Chris felt a lump in their throat as they thought about whether Nick felt just as isolated as they did.

"Yes!" Nick said loudly, looking offended. "We started the band in high school, and we were all clean then. We got our first top 40 in college, and we were still pretty clean. We were on fire, and suddenly all our old material was going well. We knew the frame of mind we had to be in to achieve that."

He pointed a finger at Chris. "We never wrote high or drunk. In the beginning, it was easy to keep our work clean, and we were even proud of that. Over time, as the others changed and I went through my detox, our outlook diverged so much it became incompatible. For years, we'd told the press over and over that we wrote when we were clean so the kids wouldn't use drugs thinking that's how they could become a rockstar, but then the band kept going down the dark road and I didn't."

"That's pretty amazing!" Chris smiled and then narrowed eyes at him. "How did the deal ruin it?"

"No music, no money, and my band wanted me out." Nick sighed. "I left, and the songs they put together without me bombed. I'm broke now, and so are they. The royalties get divided between us, and our stuff is old to the new generation, so it doesn't get played often. I find odd jobs now to keep going." Nick tamped his cigarette out and leaned back.

"You have your life and your health, though!"

"This isn't a life, kid." Nick said sharply. "I go hungry and live in squalor. Each time I try to get a job, they recognize me and it doesn't work out." He sat forward and leaned on the table. "When you go from diamonds to dust... it pales in comparison. This isn't my life. It's borrowed time." He chuckled dryly, "I've tried to end it many times already."

Chris couldn't fathom how dark depression could be to lead someone to the point of feeling like there was no alternative. Even when money was tight, Chris had never felt that way before.

"The deal?" Chris asked in a hushed tone. They silently hoped that was all it really was and not a suicide attempt.

"No, kid. My life." He narrowed his eyes. "I heard Deacon

talking with you. You're some A-lister. You're a genius but you're pretty naive, huh?"

"I guess," Chris averted their gaze. "You tried to kill yourself?" It was difficult to imagine that this man wished not to see the next day. Chris was only 21, and even at his age, such a thought seemed morbid.

"Several times." Nick nodded. Chris's eyes met his and Nick gestured for Chris to move closer. "But I can't kill myself now."

"What do you mean?"

"I mean I can't die," he chuckled. "Ironic, right? In order to survive, I paid a hefty price, and now mortality is no longer an option for me." Nick locked eyes with Chris as he began to explain further.

"Once, I was working with the band and we were on stage setting up. One of our techs messed up and plugged in an old cord that should've been thrown out. Something happened and it must have gotten wet on top of it but nobody knew. I grabbed the wire and was shocked. I mean, I was electrocuted. They said I got hit so hard, I should've had at least a heart attack. It was so bad it blew the power and there was a funny smell; but I was still standing. It creeped them all out. It creeped me out!" He held out his left hand to show a scar in the shape of a lightning bolt between his thumb and his pointer finger.

"So you got a tattoo because of it?" Chris smiled thinking it was a happy ending.

"That's one of the scars." Nick nearly hissed the words. "Each time I was supposed to die, I found one after." He looked at the raised, pink reminder and pulled his hand back to grasp the coffee cup and take a drink.

"I lost it all and sank into depression. I decided to kill myself but each time I just woke up. I couldn't die." He took a breath. "I hunted that man down and asked him why I couldn't end my own life now and he told me I had my deal." Nick chuckled, "I am cursed." He finished the coffee.

Chris stared at him with wide eyes. "Wow. It's like being immortal."

"Sure it is," Nick grumbled. "While living with a nagging hunger and no money to eat; freezing cold and on the streets. I don't have anything to live for."

Chris nodded and wondered if it was karma or irony. All they could say to Nick was, "I'm sorry."

"Think this deal over before you take it, kid." Nick stood and nodded at Chris. "I didn't know what I was getting into." With that he strolled away from the table, and over his shoulder called, "Take care of yourself, kid!"

Nick's words reverberated in Chris's mind. Questions tumbled around each other leaving Chris disconcerted.

Chris tossed money on the table for both coffees and stood, watching him go. "Nick?" The rockstar's figure was hard to see as it was absorbed by the crowd. Chris ran after him and realized quickly that Nick was gone. Chris was alone with a million thoughts floating through their mind, and not nearly enough answers.

CHAPTER 4

For the rest of the day, Chris's mind was abuzz with the possibility of cheating death. How many people would empty their pockets to find such a solution? Nick's talk weighed as heavily on their mind as Deacon's. The deal sounded sweet but only if Chris knew every detail and how to approach it.

Chris was typing out an email to their accountant, but the thoughts kept interrupting. Despite two hours of trying to type, only two sentences had been put together. It was a record of sorts for Chris.

Chris didn't have many friends and had usually ended up alone, much like Nick. It resonated with Chris to the point Chris felt a slight kinship to Nick. Being a prodigy meant that they were often leaps and bounds ahead of their peers. People Chris's age hated being outdone by their peers, and weren't too pleased about Chris skyrocketing past them. To make matters worse, Chris also managed to outshine people much older than them as well. Chris was only 21, but they often felt isolated and alone.

Finally Chris pushed from the desk with a sigh and glanced at the clock. Dinner time; a distraction sounded like a good idea.

Although their mom no longer needed to cook, she still did, just like their father still worked. Growing up, the children were taught to keep striving. They were shown that hard work and perseverance are important virtues from a young age. Meals were eaten at the same time every day, bedtime and wake-up times were always the exact same, but this also applied to sports and exercise.

Chris strolled into the kitchen to find their sibling, Taylor, gyrating away, whipping her hair and hopping from one foot to the other with music droning in the background. She seemed to be having a grand time as she swayed in tune with the beat. Her short multicolored hair was testament to how wild Tay was.

Taylor, Chris's sister, had begun to act very superior since their newfound wealth. She had always been haughty, but now that they could afford more luxurious items, she reveled in them shamelessly. While still dancing, she turned her head to give Chris a quick glance as they entered. Without saying a word, Taylor pointed at the dish cupboard and gestured to the table. Chris pulled five plates from the cupboard, but Tay stepped in and shook her head.

"Jordan isn't here yet. He's at his friend's house, and mom and dad went to do some shopping. They said they would be out late because mom is still looking for that statue figure thing," Taylor explained with a heavy sigh, sadly eyeing the food she was cooking.

"Would you rather get take-out?" Taylor was always itching to order takeout and she'd frequently be the first one to pick up the phone. It was no surprise then that she would try her hand at cooking, albeit halfheartedly, just so they could order out instead. Her attempt at a casserole in a pan was horrific. It was only brown and saucy with a pungent smell. Chris realized it must have been a little burnt too.

Chris gave a slight smile in response to Taylor's attempt at playing the older sibling. "You mean the Stafford figure she wanted over the fireplace?"

Together, Chris and Taylor returned all the other dinner plates to their rightful places in the cupboards. Chris suspected Taylor would rather order take out, like they had done earlier that week. Even though they knew all that food wasn't healthy, Tay didn't seem to care. She lived day-to-day and enjoyed each moment as it came.

Tay seemed to be trying to prove just how bad her cooking was when she pointed to the boxes of mac and cheese. It was one of her ways of testing Chris, but they didn't falter.

"Sorry, I'm late!" Jordan rushed through the door with his book bag still slung over his shoulder. "What's for dinner?" he asked, scanning the kitchen and noticing Taylor at the stove. Disappointed, he muttered, "Where's Mom?"

He clearly wasn't too pleased with the idea of eating Taylor's cooking. He groaned looking at the mess in the pan. "It's slimy and gross." Jordan picked up a wooden spoon to poke at her concoction and laughed when she slapped the spoon away.

Jordan made a beeline for the freezer, and he began rummaging around inside. "C'mon, Mom must have left us something frozen to heat up!"

Taylor looked as if she had lost in a game of cards, but tried to hide her defeat by pretending not to have heard his suggestion.

"Let's either order out or eat the mac and cheese from a

box," she suggested with her best poker face. Her siblings saw right through her bluff, shaking their heads in amusement at her ruse.

Chris groaned and went over to join Jordan by the freezer. After some searching, they stumbled across a few casseroles and Jordan gave a triumphant, "Whoop!"

Taylor groaned and whined, "We could send out..."

Instead of answering, Chris turned the oven on and put the casserole dish on top of it. "Mom left dinner." Chris announced with a smile, "It's all good."

Jordan grabbed his bag. "I'm going to unpack this fast while it's cooking."

Tay finished cooking her mac 'n' cheese, then responded with a shrug. "I think I'll order sushi later."

Chris rolled their eyes and put the casserole in the oven when the timer went off. "This looks good, Tay."

Tay mumbled at him in a condescending tone, then gave her food some angry stirring. All Chris could do was chuckle knowing what would happen. She would eat Mom's food and be too full to stuff her face with sushi... again. Chris gathered the silverware. There were no fancy forks or spoons, just simple plates and the basic utensils. They had them for occasions but didn't really bother with them for everyday meals. Chris did all but laugh knowing she had just lost the take out food war.

After supper, they went to the back patio and sat in some deck chairs to take in the simplicity of living along the river. The calm waters were gradually turning dark as night fell but Chris's gaze was fixed blankly ahead.

"I'm glad Mom left dinner," Jordan mumbled as he sat down. Chris nodded and simply stared ahead at the water.

Chris observed Tay's posture stiffen as she quickly brought her palms to her lips, desperately trying to contain the large burp that was ready to escape. The unmistakable aroma of her mother's cooking filled the room and Tay sheepishly looked away when Chris made eye contact. It was a typical move for Tay, and whilst Chris would never admit it, they loved how unique she was.

"Why are you so quiet?" She finally asked.

Chris jumped, startled out of the distant reverie they were in and took a sip from their drink to seem nonchalant. Chris pondered deeply before answering.

"I'm thinking about the meaning of life." Sitting up and gazing out at the boat they kept off of their small pier, Chris rotated their head to look back and forth between both siblings. "Let me ask you this: If someone could tell you when and how you will die, would you want to know?"

Tay narrowed her eyes, "Seriously?"

Taylor and Jordan traded a knowing look and watched their sibling with mild interest but after the meal they were happy to listen.

"What if it was something you could avoid like being hit by a bus? You know, to save your life," Chris said quickly.

"Like that movie star recently?" Tay sat up straight up looking excited at the thought of talking about movie stars. "She was almost killed by a bus, but someone pulled her out of the way."

"Exactly!" Chris smiled and realized Deacon's deal had overshadowed meeting a movie star and a rock star. Chris slowly pulled and unfolded the large photo Susan had autographed then Chris gave it to Tay. "She was downtown today and I got her autograph." Chris took a long drink of wine.

"She's really nice." A laugh escaped. "She recognized me." Chris found it amusing that few people could identify them as a famous person but skirted the topic of Chris being non-binary. Chris smirked as they silently recalled the ordeal and all there had really been to it.

Tay shook the autograph like a pennant at a football game. "That's pretty cool!" She paused and held the autographed pic out. "This is mine now." She chuckled.

Chris grinned, knowing Taylor loved celebs and knew this would tickle her.

Jordan feigned interest through his mini food coma. "How did you score meeting a movie star?"

"She knew someone at a table near mine." Chris mumbled. As the sun set, Chris watched the last of the light dance off the water. "She actually told me about the bus and her new husband."

"Whoah," Tay exclaimed with her eyes wide. "That sounds pretty cool!"

Jordan yawned. "So, if a person could avoid death like she did, would we want to know?"

Chris turned to face them both.

"Uhhhh, yeah! Duh!" Tay scoffed, "I'm far too young to die."

Chris's eyebrows shot up their forehead as Tay spoke with such certainty. Even though she was only a few years ahead of them in age, she seemed far more opinionated when it came to the subject of death.

"Yeah," Jordan agreed. "I feel people don't live long enough." He stretched in the deck chair and mumbled, "I want to be 120."

"Yeah?" Taylor pointed a finger in a mock challenge. "Then I'll be 125."

Jordan spied the time on his phone and snapped up from the chair. "I need to dip on out of here. I got places to be." He gave a noncommittal shrug. "Not sure if I'll be home but it's doubtful." He seemed to have renewed energy when he ran back into the house.

Tay cocked an eyebrow at Chris. "You good?

Chris nodded. "I am now." Chris wondered if Jordan and Tay knew they helped them make a difficult decision.

CHAPTER 5

C hris continued to gaze around uncomfortably as they sat at the same table where they had first met Deacon. Being here gave Chris the chills, not from the weather, but Chris remembered the nightmare and how everything had seemed to evolve after that. This wasn't something they did every day and it had them jumpy.

People around appeared to notice it and would peek as if anticipating something to flee, such as a sniper or drug deal. Was it that Chris's heightened anticipation made the people around them shaky or that Chris was on edge because everybody was?

Chris felt guilty but couldn't place why. Although it might have seemed insane to the vast majority of people, it wasn't illegal. Chris kept looking in the hopes of seeing Nick for more advice, but only found patrons nursing coffees.

Chris's nostrils flared and a stench hit them like a wall, disrupting the senses – the smell of foul smoke and burning fish. Chris shook their head in disbelief, wrinkled their nose in confusion and peered at the soles of their shoes. Even though it didn't really smell like a dog had pooped nearby, there was a hint of burn that made them question what the restaurant was cooking for lunch.

"You smell something?" Out of nowhere, the silky voice materialized behind them and Chris jumped.

Chris turned to fully admire Deacon standing there in a blue version of the exact same outfit he had worn yesterday. "Deacon, right?"

Again, the clothes were so dark they seemed almost black until the light hit, reminding Chris of their old house. Mom and Dad had gotten paint to freshen up the walls but they were talked into special paint. A few drops of another color made all the difference to their semi gloss. During the day, the paint looked simply white but when twilight fell the walls showed somebody had spilled a few drops of blue or green, depending on the room. The children all loved it because it felt like a magic trick every day. It was the same with Deacon's clothing.

Deacon merely chuckled and slid into the seat opposite Chris with practiced grace. "You know my name by now, mon cher." His mouth curved into a subtle smile "Ah think you been rolling it round your head since we met, non?"

"You're hard to forget." Chris took a drink of coffee and tried to relax.

"Dat's de fact, mon ami," Deacon lit a cigarette and huffed a lazy smoke ring that rose above his head then seemed to encircle his hat as it faded. "You got de money? You taking de deal or you wouldn't be here." He pulled a drag off his cigarette again and smiled.

"I think I will," Chris swallowed hard. "I have a check made out."

Deacon scoffed. He watched Chris retrieve it from their pocket, and Deacon held it between two fingers as if it were going to bite him.

"Is a check all right? If not, I would have to go to the bank..." Chris was taken back seeing Deacon hold the check like it was infectious and worried the strange man was offended.

"I find it amusing dat someone who deals in tech like you gone give me paper." Deacon smiled. "Ah t'ink a wire transfer, pay to my account." He put the check on the table and pushed the paper back at Chris. "When someone like you wan' leave a paper trail den something wrong."

Chris swallowed hard. "No, nothing like that, but checks are easier and I didn't have time for the ba..." Chris trailed off when Deacon reached in his tight coat for something. Deacon pulled his hand back out so fast, Chris jerked and hit the ground with only the table to protect them.

Deacon laughed, "You drop something?"

Chris peered up to see Deacon held a phone of his own in his hand and felt sheepish. "I slipped." Chris knew Deacon could see through that lie, but it was to save face, a little.

"Sure you did." Deacon tapped out his cig and held his candy apple red phone out as he pointed to the slit on the side. "You got a card?" Deacon cocked an eyebrow.

Chris nodded. "Okay, sure. I can do that." Fishing through their pockets they grabbed the card that sat behind their phone.

"Den swipe." Deacon held his phone closer to Chris with a nod.

Chris swiped the card on the side of his phone and Deacon simply put the phone in his pocket. Chris pointed. "Don't you want to be sure it went through?"

"You think it didn't?" He smiled. "You don't got faith all de time, eh?" He smiled but shook his head. "Yo' got faith or you would've asked to see the amount and what it says."

Chris sat up feeling alarmed. "What?"

"Dat was de deal." Deacon smiled. "Check your phone."

Chris sighed. "This is crazy." Yet Chris pulled out their phone to see new messages. "Great, you have my number too?"

Tapping the screen they had the display and noticed they had mail alerts and messages. One email was the bank about the transfer and immediately after came an email from what appeared to be Deacon.

It said 'Here's the deal,' which was followed by an outline of what Chris could and couldn't do concerning the deal. It seemed simple enough from what they skimmed. Don't speak of the deal to anybody or tell anyone about Deacon or the people involved would be 'damned and dealt with'. The thought made Chris smile and looked up from the phone.

"It seems fine. I can't tell anyone? What about Susan? She told me."

"People dat know de deal already know de deal. Tell someone who don't and dey gone leave," Deacon said as they sat back.

"Is that a threat?"

"All Ah say was dey gone leave," Deacon narrowed his dark eyes at Chris. "I don't hurt nobody. Y'all do nuff ta hurt yourself without me." Deacon said louder. "You got questions, then you got that mail on your phone." He pointed to Chris's phone.

"Okay then." Chris swallowed hard trying not to say it. Deacon hadn't said how they would die or when and if Deacon was a fortune teller then he knew Chris had to act fast.

Deacon gave a condescending smile. "When? How? Why?" Deacon tipped his top hat with his thumb, and Chris could see his face clearer.

In the light of the port cafe, Deacon's skin appeared to be incredibly taut around his face because he was so pale and the lines on his visage appeared more pronounced. Deacon's features reminded Chris of Marilyn Manson, but Deacon didn't appear to have make-up on. Still Deacon was an attractive man in a goth vampiric way. He looked like the ultimate bad boy girls brought home to anger the parents.

Deacon watched a man at the table next to them with a side glance. The man was waiting for his coffee but got up and went to the men's room. The waitress placed the absent man's drink down with a napkin and left quickly. Deacon stretched widely and it seemed he might fall from his chair but in a moment had the absent man's coffee in his hand.

Deacon sat back and scoffed, "This best not be decaf." He chuckled and took a drink.

Chris sat back. "Why did you..." Deacon's reprimanding stare rivaled the strictest of parents and stopped Chris from asking further.

"Read dat deal. You don't question me less it's bout de deal." He took another drink of the coffee despite Chris's full upset look. "You a good kid, so dis bothers you?" He chuckled. "Den I put it back?" Deacon spat in the coffee and, without turning his head to aim, he twisted his wrist as if he was tossing a frisbee.

Chris watched the coffee cup slide on air like a paper plane and glide back to the table with only a slight scrape. Chris looked around to see if anyone else was amazed by this minor feat, but nobody seemed to notice. It must have been too fast unless one expected it.

"Nice trick." Chris nodded at the mug. "Are you with the circus?"

Deacon chuckled. "Not everyone that can do tricks is on stage." He lit a cigarette. "Only the ones who want to get caught."

Chris nodded and cleared their throat. "You were going to tell me... "

"You such a good kid you can't even say it, non? You squeaky clean." He smiled. "Death, it's not a bad word but scares de good kid."

Deacon placed his nail on the cigarette's butt and flicked his ashes in the tray. He looked at Chris's expectant face and sighed. "April year after this you gone be six feet down if you don't listen to me now."

Chris sat forward enticed now and gave Deacon an encouraging nod.

Deacon puffed on his cigarette. "Tomorrow you gonna go to de doctor." He noticed Chris' upset look. "You be de good kid an' listen 'til I'm done!"

He lifted his gaunt arm and shook a bony finger at Chris, signaling for them to stay quiet.. "Tomorrow, you gonna tell dem some scuse so dey do scans of your..." He pointed to Chris's torso... "Belly and gut. Tell dem you had a bad dream or you had problems with de sick belly or de bathroom."

He pointed a finger in his face so close it nearly touched Chris's nose. "But don't let dem tell you nothing is wrong. Dey don't listen, den you go to a different doc." He sat back and took a hard drag from his cigarette. "You got de cancer in your colon and gone spread fast in a few months." He smudged his cig until it no longer glowed in the ashtray. "You almost right as rain, but if dey get this now, den no problems. Dis just started."

Chris was dumbfounded. With all Chris had noticed, things started to click. Bathroom habits had changed somewhat, but Chris blamed it on being off schedule or the start of a sickness that never happened.

"I have it now? Will I need surgery?"

"I said it just started. You gonna have to convince dem to keep looking."

Chris touched their abdomen slightly. "Where do I tell them to look?"

"De doc gonna find it." Deacon gave a nod ignoring the question. "Dat rascal waiting to be found." Then Deacon stood quickly with a wave of his hand.

"Wait." As soon as Deacon got up, Chris followed suit and threw a few bills on the table as Deacon started to move between the tables. Chris watched when the man eventually returned to the table next to them and complained that his coffee wasn't full, Chris had to control their laughter. It was the same cup Deacon had flavored.

Chris echoed Deacon's steps before snatching the blue-coated shoulder and pulling till they turned. Chris's brows furrowed as the person turned, but instead of Deacon, they found themselves face to face with a clown.

The clown grinned with their painted face, shook their head, and thrust a twisted balloon into their hands. "Balloon animal?"

Chris stood there flabbergasted looking at the mock balloon dog as it squeaked against their hand. "Thanks," Chris mumbled before backing up and making a slow exit. Chris walked past another cafe and spied a little girl accompanied by a parent and passed the balloon to the child with a smile.

"Thank you!" The girl said brightly and curtsied in her pink dress.

"Thank you," the mother said and nodded to the clown. "She wanted a balloon animal but was afraid of the clown."

"She's afraid of clowns?" Chris asked quietly.

"She wasn't before, but I guess she is today." The mother shrugged.

Chris smiled and waved as the mother and child moved on. Chris wanted to be alone with their thoughts and to take action. Fevered fingers began working the cell phone until it rang.

"Answer..." Chris mumbled.

The receptionist finally answered with the prescribed phone script and Chris spoke up quickly. "Hello, this is Chris Shepherd and I need to schedule an appointment as soon as I can." Chris gazed across the harbor, observing how the sunlight played on the water. "No, tomorrow isn't too soon. It's perfect." Chris simply nodded, feeling humbled by it all. "Okay great. Ten a.m. it is. I'll see you then. Thank you."

CHAPTER 6

After switching off the phone, Chris stood and wrapped their arms around their chest. Entranced by the water's sparkling movement in the sun's rays, Chris couldn't take their eyes away. A warning had just reached them that they were going to die in less than a year unless they shifted into action, and for some reason, the sight of water was a reminder of life. Their life was now in their own hands and it felt both exhilarating and daunting. Chris was drawn to the water, but they had never taken swimming lessons and felt wary around it.

Chris shuffled along until they found a pole to lean against, and as they stared out at the water, something caught their eye. The water was breaking randomly in a very fast sequence of bursts and a splash of color proved not to be fish. It took a few moments for them to comprehend what they were seeing: a child.

Dashing toward the edge of the water, Chris remembered the tales of how treacherous this harbor could be. The stories claimed that the harbor was saturated with so much sludge and mud that it could act like quicksand and swallow anything in its path. Standing on the shoreline, Chris watched helplessly as the young one flailed in the water.

"There's a child in the water!" Chris screamed in the hopes a boat – or someone – would hear and fish the youngster out to safety. Yet, no one seemed to take notice, as the child sank beneath the surface.

Chris scoured the area, searching in vain for someone to come to their aid. Finally, they had enough and conceded.

"Screw it!"

Chris grabbed their hoodie and cell phone, handing them over to an elderly woman nearby. Without saying a single word, Chris took a deep breath before throwing themselves into the body of water that many avoided out of fear. Chris prayed silently that everything would be okay.

From beside the harbor wall, Chris noticed a crowd of onlookers gathering to perch on benches overlooking the water. What stood out was the clown remained silent and still, though its eyes narrowed slightly and a thin, slippery, smirk appeared beneath the layers of paint.

Chris moved on adrenaline pulling along the murky water to get to where the child had sunk. Something shone from the water below. Chris took a deep breath and reached under the water for whatever it was. The water was dark, making it hard to see, so Chris began using their hands more than their eyes.

They felt something light. Grabbing hold of it, they tugged. When Chris confirmed it was the child, they pulled hard for the surface.

Breaking the surface, Chris felt something against their head. Even with water droplets clouding their vision they could see it was a life preserver. Shouts from a boat came from above Chris and they noticed a rope connecting the life preserver to the boat. Chris pulled the ring over the child's head and shoulders then waved for the crew to go ahead.

The men lifted the body of what Chris could finally see was a little girl. She had long hair and a pink dress that clung to her as the water ran off it with each tug on the rope. Chris blinked trying to clear the water from their eyes but was sure it was the same little girl with the balloon.

Chris could only watch as the child was hefted to the deck. The men on the boat called Chris and tossed the life preserver back down.

Chris eyed it but pointed to where they had given the elderly woman their things. "My stuff is over there!"

Once Chris doggy paddled to the edge, they slowed down. A strange sound filled the air over the swish of waves. It took Chris a moment to understand what they heard. It was applause. Hands were stretched out toward them and many grabbed onto Chris to help them out the water. Close by, the elderly lady stood with Chris's belongings.

Chris hardly needed to climb because so many lent a hand. Strong hands grabbed Chris' arm and yanked them up. The taste of salty seawater filled their mouth, and the image of the young girl who had been pulled into the depths came to mind. Chris willed himself to stand and trudged through the crowd, letting it trickle from his clothing.

Chris's eyes widened when they saw the older woman holding the hoodie and cell phone. They stepped closer and stretched out their hand, eager to reclaim their things. The woman smiled as she handed over their possessions. "Thank you!" Chris mumbled and then ran off.

Chris ran towards the boat, their heart pounding in his chest. They hurdled a small barrier and collided with a tall, stocky man wearing a navy suit. The man stumbled backwards as Chris scrambled to his feet and kept running. "I need to see if she's okay!"

People were gathered around with phone cameras out, aimed on Chris and they realized people were taking pictures.

"Maybe I should go before I'm on the news."

The sound of people chatting and gesturing at the spectacle was difficult to ignore. Chris shifted uncomfortably, keeping their eyes down and avoiding contact with the people around them. Chris's heart was pounding, and they could feel a chill from the salty harbor air seeping through their damp clothes. The little girl had been rescued but the crowd remained, watching on in silent judgment.

"It's too late for that." The sailor clapped Chris on the shoulder and pointed to the cameras. "Don't be shy now. You're a hero!"

Chris sighed as the girl's mother motioned them to approach. As the audience became more rapt and the noise level increased, Chris smiled and waved from the deck of the boat, but they could feel their feet shifting slowly backwards. They tried to blend in with the other passengers, desperately wanting to disappear into the shadows. Chris felt the heat rising on their cheeks as they painfully wished no one would notice them.

The girl's mother thrust her hand out with tears running down her face. The lady still had the same balloon animal in her hands the clown had given Chris but it was now wet. "Thank you!" She waved to the water. "The balloon went in the water and she ran after it before I could stop her!"

Chris started to shake the mother's hand, when the young child suddenly raced up. Chris swallowed hard and kept glancing around at all the people recording them and sure this would end up on the internet.

"It was you who saved me!" The girl looked up with a sweet smile.

"Aren't you that person that made all those apps?" The mother added quickly.

Chris felt their cheeks heat up and gave a slight nod as people began to put together who Chris was. Chris had said over and over people never recognized them, but recently more had known them.

Out of the corner of their eye, Chris saw someone was gesturing to them from a shadow off the boat. The person had eyes peeking out from under a modest hoodie and they looked honest enough. Suddenly, Chris recognized the person. It was Nick.

Chris gave the girl a quick hug. "I'm glad I could help. I have to run." Although it was challenging to dodge the crowd gathered in the little area, Chris proved fairly agile.

CHAPTER 7

"You draw a big crowd, kid." Nick joked under his breath. "Not everyone is as brave as you are."

"What are you saying?"

"I saw the kid and so did lots of people, but nobody moved except you." Nick clearly sounded impressed by Chris's actions.

"If you can't die, then why didn't you help?"

"The press. I'm a has-been and I don't want people to see me now." Nick shrugged at Chris. "Don't get me wrong. I was weighing how I could help her and get out unnoticed."

"So, to save face you would've let her drown?" Chris shook their head.

"I was going to help, kid." Nick met Chris's eye solemnly. "You beat me to it."

Chris wasn't fully convinced but dropped it. "I wondered if you'd be here today."

"Yeah, I knew you would be and thought you might need to talk."

"How did you know I was going to be here?" Chris paused and stopped by a bench to shake the water off. They observed the man on the next bench glaring as Chris tossed the dry hoodie over the wet clothing.

"Don't you know you shouldn't play in that harbor?" The nosey man remarked and clearly regarded Chris as an idiot.

"I'll keep that in mind," Chris smiled at the man and moved to the take out window of a trendy restaurant. Chris signaled to the woman taking orders as Nick followed. "Do you want a coffee?"

"No money today." Nick said quietly.

"I didn't ask if you wanted to pay for it." Chris narrowed their eyes. "I got it."

Nick looked up. "Sure, thanks."

Chris put up two fingers for the lady at the window. "Two large coffees please."

Nick nodded, "Are you cold?"

"Yes, that's what the coffee is for." Chris watched as the woman delivered and rang up the takeaway coffees. Chris gave one to Nick and paid quickly. Nick gestured for Chris to follow and moved off, "where are we going?" Chris called after Nick and followed quietly.

"Over here," Nick called behind him as he guided Chris along the narrow alleyway that was located behind the cafe. Chris seemed nervous and Nick sighed "I'm not gonna jump you for cash, kid." Nick pointed to the dumpster. "Back here."

Chris had never smelled anything so foul. The alley was chilly and gloomy, with a strong odor of smoke and urine mingling with a slight scent of mold. Chris wrinkled their nose. "People pee back here?"

Nick just nodded and walked to the side of the beaten and graffiti covered dumpster. Nick picked up a big backpack. It wasn't like the ones Chris had carried at school but much bigger like a camper's backpack. Chris watched Nick sort through it carefully.

"You're cold," Nick said, finding an old flannel shirt and tossing it to Chris. "You're also attracting attention." He tossed Chris an old pair of jeans with care-worn holes. "They're not great but dry and should fit you."

Chris's eyes widened at the offer. They were receiving clothing from a man who had practically nothing at all. "Are you sure?"

"They're clean," Nick narrowed his eyes in a mock challenge when Chris seemed dubious. "I'm homeless but not dirty." Nick pointed to a door that simply said bathroom. "The restaurant lets anybody use the bathroom."

Chris nodded and opened the door as an odor hit Chris and forced them to take a step back and to take a moment to prepare for the stench of pure excrement. "What the..." In an attempt to dispel the odor, Chris waved a hand in front of their face.

"Here." Nick chuckled with a plastic bag in his hand. "You want to put your wet things in this."

Chris took the bag while resisting the urge to retch. "Trust me. I will be fast." Chris handed Nick the coffee and took a deep breath. Chris dove into the bathroom holding their breath and began to shed and replace clothing in record time.

Finally the door burst open, and Chris ran out, taking a deep breath. "How do you do that?" Chris gasped and the air had never smelled so sweet before.

"You do what you have to." Nick shrugged and looked over how the dry clothes looked, "They're a little big huh? It was the smallest I had."

"It's fine." Chris said, straightening up and catching their breath. "Thank you."

Chris took back the coffee and took a sip. "Thanks, Nick. I feel better dry."

Nick nodded to the sunlight that played along the entrance

to the alley. "Let's get back out there so the sun can warm you up."

Chris followed him and sighed gratefully as the sun hit them. "Nick, I was thinking... I want to offer you to stay with me."

Nick looked at Chris with a stunned expression, "You're serious?"

"Yes, I've got a big house with plenty of food." Chris gestured to the clothing. "Then, I could wash this and get it back to you too." Chris hoped they could help Nick. He had a rough run of it and despite it Nick had gone out of his way to help Chris.

Nick turned so he faced Chris. "Really?"

"Yes, I'm serious," Chris nodded. "I have a car here and I'll take you back to meet my parents and family." Chris sipped the coffee. "You had ample opportunities to rob me or take advantage and didn't. I wouldn't invite you if you didn't seem honest."

Nick smiled. "Yeah, definitely. Let's go." He perked up and looked like a new man. "Four walls, here we come." He laughed and ran back to the alley.

Chris craned their neck watching Nick retrieve that old backpack and run back again. "Do you have something in there you can't replace?" Chris remarked, hoping Nick would realize he didn't need to bring the old clothes.

"Yeah, my music," Nick smiled. "I kept writing songs hoping someone would throw a guitar away so I could play by the harbor and get some money that way."

Chris gave a nod and they walked into the city streets to find the car. It was easy to see that the former rock star was a hard worker.

Chris walked up to a beautiful car and pressed their finger

on a plate on the door. Nick's eyes were wide, and when the car door snapped open, he raised a brow.

Chris nodded and spoke to the car. "Open the passenger door."

The door opened for Nick and his mouth dropped. "Uh, nice ride."

"I'll take your bag," Chris offered.

"Thanks!" Nick said and handed it to him quickly. Chris was amazed that Nick had put his faith in them by giving them his backpack, which held all Nick's belongings. Chris congratulated themself on making the right decision to bring him home.

Nick appeared to be a child at Christmas as he observed the lights and displays inside the vehicle. "Maybe it's been a while since I've been in a car. Are they all like this now?"

Chris shrugged, "I guess."

Chris was amused watching Nick climb in carefully not to scratch or scuff anything.

"Where did you get this? Tony Stark?" He joked buckling in.

As they started weaving around the other vehicles, Chris sighed. "I hate downtown traffic." There was no reply and Chris looked to see Nick had fallen asleep. Chris touched Nick's shoulder. "Are you okay?"

Nick jumped awake. "Yeah, the most comfortable seat I've had in years." Nick smiled. "Plus, sleep is a luxury when you're living on the street. Safe sleep that is. People see somebody sleeping on the street and steal or mess with you." Nick's eyes closed rapidly.

"You feel safe?"

Nick opened his eyes smiling. "Yeah, for the first time in a long time, kid." His eyes were rapidly shutting. "Thanks."

Chris kept their eyes on the road and nodded. "You can

stay with me until you're back on your feet." Chris smiled. "I've got a guitar and piano at home you can use. Maybe get those songs out and be a rockstar again." Chris paused. "Nick?"

Chris glanced over to see Nick was fast asleep and then Chris kept their attention on the road. Mom and Dad would never believe this and Chris would only be able to tell them part of it.

W hen they were home, Chris halted the vehicle and Nick woke up with a start. Chris cocked an eyebrow. "Hey, don't worry. It's safe here."
As Nick got out of the car, he put his foot down cautiously and kept turning his head around taking everything in. "Yeah," he yawned. "I can't tell you how much I appreciate this." He yawned. "Don't worry, I don't take up much space."

Chris chuckled and stopped to open the door. "C'mon, I'll show you around." Chris made their way to the door of the house and held it for Nick. "I was thinking you could use the guitar or piano and get your music out again."

"With what band?" Nick shrugged and looked around the house.

The mudroom was clean and Chris smiled that somebody had tidied up the shoes recently. The coats were hung by the door and there was a place for keys as well as a small shelf for shoes. Chris kicked off their shoes and placed them on the shelves.

Nick shrugged and kicked off his old shoes that truly looked like a bag man's. Nick sighed looking at his feet. Nick had no socks but had calluses and overgrown toenails; they were a sight. Chris sighed seeing that at least Nick's feet were clean.

"Do you want a real shower?" Chris offered and pointed at the adjoining door. "I'm sure I've got clothes to fit you."

Chris led Nick through the door and they entered a large space. They grinned as Nick looked at the piano. The way Nick eyed the piano made it obvious that he yearned to play music. Nick paused by the piano and Chris chuckled at him then led him up a carpet-lined staircase.

Nick continued to look at the halls adorned with more tables and paintings. Finally he gave a low whistle. "Big house, huh?" He said quietly and Chris shrugged. He followed to a hall on the right that led to three doors.

Chris opened the first on the left. "That's just a bathroom."

A sunken spa tub, bidet, dual sinks, a tech looking shower and beautiful marble accents looked like royalty to him.

Chris opened the opposite door on the right. "An office."

As Chris saw Nick inspecting the room with its deep-pile carpet, mahogany shelves built into the walls, and a dignified desk, Chris decided it was probably best to not disclose to him that this was their official office space. Then Nick's attention was caught as Chris tossed open the door in front of them.

"Your room." Chris smiled and stepped back to let Nick enter first.

There was more wall to wall carpet but this was a lighter color. Nick stepped in and turned his head when seagulls made a noise from the open window and Cris watched him taking it all in with huge eyes. There was a stunning view of the water. It didn't smell like the harbor and instead had a cleaner aroma. Nick turned his head in the direction to see other doors and Chris stepped in to open them for him.

Chris opened one of the opposing doors. "Closet." Chris switched a light on.

Chris' eyes widened as Nick's gaze shifted to the walk-in closet. His mouth opened, and Chris could imagine his tongue hanging out of it like a hungry puppy. A gleaming mahogany electric guitar sat in the corner, and Nick practically leapt to itbut turned to Christo Chris with an eager expression. "Mind if I exercise that for you?"

Chris nodded to the guitar leaning at the back of the closet and almost laughed that Nick noticed that over the drawers and clothing hanging up. "I forgot about that one." Chris walked in and picked it up, handing it to Nick and sighing while they turned on the light. "We all keep older clothes in here but make yourself at home." Chris pulled jeans off the hanger, then opened drawers to snatch a t-shirt.

Chris offered them to Nick and opened one of the drawers showing they were filled with underwear and socks. "These are new or practically new, so choose what you like."

Nick took the clothes and watched Chris step out. "Why do you have so many extra clothes and spare rooms?"

"We have several because my parents come from large families, and during the holidays some relatives stay over." Chris yawned. "It's just easier."

Nick nodded as Chris went by the windows to open a door near them. "This is your bathroom, and I have to warn you that my mother hates a mess." Chris smiled.

Nick looked like he won the lottery when he looked at the grand bathroom to rival the other but this one had windows that looked out to the water like the bedroom. "Nice pile of bricks."

Chris smiled. "Go ahead and shower, then I'll show you the rest of the house."

With that, Chris left Nick to indulge in a real shower.

Chris descended the steps in search of Mother but found only the television left on. The newscast was blaring loudly, drowning out all other sounds in the house. Chris stared at the screen and listened as they broadcasted from the harbor.

The anchor's voice echoed through the quiet house as they reported live from where Chris had been only a short while ago. "Our brave rescuer was too shy for an interview." The camera zoomed in on Chris padding off the boat. "They were none other than Chris Shepherd, and if you keep looking..." They trailed off as the camera panned in on Chris next to Nick. "That man in the hoodie looks like none other than Nick Dallas. He was famous throughout the '80s and '90s until he vanished."

Another reporter's voice could be heard chiming in now. "That definitely resembles Nick!"

They put an old pic of Nick side by side with the video of him walking away with Chris and one reporter laughed. "Of all the disguises. He looks like a homeless man!"

From the kitchen doorway a voice boomed in. "I guess they recognized us," Nick mumbled.

Chris turned to see Nick standing there with hair that was still damp but he looked much different. Despite a few wrinkles, he still held his attractive appearance from his prime. Chris heard somebody say the man that wandered off with the rescuer looked homeless again and Nick turned bright red.

"You're not homeless anymore." Chris said pointedly, "You're staying with us. You helped get me away from the press and gave me what little you had." Chris looked down to the care-worn garments with a wry grin.

Nick pushed his hands in his pockets. "This feels like a dream." He continued to look around with a smile playing on his lips. "Okay, I didn't know I missed this kind of lifestyle." He gestured to the house. "Walls, roof, hot showers, and warm meals." He grinned. "I'm with you, kid, but I'm gonna make a name for myself again and I'll pay you back when I do."

Chris gave a hopeful smile. "I don't need money. Just stay friends?" Chris walked into the room with the piano. "I think you're a good guy and you're worth it." Inwardly, Chris was concerned that being on the streets had hardened Nick and wanted to make sure that everyone closed their doors at night until they were certain they could fully rely on Nick.

Nick must have felt Chris's apprehension but he shifted from foot to foot. "I get it. No, I didn't go nuts; I was just a little cold, but I think you're helping me get over that." Nick looked hopeful. "I'll be a good house guest and I have ideas to get back into music."

Chris was excited to show him around the family and entertainment room. "Let's talk where it's comfortable." Chris gestured to the room they were in. "We don't use this room for hanging out but for entertaining and holidays. It's formal." Chris waved at the living room dismissively and indicated a stairwell that went down next to the kitchen. Chris began to descend the staircase and could hear Nick right behind them.

At the bottom of the stairs, motion-activated lights came on in the large entertainment room and Chris sighed, looking at it with a smile on their face. It was home to many family parties. Rather than paying attention to the long-winded lectures from the grown-ups, the younger generation would come down to this place and spend time playing video games or simply hanging out. Part was sectioned off with a large U shaped sofa and a large flat screen hung on the wall. Towards the back there were desks with computers and other electronics. To the right was an old fashioned billiards table and just beyond that was a cozy bar.

It all paled next to the immense mirror doors accompanying a view of the water. Nick looked out and beamed. "I love the water. You can be homeless anywhere. I chose the harbor because I could see the water." Nick gave Chris a warm smile. "Water's life, y'know."

Nick turned and jumped, seeing his reflection in a large mirror on the opposing wall. He gave a sheepish chuckle and a roguish grin. "I thought somebody else was here with us for a sec."

Chris joined him looking at the window and urged him forward. They opened one of the large doors showing how nice the weather was.

Nick stood on the patio and looked overwhelmed taking it all in. It was hard to tell if he was looking at the water or the pool with tables and lounge chairs around it. The pier, boats, and two boathouses that appeared to be party-ready could all be seen in the water's brilliance.

"The pool was just cleaned," Chris said quietly. "Please don't take the boats out." Chris gave an upturn of their mouth in a mock smile. "They're Dad's babies." Chris brought out their phone as they walked into the house. Touching it quickly they had the TV on. "I'll get you a remote for the house or a phone. You can control everything inside with it."

Nick approached the television, frowning at the news-caster. "We're still making the news," Nick muttered when he noticed another station presenting the same scene from several camera angles.

Chris felt a chill run down their spine as they watched the footage of the churning water on the news. The sound of the waves was unsettlingly similar to the wet slapping noise from their nightmares, and it reminded them of the pounding sensation of feet against unrelenting pavement. Chris took in a deep breath and tried to relax.

They motioned for Nick to sit. "Make yourself at home or I can show you around the rest of the house. We have a basketball hoop; you couldn't see it when we got in."

Nick grinned. Chris was delighted at Nick's reaction. Instead of tinkering with all that technology, Nick seemed to prefer to play hoops.

"You play, huh?" Nick asked with a grin. "How about after we eat? That way we can burn off the calories."

"No offense, Nick, but you look like you could use a few calories," Chris smiled then had a serious tone. "I was hoping to ask a favor."

Nick's expression revealed his doubt. His face was closed off, just like it had been when Chris first encountered him. "Sure..."

"I have a doctor's appointment tomorrow." Chris looked down and felt as if tears would burst. "I can't tell my parents yet... I need to get checked for cancer." Chris was quickly becoming misty eyed. "I could use a friend there if you don't mind going with me."

"Shit, kid. I'm sorry," Nick patted Chris's back gently. "When did you find out?"

"Remember the deal?" Chris watched Nick's face change, "Yeah..."

"That's how he said you're gonna go?" Nick laughed. "Hey, it's not gonna happen now." Obviously, it was still upsetting, and Nick patted Chris's back. "He wouldn't make the deal if it couldn't be fixed now. Hey! Don't worry. I'll go with you okay?"

Chris looked up and nodded. "Thanks, Nick. You're really the only person in the world I can talk to about this."

"No, I'm not," Nick took a breath. "He's done this deal more times than I can count." Chris stared at Nick and sighed. "The funny thing about living on the street is you're constantly in the public and you see a lot. I wasn't his only deal."

Chris nodded, but their thoughts were still racing. "How many? They can't die either right?"

Nick leaned back. "And neither can you now you made the deal, so don't worry."

Chris got up and began to pace. "Can I ask how many times you tried to kill yourself?"

"I lost count," Nick sighed and lifted his hair. "Each time I tried, I got a scar." He held his hair up for Chris to see the side of his neck and the small scar of a noose. "I got that after trying to hang myself."

Chris gasped, "Like a badge of shame? It marks you?"

"Yeah, I guess. I tried pills and got this," Nick lifted the hair by his temple to show a skull and crossbones. "I kinda like that one. It's rad."

Chris took a seat, feeling their breath escaping in short spurts. Chris and Nick seemed to travel down the same paths, like two stars crossing the night sky. Years before, Chris had considered taking their own life when confined by poverty, but Chris realized then that everyone could feel lost at points. Knowing that tomorrow always brought fresh possibilities, that was what kept Chris going. Now, Chris's days were spent in a luxurious home, with no need to worry from paycheck to paycheck. Chris's only concern was the deal. "So, once I'm healed, I can't die?"

"Pretty much. I had other small accidents after I was getting clean." Nick stood up and pulled the top of his jeans down to reveal a scar. The mark on his hip resembled a chalk body outline. "I got that from a nasty spill doing a show. I was flying above the crowd and the wire snapped holding me. I crashed on the stage but I got right back up and finished the show. Nobody could believe I wasn't hurt, not even me." He pulled his pants up and sat back down.

"Could you find some of the others like you if you wanted?" Chris narrowed eyes as the idea formed.

"Yeah, several." Nick eyed Chris suspiciously. "Why, kid?"

"Like today, I jumped after the girl but I was scared shit-less. I just prayed that I couldn't die like you said. It gave me courage." Chris heaved a hard breath. "We signed our lives away but why can't we make a difference?"

"What are you saying?"

"We can't die right? So maybe we can make a difference and help."

"I get it, but you're forgetting he targets people with money in the public eye and they're usually a pretty shallow bunch. Plus we're not the same people now."

"What do you mean?"

"One of them was the most famous fat lady in the world until he visited her. He told her she had to drop the weight and which doctor to go to and get it done. She's healthy but poor." Nick spoke so quickly he had to take a breath before continuing. "Another person was a famous professor, but he was told he would have a brain tumor. After all the proce-dures, he's not the same guy." Nick kept talking rapidly, "They don't want to be in the public eye for the same reason I didn't."

"What do you mean?"

"How the mighty have fallen? The media loves that crap and shows it to the world." Nick gave a hard scoff. "The actors or singers that got fat or poor get their pics all smeared on gossip rags. Then there's the celebs that had too much surgery or didn't age well. I hid so I could have peace from that." Nick sat up a little straighter. "I still have pride."

"But you're thinking of going back now?" Chris hoped.

"Yeah, with your help. I mean who would take a singing homeless man seriously? Honestly, I didn't even have a guitar. If I can clean up, I'm sure I can get back out there," Nick reasoned looking at the ceiling. "But I need the help."

Chris nodded. "So do I."

Nick perked up a bit and gave Chris a playful swipe. "So, we help each other."

Chris sat back preoccupied by the notion. "Maybe that's how it's done? We have to help each other to break the bad luck."

Nick relaxed and sat back. "Maybe."

"We could help the others too, Nick."

"Are you pushing for sainthood, kid? We can't save the world," Nick laughed heartily.

"No, I'm serious," Chris sat up straight. "All we have to do is find their loopholes, like yours. I figured out how to not go poor with this deal because of you." Now, Chris was talking fast and seemed ready to jump. "Also, helping them will bring all of you in the spotlight more, so a comeback will be not only expected but praised."

"I don't know..." Nick said quietly. Now the rockstar seemed uncertain.

"You've got the time, and so do I. For you, it's the best press in the world. Think about it." Now, Chris returned Nick's enthusiastic swipe on the arm. "People won't come to see you for just music but because of who you are." Chris smiled. "The rest of your band isn't doing anything now, but you can." Chris took a deep breath and looked at him earnestly. "We could save lives."

Chris's challenge seemed to pique Nick's interest, and Nick arched his brow. "What about this bulletproof hero business?"

"I'm not saying we look for trouble, but we can prevent things we see." Chris looked as the news went to commercial. "We're given a second chance so why not give back? If they definitely find cancer and heal me... I mean..." Chris waved their hands trying to find the words, then finally spat out, "If we can't die, then we're doing it."

"If he told you that you have cancer, then you do." Nick

slumped down on the comfortable leather couch. "I heard a deal a few years ago with someone who didn't believe Deacon and they were gone in a year." Nick furrowed his brow at the thought.

"Who?"

"He was a grunge rocker from the mid '90s and was told he would die on a train. Deacon told him which train and when, but this guy was a skeptic and turned it down. He kept saying he was being punked." Nick made a weak shake of his head and looked spooked. "He got on that train."

Chris's eyes were big, and waved hands about like a competitor on a game show. Chris whispered now, "I remember him! He got a deal?" Chris sat down. "Wow!" Chris returned Nick's stare with wide eyes. "He's never been wrong?"

"Not that I've seen, and sitting around Baltimore, you see a lot." Nick raised a corner of his mouth in a sarcastic smirk.

Chris heard the door upstairs close and the low murmur of voices. "Dinner time!" Chris said, clapping hands together and gesturing to the stairs.

CHAPTER 8

Music roused Chris the next dawn. After sitting up, Chris recognized the sound of the piano and a voice singing. Chris raced to the door and flung it open to hear a soothing melody that filled the home. It all came flooding back: Nick, Deacon, the little girl, the media, and – most crucially – the doctor's visit.

Chris gestured with a wave for Nick to follow him through the glass doors onto the expansive deck that overlooked the water. The late afternoon light was subdued and everything was hushed, it felt like they had entered into a dream as the sky began its slow transformation from golden orange to ever-deepening shades of purple and pink. The water was a still mirror reflecting colors so vividly that it seemed impossible, as if the two were suspended in an otherworldly portal to another universe. Long after the sun had set, they sat in quiet contemplation, enveloped by the gentle lapping of waves against the shore.

Despite the fact that the night was fuzzy after some wine, Chris recalled the brunt of it. Chris sighed and looked at the door that had been left unlocked. Nick appeared to be trustworthy and had passed the test.

"As the world falls away, I will cling to you..." Chris's ears perked up when they heard the sound of Nick's voice, recognizing the song as the same one that had made Nick famous. Chris returned to the room to brush their teeth after hearing the music. The door was left open and Nick's voice filled the room.

"We fall together, and if we fall, we fall forever..." Nick continued to harmonize with the piano.

Chris grinned widely with the toothbrush hanging out of their mouth, understanding it was a love song, and brushed their teeth more rapidly. Nick's voice was astonishing. He had the perfect tone but with that coveted slight rasp of a seasoned blues singer. Nick's voice seemed effortless and very genuine.

"As long as we're together..." Nick continued, skillfully holding the notes to emphasize specific lyrics. "Forever...together."

Chris bounded down the stairs and stopped short when he heard Nick singing. His eyes were closed and head tilted back, with his hands gripping the sides of the piano as he brought every note to life. Chris went forward, unwilling to shatter the enchantment that hovered. Nick suddenly turned to face Chris and smiled broadly.

"Can you sing?" Nick slapped the bench for Chris to join.

Chris declined quickly, "I'm not a great singer."

Nick inclined his head and exhaled loudly. "I guess it's better if we want to get an early start on the day."

Chris agreed silently. "I want to help you reconnect with old acquaintances. Perhaps they can help you get a footing in the music industry again."

Nick stood stretching. "It's not quite the same, but my voice is not as bad as I thought it would be."

Chris held their phone out to them. "If you're ready?"

Nick's brow rose in surprise and he released a drawn-out breath before speaking. He uttered the words slowly, carefully, as if trying to be both cautious and delicate. "Your father told me how he met your mother in another country." Chris could feel Nick's eyes on them, curiosity burning as their father had raised the question of Chris's ethnicity.

Chris glanced up from the floor and offered a tiny smile, one that was both proud of their shared Korean heritage and thankful for their friend's attempt at gentle sensitivity. "My mom is half Korean," Chris offered.

"That's pretty cool. We toured there back in the day. I wish I remembered it better but those days are a blur now." Nick took a deep breath and looked to the door. "Is it all right to get coffee for the road?"

"Of course!" Chris beamed, eyes twinkling. They dug into their pocket and pulled out a jangling keychain. Nick followed them to the garage, their shoulders tense as they nervously bit their lip. "I rescheduled my doctor appointment..." Chris paused, trying to make sense of the situation in their head. A few days wouldn't matter; they needed time to come to terms with the battle of surgery and the struggle felt owed to them. "Where are we going?" Chris asked with a cleansing breath.

Nick knitted his brow and lifted his hand to take the keys, but Chris was already in the car. Nick heaved a sigh. "The harbor..."

CHAPTER 9

The waterfront was already humming when they arrived, and both hid under hoodies, hoping that their antics from the day before had been forgotten. They found a seat at one of the cafes that Deacon had been frequenting, and quietly sipped their coffee while they talked.

"Does everything happen here, Nick?" Chris joked.

"Yeah, Deacon meets people here, and after their deals go bad, most wander back. I guess they're looking for him."

"Goes bad?"

"Like it wasn't what they expected."

"They can't find Deacon?"

"Only if he wants to be found." Nick muttered, but his gaze was drawn to a woman who had just breezed in. He pointed to the ethereal beauty who had captured the attention of almost every man in the café.

Chris peered at her while squinting against the sun. She emerged from the blinding blur of the sun, as if she were walking on the sunlight itself. If an angel could fall from heaven, it would appear like this. This lady covered her large, soulful eyes with a floppy sun hat and wore a flowing dress paired with gladiator sandals. The woman seemed oblivious to the attention and focused only on the table in front of her. Chris nearly laughed at how enamored Nick was of her. "She's very pretty."

"She's one of his clients," Nick whispered.

Chris turned to give her a closer examination. She had a little scar or tattoo of a noose at the base of her neck, which was easily visible on her pale skin. "I don't recognize her..."

It was hard not to look in her direction and admire her beauty. Chris was confident anyone who had met her would remember her. Even from afar, she seemed to glow with an otherworldly shine, like a sprite out of a fable. Chris could not help but think of a fairy when they looked at her.

Nick noticed Chris's stare and chuckled, "You probably wouldn't know her. She made the deal years ago." He sighed.

"I'll introduce you." Nick stood up and stumbled over himself with his eyes trained on her. He was obviously thrilled to have an excuse to speak to her.

"You know her?"

"I'm about to."

Chris' eyes widened and followed after Nick, hoping they wouldn't chase her away.

Nick stood by the lady, and she spoke before he could. "You're in my sun."

She glanced up as Chris joined them, "I know you." She smiled at Chris then she looked at Nick. "And you..."

"You do?" Nick asked, his eyes opening wider.

She raised her head and smiled. "You're both all over the morning news."

Under the watchful eye of this self-assured woman, Chris felt incredibly exposed. Chris was painfully aware of the clumsy rescue that had been made public and even more embarrassed that she'd seen it all. Chris's stomach turned slightly at the thought. Still, she seemed to cock her head in curiosity. Chris stayed quiet, so as to not make the atmosphere awkward. Anything that would disrupt the comfortable energy between them was something Chris wanted to avoid.

Nick smiled. "May we join you, Jean?" She looked doubtful until Nick added, "Ima?" With Nick's second attempt, she glanced at Chris nervously. Chris pondered if maybe she had been hurt or was just as alone as they had been. Nick slid into a chair next to her silently but kept his eyes on her the entire time.

"Don't call me Ima!" She looked insulted by it. She widened her eyes and gulped, glancing around as if searching for an exit. "How do you know me?"

Chris sat next to Nick, watching as he pulled his collar aside, revealing the scar they both shared. A feeling of jealousy washed over Chris as the two of them had a bond Chris could not relate to. Chris looked on quietly but their heart beat faster as they watched Jean and Nick together.

"Hmmm, I wonder why we both thought of the rope." She sighed as she sat back with her coffee. "What do you want?"

Nick offered his hand expectantly. "Introductions? I'm Nick and this is Chris."

She shook Nick's hand and took Chris's as Nick went on. "This is Ima, or Jean, as she's known now. Former fat lady with the circus."

Chris felt her draw her hand back swiftly and apologized but didn't know if they had upset her.

"So you know me? Has he ruined both of you like he did me?"

Chris felt starstruck. "You don't look ruined to me."

She gazed at her hands and appeared self-conscious. "I had

more money than I could count before." She whispered. "I had to do nothing but eat, and I did gain weight fast. I was so big that at times they would use trucks to get me to the tent. Then this man came to me and explained how I was really close to living my last day."

Trembling at the memory, she put her arms across her chest. "After a day and some pains in my chest, I took the deal. He saved my life but he killed Ima."

She continued to peer at the water, perhaps lost in her thoughts. "I lost weight and I got in shape, but 'normal' doesn't sell tickets in a circus. I ended up homeless and had to get a 9-5 job. I had to start over."

"You look great," Chris chimed in cheerfully.

"I never cared about how I looked, but after I lost the weight, I began to see the difference in how people treated me. They see me as normal, but I still feel like the fat lady." She sat up, seeing Nick's stare. "I belonged when I was a freak, but now that I'm normal, I don't belong anywhere." She looked down and her fingers tapped lightly on the table. "Although I look 25, I'm twice that."

"Look, Jean, you've been there and we want to find others like us." Nick said quietly.

"Oh," she said sadly. "I had thought..." She took a deep breath and grinned, "But you're the rockstar right?"

Chris observed them and wondered how dense Nick was or if he wasn't interested in her.

Nick narrowed his eyes. "Jean, we all know we can't die."

"I suppose," She muttered gently as her fingertips brushed over her scar, then she spotted Nick's other scars and studied him closely. "Really?"

Nick nodded. "I've tried many times. Jean, we're immortal but in the worst way."

Her gaze was upon her hands. "What are you saying?"

"We can't die and he ruined us. He forced us to live in poverty and to be alone. Let's find the others and band together." Nick looked to Chris for support, "Then we can face that devil and fix this." He took her hand in his and appeared to enjoy the fact that she shrank away from it. "We're broken too."

"I have a new life now. I am not broken," she murmured gently, her voice slightly quavering.

Nick let her hand go. "Bull! I can see it in your eyes. You have the dreams too."

"Dreams?" Chris whispered. It was then Chris saw Jean had dark circles under her eyes. They looked to the side and noticed Nick had shadows as well, which they had previously attributed to his living situation. Chris inhaled deeply, recalling their own nightmare of running in the cold alone. It hadn't been that frightening to Chris, and the idea of it becoming worse worried them.

"The kid here hasn't had the dreams yet," Nick eventually scoffed as Jean stared between them. "Chris just made the deal and found me here yesterday."

"Don't be alone," she remarked pointedly, grasping Chris's hand. "Never alone."

Nick nodded and patted Chris's shoulder. "Yeah," Nick took a breath, "you shouldn't be alone, but this deal is part of who we are now. We're living as part of his clause." He cocked his head, apparently recalling something else, "That and the 'don't tell' biz."

Then Nick slid her other hand into his, and the trio of them held hands. "Are you with us?"

She took a deep breath and braced herself. "There are others."

"Others?" Chris traded a look between them then sighed as

they became fixated on the idea of tormenting nightmares. "How bad can the nightmares get? We can't die, right?"

She let their hands go, folding her own in her lap. Together Nick and Jean nodded and in unison whispered, "They get bad...really bad."

CHAPTER 10

Nick strolled by the harbor with Jean and Chris. Chris and Nick's hands were deep in their pockets as they peered at the brick path in front of them. Chris groaned, observing Jean's sidelong looks at Nick, uncertain if she was drawn to one of them or skeptical of the whole thing.

Finally, Jean spoke. "The other person I know works here." She stopped in front of a quaint old bookstore. "Like us, they lost everything and had to start over." She took a deep breath peering at the glass of the door, "Don't expect him to like you." She grasped the door handle and tugged it open, letting them in.

Nick and Chris locked eyes for a brief second before pushing the door open. As they stepped inside, a rich aroma of freshly roasted coffee beans filled the air, and the low hum of conversation created a soothing ambience. Among the books sat a little coffee shop run by a single person. Looking around, they could see shelves of books, but it was modest, majestic but small, like most of the shops in the harbor. The majority of the books were aged and appeared vintage. At the register, only a modest standing display contained the newest books.

Jean exhaled sharply as she walked down an aisle of New Age books and an employee descended upon them.

"Ah!" An approaching man made the noise as he drew closer to them. He promptly handed them a flier, "let me know if I may assist you." He was a tall man with blond hair and steel blue eyes behind black rounded spectacles. He spoke with a British accent that sounded upper-class.

Nick extended his hand, but the man sneered, as if to illustrate his social position. The man exhaled and stared at Nick's hand until Nick stuffed it back into his pocket.

The man raised a brow and stifled a yawn. "The new releases are by the register and the coffee is perfect."

"They want to talk to you, Nigel,"Jean remarked slowly as she approached the small group, holding a large book in her hands. She narrowed her eyes as she met his steely glare.

"Ima!" He started in mock glee. "I suppose you're lost because the all-you-can-eat buffet is just around the corner." After he finished speaking, his look had changed to snarky and contemptuous.

Chris traded a look with Nick as this man mocked Jean. Chris wondered if they should step in or let her handle it considering she was the one to introduce them. Nick's eyes didn't leave Jean, and she seemed to have the conversation under control.

Jean smiled, not taking the bait. "They were actually interested in talking to you." She held a book in front of Nigel, only for him to yank it from her grasp.

"As if you could possibly afford it." He gingerly held the book close to his body and glared at it with thinly-veiled contempt.

"How many times have you read it? Do you have it memorized now?" She taunted him.

"Since you can't afford it, I'll just pop this back where it belongs and you can see yourselves out." Nigel brushed off her mocking.

As hard as Chris stared, they could only get a glimpse at the book but couldn't make out the title. Chris took command and took out a credit card. "I'll buy it."

Nigel barely lifted his loafers off the ground as he turned and scowled at him with narrowed eyes. "It's almost ten thousand for this book." He then turned around to try and replace it where it belonged. "I'll return it next to the Gutenberg Bible and the Codex Leicester."

"That's not a problem," Chris replied calmly, but Nigel gave them a look as if they had offered to buy his child.

"It's not for sale!" Nigel snapped.

Chris gave Nigel a look of defiance, then took out their phone. After removing the case, they pulled from it a small stack of cards and chose one without hesitation.

Jean held a hand up for everybody to stop, and laughed. "I work in a bank and I know you can't refuse legal tender. I'm sure your boss would love to know this."

When another individual entered, Chris sidestepped the door and glared at the title, 'The Immortals.' Despite the antique leather bound covering, Chris arched a brow and resisted the desire to scoff at the title. It sounded like a cruel irony.

Nigel planted his feet. "Bugger off, Ima. I'll be purchasing it."

Chris, ever the peacemaker, changed the topic and stepped forward. "Would you tell us what it's about?"

Nigel actually gave a ghost of a smile. "Everything..."

Jean rolled her eyes. "Why don't you bring it and sit down with us for a minute?"

Nigel laughed so loudly other patrons looked over. "Why would I?"

Jean breathed slowly and delicately brushed her scar. "We're all a part of the same… curse."

"Not me!" Nigel sneered and took off, but Jean followed in his footsteps, trailed by Chris and Nick.

Jean shook her head and touched his arm, but he quickly jerked away. She took a deep breath and raised her voice. "How are you sleeping, Nigel?"

With that he turned and met their eyes. Chris saw the bags under his eyes as he looked through his thick lenses, and remembered Jean and Nick had them as well.

Nigel looked at Chris accusingly. "Why don't you have them?"

"The kid just met up with our friend," Nick intercepted.

Nigel looked at Chris again. "You've no idea what you signed up for, pal." Nigel snorted and rolled his eyes.

Jean bowed her head looking at Chris sadly. "Talk with us. Just over coffee or we can go to lunch."

Chris began shifting weight from foot to foot and noticed the way Nick stared at Jean made Chris's face burn at the thought Nick might be interested in her. Chris felt red in the face realizing Nick might be interested in her.

Nigel looked between them and then at the ceiling. "I have a feeling I'm going to regret this." He regarded them as though resigned to fate. "I have my lunch break in ten minutes."

Nigel sat with the book face down on his lap. He treated that book better than some people would treat a beloved pet in public. His hand was on it or would reach for it while he sipped his coffee.

Nick watched Nigel with bated breath, while Jean appeared

indifferent. Chris felt terrified of what they had learnt, especially the dreams they would likely face soon.

"Perchance, might one of you buffoons clarify what this rubbish is all about?" Nigel said looking from face to face.

"We all made the deal, Nigel. This may be our only way to bring some peace to others if not ourselves." Jean murmured as her fingers lazily slid around the rim of her cup.

"Do-gooders? Vigilantes? What do you think will happen if that bloke finds out? He didn't make the deal to give us power!" Nigel replied sharply, wagging a finger at Jean.

"But he did give us power!" Nick hissed. "After he took all we had." Nick lit a cigarette and gazed out at the bay as a ship approached. He shut his eyes as the smell of the water wafted over them. Nick exhaled the smoke slowly from his mouth and stared intently at Nigel as he spoke. "We can't die, man. Why not use that to help people."

"Are you suggesting that we profit from our actions?" Nigel grinned and looked intrigued.

Jean rolled her eyes at his Pavlovian reaction. "Money is Nigel's only passion. He was a genius and born to an affluent household. He was one of England's top minds until his family disowned him." Nigel had opened his mouth, ready to speak, but the sound of Jean's voice caused him to clamp it shut. His head swiveled in her direction as he watched her, he glared at her looking exposed.

"Why did they do that?" Chris wondered aloud.

"Because they're narrow-minded fools!" Nigel snapped immediately. He let out a long breath before adding, "I was at the top... until I met him, my assistant."

He averted his gaze. "Benjamin told me to stay on the flight back to England. He boarded because he was desperate to see his family."

Glancing around, Nigel seemed nervous that someone

might overhear him. "He was still aboard when it crashed into the sea for some unknown reason. Nobody survived, and none of the wreckage was ever located. When the media got wind of how I got off the plane at the last second it became quite the scandal."

Chris sat up. "I remember that years ago! You were traveling with a friend and he still got on. You were national news for a long time."

"Did you happen to hear who my companion was?" Nigel waved a hand and scoffed at Chris. "Of course you did! It was all over the news how my love, Benjamin, died. He had to get to his ailing grandfather. He refused to miss the plane because I was being 'irrational' and the media loved it."

Nigel looked faraway for a moment and murmured. "I begged him to get off with me..."

"But you lived," Nick pointed out. "Like that movie..."

"We weren't known then!" Nigel snapped. "Our parents had no idea of our inclination."

"You're gay? They didn't know?" Chris's eyes widened in wonder. They understood that the world was not always as welcoming and open-minded as it is now. Nigel had endured the same struggles as Chris while growing up in an environment that was not always accepting of LGBTQ individuals. Though the world still had room for improvement, Chris felt compassion because Nigel decided to come out during a pivotal time.

"There are a few noble crests in our family, thus such controversies are not allowed. They disowned me directly. Father's last words were 'let the yanks have you'." Nigel's eyes glazed over, and his unfocused gaze remained fixed on the steam rising from his cup. He seemed lost in thought, his mind wandering to a place far beyond the harbor.

"I'm sorry," Chris said quietly. Chris was non-binary but

had never faced the ordeals Nigel had. Chris shuddered at the thought of a world where their parents, siblings, and other relations didn't show unconditional love or accept them for who they were.

Nigel smiled as he turned to face Chris. "That's all the past now, dear." He placed his palm over Chris's as he gave Chris a direct look.

Chris jumped and abruptly pulled away. "Whoa. I'm not..." Chris was sure they were five shades of red and looked over in the direction of Nick and Jean. Nigel wasn't ugly, but Chris simply wasn't interested in him romantically.

"Do you like men or women?" Nigel gave Chris a sweet smile and tried to lean in more.

Chris exhaled sharply, "No, sorry... I'm just not interested." Chris took a breath.

"Stop bothering the kid." Nick cut in. "Let's get back on track here."

Jean's laughter was like tiny fireworks going off in the night sky, twinkling and quickly dissipating. The group of friends filled the table with bright color and laughter as Nigel unabashedly professed his admiration for Chris. Chris sat there, still and smiling, happy to be among them.

Nick spoke up. "Nigel, you said you saw Deacon a lot with people like us."

Nigel sank back a bit in his chair. "Yes, I work where I see the public often. Aren't I a lucky bloke?" He looked between the other three, "I've no desire to see him, yet I do."

Nick was the first to speak after the three of them exchanged glances. "Then you know others?"

"I see them chatting away with him, then I see them come back looking for him. It's not easy for an A lister to go unnoticed. They venture in and out of the shops looking for him, wanting an explanation... just as I did." He looked bored. "Are we done?" He stood up. "I've no interest in playing superhero."

"Then tell us who they are or where to find them!" Jean said quickly.

"How can you be so mean?" Chris whispered at Nigel.

"Mean?" Nigel shot back quickly. "I'm just looking out for myself." Nigel positioned himself close to Chris. "So, are you a..." Nigel began but trailed off as if expecting Chris to finish the statement.

Chris cocked an eyebrow but didn't speak.

"What's up with the book?" Nick exhaled and used his thumb to butt the ashes from his cigarette. "Tell us about it."

Nigel set it on the table, "It's not about *him*, but about beings who resemble him." He ran his fingers over the raised lettering lovingly. "It's about immortal beings that strike deals with people like us."

"Are you saying one of them is Deacon?" Chris kept their voice low. "Are you saying he's not human? What did you find out?" Chris shifted to the edge of their seat.

Nigel smiled and continued the attention, "Well, for you..."

Flustered as Nigel's eyes sparkled with admiration and he flashed a heart-melting smile, Chris felt her face flush. They shifted uncomfortably in their seat and quickly diverted their gaze, not wanting to encourage Nigel's flirty behavior. "I'm not..." They mumbled.

"Quit stalling," Nick said fast and tamped out his spent cigarette.

Nigel winced and opened the book, showing ancient artwork of people tormented by horned demons with forked tongues. "Let's say it's not good."

"That reminds me of the nightmares!" Jean and Nick exclaimed simultaneously, then exchanged a knowing glance with Nigel.

Chris sank in the chair at the mention of the nightmares. Their dreams of being chased had scared them to the bone and the idea of the nightmares from the deal being worse scared Chris.

"You seem surprised," Nigel grumbled. He began to flip slowly through the pages. "The closest I could come up with was an ancient story about a creature named Papa Legba. Some regard him as a pitiful old man with a cane, while others regard him as a youthful and virile trickster."

"Deacon had a cane!" The other three said in unison.

Nigel chuckled at them and continued, "From older to modern appearance, the one thing that seems to be true is the cane. He's a trickster and can do things for a profit or favor." Nigel turned the page to show a picture of a person cowering under an intimidating figure. "If you try to recant or not make good on your deal, he comes back for you."

Nick huffed a breath. "Deacon took all we had; so, we made good on the deal."

"What happened to those who crossed him?" Jean inquired, peering at the image.

"It gets a bit hazy." Nigel flipped open the book to show them the exquisite drawing of a woman with ebony complexion. "This woman lived 300 years because of her deal with him." He took a breath. "Marie."

Nigel turned the book so they could see the ancient artwork of a woman with plaited hair worn atop her head and large lavish jewelry. "There's not much on her deal or how she died."

"Where is she buried?" Chris asked, their eyes huge.

"They said she outlived all her relatives so there's not much about her after 250 years." Nigel nodded. "I hope I live that long."

"What are the dreams you keep talking about?" Chris questioned cautiously, almost frightened to ask.

Nigel growled angrily, "Darling, imagine dying each night and writhing in such pain that being dipped in the River Styx would be preferable. Tormented and tortured for a crime you never committed only to live it over again each eve."

Chris tilted their head, considering Nigel's words and growing increasingly worried that their own nightmare could grow even worse. They weren't sure if they should risk going to bed that night.

"My nightmare is like being caught in a heavy metal rock band art but instead of being cool it's painful." Nick looked at the empty cigarette package as he spoke then added, "and it sucks."

"You're so articulate," Nigel ridiculed Nick.

Eyes vacant, Jean murmured, "It's like being torn apart piece by piece each night, with every nerve on fire and in agony. I die each night, but there is no rebirth in the morning, only trembling from it." She sounded haunted.

Nigel waved her off, bored. "Yes, it's all very humbling." He sat against the back of the chair. For the first time his hands weren't on the book. "What's in this playing hero bit? Will it stop the nightmares? Is there a bit of dosh involved? Notoriety?"

"Why does it have to be that way?" Chris looked annoyed. "I helped that little girl yesterday and it felt amazing. I know she will live because of me."

Nigel smiled. "Self worth?" He stroked his chin gently. "Perhaps the press might give us a little lift."

"You're in?" Jean asked hopefully

"I'm skeptical," Nigel mumbled, pushing his fingertips against each other. He looked at Jean curiously.

Jean started to get up until Nick grabbed her arm. Nick shook his head and peered at her with sympathetic eyes.

Nick sighed and looked at Chris and Nigel. "Would you give us a minute?" Nick looked to Nigel, who appeared pleased with the prospect of chatting with Chris alone and readily agreed.

Chris nodded and stood but didn't appear thrilled at the prospect of being alone with Nigel. "I've had enough coffee, so I think I'll get a smoothie."

Nigel jumped up. "That sounds delightful!" He fell in pace with Chris' step.

Chris huffed a breath, making the best of it by striking up a conversation. "Know if there is any place to get smoothies?"

Nigel walked closer and Chris kept subtly edging away. "Tell me all about you. Are you Asian? How old are you?"

Chris abruptly halted and crossed their arms over their chest. "Just ask?"

Nigel wrinkled his brow. "What?"

"You can't tell if I'm a man or a woman," Chris looked up to the sky then back to Nigel. Chris was amused by Nigel's outgoing nature, even though Chris was not as open.

They raised an eyebrow; Nigel seemed to blend into any scene, while Chris never quite fit in. Nigel laid his personality out for others to see. Chris was much more reserved; making meaningful connections had always been difficult for them and romance had seemed impossible. Despite this, Chris still hoped that one day they would find a passionate relationship that set their heart ablaze. Unfortunately for Nigel, it wouldn't be with him.

"Then tell me!"

Thankfully Chris spotted a restaurant with a takeaway window where they could get smoothies.

Smoothies in hand, Chris rushed back to the table, but all they heard was Nick whisper sweetly, "Jean…"

"We got you some!" Nigel flounced in with a styrofoam cup and smiled when Nick and Jean nearly jumped out of their skins.

Chris felt a spark of discomfort when they noticed Nick and Jean share one long, intense glance. Their eyes seemed to be dancing around each other, making Chris feel unbelievably awkward. "Did we interrupt?"

Jean shook her head but Nick had a hint of guilt on his face. Jean quickly announced, "We were saying we should do some good deeds so others will want to join us."

Nigel snorted and shoved a cup in front of each of them, as if trying to dodge the subject. "Hope you like berry!"

CHAPTER 11

C hris noticed people were racing down the harbor's quay. "What's going on?"

Jean craned her neck to see. "I'm not sure."

"Something big." Nick stood and offered Jean his hand to help her stand.

She ignored him and stood swiftly as more people ran by. Chris broke into a run in the direction of the commotion.

"Hey, kid! Chris!" Chris heard Nick call after them. Soon they heard the others running behind them.

People were gathering around a building where small puffs of white smoke poured from cracks in the windows. The building was a well-known restaurant. It was a big building, beautiful with high arches and cartoon-like sculptures that would have fit perfectly in a children's book. The architecture was far from symmetrical and reminded Chris of a child-like Picasso.

"What's with the steam?" Chris wondered aloud.

"It's smoke," a man said quickly. "A fire broke out." His eyes were glued to the building.

"Hey, kid!" Nick yelled as he caught up.

Chris pulled their phone out and dialed. When the emergency services came on the line, they said, "I am calling about a fire."

While Chris was on the phone, they heard Jean say. "Someone is up there." She took steps toward the building and Chris felt their heart race at the idea of her going inside. Chris slammed the phone in her hand before she could argue.

"Give them the location," Chris said quickly. "Help the people who get out. I'll take care of that." Chris ran.

"What?" Chris could hear Jean call after them. "I can help!"

"Kid!" Nick shouted behind them. As they ran, Chris could have sworn they heard Nick say, "This kid is gonna get me killed!" Without waiting, Chris disappeared into the building.

Nigel was hot on Chris's heels. "You'd better be right, mate."

Chris pushed into the building but it was nothing like in the movies. There were no flames, no charred rubble or apocalyptic scene, only a haze of smoke that hung overhead like an overcast day.

Nigel was suddenly next to Chris, "I must be out of my head to do this."

"How do we get upstairs?"Nick asked from behind them.

Chris turned startled. "I've never been here before!"

"Tourists!" Nigel exclaimed.

Nigel led them up the stairs where the smoke was thicker, and they all pulled their shirts over their noses to help them breathe. The air was heavy with smoke that clung to the skin like a wet blanket. Visibility decreased as the black fog thickened, blurring shapes and outlines in the distance.

"I can't see much!" Chris was feeling along the walls for the doors now.

Nigel hit the ground crawling on hands and knees. "Get down if you want to see!"

Chris broke into a sprint and stumbled over something instead of following his crawling companion.

Chris bolted upright, their eyes darting about through the tears forming in their eyes. The smoke swirled above their head, and they coughed as they strained to see through the haze. A figure materialized in front of them, its clothing and features obscured by the fog. "There's a man here," Chris croaked out, their heart thundering in his chest.

Nick reached down and tossed the man over his shoulder. "I'll get this one out fast." Chris nodded and got down on their hands and knees to follow Nigel.

"You're right, Nigel, it's easier to breathe down here!" Chris called loudly and turned to look at Nick as he disappeared back down the stairs.

"Is someone there?" A voice called.

Nigel and Chris changed direction turning toward the voice. When they drew nearer, they could make out the light from the window's shattered glass and proceeded faster when they spotted a woman's heels and ankles. The smoke seemed to gather through the open window and they heard her coughing as they got closer.

"Help!" She called louder.

Nigel grabbed her ankle and she jumped. "Get down!"

Chris dragged her down but could hear her cough. She wore a dress, and it wasn't going to pull over her nose as their shirts did.

Nigel pulled his overshirt off, "Put it over your nose and mouth."

She did, but the coughing bouts slowed her down, and they discovered she couldn't crawl very well.

Chris traded a look with Nigel. "We can't die?" Chris stood up and peered out the window to see what was below. With any luck the awning would catch them then they wouldn't have to test fate and find out if they were truly immortal. Chris was scared to find out one way or the other.

Nigel opened his eyes wide watching Chris, "You're bonkers!"

Before Nigel could move, Chris had the coughing woman in their arms. "Let's go!"

"Nick's right!" Nigel yelled loudly as they crept through the jagged edge of the window and to the ledge. "You'll be the death of us!"

Chris drew a inhaled outside and breathed air eagerly. The woman continued to cough. "We need to get you down." Chris held the woman close as they teetered along the edge and, once they had a better grip on the situation, made for the awning.

"You're right insane!" Nigel screamed.

The woman clung to Chris for dear life as the pair bounced against the striped awning. They were sent apart as they went flying off the canvas.

Chris hit the ground face first with a thud and heard Nick's voice.

"I got her!" Nick ran with arms flailing to catch the woman but ended up a human cushion for her fall. Chris watched as the air was knocked out of Nick and he lay sprawled out trying to catch his breath while the woman was pulled off him.

Chris watched as Nick staggered to his feet, just in time to see Nigel fly off the awning. He lunged forward, arms outstretched, but it was too late; Nigel hit him square in the chest and knocked him over. Chris winced in sympathy as Nick lay there, stunned.

"My hero!" Nigel called out with an over-the-top cry. Given the situation, it provided a much-needed reason to laugh. Nigel kissed Nick's cheek before breaking out in fits of laughter.

Jean ran to them and scolded Nigel. "This isn't funny!" She helped Nigel off Nick and shook her head.

"How can you not laugh at something this absurd?" Nigel continued to cackle then heard Nick finally join in.

Chris stirred from a slight daze and peeled their eyes open to see a dark stain seeping from their rolled up sleeve. With shaking hands, they peeled back the fabric and gasped at a four-inch gash oozing blood down their arm. "I think I cut myself on that window."

Nick waved for a paramedic, while Jean grasped Chris's arm to roll up the sleeve farther until the jagged wound was exposed. Chris's throat constricted as he looked away and fought off tears.

Jean tore the sleeve's fabric and exposed the wound more. She used the torn fabric and began to dab at the wound, cleaning the blood away lightly. "That was very brave or..."

"Entirely foolish?" Nigel cut in and looked at Nick. "Got a fag?"

"A cigarette?" Nick looked at him curiously.

"I think you just inhaled enough smoke!" Jean reprimanded Nigel and began to wrap Chris's arm with material she had torn off her own skirt. She shook her head. "You're quite the sight." She tossed Nigel his jacket back.

Chris's face lit up as they heard them talking. Not that long ago, they were complete strangers, and now they had managed to work together and save lives. Chris's eyes widened in surprise and reached out to touch Jean's hand in concern.

"How's that lady? She was coughing a lot."

Jean shrugged. "I'll go see." She stood and made her way to an ambulance parked right by the harbor with its lights flashing.

Sirens howled and lights flashed as the fire engine roared down the street, approaching the inferno. They watched in horror as flames licked at the walls of the building and thick black smoke poured into the sky. Suddenly, a deafening rumble shook the ground as the roof gave way and collapsed into the center of the structure, sending plumes of ash and debris shooting high above.

Nigel sat down and took a deep breath. "The fun is over! I'm not cut out for this." He looked at Nick and exhaled sharply. "The superhero life is all yours, pal!"

Jean made her way back but not alone. She had a trail of paramedics and press behind her but it looked as if she were trying to outrun them. She fell on her knees next to Nick and Chris. "The woman you rescued was the mayor's wife and she's doing fine."

Chris quickly jumped up as they heard the ambulance peel away and sound its siren. "Was that her?"

A paramedic stepped up beside Jean and looked pointedly at Chris's arm. Other medical techs went over to Nigel and Nick.

In order to obtain an exact reading, the attractive paramedic ultimately requested Nigel to take his shirt off. Nigel grinned. "Buy me dinner first?" He took his jacket off as the rescuer laughed. He smiled wickedly at the handsome first responder "This is the life!" Nigel looked at the other three. "Okay! I'm in!"

CHAPTER 12

They sat on beds at the hospital while Chris was getting stitched up on a bed by the window. Chris felt disconnected from the rest considering they were the only one to suffer an injury in the ordeal.

Jean sat in a chair next to them and watched the news story about the fire. As she saw Nigel flatten Nick, she burst out laughing and cranked up the volume so the others could hear it. "The press loves you..."

Chris watched the nurses taking blood from the others and sighed, looking up at the unflattering news footage. They still felt like they swallowed bees with all the adrenaline rushing in their veins.

The nurse was now taking Nick's blood and kept glancing up at the replay of Nick being pummeled with people. Nick groaned. "People like to laugh." He smiled as the nurse began cleaning up her supplies. Nick looked at the blood-filled vials and raised a brow. Nick kept watching the young nurse who was watching him intently. "So is this for personal or professional use?" He joked lightly.

The nurse giggled but suddenly Jean was on her feet and

the nurse sprang up. Jean opened the door. "Let me get that for you." It was plain Jean wanted the woman to leave. Chris stifled a chuckle watching them.

The nurse shook her head, looking at Nigel. "We need a little more." She put her supplies next to Nigel and wrapped his arm with the large, rubber band. "Just a pinch," she whispered and stuck him with the needle.

Nigel bounced up a bit. "That's a bit more than a pinch!" He chuckled when the nurse blushed. The nurse seemed smitten with the Englishman. Nigel sighed loudly. "Dear, you're barking up the wrong tree. Nick's the straight one." He grinned as Nick looked over, shocked, and Jean glowered. "That's if you get past his girlfriend over there."

"Girlfriend?" Jean and Nick said together, looking at each other until the doors opened.

Chris grinned at the joke but was relieved when they both seemed to deny any attachment.

In the doorway stood a tall and slender man who wore dress pants but a hospital gown for a shirt. His face was caked in soot, yet when he smiled, his white teeth lit up the room. He was covered in so much filth it was difficult to distinguish his features, let alone his ethnicity or culture.

Despite his appearance he swept into the room as if he was on a game show and made his way to Nick. "You!" He grabbed his hand and shook it tightly. "You saved my life!"

Nigel spoke up while Jean seemed to sink into the woodwork. "You're the mayor, am I right?"

The mayor seemed taken back by his accent and looked at them again. "You're not Americans?"

"We are," Nick said quickly. "Nigel is an ex Brit."

Nigel shrugged. "I've got my papers." He sounded like he took the comment as a challenge, but the mayor waved his hand as if to dismiss the notion.

"I ran back for my wife, but passed out before I found her."
The mayor spoke rapidly and needed to take a big breath.
"They said your friend found her and leapt with her to safety."
The mayor looked over to Chris and ran forward to shake
hands. "You, you saved her!'

Jean turned the TV up and pointed to it. "They got it on
video." The news showed Chris holding the woman, and they
noticed something they hadn't before: Chris saw how they
injured their arm on the shattered glass of the window.

"You were hurt?" The mayor asked Chris, looking very
concerned.

"I'm fine," Chris reassured him.

The mayor looked up to the broadcast and watched as
Chris fell with his wife and the camera zoomed down to the
amusing image of them both tumbling onto Nick. Finally, the
mayor said, "They didn't show you getting me out?"

"I guess not," Nick mumbled. "I tried to go back to help,
but they kept stopping me, and then I heard these two coming
out the window."

"They will be released as soon as they're cleared of smoke
inhalation." Jean smiled. Nigel cocked an eyebrow at her.

"I can't thank you enough." The mayor beamed and took
Chris's hand, and shook it vigorously.

"How is your wife doing? She was coughing a lot and they
took her away fast," Chris said quickly.

"She's fine and they are treating her for cuts too. Doctors
want to keep her overnight and monitor her breathing, but she
will be fine."

The mayor was all smiles as he finally let Chris's hand go.
"I need your names and contact information. I wanted to
invite you to my next party." He held his hands up and added
with a big smile, "I think we might be able to arrange
more..."

"More?" Nick asked, looking at Nigel and Jean. "That's nice and all but..."

"I'm in! Definitely in!" Nigel raised his hand enthusiastically watching the mayor. He began to pose with the mayor as Jean moved over to Nick.

"You're heroes," she whispered. "Why are you so shy about it?"

Nick sat up. "Dunno, but it should help what we're doing right?"

Chris listened as the two talked on, and glanced about, but their gaze was drawn to the window. What caught their eye was a solitary figure looking straight up at them. The figure stood with a top hat and a cane and a grin so malicious that it chilled Chris to the bone. It was Deacon and his eyes reflected back at Chris like a wild cat's might. Chris was ready to turn to alert the others, but an ambulance rushed past, and, once it had rounded the corner, the sidewalk was empty.

Chris rubbed their eyes, unsure whether it was a mirage or a message.

Later, when the group approached the hospital garage, Chris pointed to an automobile with lights that flashed when they passed by. "That must be the loaner."

Nigel sighed. "The mayor offered us his limousine." He pointed to an oncoming vehicle.

It drove slowly towards them and stopped. The window rolled down and the driver said, "I was asked to take you to your car or home.

Chris shrugged as Nigel pranced towards the door the driver held open.

Jean touched Chris's arm. "We should probably be taking it easy anyway."

Nick nodded in agreement. "I'm tired."

Nigel made sure to sit close to Chris as they all clambered into the car. Given that everyone was chatting avidly about the rescue, Jean and Nick looked unfazed by Nigel's moves.

Nigel groaned when Chris scooted aside to increase the distance between them and Chris turned to face Jean. "Is the building gone? Did everyone get out?"

Jean nodded. "They said the only people left inside were the mayor and his wife, and the building is considered a loss."

"There's something else," Chris whispered. "I saw *him*."

Jean tilted her head, "The mayor?"

Nigel began to nod off with his legs stretched out. Nick looked wide awake whereas Jean kept yawning. She waved her hand as if to wave her yawn off. "Excuse me. It's been a crazy day."

Chris glanced over their shoulder, eyes wide. They took a deep breath and leaned in close to the other person, speaking in a barely audible voice. "Not the mayor!" they said, shaking their head. Chris's face grew even more frightened as they uttered, "I saw Deacon."

At that, Nigel sat up. "Where?"

"I saw him from the hospital window and he was looking up at me." Chris' body trembled, even though the room was sweltering. Their breathing was shallow and their eyes were wide with panic as they looked around, on guard. "He didn't look happy."

"What did he do?" Jean asked quickly.

"Nothing. An ambulance passed and then he was gone." Chris watched Nick feverishly patting his pockets and rummaging through the pockets of his hoodie. He mumbled to himself under his breath as he stopped and checked each pocket, searching for a pack of cigarettes.

Nick's face lit up like Times Square when he finally found the last pack of cigarettes and removed a slightly crushed one from it. Jean noticed his greedy fingers reaching towards the cigarette, "You can't smoke that here!"

"I'm not gonna light it. I can suck the unlit cig and get some nicotine," he scoffed then turned his attention to Chris. "Kid, let me ask you something. Why did you run into that burning building?"

Chris sat back. "I wasn't scared."

Nigel looked intrigued. "Why the bloody hell not?"

"I knew I couldn't die." Chris sighed. "I should have died saving the little girl yesterday."

Nick chuckled. "You're a lousy swimmer, kid; so it took guts."

"You don't get it? I'm not a swimmer. I can't swim. I never could. I have no idea how I saved that girl." Chris met their eyes. "I wasn't thinking and it happened so fast. If I didn't die, then..."

Jean smiled. "You have a good heart." She settled back against the seat. "That's rare."

Chris blushed at the compliment but glanced at the others. "Why am I the only one who saw Deacon?"

"You're the lucky bloke? Lass?" Nigel laughed, then motioned to Jean, who was dozing off with her head on Nick's shoulder. "Send me a wedding invite?"

Chris glowered at the notion and sat back watching Jean with Nick. The image of the two of them interrupted at the cafe returned and Chris felt Jean's compliment was nothing more than an obligation now.

Nick cut Nigel a measured look. "We're all locked in the same fate. It's not like that." He looked at Jean. "It can't be. We have something to do and that would distract us."

Nigel began to croon. "I've only eyes for you..." He kept on despite Nick's angry looks.

"She's a nice lady," Chris said quietly. "I really like her." It was then Chris was sure they saw jealousy flash in Nick's eyes. Chris was a little shocked to see Nick with such a serious look on his face where Jean was concerned. Chris swallowed hard and met his eye.

Nick didn't move and appeared to be taking care not to wake Jean. "You're not her type, kid. You're too young."

Chris glanced over with a suspicious, quizzical expression, noting the way Nick's look was lingering a bit too long on Jean. They both knew they were old enough to date her, but it wasn't hard to tell that Nick had more than just a passing interest in her.

As they pulled into the deserted harbor parking lot, they all gathered their belongings.

"Kid, is that your car?" Nick pointed out the window to a wreck that hardly resembled an automobile. It looked like a balled up piece of metal with protruding bits of rubber, metal and plastic.

Chris gulped as they spotted the license plate from the car sticking out of the wreckage. The vehicle was the first item Chris had purchased with their hard-earned money and it felt like the loss of an old friend. It had been the only companion when Chris came to the harbor, ran an errand, or needed respite. It had been a shelter when a rampant storm started up and the welcome seat when they were tired from shopping and could no longer walk. Taking a deep breath, Chris felt violated at the absence of their beloved automobile and it left them hollow inside. Sure, Chris had rentals on their insurance, so other means of transportation was not the issue, but it would never be the same as the car that had been named Buddy. Now, Buddy was gone and Chris felt like they had lost something beloved.

CHAPTER 13

The small group sat inside of Jean's small sedan on the way back to Chris's house. They were all very silent, but they felt that was due to Nigel having claimed the front seat so he could command the radio. Or maybe it was because of what the police had told them about Chris's car.

"We need the others," Nick mumbled, staring out the passenger window. "There's power in numbers."

Nigel fussed while tuning the radio. "Don't you have satellite radio? Anything?"

"Said the man with no car?" Jean scoffed.

Nigel turned back and sighed. "If they're targeting Chris, we just don't leave Chris alone." He dusted his hands. "There, all sorted."

Jean rolled her eyes. "That make sense to you? I'm not abandoning anybody." She glanced at Nick and Chris in the rearview.

Chris smiled. "We should have enough room at my house. My parents are pretty cool."

Nick laughed. "Don't you own the house?"

Chris shook their head. "Not anymore. After you told me

about the arrangement for the deal with Deacon, I divided my assets up among my parents and siblings so I have nothing already."

Jean looked back impressed. "Is that why you saw him? You outsmarted him with Nick's help..."

"I paid him the outlandish fee." Chris sighed. "I kept my part of the deal."

They exhaled deeply, knowing terrifying dreams would remain a part of their life. The thought that nightmares might become more frequent filled them with trepidation. It seemed like the deal was growing even worse.

"Maybe it has nothing to do with you?" Nick shook his head. "The rest of us weren't looking out of the windows, so we didn't see anything." He met Chris' eye, "You probably imagined it with all the drugs you're on."

Chris scoffed loudly and gave Nick a sidelong glance. "Antibiotics?"

"Others have seen him after!" Nigel said loudly. "He's around when he wants to be."

Jean exhaled loudly. "What about that woman you read about? The French one?"

Nigel crossed his arms. "Some foul git stole my book while we were saving lives." He scoffed, "I don't have it memorized."

Jean chuckled, "I thought you were a genius?"

Nigel raised an eyebrow and looked as if he was bursting with news but said nothing.

Chris pointed to the driveway from the back seat. "That's our driveway."

Jean gasped seeing the spacious drive before the large house Chris was pointing at.

"There." Chris looked around, watching for Deacon – a little worried..

Nigel glanced up from the radio and the corners of his mouth curved up. "Doing all right for yourself, aren't you?"

Nick gave a shrug. "I've seen the house." Nigel and Jean looked at him incredulously. Chris supposed it was surprising how Nick seemed to regard this home as just four walls and a roof. It was impressive with the water behind the house but it was also serene.

As if to abate their stares, Nick took a deep breath and nodded. "It's a nice place."

Chris held a laugh back knowing the rockstar probably had bigger guest houses in the '80s but for others who might not have lived in pure luxury, it could be seen as a palace.

"Nice?" Jean mumbled as she approached the small gate. "How do we get in?"

"I have it." Chris pulled out their phone and tapped the screen. "We can do everything by phone now."

Nigel raised a brow in mock challenge. "I could hack them easily, mate." He watched as the gates tumbled open.

"Not if I lock you out manually." Chris smiled. "When we're all in, then we use physical locks." Chris shrugged at Nigel. "It's not all electronic."

Nick shook his head. "On foot it's easy to hop."

Chris didn't like that they were pointing out the possible weak spots and Nick gave them a teasing grin.

Jean pointed at the ground lights as the gate opened. "I have a feeling they have other things to keep people out."

"The doors have a second set of doors and there's a gate to get on our patio, porches, or dock." Chris pointed to the double doors. "We have a mudroom past the main entrances, so it acts like another set of doors."

"So you've got a moat?" Nigel snickered.

Chris rolled their eyes, but Jean intervened and spoke up, "Jealous?"

Nigel smiled. "If we're superheroes, we'll need a moat for the secret liar."

They all laughed as Jean pulled in front of the circular driveway and stopped by the garage. "Where do I go now?" Chris could feel Jean's eyes on them but they already had their phone out and opened the doors.

The garage opened to reveal a large, yet simple, area. The occupants of the car collectively held their breaths as the lights flickered on, illuminating everything in a sharp glare. "Park anywhere?"

Chris pointed to an SUV. "Next to that is fine."

Nick nodded and took a breath. "I'm going to grab a cigarette before I come in."

As they got out, Nigel snickered, "Don't want to scare the fam with a rockstar too soon, or do you need a grand entrance?"

Nick shook his head and mumbled, "I'm no rockstar now." His head was low as if mourning the thought. He moved outside the garage and they could see his shadow against the light.

Chris watched him go. "He's already been here." Then nodded to the door. "It's unlocked now."

Nigel tapped Chris's shoulder and gestured at Jean who was staring after Nick. She was completely fixated on the former rockstar.

Chris cleared their throat. "Come on in." Chris looked down at their feet rather than at Jean, seeing how enamored she was with Nick.

Jean looked resigned to following them and whispered, "I'm coming." She moved behind them. "Is he okay?" She glanced back in Nick's direction.

Nigel sighed. "He sees what I did and what you did, a life of fame and fortune that's forgotten us."

Jean trudged behind them. She took a deep breath and followed quietly.

Ever the gentleman, Nigel waited for her to go in first where Chris waited in the mudroom.

"Shoes off here please," Chris fussed.

Jean and Nigel began to pull their shoes off and Chris gestured to the shoe rack. When their shoes were lined up, they looked to Chris for instructions.

"Do you need slippers?" Chris gestured to another rack with a line of pristine slippers.

Jean nodded with her now bare feet and chose a pair of slip ons. "Thank you."

Nigel cocked his head to the side. "Thank you, but do they come with a dinner jacket and pipe?" He gave Chris a teasing smile. They held out a pair, but Nigel shook his head. "No thanks, luv. I'm sorted." He showed off his white socks and smiled.

Chris hushed them. "Be quiet in case somebody is in bed..."

The other two watched Chris open the door and turn on dimmer lights, just enough to light the way.

"We'll wait in the kitchen for Nick, then I'll help you get settled in your rooms," Chris mumbled, watching Jean with a side-long look, hoping not to get caught staring.

Jean kept her arms wrapped around herself as if to keep warm and from time to time she glanced around the tidy kitchen.

"Do you need something to get warm?" Chris offered quickly.

Nigel peeked around then fell into a chair and rummaged through the small snack dish on the table. He sat there with an air of boredom, watching Chris who doted on Jean.

Chris stepped around the corner but heard Nigel say,

"Don't lead the kid on, Ima. It's quite plain you're mad for Nick."

Chris heard Nigel calling her Ima and raced back to the kitchen. Chris would face Nigel if he kept doing it because they'd noticed how Jean hated her old name and the reminder of everything she'd lost.

Jean huffed at Nigel but only responded with. "The only mad person here is you."

Chris heard them in the other room and this time peeked in to see Jean's cheeks tinted red.

"Am I?" Nigel cooed at her and leaned his head on a single finger.

"Chris is a kid." She waved his suspicion off.

Chris came in quickly holding a plush blanket with a proud smile. "Microfiber."

Nigel nodded mocking their excitement. "Is it?"

Chris cut Nigel a sharp look almost daring him to continue after hearing how he'd mocked Jean as well.

Jean rolled her eyes and took the blanket before Nigel's sarcasm could fade Chris's smile. She wrapped it around her shoulders gratefully. "I guess I was cold. Thank you."

Chris moved to the cabinets and pulled out several mugs. "Coffee? Tea?"

"Or me?" Nigel winked at Chris.

Chris didn't fall for teasing. "I was thinking of cocoa..."

Jean gave a nod. "Anything warm sounds good."

"Cappuccino?" Nigel said jokingly but nearly gasped when Chris dutifully opened a cabinet that had been hollowed out inside and instead of cabinets it held a fancy coffee maker that sparkled, it shined so bright. Chris switched it on and put mugs down.

Nigel rubbed his hands together. "Dear Santa, this year I

want..." he chuckled, not finishing his sentence when he instead pointed to the table top. "One please!"

Chris sat with a mug of cocoa while Jean finished her coffee and Nigel sipped his cappuccino. Jean and Chris tried to hide their amusement seeing Nigel raise his head from his cappuccino with foam on his nose.

Chris watched Jean who was pensive, her eyes lingering on her mug. Chris shared the same expression, but not for the same reason. It was apararent she yearned after Nick, though she kept that to herself.

Nigel cocked a brow at her forlorn look. "Missing someone?" Nigel seemed to miss nothing.

Chris watched her turn red and she shook her head as if to brush it off but said nothing. Focusing on the mug, Chris took a sip as a diversion from thinking of Jean with Nick.

The night was pierced by a scream. A moment of silence followed and then a shriek echoed all around.

"That's Nick!" Jean exclaimed.

The trio flew from their seats and ran out the house to the open garage doors. Chris searched for Nick but couldn't see him in the darkness. When they looked down, Chris noticed a darker shadow on the ground.

Jean saw him at the same time and fell to her knees next to Nick, her hands frantically searching for any sign of life. Chris and Nigel followed suit, lowering themselves down and pressing their ears against the man's chest, as if hoping to hear something encouraging.

"I found a heartbeat..." Jean murmured in relief.

Without warning, Nick inhaled sharply, and Nigel and

Chris snapped their heads back to look at him. In a frenzy, Nick's arms flailed uncontrollably until Jean grabbed hold of his head to steady him. He calmed down and filled his lungs with air, taking hold of one of her hands.

"That dude was here!" he exclaimed.

Chris frowned as they observed the interaction between them but was glad Nick was all right. "Who else was here?"

"Deacon," Nick rasped, his voice heavy with weariness. Nigel and Chris boosted him up and nodded. "He did something to me. I feel so drained."

Nick attempted to stand, but his legs wobbled. Nigel and Chris took hold of either side of him in order to provide him balance.

Jean let out a gasp. "Nick?" she questioned, her expression tense with worry.

Nigel gave a quick glance in Nick's direction. "He's out."

Together, the trio all hefted the sleeping rockstar to get him safely inside. Chris led them around the back of the house to avoid traipsing Nick down the stairs.

Nigel grumbled the entire time.

Chris kept hushing the noise, not wanting to wake anyone up in case their parents were home and already asleep.

"We need to be quick," Jean suggested. "We don't want the police getting involved."

Nigel laughed, "What would we tell them? That some sort of bogeyman is after us?"

They opened the patio doors to the basement family room and the lights came on automatically, lighting up the large space. Nigel was so amazed he almost dropped Nick. His eyes locked on gadgets and technological devices at one end of the room.

Chris was jerked roughly when Nigel squealed loudly and dropped Nick. The bookstore genius tossed his hand to his chest and exhaled at the sight of a full length, ornate mirror on the opposite wall. Nigel's reflection stared back at him, terror written on its features.

"That bloody mirror gave me a fright!"

"Nigel!" Jean shouted at the Englishman. She struggled to keep her grip on the unconscious Nick.

When Nigel had gathered up the leg he'd dropped, Chris guided them to the couch and they placed Nick gently on it. Running back to the door, Chris locked it and drew the blinds.

Jean moved to the window, observing the water. Chris smiled and opened the blinds again. "You like the view?"

Jean nodded, transfixed. "I've always been a fan of the water. That's why I go to the harbor."

Chris could hardly believe the smile she beamed at them and noticed her reddened cheeks but she quickly looked away. Chris paused to take a deep breath, feeling much more protective of her in the face of the palpable tension surrounding them.

"We should close up," Chris said quietly. "I have a strange feeling. It's like we're being watched." Chris shivered as they spoke, their voice echoing around them eerily.

Jean and Nigel gasped. "You feel it too?" they asked Chris in unison.

With that, Jean closed the blinds. She moved to the couch, asking "How's he doing?"

Nigel hardly seemed to hear her. His attention was still focused on the computers, television, and other devices. "Nick will be alright," he mumbled.

Jean sighed and checked Nick's pulse. "He's okay, I guess..."

CHAPTER 14

A moment later, an eerie creak from the stairs echoed through the room and sent chills down Chris's spine. They grabbed a pool stick to prepare for the worst, and noticed how Jean and Nigel scrambled to their feet.

The sound of the intruder coming closer caused the small group's shadows to grow longer when suddenly the lights flickered on and all three of them screamed in surprise.

Chris lifted the pool cue toward the single, small, illuminated figure atop the stairs. Chris finally sighed loudly when recognition came to them and they placed the pool stick onto the table.

"You scared us!" Chris exclaimed, gesturing toward the newcomer. "Everyone, this is Taylor."

Chris watched Taylor's almond-shaped eyes, markedly different from Chris's own, move across the group, looking like she caught Chris doing something wrong. Taking in her hairstyle, with two tones merging together like a stream, Chris thought the blue dye made her look like she was from an anime. Her hair had a waterfall-like feel as the layers cascaded down. Although her build was athletic, her plain tee and plaid pajama pants made it difficult to tell if Taylor was male or female. It made Chris feel mischievous.

Nigel's attention was fixated on the two siblings and Taylor raised a questioning brow in his direction.

"Are they stealing the computer?" Taylor spoke in a hushed voice, similarly to how Chris usually talked.

Chris took a look at Nigel who still gripped the keyboard like a bat. "Nigel..." Chris nodded to Nigel and met Taylor's gaze. "That's Nigel."

"Pleased to meet you!" Nigel crooned to Taylor.

Chris pointed to Jean standing up. "This is Jean, and Nick is the sleeping one on the couch. You would know him if you had been here when he met Mom and Dad."

Taylor tilted her head and hardly a strand of hair moved. "Do Mom and Dad know you have all these old people here?"

"Old?" Nigel scoffed.

Jean giggled as Taylor stepped up, eagerly offering her hand to shake. "I'm Taylor," she said. "Chris is my..."

"SIBLING!" Chris interrupted with an impish grin.

Taylor stared at Chris and sighed. "You mean they can't tell whether you're male or female?"

Chris merely chuckled at the comment.

Taylor sighed and shook her head. "I'm Taylor. I'm Chris's sister," she said, gesturing to the stairs. "Is the chaos in the kitchen yours?"

Chris groaned in response. "I completely forgot about that!"

"I'll clean it up before I go back to bed," Taylor replied, rolling her eyes. "You owe me. Even more so if you want to remain gender ambiguous."

Chris rolled their eyes at Taylor and instead focused on the fact she had been home the entire time. "You were here? I've been home for a while now. You could have said something, like hello."

Taylor ignored Chris and made it a point to be polite. She came forward and offered her hand to the nearest person.

Jean laughed as she shook Taylor's hand, but Nigel merely smiled politely in response.

"Are you sure you're a girl?" Nigel whined. "You're too hot to be a girl!"

Taylor studied him and replied, "You're English? Sorry, I don't go for old men."

She then flashed a glance at Chris but kept reaching her hand to her face as if she was trying not to rub her eyes. "I'm going back up, but keep it quiet. The screaming woke me up."

"Okay, see you in the morning." Chris mumbed, as Taylor trudged up the stairs.

"Old? She is too hot to be female!" Nigel grumbled, pushing the keyboard away.

"Should we stay the night here?" Jean asked, glancing up the stairs.

"I think it's safer to stay together," Chris suggested softly. "Unless you want to go."

"I'm afraid to go home alone now," Jean mumbled slowly. She wrapped her arms around herself protectively, as if shielding her body from harm, and uttered in a near-whisper

Chris pressed their lips together hearing how scared she was and knew this would be their fate too soon.

"I'm not too keen on that either," Nigel kept looking around the room. "If there's a place I can set up camp, then I'll claim my area."

"The couches have recliners to relax in or fold down into beds," Chris gestured to the three couches arranged in a U shape.

"Nice, mate," Nigel plopped down on one of the vacant sofas, looking exhausted.

Chris exhaled. "There's also a bar if you need it, and over there is a full bathroom with a shower."

Nigel's eyes lit up. "Bar?"

"Please, please moderate your drinking," Chris exhaled. "There is a soda machine back behind the bar for sodas and snacks. And that," Chris pointed to the stairs Taylor had used, "those stairs lead to the kitchen."

The faint sound of someone stirring around upstairs caught Chris's attention. "Taylor?" Chris called out.

The noises stopped, followed by the sound of creaking stairs as Taylor descended a few steps.

"Yes?" she replied.

"Could you make sure the garage doors are all shut and locked?" Chris asked rapidly. Following Deacon's unexpected appearance at the hospital and Nick's subsequent report on his sighting here at the house, they had no choice but to err on the side of caution. Tay gave Chris a skeptical look that suggested she thought they were being overly paranoid.

Taylor shrugged and went back up.

Chris nodded. "I can lock the doors with my phone, but they have to be physically closed first."

"I like your sister. Too bad she's a girl," Nigel commented from across the room. He made his way toward the bar. "Sorry, mate, but I need a drink..."

Chris stirred in the giant bean bag and wiped sleep from their eyes. They surveyed the room, taking in the peaceful slumber of the new friends they'd made. The memories of what had happened over the past few days came back to them. Nigel snored away, after having claimed his space.

Jean stayed with Nick, ensuring his breathing was steady and that he was safe. Somehow, she had drifted off to sleep beside the rockstar while he held her close like a teddy bear. Chris noticed the couple together, drawn to each other like magnets from afar. Chris let out a deep sigh of relief when they saw Nick in the arms of Jean. A fleeting sense of jealousy twisted their heart; after all, everyone deserved to have someone look at them the way Jean was looking at Nick. Chris's eyes flitted between the two lovers, and they couldn't help but feel a pang of longing for their own soulmate.

Nigel's snoring rumbled and resonated, and Chris was surprised it hadn't woken Jean or Nick. Sounds filtered down the stairs from the kitchen and Chris assumed someone was getting food. Thoughts crossed their mind of getting breakfast for the whole crew When Nick stirred awake. He noted Jean sleeping peacefully next to him, clutched his chest, and shuddered. Stretching, Nick looked pleased at the sight of Jean.

Chris gave a fake cough in hopes of splitting them apart then spoke softly, not wanting to wake Jean or Nigel, "Breakfast?"

Nick glanced up, one eyebrow lifting in agreement. He carefully extricated himself from the blanket, tumbling to the floor with a thud.

Chris stifled a laugh and gestured upstairs.

When they arrived at the top, Chris peered into the kitchen and saw Taylor. She was oblivious to their presence as she bopped to her own beat. She moved with such ease and grace while cooking eggs, tossing her head in time to the rhythm of her music as it played from her headphones. Her thick blue hair obscured the band of her earphones.

Nick gave Taylor a curious look. "Who's this?" he asked.

Chris gave a one-shouldered shrug. "Taylor." Chris reached out and tapped Taylor's shoulder, which made her jump.

Taylor eyed Nick curiously before turning to Chris. "No, seriously who is this?" She asked, examining Nick. "You look really familiar."

Chris cleared their throat before explaining, "This is Nick; he's staying with us for a while. Mom and Dad already love him." Chris turned to Nick and introduced him to Taylor. "This is Taylor, my... "

She stuck out her hand and spoke over Chris, "Sister!" She smiled before returning to her eggs. "Are all these people staying here?" She tossed her head back and looked at the ceiling as if praying for strength. "You realize you're not the only person living here, Chris. We should all have a say who's going to be here. It would be so easy to slip a correct pronoun if they're here too long."

"It's just Nick who's staying with us," Chris explained with a distant gaze as they remembered what happened that night. "My car had some trouble after the Mayor's rescue and it was late..." Chris rushed out the words, talking faster than the fastest auctioneer could manage.

"Mayor?" Taylor watched the sizzling bacon before glancing at Nick again. "Does this make sense to you yet?"

"I was there too." Nick shrugged. "There was a fire downtown and Chris ran into the building to help before firefighters arrived." He tapped his smokes to pack them before using them and Taylor glared at the cigarettes. He tucked the pack in his pocket again, and held his now empty hands flat in front of him. Running his hand alongside his head, much the way a greaser used to in the '50s, Nick said, "I won't smoke inside."

Chris swallowed hard and looked down to their feet hoping Tay wouldn't pry. Going into detail on what happened at the harbor the past two days could mean a lecture from Tay and their parents if they found out how reckless Chris had been. Even though Chris glanced up at Nick to beg his silence, Nick didn't seem to pick up on the request.

Instead, Nick reassured Tay. " I helped so the kid wouldn't get all the credit for saving everyone." He ruffled Chris's hair playfully.

Taylor crossed her arms, letting them intertwine. Her sweet, brown eyes narrowed in suspicion. "Who are you?"

Nick smiled nervously, casting a hopeful glance at Chris, who was searching the refrigerator for something to drink. "Just Nick..." he said in a quiet voice.

Chris clumsily held a bundle of frozen sausages, waffles, and juice in their arms and declared, "We should make breakfast for everyone."

Taylor let out a deep sigh and pointed to the toaster and the sausage that was already cooking. "I do have manners..." She reached for a plate for the bacon then said. "Let's start getting these plates ready and I'll finish up with breakfast." Taylor's face lit up and her her eyebrows shot up when Nick stepped forward to help.

"Are Mom and Dad home?" Chris set the table while Nick helped Taylor with the food.

"They went to a rummage sale super early. She's still looking for that statue, but now she's also got some other stuff on her list too," Taylor said as she loaded food onto the plates that Nick handed her. She couldn't take her eyes off him.

Finally, she broke the silence. "Where have I seen you before?" She squinted her eyes as if trying to see him better and cocked her head to the side. She pulled her bottom lip in her mouth and heaved a sigh.

"I used to make music..." Nick said with a casual shrug.

Taylor's eyes widened to half dollars and her mouth hung open. She looked like she might say something but instead she pointed her finger at him.

Chris laughed, "Yes, he's *that* guy..."

Taylor still stood there with her mouth open and dropped her hands to her sides. She nearly dropped the cooking utensil she had been holding. Finally she regained the power of speech. "Seriously?" She seemed to have a newfound interest in him. "My Mom loves your stuff!" She observed him closely. "Why did you stop making music?"

"Things happen," Nick mumbled as he drifted toward the plate rack. "Should we wake up the others?"

Chris glanced at Taylor then back to Nick. "Yeah, it's probably a good idea. It's getting late." With that, Chris ran down the steps and heard Taylor bombard Nick with more questions. It seemed she was more comfortable with a former rockstar in the house.

Chris tiptoed into the family room, hoping not to rouse Jean who slept deeply. It felt almost sacrilegious to awaken her. After all, she had stayed up late, worrying about Nick. Chris hadn't made it through the night and had retired while Jean kept a watchful eye over their sick friend. Wondering how late she'd been up, Chris remembered how none of them knew what to expect. They had both been deeply concerned Nick might not make it through the night..

Chris tried to wake Jean with a slight tug to her shoulder, but nothing worked. They grew apprehensive. "Jean?"

CHAPTER 15

Chris shook Jean a little more and with a bit more pressure on her arm until she bolted awake. She breathed heavily and started to gag, taking huge gasps of air, almost as if she were guzzling it down, and Chris reached over to her in support, hoping to offer a reassuring touch.

Jean grabbed at her throat with both hands, much the same way the man had at the Inner Harbor when he nearly choked to death. Finally, Jean clasped a hand over her mouth and ran for the bathroom.

"What's up with her? She's sick?" Taylor asked from the bottom of the stairs. She moved slowly and curiously.

"I'm sure it was just a dream. No one else here is sick," Chris offered quietly.

"Her dream made her sick?" Taylor scoffed. She kept watching them all suspiciously and then took a deep breath.

"More like a living hell..." Nick muttered, sliding into a chair with a raised eyebrow but he looked haunted.

Chris smiled and looked at Nigel. "Nigel might know how

to help. He is extremely smart. He's like Steven Hawking and Einstein smart."

Taylor stared at the small group with her arms crossed, clearly not believing them. Her gaze shifted to Nigel, as if in sudden recognition. "Wait... I know you! You're that guy who vanished after the plane crash! Weren't you one of those brainiacs in the think tank?" Taylor looked around with wider eyes now.

Nigel lit up at the thought. "She knows me!" he exclaimed. "That's me. Yes, I am that bloke!"

Taylor fixed her gaze on Chris and asked, "What are these famous people doing in our home?" She looked towards the bathroom and tossed her hand on her hip as a silent dare for Chris to not tell her the truth. "Is *she* famous too?"

Nick let out a heavy sigh and said, "I've seen Chris get recognized down at the harbor." He glanced across the room at Chris and added, "You're a celebrity, right? Famous people know you."

"Chris, I can count how many people you've brought home on one hand and today you doubled it!" Taylor had a cynical and determined expression as she spoke. "So, you bring home famous people now?" She gestured over to the bathroom. "And who's that?"

Taylor held up a hand. "This is all after you were at the harbor talking about famous people and the deal with Jordan and I?" She narrowed her eyes.

Nick let out a heavy breath and looked at Chris worriedly. He mouthed the words, "She knows?"

Chris came to a sudden stop, realizing that Tay had already known about the deal all along. Chris stood open mouthed, and gave Nick a subtle nod in hopes of avoiding drawing Tay's attention.

Taylor scoffed loudly. She was used to secrets among the

siblings and caught Nick's not so subtle gesture. She glared at Chris accusingly.

Chris shrugged feeling very sheepish now and thought of the deal and if they had done anything wrong. Chris took a hard breath almost feeling resigned, "I told her and Jordan part of it when I was making the choice. The night before I …"

Taylor laughed dryly, "I call BS then, Chris. This is a joke. Right?"

"Sorta," Chris mumbled in agreement and turned, hearing the bathroom door open.

When Jean stepped out, Chris was happy Taylor forgot the argument, but it was unfortunate that Jean was the reason why. Taylor gawked at how wan she looked and didn't let the sick woman leave her sight.

It was clear to everyone that Jean was in bad condition. Her skin had taken on a pasty hue and she moved at an agonizingly slow pace, hugging herself close as if her arms were the only things preventing her from coming apart.

Nigel rose to the occasion and taunted, "Would you care for a spot of breakfast?"

Jean didn't respond and Chris watched her hollow eyes – worried. Jean moved to sit in an empty chair alone, her face unreadable.

"I'm not hungry," Jean finally said in a voice just below a whisper.

"That's a first," Nigel remarked and when the others gave him a disapproving glance, he quickly apologized under his breath.

Chris gave Nigel a slight slap and whispered, "Quit it."

Nick dropped to his knees in front of her until they were eye to eye. "Would you like a cup of coffee? Or maybe tea?" He looked at her as she gave a subtle nod, then he glanced at

Taylor. "The other kid is a good cook, and they have some extravagant coffee stuff."

Chris glowered at Nick on his knees in front of Jean and how he lavished attention on her, but Chris was also happy Jean was gaining her color again.

Nick extended his arm to help Jean up, but she brushed it away and used her own strength to get to her feet. As the others started to move toward the stairs, she slowly followed.

Once upstairs, Jean sipped her coffee but Taylor's curiosity was not dulled. "What's going on here?" She glanced from Chris to the other three people in the room. "How do you know them, and why is everyone acting so strange?"

"It's a long story, Tay..." Chris frowned, peering around at the others.

Jean glanced up, her voice firm and unwavering. "No," she said. "We're haunted."

Taylor chuckled, but when none of the others joined in with a laugh or even cracked a smile, she realized they were serious. "Oh, I'm sorry. Is this for real?" She looked at Chris and sighed. "Do you think you're haunted?

"Not as much as they are, but I have witnessed some incredible stuff." Chris murmured.

The landline telephone rang and Taylor plucked it from the wall.

"Hello...This is them," Taylor announced quickly and glanced at Chris. "Chris is here..." she started to offer them the phone, but Chris shook their head, cheeks stuffed with pancakes. "Can I take a message?" she asked, covering the receiver. "It sounds like it's the insurance agency about your car?"

Chris made a muffled noise as Taylor went on and tensed up in anticipation. Chris adored their car and the suspense of waiting for Taylor's news was agonizing. As Chris listened to

Taylor on the phone, they observed her eyes gradually widen with surprise, or was it disbelief?

"I'll let them know..." Taylor ended the call and turned to Chris. "What happened in the car wreck?"

Chris looked up and wrinkled a brow. "What did they say?"

"They said the car was destroyed beyond repair – they had never seen anything like it. They said it looked as if God had picked it up and used it as a bowling ball!" She stepped toward Chris, tears forming in her eyes. "Are you alright?" she asked, her gaze shifting to the others in the room. "What's going on?"

Nigel sighed. "We were bowling with God and lost."

The others groaned at the joke but Taylor went to Chris and stared hard into their eyes. "You're okay?"

"It happened while the car was parked," Chris admitted quietly. "Right after we helped rescue the mayor and his wife..."

"Help nothing!" Nick scoffed. "We did it all!"

"That was you?" Taylor looked astonished and covered her mouth with her hand. "I saw it on the news." She put her arms protectively across her chest. "I thought the person bouncing off that awning looked familiar!"

"The car was wrecked while we were off doing that," Chris muttered sadly. Chris loved their car so dearly that even Chris's parents refused to drive it for fear of scratching it or just changing the seat. The car had been more like an old friend rather than an automobile but compared to the real friends being tormented, it meant nothing.

Taylor sat next to Chris and swallowed hard. "But are you okay?"

"We were checked out at the hospital and they said we're fine but the kid had to get stitches," Nick pointed at Chris who peered out the window. Chris gave a rueful grin holding up the arm that was already healing. "I'm fine." Chris was filled with a feeling of invincibility. Yet at the same time, when Taylor glared at them, they felt like a scared rabbit.

"So, God trashed your car?" Taylor scoffed.

"No," Jean gave her a deadpan stare. "The devil did."

Taylor waited for them to laugh or explain further but they all seemed to agree. "The devil?"

"We've made a deal with the devil, love." Nigel stared over his coffee mug. "Or something bloody close…"

Taylor shook her head. "You went nuts?"

Nick sat with his coffee and patted himself down, looking for his smokes. "I wish it was just nuts, kid. Truth is we all made a deal to save our lives and had no idea what we were in for."

Chris gave a nonchalant shrug and said, "Nick tried to warn me but I thought I could beat them at their own game."

"You're all serious or there's a hidden cam?" Taylor looked around lightly and found nothing. "You're just nuts?"

The doorbell rang and the siblings ran towards it, excitedly hoping it was a delivery, while the other three followed more slowly.

Taylor and Chris raced toward the door and Chris pulled out in front of her, "I have it, Tay!"

Tay tripped Chris and jumped over them with a sly grin. As she reached for the door she tossed her hair over her shoulder and said, "Relax, I'll get it."

Chris got to their feet and saw Tay staring at the door then shake her head. Chris peered out and shrugged because they had no idea who it was, "Amazon?"

The two of them shot each other a nervous glance when they saw a man wearing a chauffeur-like uniform who held an oversized box.

Tay opened the door but Chris stepped forward to deal

with the man. He simply put the box in Chris's arms and gave a wave, turning to leave.

Chris accepted the package from the man and Nigel stepped next to them. Placing the box on the hall table by the doorway, Nigel stared at it while Chris produced a pair of scissors from the table drawer and started cutting through the packing tape.

"As long as it's not a bomb," Tay giggled and tried to peer into the box before Chris, then turned to lock the door up.

Nigel snagged the book in the box before Chris could get their hands on it and shouted out, letting anybody in screaming distance know, "The book is here!"

Chris, undisturbed by Nigle's rooting around the box, continued to search for the things they had at the café table when they helped rescue the mayor. Chris managed to locate the car keys from the demolished vehicle, Jean's sunglasses, and a pack of Nick's cigarettes, as well as other miscellaneous items.

"What's this?" Taylor looked at the book Nigel held.

"The creature that's haunting us..." Chris whispered.

They turned the corner, hearing Jean and Nick talking quietly so they moved slowly into the kitchen. Nick and Jean seemed so engulfed in their conversation they didn't see Chris standing there.

Jean held a cup of tea in her hands and stared off into the distance while Nick intermittently glanced between her and his plate. He took a bite in an attempt to encourage her to do the same, yet he was subtle and kept his gaze on her as covert as possible.

Jean exhaled deeply and took a sip of the drink in her hand. "You don't have to babysit me," she said. "You can go."

Nick shifted uncomfortably and finally looked in her eyes.

"I'm not... it's not really a good idea for any of us to be alone," he said.

Chris finally coughed to alert the two they were at the threshold of the kitchen, listening.

"I understand," she murmured with a dismal expression, her gaze drifting away to the window and the ocean view beyond.

"It's not like that," Nick said, inhaling deeply and looking between Chris and Jean. He covered her hand with his own. A smile lit up her face as her gaze met his. Nick intertwined their fingers and sighed. "Jean..." He seemed to be gathering up courage. "I don't think you understand..."

Chris inhaled sharply, unsure of what they were witnessing. Was it a romantic proposal, or a kind man trying to console a woman who felt lost and isolated by fear?

"Bloody hell! You won't believe it!" Nigel burst through the door, holding aloft the book in his hands.

Nick and Jean jumped up in shock while Chris remained frozen, unsure of whether they'd scream or burst into tears from the fright. Nigel had pulled off the ultimate surprise, and he was now undisputed master of the jumpscare.

"Where did you find that?" Jean's eyes were wide with astonishment as she moved closer to take a look.

Nick took out a cigarette and shook his head, "I need a smoke."

Jean looked worried that he would be alone again and shook her head and snapped, "You can wait."

Chris raised an eyebrow at Jean and tilted their head when she barked orders at Nick, in the same manner that a protective mother would.

Nigel arched an eyebrow and snickered then made a whip sound. "Oh honey, the kitten has a whip."

They ignored his antics and Chris held up a coffee mug in

Nick's direction in a silent offer for java. Chris hoped the coffee would help him resist his cravings for nicotine.

Nigel had not finished his taunting inquiry. "When's the date?" He said with a playful inflection, but the curt looks from Jean, Nick, and Chris stopped him in his tracks. "Sorry I asked."

Taylor stepped in the room popping her gum. She held a phone in her hand, which held the majority of her attention. "Did you see what was sent?" Taylor stood there with arms folded and listened but then reminded Chris, "Did you get everything out of the box?"

Chris nodded, "I guess they found our table and packed it up because all the things we had are there."

Jean snatched the book from Nigel, eager to get started. "Okay, if this book can really help us then let's get to it..." She put it down on the counter and the others clustered around, each taking a bar stool. Flipping the book open, Jean riffled through the pages, trying to find where they had left off. "You mentioned a woman who lived hundreds of years because of some kind of arrangement..." she said to Nigel.

Nigel nodded and took command of the book. Soon he found a photograph of a woman who resembled a gypsy or voodoo queen. He looked up and said, "No one knows what happened to her; her descendants have no clue either."

Taylor raised a brow. "She's pretty. Where's she from?"

"New Orleans." Nigel exhaled loudly. "Her descendants still live there."

Chris took out their cell phone and opened the search engine. "Let's see who we can contact," they suggested.

Tay laughed and sat down looking at the table and the items left there. She tried on Jean's sunglasses until Jean held her hand out for them and Tay put them in her hand reluctantly; Taylor narrowed her eyes at Chris then the others. "So what? You're going to work Google and look for her relatives or something?"

"Exactly," Chris smiled. Chris was very good with finding things online; to them it was like coding.

After numerous phone calls with no success, they became disheartened and frustrated.

Taylor's phone buzzed and she read a text in silence. "Mom and Dad said they're staying at a hotel for dinner for their anniversary." She glanced up at Chris with a meaningful gaze. "We totally forgot about it..."

Chris nodded. "We can get them something. Flowers, candy, and a spa day."

Taylor's shoulders rose and then fell, a sign of her resignation. She typed out a message on her phone and moaned, "We should have done more."

Nigel tried to lighten the mood with a joke. "Well, you made them breakfast and they didn't show..."

"Tay," Chris sighed. "They're at a hotel to be alone. It's their anniversary."

Taylor just shrugged and took a seat next to Nick. "Whatever."

Chris's phone hummed as it came to life, and Chris glanced at the display. "No name..."

All eyes went to them as they answered the call in a hushed voice.

"Hello?" Chris shot a curious glance at the other people. They all started to speak simultaneously until Chris held a finger up in the air in a meager attempt to hush them so they could hear. "I'm still here..."

Jean, Nigel and Nick became silent as they watched Chris walk back and forth. Taylor settled into a nearby chair and let out a deep yawn.

"Indeed, we're searching for anyone related to Marie..." Chris paused before he added with a grin. "Yes, her."

"We found her?" Nick chuckled.

"No, it's not possible," Nigel shook his head. "I've been looking for years."

"Is that why you put that book on lay-away? You've been looking for her all this time?" Jean asked in a hush. But as Chris started to talk louder, they began to miss out on what was being said on the other end. That was until Chris took the phone and left the room.

When Chris reentered, they could hear a murmur of conversations regarding their gender. People were attempting to get Tay to spill the details everyone in the room desperately wanted to know. Although Chris couldn't help but be amused by this curiosity, they had no intention of revealing such insignificant information in a time where other things were far more important.

Thankfully Chris had a distraction to get them off the topic. "I think I've got a connection to this lady," Chris said as they sat down and drank some of the now cold coffee. "But the informant said it would be better to meet in person. We should travel and talk face to face." Chris looked at them. "Does this feel crazy to anyone else?"

Nigel jumped up and yelled, "I'll go by myself if no one else wants to!"

They all traded a look and stared at Nigel dead on for an answer. Nigel was usually not the type to offer his help, and something seemed off about the sudden offer.

"You have money for that ticket laying around?" Jean countered quietly.

"I'll get it. I have mates who owe me," Nigel smiled.

Nick laughed. "Yeah, you just volunteer? No, I think we all need to go then."

Chris gave Nick a quick nod, both seemed to suspect that Nigel had ulterior motives for offering his help. Chris furrowed their brow with determination to uncover the truth behind Nigel's unexpected generosity.

"Why do you want to go alone?" Taylor stared Nigel down.

Nigel exhaled heavily. "I think she's the answer and I don't want you lot to muck it up."

Taylor scoffed and Nick spoke up, "I'm with her." He pointed at Taylor. "There's more to it, isn't there?"

All eyes turned to Nigel who was hiding in his cup of coffee. After a brief moment of silence, he said, "New Orleans is a sexy city!" He mustered a smile and added, "I've always wanted to go there."

Chris raised a brow. "How did you know it was New Orleans?"

"Because that's where Marie lived." Nigel nodded to the book he kept in his lap.

Taylor shook her head incredulously. "Are you actually suggesting that we go there now?"

Nick got to his feet. "Not suggesting, doing." Nick looked to Chris who cocked their head.

Taylor shot him an intense look. "Who is paying for it?"

Chris let out a deep breath when they realized that Taylor was trying to protect them from being taken advantage of. Chris had been about to offer to pay, but it appeared to have agitated Taylor that Nick already assumed they would. Chris gave her an intense look, which warned her to back off.

"I've walked further than that..." Nick shrugged.

"I'm paying," Chris said quickly. They were sure Nick

would walk it and didn't want that. It was clear to Chris that Nick had not been counting on Chris to pay his way there.

Taylor lifted her head and tapped her phone to reveal the money transfer. "You moved all your funds over to me and Mom," Taylor countered. "You really want to go there?" she asked, holding up the screen.

Nigel enthusiastically chimed in, "Where's your sense of adventure?"

Chris stared at Taylor with a meaningful look, "I need to go."

Taylor gave a small smile and quickly glanced at them, "You've gone nuts!" She tossed her hands up dramatically. Then her eyes fell on her phone as she began to type and talk at the same time. "I suppose I'm coming along too," she sighed. "My social media will love this."

Chris glanced over to see what she was typing and almost chuckled at the words on the screen. *'Heading to New Orleans on vacay!'* Taylor put up two fingers in the shape of a peace sign and took a selfie to add to herpost. Chris scoffed and shook their head in disbelief.

Jean softly smiled and met their eyes. "Thank you both for taking on this journey," she said.

Taylor ended up seated beside Chris on the plane because Nick snatched the spot next to Jean, and Chris didn't want to sit near Nigel. Taylor kept taking photos out the window and documenting her experience with videos and selfies, which usually would have been amusing to Chris.

Chris was happy to be in the seats in front of Jean and

Nick. It was easy to hear their conversation and offered a welcome distraction from Taylor's incessant rambling about things off the top of her head. Chris could even steal looks without being too obvious and felt stealthy as they eavesdropped.

Jean gazed out the window and not at Nick, which made Chris smile. When the stewardess offered snacks, Jean waved the woman away.

"That's how you lost all the weight. You hardly eat anything," Nick said quietly and was clearly trying to drum up a conversation. Chris knew Jean didn't like talking about food so Nick had to be grasping at straws.

Jean snorted, "That's part of the paradox, the double-edged sword."

"What do you mean?" Nick inquired in a whisper.

As they talked in lower tones, Chris pressed back against the seat to hear them better. Chris wished Tay would hush because it would make hearing the whispers so much easier. Still, Chris wondered if they should be listening at all. It seemed like a betrayal, but Chris couldn't stop listening. They finally reasoned that they wanted to know how to help their friends better and felt allowed to listen.

"My nightmares involve food," Jean mumbled. "Terrifying choking or consequences of eating... I can scarcely glance at food without wanting to vomit."

Chris glanced back to see Jean and Nick trade a sympathetic look, but Jean turned her head away quickly.

"They're worse now." Jean said through a long sigh.

"Worse? How?"

Chris's heart wrenched on hearing the sorrow in Nick's voice.

"The smell and sight of food triggers a wave of nausea in me," Jean admitted. "I can drink without issue but when it comes to eating, especially anything fatty or greasy, it's too much for me. Things like pork rinds, chicken wings or cheese-cake... I can hardly bear to think about them."

Jean sounded like she was gagging and when Chris turned slightly, they saw Jean covering her mouth with her hand.

"I get what you're saying," Nick groaned. "My dreams are related to my drug and alcohol abuse."

Chris heard Nick take a deep breath as the former rockstar continued, "It was the start of spring when I first saw you in the circus... The band didn't always stay together and I would wander off by myself. I loved the circus when I was younger because my dad would take me. The smells and the sounds would remind me of my childhood."

Nick paused and Chris glanced back to see he had a wide grin on his face. "I wanted to be a lion tamer or the ringleader," Nick chuckled. "I didn't think of it as a freak show but as something extraordinary. You and the others were capable of doing things I could only dream of." He smiled at her.

"I was fat," Jean scoffed. "That takes no special talent."

"You used to love your life for who you were, no matter what you looked like," he said. "I can see what I see now... a beauty... a knockout..." he stammered, turning red. Chris peered between the seat backs to see Jean stare at him incred-ulously.

"You're perfect," Nick sighed.

"I wish." Jean muttered and diverted her eyes. "It seems like I used to be a magnet for carnies, and now all I seem to attract are shallow men who want to take advantage of me..." She stopped and blushed at her bold revelation.

"I can be shallow," Nick admitted and sank down in his seat.

As soon as Taylor caught Chris listening in, she turned her attention to the two seated behind her. She met Chris's gaze with a playful glint in her eyes, and Chris couldn't help but wonder if Taylor would ruin their cover.

Chris spied the movie screen and raised a brow, "Wait… that's Nick."

Taylor eyed the outdated video before them and began to guffaw. Chris and Taylor turned to face them and gave up hiding to listen in. They made no effort to hide how funny they thought it was.

Tay cocked an eyebrow at Nick, "You're actually in this movie?" She pointed to her screen.

Instead of answering, he snatched the sunglasses from Jean's purse and put them on, then pulled his hood up.

Jean watched him and settled down to watch the movie.

Nigel flailed around on his seat, drawing everyone's attention. Chris stood up a little, and could tell from Nigel's wide eyes and panting breaths that he was very scared.

Taylor sat up with her knee in her seat to see what the ruckus was. She was more inquisitive about the situation and didn't seem to care who saw her. Chris looked out the window, grateful they did not have to take this whole situation on alone.

"Were we being too loud? We didn't mean to wake you," Taylor said to Nigel as she sank back into her seat, and resumed scrolling through her phone.

"Everything alright?" Chris queried in a hushed voice and peered at Nigel between the seats.

"No!" Nigel snapped.

Taylor sat up a little to meet his eye and had a subtle smile on her features. "You were shaking around and talking to yourself and stuff."

Chris gave Taylor a noncommittal shrug and addressed Nigel, who appeared to be frightened. "Are you all right?" they asked again.

"No!" Nigel said louder now, "I am NOT alright." Nigel looked petrified yet insulted that Chris was speaking to him. "In my nightmares, I DIE ON A PLANE!"

Everybody within earshot looked over at them and Nigel's face flushed. Chris looked at the other passengers worriedly. It was not the kind of thing to say on a plane, much less to scream it for the whole cabin to hear.

Nigel was curled in a fetal position, the book cradled close like a teddy bear. Finally, he sat up to compose himself and held a finger up as the flight attendant came over.

"An appletini please..." As an afterthought, he added, "Make that two..."

Chris sighed and turned upon hearing Jean giggle at the movie with Nick featured in it.

"I can't get over that guy is in this movie..." Taylor asked with surprise, popping a peanut into her mouth. She knit her eyebrows together as she looked at Nick on the screen "It's a really old movie but he doesn't look any different. Isn't that odd?"

Chris gave a slight nod and noticed Nick had disappeared into his seat. Chris raised an eyebrow in confusion, wondering why Nick was acting so odd. However, it was obvious from watching the movie that Taylor was right – he hadn't aged. Could he be scared someone might recognize him and notice the discrepancy?

Chris tapped away at the screen of their phone, looking for information on Nick Dallas. They eventually found that he was 68 years old, despite looking much younger than he ought to. Chris checkedup Nigel Collin's age; he was supposed to be around 60. It took longer to search for Jean or Ima since the circus wasn't as coveted as the silver screen or vinyl records. Before long, the plane began its descent, and Chris glanced at the phone one last time before putting it away. According to the records, Jean was 54; however, she appeared not a day over 25.

Nick, Jean, and Nigel had faded from public consciousness. They were no longer monitored by the press and had been forgotten. Nick lived on the streets, Jean had taken on several aliases, and Nigel had been forgotten as a great mind. They seemed to keep to themselves, and found it hard to make ends meet and earned minor monies if at all.

Chris noticed the airline staff announcing their arrival in New Orleans and peered out of the window of the plane. The airport didn't appear any different from Baltimore.

Taylor was already gathering her belongings, Nigel stood in the aisle to get off the plane, Nick had pulled his hoodie up, and Jean was giggling behind her hand.

Chris handed Taylor her luggage, and she took it without a word. Her stuff was always new, with the trendiest labels and logos, whereas Chris's were simple and functional. She pulled out her wireless earbuds and placed them neatly in their pink case. Next, she took her phone out to snap a selfie before putting it away and grabbing her small backpack from Chris. With a smile and a wave, she floated off the plane. Life was just easier for Tay than it was for Chris.

Everyone had always told Chris that the oldest sibling had it the hardest, but that didn't seem true for Tay. Chris watched her prance around with the signature and trendy things and thought it was a waste of money for a label, but as long as it made her happy, Chris couldn't say no.

When they entered the terminal, Chris noticed how new and tidy the airport was and let out a deep sigh.

As Nigel, Nick, and Jean followed behind the siblings, Taylor couldn't help but giggle at Nick who kept his hood up.

"You look like the Unabomber with that hood," she teased.

Jean pushed down NIck's hood and ruffled his hair. "He's just trying to hide his boyish good looks."

"Will a single Uber work for all of us?" Jean surveyed the group.

"I think we should rent a car." Chris pointed to the rental signs in the area.

Taylor followed Chris to the rental and murmured, "You really do have weird friends, Chris."

CHAPTER 16

Taking the front seat next to Chris, Taylor set the GPS on her phone and began navigating towards the address it gave her. Tay gasped and pointed at the sights, and Chris agreed; they were captivated by everything they saw.

Jean struggled to keep her eyes open despite the overwhelming energy of the French quarter. In the rearview, Chris noted she had reached the point of exhaustion and could no longer battle against it.

Nigel sat up straight with an idea. "Why don't we drive home? We can drive across a few states and be in springtime weather in no time." His suggestion was met with astonished looks from the others.

"It's only a ten-hour drive!" Taylor pointed out jokingly.

"Afraid of the plane ride, Brit?" Nick remarked with an inquisitive look.

"No... well, yes, but that isn't why I suggested it", Nigel stammered, uncharacteristically unsure of himself.

As Taylor's phone spoke up with directions, Nigel stopped complaining. Taylor surveyed the bustling cityscape before saying, "Okay, it looks like we're going to a business instead of a house."

"Maybe she doesn't trust us?" Chris said with a deep breath but kept eyes on the road and ears attentive to Taylor's directions.

Nick inquired from the backseat, "Does she realize how many of us there are?"

Chris gave a soft reply, "I don't think so."

"Then she never had reason to trust us, did she?" Nick reasoned.

"I always suggest meeting new online acquaintances at neutral places," Nigel said in a hurry. "You never know who you can run into nowadays." His eyes surveyed the vivid characters on the streets.

"You have arrived at your destination," the phone barked suddenly.

Chris pulled into a parking space and Taylor added, "It looks like a restaurant."

"Actually, it's a cafe," Nigel said with a shrug and stepped out of the vehicle, giving himself one long stretch.

When he got out of the car, Nick accidentally woke Jean and, as soon as his feet hit the ground, he tapped his pockets for his smokes. When he lit up a cigarette, his gaze fell upon a woman and he gestured to draw Chris's attention.

The woman in the cafe carried herself with the ease of a wildcat. Her movements were so fluid it seemed as if they came from an innate sense of confidence rather than honed skill and each compact motion felt like a wave of allure.

Chris watched Nick quickly look from this woman to Jean who stood beside him. Jean's eyes were wide open and her mouth formed a small "o". Nick let out a chuckle when she snapped her jaw shut and he glanced back and forth between the two women. Chris considered that Jean had a much different beauty from this other woman. Jean's was sweet, while her counterpart oozed with danger.

Chris tried to hide their smile as they got out of the car and could only think, *Caught like a mouse in a trap.*

"Aiyeee!" Nigel squealed. "Put your best French foot forward!"

Chris shut the car door and donned a pair of sunglasses, as if to reinforce the message that they should not draw too much notice. Speaking softly, Chris suggested, "Let's sit near a table so we can hear the conversation, but let me do the talking. I don't want to frighten her away by all of us showing up together."

Taylor wandered around snapping pictures like the perfect tourist, while the rest attempted to go unnoticed. Chris grabbed one of the tables and the others sat at the other. Chris kept looking around as they sat alone.

Suddenly, the alluring woman showed up by the table and purred. "Coffee? Beignets?"

Chris attempted to remain nonchalant, casually raising their eyebrow in response. The woman had the same accent as Deacon and that made Chris think back to their conversation at the harbor cafe.

"Please," Chris said simply.

"One or both?" She asked with a hand on her hip.

"Both, please," Chris nodded.

She hesitated, her eyes falling to the ground. "So, what about your friends at the table with you?"

Chris sat upright. "What do you mean?" She waved her hand dismissively. "Oh, come on now. You're the Yankee that contacted my daughter and asked for a

meeting."

"Abigail?" Chris croaked.

She finally seated herself at the table across from them,

propping up her elbow and resting her chin upon it. "Non, mon cher," she said. "I am Marie."

At that moment they were both aware of a loud cough and Chris knew it was Nigel attempting to get their attention.

Marie chuckled and said, "Let's sit with your friends because we're gonna need this table for real customers." She rose from her seat and beckoned a woman of an age similar to hers. "Gail, coffees 'n beignets!" She pointed to the table as she sauntered over to it.

Chris quickly rose and introduced the four of them to her. "Marie, this is Nigel, Jean, Nick, and Taylor." Chris gestured to the beauty standing beside them. "This is who I was meeting... Marie."

Nigel spoke up quickly. "Marie?" He cocked his head, and his eyes so wide they were ready to pop out of his head.

Marie gave a slight nod and slipped into a chair. She watched as one of the waitresses brought Chris a chair.

Nick couldn't take his eyes off her and made no effort to hide it. "You work here?" Nick squeaked and Chris was surprised at the strangled sound coming from their friend who usually took everything in his stride.

Taylor let out an exasperated sigh and started pulling apart a napkin.

"Child, don't you make no mess!" She chided Taylor with a toss of her chin and an elbow propped on the back of her chair. "This is my cafe. I own it, and everyone who works here is part of my family."

Taylor crumpled up her napkin and grabbed her phone, taking refuge in the beeping and blinking of the device. "They said you wanted to meet somewhere public."

"I did!" She replied hastily. "I don't know y'all! This is a safe place with plenty of patrons."

"And tourists," Nigel interjected. "How did you pick us out of all the strangers?"

"You English, mon cher?" She laughed "I missed that now, did I?"

She eyed Nick's cigarettes and slyly took one. She waited, and Nick quickly lit it for her. Her air of cool self-confidence seemed to be a part of her nature. As soon as he ignited the cigarette, she grabbed his arm, revealing the scar on his wrist. Of all the many scars he bore, it was the easiest for her to point out. "You got the mark!"

The woman leered at Jean pointing at a scar Marie spied on her neck. Swiveling her head, Marie looked at Nigel, who covered up when she glared at him as if to call him out. Last, she looked at Taylor and Chris, asking, "Don't y'all have it?"

Taylor seemed to shrink back from her. "I'm not contagious if that's what you mean!"

Marie ignored Taylor and turned to Chris. "What about you, honey?"

Chris gave a sudden yelp of surprise. "What?"

"You made the deal, no?" She took a small puff of her cigarette. "But no mark?"

Nigel, Nick and Jean all sat up straighter in their seats, but only Nigel spoke up. "How do you know all this?"

A deep laugh left her lips and her long braids danced with her laughter. "Let's just say I got my own ways." In the blink of an eye, her expression hardened again. "Why did I want to meet in a public place? I ain't scared of you children. I wanted to be sure that you are what I think you are and it's easier to shoo away a pest when there's people around." She laughed mockingly.

A waitress delivered a tray of coffees and a plate loaded with a fragrant dessert covered in powdered sugar.

In a hushed voice, Nigel exclaimed, "You're not related to Marie, you ARE Marie!"

She chuckled but her stare fixed on him. "There's many women named Marie, chile." Her voice was low and husky, like a saxophone's melody, and although she spoke softly, the words were sharp daggers to the heart.

"You're her." Nigel's eyes widened taking it all in. "Blimey! I've read all about you. You were said to have practiced voodoo." He looked like an impressed admirer.

She let out a laugh, but it sounded strangely like Deacon's. It was as if two voices were talking at once, and the laughter had a seething tone. "You got some stories?" She took her coffee and waved fingers while her elbow still balanced on the back of her chair, beckoning him to speak.

Nigel scooted closer to the table and asked, "Did you make a deal? What is it?" Nigel sat forward and leaned on the table. "You know him, don't you?"

She feigned innocence in response. "Know who?"

At this point, everyone's eyes moved quickly between Nigel and Marie as if watching a tennis match except for Taylor who had her phone in her hands under the table.

Nigel looked her straight in the eyes. "He's Papa Legba, isn't he?"

Astonished, she burst into a laugh, "Papa? You think you struck a bargain with him?" She took a long drag of her cigarette. "Why you think that?"

Nigel pushed his glasses up by the nose feeling sheepish, "I was sure before but not now..." he said quietly.

"Papa?" Marie chuckled, eyes twinkling as the others hung onto her every word. "Do you know what you gotta do just to get Papa's attention?"

Taylor looked up at her curiously, waiting for an answer. "What?"

Marie smirked at their entranced faces and gaping mouths. "First you get his attention with an offering of something he likes to indulge in." She sighed and shrugged until her arm was finally off the back of the chair. "Then you gotta make a deal and keep that deal without attracting attention."

"He took our money with a signed contract," Chris added calmly.

"Then that ain't Papa," she added as she snuffed her cigarette out. "With Papa, it's all a deal, and if you break it, he gets you." She sat back with a sigh and stared Chris dead in the eye. "Your deal ain't with Papa, Cheri." She propped her elbow on the back of the chair again then crossed her legs.

"How do you know all this?" Jean inquired quietly.

"Bad news always travel fast." Marie nodded to Nigel. "I heard about someone digging up my past." She seemed almost angry then waved her hand dismissively. "So, I did some asking of my own."

"You spied on us?" Nick seemed impressed and leaned back in his chair now.

"No need to. All I had to do was ask around," the witchy woman replied with a grin. "Y'all been on the news saving people and something wasn't right 'bout it." She lifted her coffee cup and took a sip. "Try the beignets. Best in New Orleans!" The air was thick with the aroma of freshly cooked beignets, cinnamon, and melting sugar, making bellies grumble, but they kept on subject.

"Is all of this real?" Taylor narrowed her eyes. "Or she's in on this joke?"

"This ain't no joke!" A low snarl erupted from the woman's throat, thick and threatening. She stared Taylor down, daring her not to meet her gaze. When Taylor attempted to ignore her by staring at her phone, Marie grabbed the device and Chris watched Taylor become dumbfounded. It cut them to the quick. Marie released her grip and pointed a finger at Taylor. "Now, put that phone away, chile! No toys at the table."

"What answers you want? You sure you want them?" Marie looked around the group like a teen playing truth or dare.

"Of course," Chris said without hesitation.

"Do I know people who do voodoo and dabble in dark arts? Oui!" She announced quickly. "I also been around long enough to know when something's wrong." She gave a knowing look. "You see the news you made? Tricks no human can do?" She scoffed. "They think you're a superhero because that's what they wanna believe." She pointed to herself. "Me? I read between the lines."

Nigel grew more excited. "We made the telly down here?" He grinned at the others, clearly impressed.

"You gone save some mayor and it's gone be big news," she scoffed. "But they put it together and how nobody got hurt and that other saving you did with that chile." She gave a low sound. "None of it looked normal."

The others glanced at each other curiously, obviously not understanding what she meant.

Marie let out a heavy sigh. "That stunt you pulled saving that chile looked like some computer game. You ain't swimming but the water was moving you. They got the rescue on video and it's all the talk." Marie's face and all her features were clearly visible against the cafe's ambience. The lines on her face were sharp, her frown pronounced and a scowl playing on her lips.

Chris looked sheepish. "I can't swim. I have no idea how I did it."

Taylor nodded in agreement. "We live by the water and have a pool but Chris can't swim."

"I sink like a rock. Dad had to pull me out twice," Chris admitted.

"But you saved a chile in that water? I heard that water is cursed. Got muck piled so high even best swimmers struggle." Marie chuckled at this thought, her face lighting up with mirth. "I also heard you got your own Loch Ness monster there."

They all nodded in quiet confirmation.

Marie sneered. "You quick to believe all this with demons, deals, voodoo and monsters."

Nigel pointed his finger defending the facts. "I'm not barking. Things happened and there's no other reason for them."

She laughed again as her braids swayed with her motion. "Famous people died in there, and the curse of the Chesapeake ain't no joke."

"What are we dealing with?" Nick lowered his voice. "Did we make a deal with the Devil?"

Marie burst into peals of laughter, her head thrown back as if the crescendo would be loud enough to break glass. When she finally regained her composure, she said, "This boy thinks he made a deal with the Devil." She took a deep breath before continuing, "This ain't nothing like the devil or Papa but probably some fantomes or demons."

"Demon?" Taylor asked in a doubtful tone. "This is nuts. You're all going through some midlife crisis."

Marie chuckled softly. "Little girl, how old is this rockstar?"

"I Dunno 40 or 50?" She shrugged.

"But he had hits in the '80s?" Marie arched a brow at her.

Nick cleared his throat. "I'm 68 this year."

Taylor's jaw dropped as she swung around to look at Nigel and Jean.

"60," Nigel laughed, knowing he didn't look a day over 30.

"54," Jean glanced away, her cheeks coloring.

"Nu-uh," Taylor exclaimed in disbelief.

"They can't die and they stuck looking at the age they

made the deal!" Marie challenged and as she watched Taylor start searching on her phone. "That rockstar been all over the news lately, and they can't figure out how he looks so young!" Marie chuckled.

Chris inclined their head and inquired, "Is it wrong to ask your age?"

"Older than all y'all." Marie swept her hand around the group. Although it was clear she didn't appear much older than Taylor, there was something about her eyes that suggested she had seen more in life than could be perceived on the surface. Her eyes radiated with a wisdom far beyond her years.

"How do we get out of this?" Nick questioned quickly

"You don't," Marie said wearily. "Why would you?"

"You don't have nightmares?" Jean asked in a whisper.

Marie shook her head. "What I did was different than y'all." She laughed mirthlessly. "I got ways y'all ain't never heard of!" She laughed. "What I am ain't the same."

Jean appeared to accept her remarks as she cast a gaze down at her crossed hands on her lap.

Marie glanced at the clock then to the other guest leaving. "I gotta help my family clean up the cafe." She gave them all a smile before standing, "We're a number one tourist attraction." Then she stood with a wink. "Y'all take care." She made her way to the kitchen.

Taylor checked her phone and raised an eyebrow. "Really? You guys are all older than my parents?"

"Nobody lied, Tay," Chris said quietly as Nigel filled his pockets with pastries. "Tay, go pay for it so we can get a fast flight home."

Nigel nearly choked on the piece of pastry he was eating. "We're flying?"

"I have a doctor's appointment tomorrow," Chris mumbled, but knew it would be Angellkittyhard to go to something that seemed so frivolous right now. If the appointment was missed, then it would be easy enough to make another.

Nigel seemed disheartened and nodded once. His gaze was diverted to Taylor, who had already gone up to the register to pay for the coffee.

Jean kept her peace, while Nick shifted in his chair, clearing his throat. "Guess we're stuck," he said.

"I guess we are famous," Nigel commented, gesturing at the television that hung from the ceiling in the cafe.

The entire rescue from the fire was remarked as death defying, but it was pointed out that everyone escaped damage-free. The press did its best to make a story of how they had all made lucky jumps away from the blaze. The highlight was probably Chris, who had tried to protect the mayor's wife with their own body, as if they knew they couldn't get hurt.

The news shifted to the water rescue, where Chris flailed instead of swimming but stayed afloat. It was almost as if they were walking on water. It truly looked like a miracle.

Chris swallowed hard and felt called out by the media and half expected people to think it was a deepfake.

"I didn't know you could walk on water, mate," Nigel quipped.

Chris's face flushed, and uncertainty over the newscasters labeling the group "The Immortals". The reporter marveled at the fact that Nick, Nigel, and Jean looked the same age, maintaining a youthful appearance despite the years passing by.

Jean merely shrugged in response. "It will pass." She had yet to save a life or perform a daring feat. For the time being, she wasn't really seen as one of the heroes so she could move with less notice.

Nick glanced over at Taylor as she began heading back to the table, muttering to her, "We should still go."

"Did you see the television?" Taylor exclaimed with her eyes wide open.

"C'mon, Tay. We're going home." Chris mumbled and the group strolled down the street together. Tay was the first to run forward, her phone already in her hand as she snapped selfies with anything that caught her eye.

Chris rolled their eyes in exasperation as Taylor continued to be her usual self. Nick found her antics amusing and marched forward, with Jean right behind him. Though Marie had provided little assistance, Chris was still joyful. The prospect of returning home with a new family had them feeling hopeful and upbeat.

Chris didn't notice the car coming until it was too late to issue a warning. Taylor shrieked when the vehicle careened towards her. Nick, who was closest to her, lunged and pulled Tay to the ground underneath him.

The car's horn blared a panicked, high-pitched wail, then cut out when the scream of metal being wrenched took over.

CHAPTER 17

Taylor's cries for help drowned out Chris's scream for her. Jean rushed towards them and was by Nick's side first. All Chris could make out of Taylor was a leg sticking out from under Nick.

Chris eyed the crowd with camera phones out that had begun to gather to see what happened. Gawkers trying to get some morbid click for social media and their 15 seconds of fame. Chris glowered at them and their rude fascination with the accident. This was Taylor, and Chris panicked as they made their way past all these *people*.

The car was slumped over Nick, his clothes torn and yet, miraculously, he was free of blood. The car had contorted around Nick's body, as if he were fashioned out of metal instead of flesh and bone.

Chris's voice cracked with urgency as they urged Jean to tell them what had happened to Tay. Their face was tight with worry, and their fists clenched in frustration as they attempted to push their way through the crowd. They were only able to observe Jean as she squeezed Nick's shoulder. The former musician looked up at her, his face covered in grime. A moment later, Taylor emerged from beneath Nick. She appeared petrified but unscathed. As the two survivors stood side by side, the hoard of people around them began to clap.

The driver hobbled out coughing, holding onto his arm. He gestured towards the car, which now had an airbag protruding from the steering wheel. "My brakes... must've gone out. Are you okay?"

Nigel raised an eyebrow as he studied the man's arm. "Are you okay, sir? Your arm looks off."

The driver finally seemed to realize the damage done to his limb and he groaned in pain, "I think it's broken." He glanced around the group and asked them, "What did I hit?" A woman jabbed her index finger toward Nick as other people furrowed their brows at him, suggesting that Nick was the obstacle the driver had collided with.

Chris rushed to Taylor's side and anxiously scanned her for signs of harm before embracing her. Once satisfied, they both looked at Nick with relief and Chris let out a long sigh of gratitude.

Nick began ushering everyone away. "We really should go," he whispered nervously to the siblings.

Before they made it anywhere, a voice called out from behind them, "It's those immortals from the news!"

Marie came out to the parking lot and surveyed the area. She grabbed Chris's arm and whispered harshly in their ear, "Y'all got to go now! I can't have eyes on us!"

Her glare was sharp with anger, and for a second Chris thought that her eyes had turned red. Chris nodded and started towards their car.

"Where is my phone?" Taylor asked in a squeaky voice. It took her a moment to notice all the phones pointed at them. Nigel shoved the requested device into her hand and pushed her to leave.

As they reached the car, the sound of sirens cut through the loud applause and people cheering, "The immortals!"

Taylor was visibly shaken as Chris drove. She sat with her knees drawn up to her chest. "Well, that happened." Chris tried to comfort her by patting her shoulder, but she flinched away. "Just keep your eyes on the road." She stared ahead. "I'm not one of the immortals."

Jean spoke up quickly, "You don't want to be." She turned her gaze to Nick, who was changing into a new shirt that Chris had packed. "Where did this come from?" Jean asked.

Chris glanced up in the rearview mirror to see Nick changing into the shirt. Chris was smaller than Nick who fought to get the shirt on. The next time Chris looked in the rearview mirror , they saw Jean point out a small scar on Nick's lower back.

Jean's eyes widened at the red mark that depicted a car. "What's that?" She touched next to the red spot and bit her lip looking at it.

Nigel glanced over and raised an eyebrow. "Do you already have a tattoo of a car on your back, mate?"

Nick quickly pulled the tightly clinging shirt down and mumbled, "We know why it's there."

"You have a tattoo of a car?" Taylor glared at him as he attempted to hide it. She held up her wrist for him to see a blue crab tattoo. "I have a crab." She shivered and pushed the air vent away from her. Pointing to Chris with a smile, she added, "Chris has a bell tattoo."

Jean shook her head. "That's not a regular tattoo. We get these marks when we survive death. When we try to kill ourselves, it doesn't work. We always wake up with some kind of mark to commemorate the near-death experience."

Nigel looked at Nick. "I think Nick has the most of those scars."

Taylor curled back up, as if she felt overwhelmed by the situation. Her voice trembled when she asked Nick, "Is this all real?"

Nick sighed. "I've tried cutting my wrists, overdosing, hanging myself, jumping off things..." He gestured at his body, covered in various marks. "I don't even know how many times I've tried anymore."

Taylor offered a little smile. "You're teasing me now." She glanced at Nick bashfully. "Thanks," and Tay's cheeks flushed with color.

Chris did a double take. That was unusual for Tay. Nick returned her gaze thoughtfully, and she paused while her eyes roved up and down his body.

"Th... thank you... for saving my life," she stuttered. Nick's eyes met hers and she froze, her smile dimming a fraction.

"You're welcome."

"You're staying with us? Living with us?" Taylor asked eagerly. "I feel better with you around."

Nick gave a light chuckle. "Then I will stay as long as I can, kiddo."

"So you all made some deal to stay alive and now you're indestructible?" Taylor raised one eyebrow skeptically. "Sounds like a great deal."

"It isn't," everyone replied in unison.

Chris kept quiet, feigning disinterest in the conversation while keeping their eyes on the road, then Taylor pointed for them to turn into the airport.

Nigel's phone began to hum with a default ringtone and he answered it. A smile graced Nigel's face as he began speaking in hushed tones. They could all hear him mumble, "I'll call you back in a bit."

When Chris paused at a traffic signal, Nigel exchanged looks with them as though trying to make them envious. He gradually made eye contact with the other curious stares.

"That was that snack of a man – that paramedic who came to our rescue after helping the mayor." He all but squealed in delight, "We're going to chat when I'm not around you lot." Nigel winked.

Chris knew Nigel was scared of the plane ride home but hoped thoughts of the EMT would keep Nigel busy and reduce his anxiety.

Chris's thoughts were plagued by worries worse than they could express. The doctor's appointment dimmed in the shadow of fresh blemishes on Nick, and the near-fatal accident with Tay. The worst fortune imaginable just kept on piling on.

Once they were on the plane, everyone took their seats. Nigel had a deep furrow on his brow and Chris thought it might be because he didn't want to sit alone again..

Taylor eagerly shoved Jean to the side so she could take the spot beside Nick, who stepped through to his seat with an amused expression.

"Can I please not have to sit next to Nigel?" Chris stopped next to Jean and glanced towards the flamboyant man. "I'd rather avoid his flirting."

Jean observed Nigel. "I hope he sits close enough that we can keep an eye on him. I can only imagine how he must feel about planes."

Chris looked up, and Nigel's anxiety couldn't be denied. "He did choose to come with us, though." Chris gingerly took a seat, making sure not to show too much joy at the prospect of sitting next to Jean. The fragrance of her perfume wafted through the air as they drew near.

Averting their gaze, Chris felt a little sheepish. A moment later, they were distracted by Taylor. Her voice echoed off the walls as she animatedly talked to Nick, and it was almost like a weight had been lifted, hearing her light-hearted banter. She was back to her old self again. Chris beamed at the thought of Tay behaving like she used to and kept a watchful eye on her as she carried on with Nick.

Chris's ears perked up hearing Taylor kept talking to Nick about her phone. "You never had a cell phone?" She held hers out showing him her apps. "Chris made money creating apps for cells." Chris narrowed their eyes, sure the whole plane could hear the exchange. Couldn't she keep her voice down?

"Yeah, seems like a smart kid," Nick said as he watched Taylor scroll through the device. "Can I take a look?"

Chris ignored Tay's blathering. It was clear she was smitten with him after he saved her life, so she was trying to amuse him, or maybe she just felt safe with him now.

Jean glanced over at Chris with a little smile. "You're protective?"

Chris nodded then cleared their throat. Glancing at Jean, they steeled themself with a deep breath before saying, "So... what about you and Nick?" Chris stole a glimpse at her from the corner of their eyes to gauge her reaction.

Jean raised her eyebrows and said nothing, as though expectantly waiting for Chris to finish.

Chris finally exhaled then stammered, "I thought you like him."

Jean smiled and cocked her head toward Nick and Taylor

who had their heads together, talking. Words couldn't seem to pour out of Taylor fast enough, and her hands waved around. Jean gasped when Chris's words dawned on her and the corner of her mouth turned up slightly. "Are you asking if we're dating?"

Chris nodded hesitantly and attempted to match Jean's deep, steady breaths. It was difficult not to take in a large gasp of air when, after days of anticipation, Chris finally had the courage to ask.

"No," she cocked her head. "We hardly talk." She looked out the window with a far away look.

"Still..." Chris's voice trailed off as they tried to find the right words. Chris's unease was clear, and they began fidgeting in the seat while their face grew hotter by the second. "I thought you had a thing for him or that he liked you."

Chris could see Taylor bouncing in her seat a bit and waved her phone in one hand as if it was another appendage, then she practically screamed, "Chris is muy smart and people hated them for it. You're probably Chris' only friends."

Chris heard every loud word and wished she would stop talking. If they could hear her, they knew Jean could too. Mortified, Chris tried not to breathe, held back every possible sound, so as not to alert Nick and Taylor that the conversation was being overheard. Chris waited in the hope Nick might declare his lack of interest in Jean.

Taylor wasn't done talking and turned. "See, it's kinda like this." She took a deep breath and began to say everything in one excited breath. Taylor was known to spill tea and pointed her phone at them as if it was an extra finger, "Chris was so smart they ended up in lots of my classes too! I could see the kids didn't like smarty pants or somebody that young knowing more than they did but..."

She inhaled, and continued. "Chris got the answers fast

when it came to books and tech." Taylor waggled her phone for emphasis. "So, when Chris talks they're usually right and people learned to listen... like really fast." She gave a dry chuckle. "Try living with that at home!" She gestured back to the phone, but Nick looked on in shock, as if Tay had sprouted an extra head. Chris stifled a chuckle but hoped Jean didn't hear Taylor's prattling.

"Okay?" Nick looked overwhelmed by her tirade and the strangeness of the complicated tech.

"Go ahead," Taylor urged, placing the phone in Nick's hand. "I have no secrets." She glanced at him as he navigated through the phone very slowly and smiled. When he pressed the camera icon, she let out a laugh. "Press this one to take a selfie!" She flipped the display around.

Jean turned her head to face Chris and rolled her eyes before responding quietly. "Nick is used to date women with model-looks like the one we saw at the restaurant earlier. I'm not exactly a bombshell."

Chris lifted an eyebrow and remarked, "You're prettier than that woman." When their eyes met, Chris quickly looked away, feeling exposed as if they had just been caught cheating at a game of poker. Chris yearned to express how they felt, yet admitting it to her filled them with fear. Chris had never been in a serious relationship due to their picky disposition when it came to romantic interests. Chris's non-binary identity also made it difficult for them to find someone they accepted, let alone someone that they liked. The intensity of their sudden attraction to Jean was over-whelming, but they couldn't ignore their emotions any longer.

The aircraft started to move down the runway, startling Jean. Herhands collided with Chrsi's on the armrest, as if by destiny. "I should have paid attention when the stewardess was speaking." Jean said, embarrassed as she slowly removed her hand from Chris'. "So are you like..."

Chris met Jean's gaze and waited for her to continue her query. The plane lurched, pushing Chris closer to Jean than anticipated. They felt a wave of emotion wash over them when they noticed how close they were. The scent of her perfume was intoxicating, and Chris couldn't tear their gaze away from her hazel eyes.

At last, they gently exhaled the words, "Do you want something to drink?" Despite their nerves, Chris wasn't about to give up.

Nick let out a chuckle and Taylor repositioned the phone to get his face in the middle. "You have to aim it!" She grinned, making a peace sign with her fingers and demonstrating how to take a selfie. "You try!"

Aiming it, Nick agreed, "The angle makes all the difference."

Nick glanced over and tried to catch Chris's attention, but they didn't acknowledge it, not wanting to break the moment with Jean. It took concentration to shrug off Nick's stare, and Chris was glad they were strong enough to do it. That was new... a good type of change.

Chris leaned in towards Jean, like two magnets coming together. They could feel Jean's breath against their lips and Chris's cheeks grew warm. Entranced by the moment, they leaned in even closer.

"Drinking makes me sleepy," Jean blurted out, looking back to Nick and Taylor's seats with a worried expression. Both he and Taylor were intently observing Jean and Chris.

Taylor giggled as she glanced at Chris, blushing hard.

"I need the restroom," Jean deflected. Chris grumbled and they stood up to let her pass. Chris narrowed their eyes at Taylor who seemed to be enjoying this live show far too much.

Chris was sure the whole thing showed up crimson red on their face.

"Omg!" Taylor exclaimed in a hushed voice. "Was she really going to kiss Chris?"

Chris's ears burned even hotter when they heard Taylor sigh with relief, as Jean made her way to the restroom. "I'm glad that didn't happen," Taylor scoffed. "She is definitely too old for Chris."

Nick and Jean locked eyes for a moment as Jean moved down the aisle before she averted her gaze. Chris watched the interaction intently and hoped Jean's reaction and Nick slumping in his seat with a deep sigh meant Chris had a chance for a do-over.

Nigel piped up from behind the group. "It's like a soap opera on this plane!"

Chris sank into their seat and groaned. Nigel must have heard it all too, and Chris wanted to pull something over their head and disappear for the rest of the flight.

Nigel swept his arm wide and announced, "Over my airways!" Although Chris didn't share the sentiment, Nigel continued with another quip, "Air yuck?"

Taylor rolled her eyes and Nick scoffed, but Nigel remained unruffled. "Did this offend you?" Nigel purred in Nick's ear. "Don't worry, plenty more plump women around."

Taylor spun her head around, astounded. "She was fat?"

Just then the plane started to shimmy and shudder, and Nick stood enough to give Nigel an abrupt shove back into his seat. Nigel clung desperately to the armrests, terror evident in his widened eyes. Nick's timing couldn't have been worse.

"Nigel, calm down," Chris called. The poor cell signal on the plane was likely why Nigel had not phoned back his new romance – the EMT – like he was supposed to. Chris was sure that if Nigel had been chatting on the phone, he might have been distracted enough to miss the turbulence and all the worrisome scenarios that must be going through his head.

Instead Nigel threw his arms over his face and let out a shriek. After the turbulence calmed down, Chris watched him peer between fingers. Even Nick and Taylor looked concerned.

Nigel groaned and recovered his calm. "Sorry, I seem to be aboard scary airlines."

Taylor looked away and put on her shades as if to hide from the scene. She sank down in her chair. "Why does he keep doing this near me?"

Chris sighed, silently pleading with everyone to cease the exhausting chatter until they got off the plane.

Chris was relieved nothing else happened on the flight, and they landed and exited without further incident.

After reaching the car, Taylor and Chris rushed to claim the front seats. The drive from BWI Airport was silent, with each of them on edge. This time Jean wasn't napping on Nick. Chris drove up to the house and opened the gates, maneuvering around the circular driveway to the garage.

"Don't you have to return this car?" Nigel asked quietly.

"This is the rental," Chris moaned thinking of their long lost car. Taylor opened the garage door with her phone for them and Chris fussed. "My old one is gone, so until I get another..." Chris trailed off not wanting to whine about how they missed their car. It seemed silly to go on about a car when Tay nearly died today.

As the group exited the vehicle, Jean kept up a noticeable distance from Nick who was despondent and tired. Chris couldn't help but wonder how much of their conversation with Jean Nick had witnessed. Chris opened the door as Tay raced to Nick and hugged him around his waist. Chris felt replaced by Nick and it was Chris's turn to feel a little jealous.

Jean smiled warmly as Nick kissed the younger girl's head, watching them all together in a familiar setting.

Nigel still had that book tucked away in his backpack but held the bag close to his chest, like a baby. He didn't seem to pay attention to anyone or anything else. The plane ride had obviously shaken him, and he remained uncharacteristically reserved.

He had his phone out and was dialing quickly, "Jeremy?"

Chris knew Nigel would be cheered up fast and Chris was very happy for Nigel.

CHAPTER 18

"Looks like we're the first home," Chris said as they entered the mudroom to remove their shoes.

"Mom and Dad must be having a good time then," Tay smiled, although she shook her head. "How are we going to explain this to Mom and Dad when they get back?" Taylor groaned.

"That you almost got killed?" Chris opened the main door and set down keys.

"All of it." Taylor whispered. She bit her bottom lip worriedly.

Chris threw out a suggestion. "We don't?"

Nigel hung up the phone and agreed. "That's probably for the best. We don't know enough about what happens when someone who shouldn't know about the deal finds out or what will happen to us if we tell anyone."

Nick nodded at Taylor. "You might be in danger because you know."

Chris's eyes darted as thoughts fell into place. "Do you think that's why she was almost hit by that car?" Chris wondered worriedly.

"It could be," Nigel contemplated.

"So we need to keep her close," Nick stated decisively.

Taylor slumped into a kitchen chair. "Let me make this deal too, so you don't have to worry about me."

"No, you won't!" They all cried out in unison.

Tay stuck her lip out and crossed her arms on her chest. "I can if I want..."

"She's used to getting her way," Chris breathed out in an exasperated sigh and hoped teasing Tay would get her mind off making such a deal of her own.

Taylor gave Chris a playful swat and Chris turned to the others. "So, it looks like we're the only ones home. Do you want to stay with us?" Chris tried not to look directly at Jean, then darted their gaze to Nick and Nigel.

Nick simply shrugged, "I'm the extended guest already."

Nigel nodded in agreement. "It's probably best to stick together and I won't miss my flat."

Jean agreed, "That works for me too, but I still need to grab some stuff from home."

Nigel questioned incredulously, "What do you need that they don't have here?" He gave her a skeptical glance, "Medicine? Photos?" Laughing, he said, "I was healed from my ailments shortly after the deal and photos can wait a week."

Jean shook her head. "I'm okay, mostly, but I find it hard to sleep without something special," she said with a blush. "It helps with the night horrors."

"Do tell!" Nigel looked instantly interested and cocked his head to one side, awaiting her explanation.

"It's nothing like that," she replied, her cheeks flushing darker.

"I'll go with you if you like," Nick offered.

She responded with a shrug and glanced around at the others, "I'll grab some clothes too."

Nigel leaned back in his chair. "Not me! I'm looking forward to chez Shepherd! I bet you have much nicer clothes than I do."

Chris shook their head at Nigel for thinking they were in a hotel. Chris kept to themselves, observing the rest of the crowd but their gaze continually fell on Jean.

Taylor stayed in her seat and seemed to be deep in thought.

Nigel released a heavy sigh, then looked towards Chris and Taylor. "Where can a bloke get a hot shower and some warm clothes?"

Chris nodded. "I'll show you." Chris motioned for Nigel to join them and they began ascending the stairs. Chris urged Nigel to keep up, as their own urgency was causing them to pick up the pace. The idea of finding out what Jean and Nick were discussing had made Chris move faster. They soon pulled up in front of a room. "Here, help yourself to clothing in there and there's a stocked shower."

Before Nigel could offer a reply, Chris beamed a smile and darted away to try to rejoin the group. Feeling torn between their feelings for Jean, and how things were playing out between her and Nick had become a challenge for Chris, but they were sure that it would all work out in the end. This thought comforted them. After all, Chris's mother was always so certain that everything happened for the best. In moments like this, Chris yearned for her wise counsel.

Chris could hear the chatter as they approached the kitchen and hurried back in to see Jean with her keys in hand. Chris glanced around worriedly. "What's going on?" Chris worried their conversation on the airplane journey had been too much for her, and made her decide to leave earlier than planned.

"I need to get my things," Jean replied simply.

"I said I'd join her so she wouldn't be alone," Nick remarked.

"I'm gonna order pizza when they get back," Taylor said casually as she popped the gum in her mouth.

Chris felt a twinge of envy after the near encounter with Jean on the plane but it was soon replaced by concern for both friends.

"You sure you have your phone?" Chris wanted to go in Nick's stead but the idea of leaving Nigel and Taylor alone in the house was a no. Chris smiled a little at the thought of the two of them driving Nick crazy while Chris accompanied Jean. Chris knew it would be rude to leave Tay to entertain, especially when Chris didn't want her to introduce Nigel to the Karaoke machine.

Jean gave a brisk nod and mumbled, "We won't take too long."

Nick merely shrugged, looking worn out, and followed her to the garage. "Make sure you lock up after us." He nodded toward the door.

Taylor stood up and added, "Give us a call when you're close so we can buzz you in!"

Chris remained in their seat until the car drove off, then stood to lock up the entrance.

Chris was puttering around the kitchen making coffee, and tossing around dinner and breakfast ideas with Taylor and Nigel. Those two were getting along famously, and while Chris listened, they hoped Taylor wouldn't drag Nigel into a loud activity. Chris hated it when Tay had friends over and tried to sing, and Nigel definitely seemed the type to join in.

Taylor laughed and said, "Do you all have your own super-hero names?"

Nigel replied with enthusiasm, "That could be fun!"

As if on cue, both Taylor's and Chris's watches shook to life and both looked to find out why.

Nigel chuckled ruefully at the noise and exclaimed, "I miss being able to afford tech too!" Then his gaze fell upon their worried expressions. "What is it?"

Taylor extended her arm towards Nigel, pointing out the tiny words that had appeared on her wristwatch. Tay and Chris had programmed their phones to send alerts when certain keywords were detected; Chris's watch was vibrating now as they opened the phone to see what else had triggered it.

"Bubble Buddy, turn the news on!" Taylor commanded.

"Is the whole house controlled by AI?" Nigel asked as he scampered behind Taylor with eyes wide in wonderment.

Taylor led them into the living room and nodded in affirmation as the walls began to unfold and a TV appeared before them.

Laughing, Nigel asked, "Your AI is called Bubble Buddy?"

"That's what Tay calls it," Chris mumbled and held back from rolling their eyes. Taylor was notorious for naming things to her liking and nobody usually cared until it was embarrassing in front of guests. "We'll get you all set up here for the week."

Nigel grinned and joked, "I may never leave!"

Taylor motioned to the television, saying, "Hey, you're on national news."

A reporter said, "We were unable to get a comment from them but did spot two of the self-proclaimed Immortals with another interesting figure." The camera zoomed in and they could see Nick and Jean standing close together and smiling very happily. Nick opened the passenger door to let Jean enter before putting Jean's bags in the trunk then getting into the driver's seat himself. They zoomed in for a closer look at his face, then panned out to show Jean in the front seat holding something next to her purse.

"Self-proclaimed?" Chris scoffed. "We didn't start that."

Of course, Nigel was first to notice it. "Does the fat lady have a stuffie toy in her hands?"

Chris gave Nigel a sidelong glance and jumped to her defense. "That might be what she wanted to get. Something sentimental." Chris cleared their throat pointedly. "It is good to know she's not hung up on something just because it costs a lot."

Watching how Nick seemed to dote on Jean, Chris could hardly tear their eyes from the scene. Nick also kept in close proximity to her and Chris inhaled, wondering if it was simply a protective gesture or if something had happened between them. Nick's hand touched her back, forearm, and hand as he guided her into the car but Jean didn't pull away like she had with Chris. With an eye on Nigel, Chris made sure that he got the message not to bully Jean.

The news team continued on as a banner flew across the screen with the words: TRAGIC DEATH. "Just in, we are sad to report that a young lady who has lately been in much of the news has tragically died." The footage of Chris's water rescue came up and cut to the little girl, standing drenched in the boat.

"Persephone Rogers," the newscaster said louder, zooming in on her face. "Was tragically killed at the same harbor where she'd recently been saved." The image switched to show a woman walking from an ambulance with her head in her hands. "Just the other day Persephone was rescued after falling in the harbor, but today her life was cut short."

They showed a traffic light with stopped traffic and Persephone's mother standing by, crying her eyes out. Next, the video cut to show a person with a microphone shoved in their face, "Yeah, she just ran out into the street chasing some balloon animal and nobody could stop fast enough."

Chris sank back into the overstuffed chair with their breath escaping in small, panting gasps. "What?" They shook their head. It felt like the air had been knocked out of them.

"Is that the lass you rescued?" Nigel asked wide eyed and rubbed his jaw thoughtfully.

Chris nodded dumbfounded and grabbed the remote to click the sound up.

They were already back to the newscasters at the desk and had the little girl's picture behind them on a screen with a caption that read: LIFE CUT SHORT. One of the reporters tapped the papers on the desk. "Tragic, tragic news."

"Now, has anybody heard anything from her rescuer?" The other reporter asked as if he were an actor on cue.

"We have reached out but have not been able to contact Chris Shephard about this," She looked right into the camera as if she were talking directly to Chris. "I am sure Chris Shephard feels this loss as much as we do,"

"Indeed," the other newscaster said to help wrap it up. "We'll be back with move coverage as it comes in." With that, the news went to commercial and soon somebody was yelling about car insurance.

Chris turned it down, a lump forming in their throat. "She was chasing a balloon animal that I gave her the other day?" Chris shook their head feeling responsible for her life and now her death.

Nigel and Taylor traded a worried look and finally Tay spoke up, "How did they track down Nick and Jean?"

"It wouldn't be hard to find us, except for Nick?" Chris opened their eyes wide in sudden surprise. "When was the last time we checked the security cameras?"

"Bubble Buddy, front cameras!" Taylor exclaimed.

The television screen split into two halves and they could see a strange van right outside the house.

"Is that a news van?" Nigel squinted his eyes as he got closer to the TV. "It is." He exchanged an astonished look with them. "The news is stalking us?"

Chris started typing into the phone, trying to warn the others and ask them to call when they got close so they could sneak in without being noticed.

"They'll see the cars!" Taylor changed the channel back to the news where the anchors were still talking about the Immortals. Every person on their team was shown on screen, with a detailed profile of what they had done during their travels from Baltimore to New Orleans.

Chris had always had their privacy, even after their apps sold. Now these news people were pushing into Chris's life.

Tay must have picked up on their mood or read their mind again. She crossed her arms and shook her head. "Def stalking." Taylor sighed. "Cool but creepy." Tay smiled and took a selfie with the TV screen.

Chris raised an eyebrow at their sister, but this wasn't the time to grill her about her selfies. They pulled their phone out and began to text Jean's cell to warn her and Nick. No answer. Chris started to send more messages hoping Nick understood how to text if Jean was driving.

Nigel glanced up at the grand staircase. "I'd like to claim my bed for the night, innkeeper."

"I have to get ready before they arrive," Chris heard Taylor moan at the TV and then at Chris who was still texting away. They continued to ignore her, and she eventually surrendered, heading towards the stairs. "I'll show you your room so we can stop having group sleepovers in the family room." She groaned as she waved for Nigel to follow her. Chris smiled triumphantly at getting Taylor to finally help out a little – and they hadn't needed to fight.

Chris watched Jean guide her car into the garage after pushing past the media. They stood behind the door, out of sight, until the garage door shut. Jean and Nick parked Jean's small sedan and they looked to the others waiting by the door.

A wide smile spread across Nick's face as he helped Jean out of the car. "Wow! I haven't seen the press like that in years!"

Jean threw her plushie behind her back quickly, but Chris had already seen her holding it.

Nick and Jean peered up at the doorway where Nigel, Tay, and Chris shared a look of surprise. Nick flashed them a brilliant smile, and Chris caught Taylor ogling Nick in admiration.

"I guess they think everyone with us is an Immortal now?" Nick joked with an amused twinkle in his eye. "More immortals?"

Taylor scoffed. "No!"

"Let's go inside before the press hears us," Chris interrupted cautiously.

Nigel beckoned them cheerily. "Come on! We've got cappuccino brewing!"

CHAPTER 19

W hen Nick and Jean entered the room, it was obvious something positive had happened between them. From his relieved look, it seemed like maybe Jean had let him drive home. Nick stood tall and beamed from ear to ear; a wave of happiness surrounded him.

Chris shifted their weight from foot to foot and watched Nick and Jean carefully for any clue to what had transpired between them.

Tay laughed. "You look like a rockstar again!"

"I'm not that guy anymore," Nick responded humbly, trying to downplay his past fame.

"You're still Nick," Chris said, vying for his attention. The sudden smile directed at Tay had Chris a bit jealous and all they could do was swallow hard, because not only was Jean under Nick's spell, but so was Tay too.

Taylor sighed and popped her gum loudly as she spoke. "So, you got yourself a sugar momma then?" She gave Jean a side-long glance.

Chris had long been aware of Tay's confidence even in their

days of poverty. She had always carried herself with a certain swagger. There was no mistaking that her gaze toward Jean was one of rivalry. It was clear that Tay wasn't afraid to take on a challenge. Taylor kept staring at Jean, and when she met Jean's eyes, Jean bit her lip and stared down to the floor.

"Why don't we take a seat?" Chris gestured to the living room through the door to the house. The way Taylor stared at Jean was something Chris had to stop, fast. Tay seemed to want all of Nick's attention now, and that made Jean a threat to Tay. Chris gestured for them to follow, and hoped to diffuse the situation, or at least distract everyone.

Nick nodded and popped the trunk to grab Jean's things. "Sounds good."

Taylor moved closer to Nick and narrowed her eyes at Jean's proximity. "Want some coffee?" Taylor batted her eyes at Nick.

Chris cocked their head and watched Tay with interest. She had been taken with Nick since he saved her life in New Orleans, and it appeared as if she was bewitched by him. Chris motioned for the group to follow into the living room. Taking a seat by the fireplace, Chris settled in, feeling glum. Nick seemed to have Jean and Taylor fighting over him, and the little girl Chris had saved, had passed on.

"So, the media is constantly here, huh?" Nick mumbled as he eyed the news still on the television.

Chris looked at him. "Yeah, that's not all." Chris's mood sank deeper and they met his eye. "That little girl from the harbor died today."

Nick raised a brow, "What? Did she have injuries they didn't find?"

Chris rose from their seat. "She ran into traffic after something today and she didn't make it." Chris shook their head and took a hard breath. They couldn't bring themself to say she had been chasing the very balloon they had given her.

Nigel cocked his head to the side. "Have none of you lot figured this out yet?" He crossed his arms and took a deep breath. "The deal is not as simple as it seems..."

Nodding meaningfully, Nigel added, "That's why I've been avoiding people and haven't made friends. Once you have a nice mortal friend their life is in danger."

"I have no friends aside from all of you. I have been afraid to make friends because everyone I got close to died," Jean added with a shrug. "I've been alone for years."

"Nobody could tell who I was until recently," Nick chimed in, his eyes narrowing slightly. "I've been living on the streets and no one expects to find someone who had top 40 hits out in the harbor begging for change."

Nigel sighed at that. "You'll have to do something soon, since you don't look your age, Nick. You could just claim that you're your own kid; that's what I plan to do if I get caught."

"You?" Jean queried softly. "A love child? How?"

"Wild nights with too much vino!" Nigel joked with a smile. "Maybe it's before I realized which way my porch door swung?" He held his pointer finger up to initiate swinging, but it was clear he wasn't serious.

Taylor tightened her eyes and blurted, "I didn't make any agreement so I'm making my way to bed." In an exaggerated show of reluctance, she marched off toward the stairs and dragged her feet across the floor.

"Tay's mad." Chris sighed quietly. "But I'll speak with her tomorrow..."

Nick just smiled as she stormed out. "She's still a cute kid."

"If she doesn't drink my blood," Jean rolled her eyes.

"Tay is team Nick?" Nigel laughed.

Nick shrugged. "I didn't mean to make things hard on anybody. Is she mad at me?"

Chris spotted Taylor peeking around the corner. Chris held back a chuckle at seeing her eavesdrop, and Taylor quickly eased back into the room.

"Will you vanish again?" Chris questioned Nick quietly with the corners of their mouth hanging down.

Nick stretched and suppressed a yawn. "I'll stay as long as I'm wanted."

Nigel rolled his eyes. "That is if you can peel Taylor off your leg." Then he sat up. "I never looked for another mate and do you know why?" When all eyes were on him he pointed his finger at each of them. "It's hard to find another immortal, much less one with the same inclination."

He paused and took a hard breath as if he were trying to keep from getting emotional. "Normals don't live forever like we do!" He wiped away an invisible tear from the corner of his eye. "Remember my boyfriend was mortal. He's left me here with nothing but time to grieve for him."

Taylor's face tensed up into a frown. "I'm not one of you though," she said quietly.

Nick looked around the group. "I thought people who found out about this died..."

Chris sat up, asking, "But she wasn't told... She sort of guessed and it started before I made the deal." Chris struggled to hold back their worry when they realized what Nick was hinting at.

Nigel replied in a quiet voice. "She figured it out? Maybe that will work in her favor..." He lowered his gaze sadly. With a sigh, he went on. "Most of the normal people I've known are gone by now and the slightest relationships were cut... short."

Taylor stared at him in terror, murmuring, "So now I'm

going to die because I know?" Chris shook their head in denial, but it was all beginning to make sense.

Nick glanced at her with worry. "The car was coming for Taylor in New Orleans," he said. "I lost a mortal friend like that back in the 80's."

Jean murmured softly, "We better not leave her by herself."

Taylor looked at them all, her face expressing her obvious fright. "Well, this sucks." She edged closer to Nick and mumbled, "I really don't want to die."

"She could just make the deal," Jean proposed.

Nigel quickly interjected, "Deacon picks who he wants; she's not famous or wealthy."

Taylor exhaled hard. "So, I'm the liability," she said sadly and started pressing buttons on her phone as if to distract herself.

Chris shook their head. "No. This is all my fault. Don't worry, we'll keep you safe."

Nigel scoffed. "Didn't you say Taylor had your fortune?" He gave Tay a sweet smile and sighed. "Alas, he decides who he makes the deal with. Plus most he makes a deal with are about to die, which is why he preys on us." Nigel tried to make a scary yet funny face as if to dismiss it all.

"So she can't make the deal unless he wants her?" Chris turned their head in wonder.

"I was about to die," Nick offered with a long exhalation. "We all were... maybe he can only make deals with people who are dying?"

Nigel chuckled and said. "Mwahahaha."

Jean ignored Nigel and nodded at Tay. "We could share a room if you'd like."

Tay nodded slightly but kept typing away on her phone with an air of resignation. Chris could see she was afraid, but tried not to let it show. She usually had a firm handle on the situations she faced, but this time she had no control over what might happen. Taylor was acting like she didn't care at all, but they heard another sigh escape her lips.

Chris, Nick, and Nigel all headed up the stairs together, but Jean moved closer to Taylor. Chris' heart went out to Tay and they were extremely worried. Suddenly, a faint buzzing noise filled the room, and everyone except Nick looked towards their phones. Chris took a deep breath before producing the device. "It's mine," Chris announced and let out a cry of surprise at the caller ID. They showed the screen to the others, all but Tay gaping at the name, Hunter James.

Taylor wrinkled her brow in confusion. "Who is it?" She crossed her arms and scowled. "Another old person?"

Chris hushed her with one hand. "He was an Olympian, Tay... In the Olympics." Chris left the room with their phone.

When Chris came back in, Jean was the first to venture a guess as to what the call was about. "I guess Hunter saw what everyone else is seeing..." She gestured toward the TV screen that still showed news about the immortals.

Chris looked up from their phone. "Hunter wants us all to meet tomorrow. We'll meet here if the press has cleared out, but if not, we'll do it downtown." Chris noticed Tay's questioning stare and took a breath to explain. "Hunter was an Olympian who disappeared during the '90s."

Nigel scowled. "Downtown area again! Why does it always have to be that bloody harbor?" He glared at each of them. "She warned us it was cursed!"

Jean raised her brow. "Who?"

"Marie..." Nick mumbled.

"That hoochie momma we met in New Orleans?" Tay scoffed.

Nigel uncrossed his arms and gestured to the book on the table. "Remember we read about her in the book."

Jean nodded. "You weren't specific..."

Tay scurried into the kitchen and returned with the book in her hands. "This old thing?" She was about to hand it off to Nick when Nigel jumped up.

Nigel snatched the book out of Tay's grasp, "This book... is the whole reason why I took a job at that bookstore!"

Chris felt their phone buzzing again, and snapped it from their pocket, looking at the others. "Peresphone's mother invited me to her funeral tomorrow." Chris had unshed tears that threatened to spill and their bottom lip trembled slightly.

Jean stifled a yawn but it didn't go unnoticed by the others. Despite their grief, Chris noticed. "We should get a bed in Tay's room and get rooms together for everyone else before it gets too late."

Everyone in agreement, they got up and followed Chris.

The group managed to moved a bed into Taylor's room so Jean could stay with her. Chris was astonished at how quickly Jean dozed off. She clearly hadn't been able to fight the exhaustion and was snoozing by the time they left the room.

Nigel gave a small wave and yawn. "I need a bit of a respite too." Chris nodded seeing he looked asleep on his feet and hoped the nightmares wouldn't haunt Nigel and Jean.

I n the kitchen, Nick and Chris chatted quietly. Taylor stepped in with a small wave of acknowledgement toward them both and made a beeline for the coffee.

"What I'm saying is that we should postpone our meeting with this guy, out of respect now that... Persephone has died," Chris whispered while looking down into their mug. "It's respectful..."

"I get that," Nick replied with a weary groan. "But we don't want to leave this other guy alone. What if something happens..." Nick stood up then sat back down running his hand through his hair. "Before, you wanted to get together as many immortals as we could find to change things. Maybe he knows something to help Tay."

Chris shifted their gaze from Nick to Tay, who was listening intently. "Do you think it wasn't a coincidence?"

Tay scoffed at the idea. "Yeah, like that kid got hit by how many cars the day after you saved her life?"

Chris nodded in agreement but still felt tearful. "I thought about it and the same balloon animal that I gave her could have stayed inflated and maybe she treasured it because she saw it as a good luck charm. We don't know..." Chris tapped fingers together atop the kitchen table and looked away from Tay's worried face. "I didn't want to ask her mother about it."

Tay shook her head in response. "If I don't make this deal, I could be the one in trouble next."

Nick grinned. "You don't need a deal..."

Tay stirred her creamer and sugar substitute into her coffee but still shook her head. "You don't get it."

Chris sat on the bench next to Taylor and knew she was sad. She was really used to having things her way.

"Tell me you haven't connected the dots. Mortals around

Immortals die. It's some punishment or something." Taylor insisted with pleading eyes. "Am I going to be the next to die?"

"We won't let that happen, Tay." Chris nodded in agreement then glanced back to the phone. They couldn't stop thinking about Persephone. "I feel sorry for Persephone's mother. It can't be easy to lose a child, and Persephone was so young."

Chris stopped looking at Nick and Tay. She was continually looking at Nick like he was a celeb again or like she had a huge crush. Nick gave her a playful nudge with his elbow. "You're up early." Chris was happy Nick veered away from talking about the mortals tied into their fates.

"Yeah, there's some old lady snoring in my room." Tay shrugged.

Chris glanced over at Nick with a furrowed brow. "Should we check on Nigel and Jean?"

"I heard weird noises coming from his room," Tay said as she took a sip of her rapidly cooling coffee.

Chris noticed light peeking through the windows and realized they had been up all night.

Nick groaned. "My morning could have done without that."

Chris looked between them then realized Taylor was referring to but shook their head. "It could have been a nightmare," Chris nodded and then turned to Tay. Chris wanted to get her off the subject of people alone in their rooms. "Let's get some breakfast started." Chris was exhausted yet energized from being up all night. Nick had been very reluctant to sleep but Chris didn't mind remaining awake.

Nick yawned and stretched. "I'll get them both up and you two make more coffee." He smiled, taking his mug with him. As he left, he ruffled Tay's hair like she was his little sister and gave her a big grin when she fussed with her hair to fix it back.

Chris flinched seeing Nick acting like Taylor's sibling but

didn't say anything. They watched Nick go and noticed Tay kept an eye on him too but it seemed she watched for different reasons. Chris chuckled, sure she would make gooey eyes at Nick when he returned.

Taylor exhaled hard when Nick left and got up for some coffee. "She's sleeping... What's he going to do?"

Chris glanced around nervously and sighed. Chris was sure Nick was in love with Jean and the idea of them being alone together stung. Chris tried to be nonchalant about it. "Tay..." Chris chuckled as Taylor brought a cup of coffee over.

Instead of answering, she sat there looking down at the creamer making clouds in her beverage.

Nigel moseyed into the kitchen carrying the book and perked his nose up. "Is that coffee?" He made a beeline for the machine, ignoring the siblings. Taking in their reclusiveness and pensive faces, Nigel said, "Ohhhh." He smiled and poured his coffee. "What have I interrupted?" Juggling the book and coffee mug, he drew closer to the table.

To Chris, Nigel looked like a hungry shark as he circled the table, looking for a seat. He finally flopped down with a deep sigh. "Is Nick off somewhere snogging Jean?" Nigel sent the taunt with a big smile on his face.

Tay's piercing gaze focused on Chris, and Chris instantly shrank back in their seat.

Nick came back to the kitchen and gently shoved the back of Nigel's head to stop him talking. "We weren't doing anything." Nick went to get a new cup and shook his head at Nigel. "You know you're a pain, right?"

Nigel prattled on despite the playful shove, and kept going as if oblivious to Chris's sad look over the comment about Jean. Sipping his coffee, Nigel hugged the book close with the other.

Taylor raised her eyebrow. "Did you sleep with that book?"

Nigel scoffed, "I've known it longer than any of you!"

Chris stood at the counter cracking eggs and tried to ignore the banter. "Is she ready to go downtown? Persephone's mother sent a text asking if we would be at the service." Chris gestured towards the TV, saying, "They're talking about it all over the news again."

Nigel glanced at the TV, where words flashed across the screen, indicating a new report on the story. "Turn it up!"

Chris found the remote and pressed the volume up so they could all hear. "The funeral for Persephone Rogers will commence in a few hours," the woman spoke rapidly on the TV. She changed her tone, becoming more somber as images of a home engulfed in media coverage came into view. "Her mother asked people to please send donations to the local Children's Hospital or St Jude's instead of sending flowers."

The camera zoomed in for a tighter angle on the news reporter's face. She added, "There will be no viewing or public funeral. Mrs. Rogers is overwhelmed and requests privacy in her grief. Therefore, Persephone's funeral is for invited family and friends only."

"Yet she invited you?" Nigel exclaimed in disbelief.

The TV blared on. "Persephone was the same child who was rescued from the harbor a few days ago. Entrepreneur Chris Shephard and a man who turned out to be none other than '80s singing legend Nick Dallas." The female reporter seemed to swoon.

"Why do we always have to find out what matters to us through the news?" Jean observed from the kitchen door. She had a far away look as she stared at the TV.

Chris's pulse raced as they saw her. Her hair was still damp and she had bright, alert eyes compared to Nick's dark circles. Chris turned the volume down and gestured to coffee for Jean. "Breakfast? Eggs Bagel?"

Jean handed Nick his coffee cup that he had left on the counter. "You forgot this."

Nick handed Jean the untouched cup of coffee he had gotten with steam still pouring off of it. Jean beamed at him. "Thanks." Chris was surprised by the change in behavior between Jean and Nick, almost as if something had happened between them. Chris raised an eyebrow at their newfound closeness.

Rising from the tale, Chris busied themself with gathering eggs, bacon, cereal, and other breakfast food items in an effort to ignore the intense glances passing between Nick and Jean.

Nigel rolled his eyes at them playfully. "Get a room."

Chris glanced at the news channel's banner that informed everyone of Persephone's death and sighed. "We should check up on her mother. I cannot imagine what she must be going through." Chris fumbled with cooking the rest of the eggs to keep their hands busy.

Taylor scrolled through her phone then lifted her head. "When are we going to meet that dude?"

Chris glanced at Taylor's phone, laden with pictures of Hunter, and scoffed, "Another crush? Really, Tay?" Chris returned their attention to the eggs they had been making. "When he calls." Just then, Chris's phone buzzed on the countertop. "There's Hunter now."

"We don't know which way his pendulum swings!" Nigel perked up with interest and moved closer. "Can we listen?"

"Let's FaceTime him," Chris suggested as they tapped the phone.

Everyone gathered around the device to get a better look at the man on the other end of the line. Chris watched Nigel's stunned expression at the ebony man who looked exactly like he had in his twenties. Hunter's intense gaze pierced through them with light brown eyes. His short buzzed hair showed off a youthful face. In a deep voice Hunter chimed in, "Hey, I guess y'all seen the news 'bout that girl?" He took a breath. "You're all over the news."

Chris nodded and replied, "Yes, we knew her…"

"Yeah, it's the timing for me because you just rescued her and now she's gone. That's messed up." Hunter looked at each of them in turn and took a deep breath. "I think I'm out. I don't want to end up like that."

"Wait… What?" Chris said quickly. "What do you mean?"

Jean moved forward so she could meet Hunter's eyes. "What do you know?" She touched Taylor's back much the way their mother had. "One of us isn't immortal here."

"Y'all made that deal then?" Hunter just stared at Jean in awe until he remembered to say, "Is it you? Are you mortal?"

She shook her head. "No, I made my deal a long time ago."

Hunter smiled, looking directly at Jean now. "If I go, then you'll be there too?"

Jean mumbled an uncertain response, "Well… yes…"

"Count me in," Hunter agreed. "We'll meet up at 1:00 pm at the cafe by the harbor. You know, between the aquarium and the world trade center?" Abruptly, the call ended.

Chris took a hard breath thinking about Hunter's fascination with Jean and how ill timed this all was.

Nigel sighed in exasperation. "Why does it always have to be that bloody harbor?"

Taylor glanced from one to the other. "Do I get to go?"

Nick looked at Chris. "We should have enough of us to keep her safe."

Chris nodded but looked down at their now silent phone and sighed. Nigel did have a point. They had a run in with a car trying to kill Tay and their own car had ended up totaled. Was there a connection? Why didn't the others think of it? Nigel did have a point. Why was it always that harbor?

The cafe was jumping with patrons and staff who bustled to take care of everyone. There were no empty tables, which had Chris feeling a bit guilty for holding up the table when they were in a group with only drinks. Still it was where they said they would meet Hunter.

Chris caught a glance of Taylor's phone and the social media post she was preparing. Chris did a double take when they caught the pic of her at the cafe with the heading, "Meeting a hottie by the harbor."

The television monitor had the news on, and they watched it not for the news but to make sure it wasn't about them.

"A city will mourn the little girl who was rescued only to be lost days later," the newscaster said quickly. They showed the rescue by the harbor with Chris and Nick, which caused Chris to pull their hoodie up with a sigh.

The news video shifted to show the scene of Persephone's accident. "She was saved by one of a group now dubbed the Immortals," the newscaster said in her monotone voice. The picture changed to show Nick rescuing Taylor from the car, and next to Chris the former rock star pulled his hoodie up too. "In the same strange turn of events, the group rescued a girl from certain death, but this reporter has learned that the driver of the car did die from their injuries."

"What?" Nick breathed out in a hard gasp. He hardly seemed aware that he spoke and the group exchanged a look.

"He wasn't hurt that badly, was he?" Chris mumbled, then began to feel eyes on them and some murmuring. "I think we need to move..."

Fear clenched deep within Chris as they looked out at the

faces of the crowd, afraid someone might realize who they were. A chill ran down their spine.

At last, they spotted Hunter coming toward them. Chris threw some money on the table in payment for their drinks and stood to stretch out a hand in greeting. "I'm..."

"I know who you are." Hunter smiled. "I know who most of you are, except for you..." He looked at Jean expectantly.

"Jean," she replied as he took her hand and kissed it.

Chris furrowed their brow in response, but Nick took more direct action. He moved forward abruptly and held his own hand out before Hunter could reach for it. "Nick."

Hunter nodded. "Yeah, I remember you." He finally noticed Taylor and grinned from ear to ear. "You must be related to Chris!"

Chris nodded in the direction away from the cafe. "Let's talk where it's not so crowded."

Taylor followed Hunter as he headed for the World Trade Center. When they arrived, their eyes fell on a sculpture erected to honor victims who had perished in the 9/11 attacks. The structured piece of art was made of a slab of marble beneath two mangled beams that had once been part of NYC's iconic Twin Towers.

Hunter leaned against the marble and looked in the direction of the National Aquarium. "I really like it here," he attempted to relax but his body language indicated the opposite. He offered a smile but his eyes were wild with anxiety.

Taylor moved closer to him with her eyes open wider and asked, "Why?" She kept going closer to Hunter as she did. Chris groaned inwardly watching Taylor's attention flit from Nick to Hunter the same way a butterfly went from flower to flower.

Hunter gestured to the memorial behind him. "I was

supposed to be in the Pentagon that day, but Deacon told me not to go. I was taking my girlfriend on a tour of DC, showing her all the places we'd been for the Olympics and everything. We used to meet politicians and celebs all the time when we were there, so I really knew my way around the city. That Deacon guy said to put off going to DC for a week, so I did. If only I'd known what that Deacon meant..."

He glanced at the marble beams. "No wonder his words sounded so strange." Hunter shoved his hands into his pockets. Hunter looked chilled suddenly and stared at the water. "Now I have nightmares of the plane crashing in the Pentagon and..." He looked scared and pressed his lips together.

Taylor threw her arms around him, as if they had known each other for years. "It must be scary."

Chris stepped forward and introduced her. "That's my sister, Taylor."

Chris watched Tay lavish attention on the newcomer and smiled. Chris hadn't approved of her interest in Nick because he acted more like their father. Chris was certain Tay would eventually lose interest in Hunter and move on to somebody else... par for the course.

Hunter looked spooked. "How old?"

Taylor sighed before replying, "I'm 23."

Hunter chuckled uneasily. "Sorry, I thought you were a minor and it tossed me. I don't need any legal stuff. Plus, it won't do me any favors to hang around with people who don't look their age."

Nigel moved closer, pushing Taylor gently aside. "None of us really do... we get by," he said with a smile. "I'm Nigel."

"Yeah, I know you," Hunter began. "My parents really enjoyed your talks on physics and reading the things you published."

Nigel was evidently taken aback by Hunter's recognition of him. He grinned broadly. "Do tell!"

Hunter's eyebrows shot up. He was clearly taken aback by how exuberant Nigel was, "They still have magazines with you on them."

Nigel seemed very interested in what Hunter had to say and waited with bated breath. The Nigel they'd seen back then seemed so bland, standoffish, and devoid of personality; now it was hard to tell what he was thinking under the enigmatic façade. "You're different than I expected you to be."

Nigel cleared his throat. "Like most of us, luv, that person is gone. I have all the same knowledge and skills, but I can't help save the economy now."

Hunter watched him intently as he spoke. He seemed to be silently weighing in on his opinion of it all. "So, are there a lot of us?"

Nick lit a cigarette, distancing himself from the group to avoid the smoke bothering the others. "We're still finding that out." He blew the smoke away from the small group.

Nigel nodded in confirmation, adding, "You'd be taken aback, mate." He glanced around at the company present. "I work in a bookstore nearby and I've noticed that chap makes deals every other week or so."

"How do we track them down?" Hunter grinned. "It would be nice to know more people like me... us."

Before anyone could answer, a loud boom echoed through the air, causing everybody to jump.

"Was that thunder?" Chris asked, squinting at dark clouds approaching in the distance.

"Sounds like it," Nigel said, pointing beyond the harbor. "The weather here can be unpredictable. I hear folks telling stories about storms they experience out on the water but that the land never sees. It usually scares the tourists how fast the weather can change in these parts."

Taylor inched closer to Hunter; Tay kept stealing glances at Hunter and fussed with her hair when she thought he wasn't watching. "What have you been up to since your deal?" She asked.

"My girlfriend and I split, and I haven't felt close to anyone but my immediate family for a long time," he responded, his voice filled with sadness.

Chris jumped in quickly, "Do they know?" Chris hoped Hunter's family knew because if they had done so a long time, then Taylor might beoff the hook.

Hunter forced a smile. "No, I didn't tell them but I think they guess something's up. They just keep saying I look young."

Nick put out his cigarette and shook his head as the sky darkened. "Let's move. We might be immortal, but Tay isn't." He shook his head as the sky seemed to go black. "I don't like this."

Before he finished speaking there was an intense thunder-clap, causing them all to jump. Tay looked especially scared and gazed at her companions, eyes wide and darting around.

"Can we please go home?" Tay begged.

Hunter stayed close and put a hand on the small of her back to usher her toward the car. Chris cocked an eyebrow at the newcomer taking an interest in Tay but also at the sheer fright Tay showed. Chris nervously stepped closer to Tay but she lightly moved them away with a gentle shove. Chris smiled understanding that they got in her way and allowed her the personal space she needed.

Another loud *boom* echoed through the air, prompting Hunter to look up. A long arc of light blazed down toward the group, aiming straight for Tay. In one swift motion, Hunter pushed her out of harm's way as the bolt made its descent. Lightning blasted Hunter; his body writhed and jerked from the electricity.

Chris' mouth dropped. It happened so quickly, in nanoseconds. Rushing toward Taylor, Chris helped her get back on her feet after Hunter had pushed her down. Chris stopped abruptly and watched Hunter, transfixed as the lightning's wrath took effect.

Tay leaped to her feet and made a dash for Hunter, but Nigel hastily dragged her back to where Jean and Nick stood. "Don't you know how electricity works?"

Taylor's eyes brimmed with tears. Chris knew Hunter had saved her from this torment because it had been meant for her. Did she feel responsible? Seconds felt like an eternity as they watched Hunter crumple onto the ground, tendrils of smoke rising from him. His clothes appeared charred and his eyes darted around.

Chris shifted their gaze from Hunter to a group of people huddled for shelter and more watching from inside the building, with several cell phones pointed at Hunter.

Hunter stood there looking warily at the people with cameras as he surveyed the scene. Taylor dashed forward and threw herself into his arms. He held her tightly and glanced at the others.

"It's the Immortals!" someone shouted, and Hunter looked like a deer caught in headlights.

"Are you okay?" Chris demanded of Tay.

She stepped back and her hair stood up a little. "He feels all fuzzy!"

Nigel pulled her away. "That's the electricity, luv."

Nick looked around nervously. "Let's get out of here before something else happens."

Chris agreed and nodded at Hunter, suggesting, "Why don't you come with us?"

Hunter followed along as they moved away to escape the thundering cheers coming from the harbor. Chris took a deep breath, wanting to put as much distance as possible between them and that dreadful place. Marie was right, it was cursed.

CHAPTER 20

Chris rattled off the rules about taking shoes off when Tay shouted from the kitchen, "Don't bore him!" She ran over to Hunter and asked, "Do you want coffee?" She popped her gum trying to act casual but Chris was wise to her.

"Yeah." Hunter smiled. "That would be good."

Tay smiled and sprang away. Hunter stared after her then turned to Chris and asked, "Yo, is your sister seeing anyone?"

Chris's mouth fell open. "Tay? No, I don't think she's ever had a serious relationship."

Hunter grinned. "She's pretty cute." He looked at the door where she had disappeared and smiled. "I'm still twenty no matter what, right?" Hunter chuckled. "It's like I never left my twenties, mentally or physically. I didn't go out much after 9/11, and it feels like I missed out on a lot of things."

"Hmm..." Chris sighed and gestured toward the kitchen.

The smell of coffee filled the house and Chris knew Tay was the one to start it all up. She wasn't in the kitchen, but the coffee machine could be heard hissing and bubbling.

Noise reverberated from the television in the living room,

quickly drawing their attention. The others sat looking at the news on the flatscreen. They all stood in silent awe at the footage of Hunter pushing Taylor out of harm's way moments before being struck by lightning.

Chris couldn't help but murmur under their breath, "You have my blessing after that." It was a half joke, but anybody who would give their life for somebody as crazy as Tay had to be worth it.

Hunter turned his head as Chris turned up a corner of their mouth. "That's a joke?"

"Another immortal seems to have emerged and it looks like he's none other than Hunter James, the Olympian." The reporter bellowed.

Hunter just sighed and stared ahead blankly, lamenting, "I had such a quiet life."

They saw a house on TV and Hunter moved closer to the screen, pointing. "That's my house!" They could see Hunter's family being hounded about his whereabouts, and an old woman kept saying, "He's not home."

Hunter slumped on the bench beside the TV. "I can't go home for a while," he mumbled.

Taylor rushed into the room. Her sight was set on Hunter and suddenly she was by his side with a huge smile and starry eyes. "Are you still all tingly from the electricity?"

Nigel went to get a cappuccino from the coffee bar and spoke up, "It can take some time for the effects to wear off, my dear." Nigel cocked an eyebrow at Hunter. "I'm not sure what all the effects are of an immortal struck by lightning..."

Nick held up a hand to show a scar with a lightning bolt. "I grabbed a live wire and it should have killed me..." He took a deep breath. "They couldn't explain how I was still alive." He shrugged. "I had a fuzzy feeling for a few hours... I got shocked easily too."

Taylor and Hunter exchange whispers, their voices barely above a murmur. Taylor was undoubtedly flirting and Hunter seemed to be enjoying it.

Jean watched the dynamics between Hunter and Tay, and nudged Nick with a smile playing on her lips. "I don't think he heard all of that."

"Yeah, I know…" Nick whispered.

"Jealous?" Jean teased.

"Protective," Nick hissed loud enough for Jean and Chris to hear.

Hunter turned away from Taylor and said, to the room at large,. "So, you rescued a small girl, along with the mayor and his wife, who had nothing to do with the deal?"

Chris gave Hunter coffee and placed condiments on the table. "We can't die, so why not lend a helping hand?" Chris muttered, though they felt uncertain of their own words. Chris offered the coffee on the tray but kept an eye on Taylor and how she flirted with Hunter.

Taylor jokingly offered herself as a sacrifice. "Start with me! If I make this deal, then I can help instead of needing to be rescued all the time." She pointed to the television showing Hunter's face again with scrolling words that said, 'DARING RESCUE AT THE INNER HARBOR.'

Nick sighed heavily. "We can't control that, kiddo."

Chris nodded. "I'm sure we could dig up the money if we had to, but we can't force Deacon to make a deal for you."

"He scares me," Jean said and wrapped her arms around her chest as if she suddenly couldn't get warm.

Nigel cleared his throat, "I think this might be a problem." He pointed at the television set.

"How is it that each one of them looks so young?" A female reporter asked loudly. She looked at the photo she shuffled and then to the camera.

"Well, Chris Shepherd is only 21 years old," the fashionable guy beside her replied.

The lady reporter persisted. "Today we're adding another one of these proclaimed Immortals who doesn't look their age." Hunter's picture from earlier at the WTC was displayed on the screen alongside a photo from the '80s Olympics. "It's incredible that he hasn't aged a day, considering Hunter James is supposed to be in his fifties."

"He must be using a good lotion!" she said quickly, as his photo appeared on screen. "And Nigel Collins," Nigel's picture was next to it. "And Nick Dallas?"

"Good moisturizer," the other reporter commented half-heartedly.

Nigel sighed. "They are playing good cop and bad cop with us to make their point without looking like idiots."

"Why didn't they include Jean in the story?" Taylor said with her eyes on Jean's now.

When Tay brought it up, Chris noticed Jean seemed relieved by the exclusion, but Taylor looked suspicious.

"They don't recognize her," Nick whispered with a smile.

"But how are you famous enough to make the deal?" Hunter blurted out.

"I'm just an ex-rich circus performer and I look different now. I even changed my name," Jean said humbly.

Nigel scoffed. "She hasn't done anything daring or noteworthy. Why would they ever think she was one of us?" He gestured to Taylor. "They probably think she's a groupie like Taylor."

"Groupie?" Taylor almost leapt up in shock, but Chris and Hunter pushed her back into her seat. Chris laughed watching Tay's eyes wide in surprise at being thought of as a fangirl.

"Better sleep with one eye open tonight after that comment," Chris joked at Nigel, before the phone buzzed in their pocket. Chris sighed reading the text. "It's Persephone's mother. She's seen the news." Heaving a sigh, Chris knew this was the last thing Persephone's mother needed. Chris could see the dots indicating that she was still typing. Chris paused reading it and then said. "She sent the details for funeral arrangements."

"She's probably lonely without her kid," Nick said, shoving his hands into his pockets.

"Can we go?" Jean looked around. "The press is looking past all the good deeds now and thinks something is up."

"They're not wrong..." Hunter blew on his coffee as he watched the steam drift away and the creamer create a pattern on the surface. "There's no turning back."

Chris inhaled and said, "We should all go to the funeral to show our support for her."

"Alright then, that's settled," Nigel exclaimed, clapping his hands. "We should get to know Hunter better." He sat up on the bench beside him and placed a hand on his leg, ready to listen. "Why don't you tell us about yourself?"

Hunter looked away and took a deep breath as Taylor giggled.

Nick stopped laughing long enough to pat Nigel on the back. "Sorry, but I think he's straight."

Nigel slumped next to him and slowly slid out of the seat to find a new place nearer his cappuccino. With a start, he looked around, eyes wild. "Where did my book go?"

Jean mocked, "It's not yours until you buy it." She approached the counter to pick up the book. But Nigel was one step ahead and snatched it from her.

Chris raised an eyebrow at Jean's rebuttal of Nigel, who hadn't held back from teasing her. A small smile tugged at the corner of Chris's lips at the sight of Jean seeming more confident than usual.

The news blared about something new. Jean gestured toward the screen and they watched in horror as Hunter James' house exploded on the TV. In moments, only a few beams were left of what had been a home.

"It seems the house must have had a gas explosion. Our news crews were already on the scene." The report showed the intact house from before, followed by a deafening boom, and a cloud of smoke, which consumed everything in sight.

Chris's mouth hung open and they traded a worried look with the others. Hunter stared at the screen dumbfounded, as if willing the news to change. He sat there petrified until Taylor touched his shoulder gently, then he came to life.

Chris gulped as they thought of the implications of Hunter's family finding out about the deal, and Taylor knowing. Chris felt a void in their chest as they looked at both the television and Taylor. This wasn't good.

Finally Hunter's stone-like stare shifted, and he screamed. "WHAT?" Hunter jumped at the sight, his arms and knees quivering underneath him. He let out an anguished cry. "Wait! What?"

"We were expecting the James family to give us Hunter's whereabouts when suddenly, their house was destroyed," the news reported. "It seems nobody survived the explosion."

"No, no, no, no!" Hunter shook his head anxiously tapped on the screen of his phone. He dialed the number and paced, murmuring that it couldn't be true."Pick up! Please." He moved in an anxious dance and kept his head low. "They can't be!"

Taylor moved closer to him and touched his hand gently. Hunter looked at her with tear-soaked eyes and a quivering lip. He held up his phone so everyone could see it ringing until it finally switched to the message, "The wireless customer you are calling is not available. Please try again later". Hunter's eyes were wide and he only said, "No..." Taylor wrapped her arms around Hunter, hugging him tightly.

All Chris could do was watch while it unfolded. They were stupefied, felt helpless.

Nigel took the center of the room and held his finger up much the same way Chris had seen Fred do on Scooby Doo all those times when Fred had an epiphany. Being the center of attention seemed natural to Nigel, who waited for everyone to calm before he raised a brow dramatically. Once all eyes were upon him, he cleared his throat. "Does it seem peculiar to anybody else that after we 'save' someone, they or somebody else dies?"

Chris traded a curious look with the others.

Jean said simply and crossed her arms in defiance. The little war between Nigel and Jean waged on.

Chris shook their head. "The first rescue was Persephone..."

"Gone," Nigel chirped and made an invisible check in the air with his forefinger.

"Next was the mayor and they're fine..." Chris said and was happy to prove Nigel wrong.

The news rang in louder about the carnage at Hunter's home. Suddenly, it stopped and the words BREAKING NEWS flew across the screen. A reporter's face popped onto the screen.

"Just in..." she said quickly, and the camera cut to the mayor emerging from the hospital. He pushed past microphones when asked about his wife. "The mayor's wife was killed today after a downtown mugging." Microphones were shoved in his direction as he shook his head, tears welling up in his eyes as he walked away. "The Mayor's office declined to comment." Another reporter looked up and added, "Our thoughts are with the mayor as the city mourns with him."

Chris clicked the television off. "Okay, so there has been a death with each rescue..." Chris shuffled their hands in their pocket and sighed deeply. "It's a coincidence..."

"How about the bloke who was driving the car?" Nigel scoffed and rolled his eyes. "Serves you right for not listening to me."

They all watched Taylor hug Hunter. Hunter suddenly stopped hugging her back. He looked down at her and held her even closer, speaking so quiet that Chris had to strain to hear him. "He's not going to get you." Hunter met Chris's gaze. "I'm in. Whatever this is, I'm in with both feet."

Chris was overwhelmed, and they prayed they could keep Taylor safe. Deacon was in control no matter what anyone did; it felt like they were nothing but playthings for a deity – Deacon, the true immortal.

CHAPTER 21

Hunter stood with his arms crossed, looking at the water through the glass doors r. His haunted expression spoke volumes.

Chris took a hard breath, still plagued by the worry that Taylor knew about the deal. Had Hunter's family known? Tay had escaped death twice now and, if not for Nick or Hunter, she would be gone. A chill crept into Chris and they trembled.

Taylor stood next to Chris watching Hunter and bit her lip. Sheglanced at Chris, her eyes glassy. "His whole family is gone," she said in a low voice. "Do you think it's our fault?"

"That's what worries me," Chris murmured, thinking of the other tragedies.

"I'm going to talk to him," Taylor said quietly. "He needs a friend or someone to open up to."

Chris nodded, watching Taylor make her way toward Hunter with two blankets over her arm and drinks in hand. Chris swallowed hard and mumbled, "Just don't be alone."

Jean came over to Chris with a heavy sigh and asked, "How are you going to make that work? She needs alone time."

"One of us can stand outside the bathroom door when she needs it," Nick suggested.

Jean placed her hand on Nick's back in admiration. "You two are so protective. It's adorable." Chris was jealous, but Nick had saved Tay's life and still was undeniably protective of her. Chris held no grudges against Nick, yet a deep longing for Jean still lingered in their heart.

Chris smiled and looked at Nick. "Thank you for everything."

"You're family to me now," Nick replied softly enough that almost no one heard him. "I'm fond of all of you."

Jean let out a giggle but stifled it as if she couldn't help letting it out. Raising an eyebrow in surprise, Jean observed how Taylor joined Hunter, and the way the young, blue haired woman fawned over the former Olympian. With a smile, Jean cast her gaze toward Chris and Nick, and said, "Thank you both. It's been ages since I've felt comfortable around other people."

Nick craned his neck. "Speaking of comfort and so on... where's Nigel?"

In answer, Jean merely pointed around the corner to the kitchen where Nigel sat alone, acting very suspicious.

Chris wrinkled their nose as Nigel pored over that book, leafing through the pages at a feverish pace. Nigel acted as if he was alone and the book was his long lost friend. His finger traced over the pages until he eventually stopped.

"What are you doing?" Nick enquired abruptly. Jean and Chris stood behind him.

Nigel jumped so high it looked like his feet left the ground.

"Nothing!" He squeaked out, blushing. "You gave me a fright..." He put a hand over his heart and casually, but purposefully, closed the book. "Never do that when I'm reading."

Chris's eyes crinkled with laughter as Nigel's face contorted in surprise and frustration. His mouth hung open, his eyebrows knit together, and his cheeks turned a bright shade of red. Chris couldn't contain his amusement at the sight.

Nick glanced back at Jean whose eyebrows were already scrunched up in suspicion. "It wasn't like we caught you skimming through Playboy," he joked.

Jean snorted and suggested, "Playgirl?"

Nigel scoffed and looked at Jean. "Don't you yuck my yum!"

Chris couldn't resist and finally let out a chuckle. It felt refreshing in the midst of all the grim news going around. The laughter wasn't meant to be malicious, but rather they appreciated Nigel's momentary humiliation.

"When I read anything, I shut the world out," Nigel informed them in a low voice. "I suggest you be careful with hot beverages around me. People have been scalded before." He grabbed his book and changed the subject. "So who has Taylor watch?"

Jean raised an eyebrow skeptically, "She's keeping Hunter company. You know, the guy who lost his entire family today?"

"So did the androgynous Chris offer him a room to stay here?" Nigel crossed his arms and looked at Chris as he held the book to his chest. "There is more than enough room here."

"I think they probably will," Nick continued, observing Nigel.

Chris stood there with their mouth hanging open. It was the truth, but Nigel put it so rudely it felt like an insult, and all Chris could do was stare at him. "Of course I will offer Hunter to stay here. He has no place to go."

"Are you jealous or do you just hate Chris?" Jean gave Nigel a hard-hitting stare.

Chris gaped at Jean with a silly, yet proud, grin. She had been quick to defend them.

"Not at all," Nigel cooed, "I'm here to reap rewards too and Hunter or that EMT lad, Jeremy, might be among them."

Nick nodded. "So what were you looking for in the book?"

Nigel huffed. "Answers, but none were to be found." He pushed up his glasses. "I suppose we're all doomed to be one big dysfunctional family."

Chris scoffed, "Define dysfunctional?"

Nick chuckled, "Don't worry about Hunter. He's got his sights set on Taylor."

Jean shook her head. "Yes, but for how long?" Nick looked puzzled and she threw her hands up. "Men!" She took a deep breath and turned to Nick with a straight face. "How old is Hunter? In his 20s during the '80s, he must be at least 50 or 60 now. And Taylor is only 23?"

Nigel snickered. "He thinks he's still got it? A cad perhaps? A nonce?" He waved his hand in jest.

Chris scratched their head. "Nonce?" Taking a deep breath, Chris said, "Hunter seems like a good person." Chris usually found Nigel a bit amusing, but his nitpicking was wearing thin.

"Maybe he'll take things slow." Nick shrugged nonchalantly, ignoring Nigel's howl of laughter.

"I think Hunter sees Taylor as we do. The younger generation didn't live through the '70s or '80s, so they have no idea about how we and others lived our lives until this point. We have experiences they could never fathom, so it might be tough for them to see things from our perspective," Jean stated with a shrug.

Nigel interjected, "Oh, it appears genderless-Chris is taking a back seat."

"Nigel, why are you so hung up on gender? Could it be because you're attracted to Chris?" Jean shook her head at his immaturity. "Chris is an incredible human being without any need for explanation... end of story."

Chris cocked an eyebrow at Nigel and met his stare dead on, reminding him they could hear everything. They puffed up their chest with pride and rode the high after listening to Jean's words.

"I'll offer Hunter a room here. We have vacant rooms, so we can share if other people arrive. My parents' room isn't occupied right now," Chris trailed off while staring at their feet.

They were relieved their parents were away celebrating an anniversary with no knowledge of the chaos unfolding at the house. In contrast to other children who took the opportunity to sneak out and have a good time when their parents were away, Chris was faced with a funeral and close calls with death.

"Soon we'll need a bus," Nigel said with a cheerful grin.

"We have a minivan in the garage," Chris replied offhandedly. "I think it'll be suitable even for your fancy taste, Nigel." They smiled.

Nigel raised a finger with a smirk at Chris but before they could whip out a witty remark Chris turned around ready for another battle of wits with him.

Instead, Nick nearly lunged in Nigel's face. "Leave the kid alone. All they have been is a good friend and that's all they have to be." Nick glanced up realizing Chris heard his words.

Nigel looked abashed and a little scared of Nick as he shook his head. He kept his eyes down, focused on the book in his hands before tossing it in his bag. He met Chris's gaze.

Chris sighed, feeling the tension. Why couldn't families be less argumentative? Nick and Jean stood up to Nigel's rudeness, something families didn't always do – but ought to. Chris knew Nigel was the only other person present who was also of the Pride community and Chris had hoped that would bond them. However, Chris could see that Nigel regarded them and the others in the group with a less than favorable view.

The road leading to the funeral was busy and the cars barely moved. Chris drove, but Taylor seemed more interested in playing radio commando than navigator through traffic. They crept along, surrounded by fancy cars parked in the lots adjacent to the funeral home.

"No turning back now." Chris mumbled.

Nigel eyed some of the high-end cars, and grinned. "Why would we want to?"

It was clear Persephone's family was well off, but the media presence might also have brought in rich gate crashers.

Hunter gestured to all the news vans nearby. "That's why," he said. His breath hissed out as he spoke, and a look of gloom crossed his face. "I've got to do this for my family too, but I have no idea how to begin."

Chris felt guilty. They were sure the explosion had something to do with Hunter meeting them and saving Taylor. Chris took a deep breath and set their sights on the circus that the media had made of this, but all in all, Chris felt responsible for the death of Hunter's family as well as for Persephone's.

"Is that the mother?" Jean asked, her gaze directed towards a woman at the center of all the attention.

Nick nodded. "That's her."

The small group piled out of the van and they made a beeline for Persephone's mother. She saw them coming and met them halfway, extending her hand to Hunter, "Hunter James, correct?" A quick smile of admiration accompanied her greeting.

Chris noted how red her eyes were as she continued to stare around uncomfortably with the press.

"I'm Bessy. Persephone's mother." She turned her head as

the flashing cameras caught her attention. "I requested privacy at the funeral home, but this is a public road so we're on public property here."

Taylor nervously bit her lip as she moved closer to the group. "It looks like it."

Chris never found it easy to stand still, but with all eyes on them doing so seemed harder. They kept shifting from foot to foot and sighed often. They felt so helpless and useless. What had been the point of saving Persephone's life to be the cause of her death days later.

Nick approached Bess, expressing his remorse. "I'm really sorry, ma'am."

Bess glanced at him with tears ready to spill. "It wasn't your doing. It was an accident."

The small group seated themselves directly behind Bess. Chris looked around, noticing the small turnout of relatives. Most of the people in attendance were from the press, famous well wishers, politicians and such.

When Bess was left alone at the front of the row, Chris prompted the others to move up and sit beside her. Jean took Bess's hand in hers, and Nick and their friends filled in the rest of the seats around the two women.

Bess glanced up with puffy and sad eyes, and barely managed to mutter a thank you. But no one responded vocally and the only response was from Jean's tender embrace of Bess's hand.

Hunter was an emotional wreck. He hardly stirred when it came time for the holy man to give his speech. Bent in prayer, with hands clasped together, Hunter rarely even lifted his head. When they began to lower Perephone into her grave, Hunter let out a tearful sob. It struck Chris how heartbreaking it must be for Hunter to mourn for his family as well as the fallen child.

Taylor sat beside Hunter, softly placing her hand on his. Her eyes were filled with tears as she looked at him.

"I don't even know if there's anyone for me to bury." Hunter's expression dropped.

Chris heard the hushed whispers of those around Hunter speculating how close he must have been with the family to be so affected.

Bess stood motionless as she bade Chris and their friends goodbye. Chris nodded and pointed toward a familiar face. "Isn't that Susan Click?"

Looking over in the direction of Chris's finger, Bess gave a humble wave. "I think she goes by her married name now. Harrison."

The rest of the group caught up, and Jean straightened when she saw the actress walking over.

Nigel chuckled, noticing how uneasy Jean felt with the beauty bounding over to them.

She heard Nigel's laugh and she gave him a puzzled look, only to narrow her eyes trying to demand respect for the solemn situation.

Before anyone else could speak, Susan interrupted. "My Lord!" She rushed over to Bess. "This is heart wrenching."

"Susan and I grew up together and lost touch..." Bess explained and stared at the ground. "Thank you, Susie."

Susan tossed a carefree hand. "Your girl could've been your twin."

The group looked at each other, unsure whether Susan recognized any of them now that they were all immortal. Susan looked around and soon pointed to Chris, "I know you!"

Susan's eyes lit up as she recognized the rest of them. "Oh, you're those *immortals,* aren't ya?" She gave them a smile. "I'd love to know your beauty tricks. What moisturizer do y'all use?"

Bess laughed as if she were used to her friend embarrassing her. "We were about to leave. I wanted to thank you personally for being here and all you did for Persephone." Her voice was wrought with emotion as she added tearfully, "I wouldn't want any more mourners either." Bess raised a hand as a thought occurred. "I need some time to be alone... Without all this press."

Chris looked at her sheepishly. "We were all going back to my home to decompress. You're both welcome to join us."

"I would really like to be alone," Bess said and took a deep breath. Her eyes brimmed with tears again. Chris met Bess's gaze and immediately regretted it. She was ready to spill tears again, and her chest heaved a bit. Chris could hardly fathom such grief and their heart lurched hoping they never would.

"Well..." Susan began and gestured for her husband to come closer. "Let me see what Tom thinks." She seemed either oblivious or used to her friend being upset like this and focused on the man as he walked.

Chris followed Susan's gaze and took note of a man they had not noticed before. Chris's eyes seemed to glide over the man without taking anything in and they knew if they'd passed this man on the street they would not remember a thing about him, with the exception of his glasses. The spectacles were plain black, with thick rims and thin wire frames. They were no more than spectacles to correct his vision, yet they fit him oddly.

His face was round, and his jaw was slender. His light brown skin looked almost untouched, the only indication that he might be a celebrity. It was the only proof of his status. His clothes looked as if he'd picked them out at a thrift shop. He wore a suit jacket that looked like it had lived in another era and pants that might have fit him once but were too loose now. His brown locks and athletic body seemed to say this simple look he bore was nothing more than him acting the role of an average man. He didn't seem to put on airs or push his way as if he was entitled. Instead he gingerly pushed his way through the crowd until he got to his wife.

"They're getting together and invited us to join them," Susan murmured as Tom offered a handshake of introduction.

Tom nodded and replied, "We can follow them in our car. I'll drive."

CHAPTER 22

The group glanced at Tom uneasily. As they strolled to their cars, Chris sidled up to Susan and whispered, "Does your husband know about the arrangement with Deacon?"

Susan let out a laugh. "Well... he put two and two together after noticing my bus scar and hearing my nightmares. I didn't come right out and say it, but I did confirm it."

Chris wrinkled their nose at her. "He knows? Then he isn't safe." Chris swallowed hard when they saw Tom walking ahead of them with the car keys swinging in his hand. Chris called over their shoulder to Susan, "Let's catch up to him."

When Chris was almost by Tom's side, a shrill cry drew their attention. A piece of lawn equipment with huge blades spun out of control and careened towards Tom. The worker in charge of the machinery was fiddling with the stick shift, a frantic look on his face. Blades of grass whipped in all directions as the monster of sharp, spinning iron edges tore up the pristine turf.

With their heart pounding in their throat, Chris sprinted and grabbed Tom by the jacket, jerking him backwards. Chris crouched over Tom's prone form just as the vehicle's clippers blazed past and a gust of wind rustled Chris's hair.

In the next instant, the swirling machine of death thudded into a nearby tree. With a loud crack, the trunk split it into two and half of the tree careened toward where Chris and Tom huddled. In panic, Chris pulled Tom until the larger man was pinned under their body... like Nick had done for Taylor.

Chris's body throbbed with pain as a giant branch crashed into them. They could feel people pulling at them under the leaves and branches. The voices around them sounded far away but soon enough, Susan's shrill voice grew nearer.

Chris felt someone pick them up and screamed in agony. They could barely think through the searing pain. "Is Tom alright?" they moaned, their gaze falling upon those assisting Tom to stand.

"I'm okay," Tom uttered in a hushed tone.

Nigel, Nick, and Jean arrived at the scene of the accident with Taylor and Hunter in tow. Nigel gasped when he saw the enormous tree and Chris who emerged from underneath it.

"That's what we call a widow maker," Nigel shook his head and looked at Tom. "Who do we have here?"

Susan surveyed Tom to make sure he was uninjured while Bess held back and contained the media so the group could examine what damage had been done.

"Well then," Susan let out a sigh and dusted off Tom. "Not even a bruise." She beamed at Chris and whispered, "Thank you."

Chris offered a nod in response but still had the surreal impression the whole thing must have happened to someone else. When the pain resurfaced, they had to admit the truth. "I think I broke something."

Taylor took in the way Chris clutched at their side and

inhaled with shallow breaths. "You're hurt?" Panic surfaced in her voice.

Hunter raised a brow. "I thought immortals didn't get hurt."

Nigel snickered. "You still smell like a barbecued Olympian, luv."

Chris moaned in agony. "I think someone else should drive."

Jean shook her head. "You ought to see a doctor."

Chris sighed in frustration. Their eyes fell on a cameraman and they frantically searched for a way to get away from the scene before the media caught onto what had happened. The last thing Chris wanted was for the media to complicate an already difficult situation that brought a stream of thoughts in a cascade through their head.

Bess looked them over and back to the media that closed in on them. "Do you need medical attention?"

Chris shook their head. "I just want to go home. I'll be fine."

Jean nodded vigorously and put a possessive hand on Chris's shoulder. "Chris got hurt trying to protect Susan's husband."

"If you don't want to make the news you'd better run," Bess pointed to a camera crew rushing closer.

Chris won the argument and the group agreed to drive them home. A multitude of vans, with people milling around them, stood outside the gates to Chris's house. More reporters loitered in their cars, parked on the curb.

Chris had to insist over and over to go home. Why would an injury take them down? They were immortal. A thought crossed their mind: they had seen Hunter and Nick get scars after their brushes with death, while the pain in Chris's chest indicated they had a bone.

Sitting in the car, Chris took in the chaotic scene. "We'll get you on the security system and something to work with the A.I.," Chris mumbled to Hunter. Chris wanted to make sure any of their friends could come and go without trouble from the press.

Hunter gazed at all the cars. "Ah, the perks of fame!" His attention caught on Chris as they used their phone to open the gates. "I don't miss this part!" Hunter gave a dry chuckle before exhaling and looking straight ahead. Chris couldn't help but wonder if attending the funeral had brought back Hunter's memories of his personal tragedy.

Chris wondered about the numerous posts Taylor had shared on social media lately. In the past, Taylor always shared about her posts, bragging about her engagement, even if it was low. Now Chris thought about it, she seemed to hide her phone from view whenever they looked over.

With a shrug, Chris gave her the benefit of the doubt. "Let's go out later and pick up food," Chris suggested with a smile. "It'll give us something to do."

Taylor chuckled. "Field trip?"

They pulled up to the gate and parked in the garage along-side other vehicles. Chris quickly pressed the button to close the doors and escape the media, but they still felt hounded and rushed inside to put more distance between them and the reporters.

Jean was right beside them and ushered Chris inside. "Let's get you in."

"Well... Is it okay if we sit here?" She gestured toward Tom stretching out in the living room.

"It's fine," Chris gestured toward the opulent chamber with an expensive piano at its center, and plush couches that caved in on their own. They involuntarily flinched as they raised their arm, before quickly letting it fall to their side.

Susan touched Chris's arm. "Are you okay?"

Nodding, Chris entered the growing crowd in the living room. "I feel like I have a bruise."

Tom made a beeline for them. "I am so sorry for what happened."

"It wasn't your fault," Chris muttered.

Tom's eyes were difficult to make out beneath the thick lenses of his eyeglasses. It was impossible to tell if they were blue, brown, green, or some shade of hazel. Tom had an undeniably friendly face, with small smile lines at the corners of his eyes. The worry lines now creasing his brow took away from his normally happy expression. He adjusted his glasses before pushing his hands into his pockets. "I'm very sorry," Tom said.

Chris shook their head. "Sorry you're alive?" Chris joked feebly. "You would do the same if you could, right?"

Tom nodded. "If I could I would, but wishing doesn't diminish what you did." They all knew too well about the tale that had graced the national news and all the gossip rags. Tom had saved Susan's life when he pulled her out of the way of a bus.

Susan pulled Tom onto the plush couch with her and grinned at Chris. "You're a hero," she declared.

Chris nearly smiled but noticed Taylor kept her gaze fixed on Hunter, who was sitting in a chair close to the fireplace. She looked away and lit the hearth. Flames danced to life.

Nigel quickly grabbed the remaining armchair. Soon all the single seats were taken.

Hunter stood up with a playful grin and joked lightly to Chris. "Take my seat, hero."

The former Olympian settled on the floor between Taylor and the chair he'd offered to Chris. Settling into the indicated seat, Chris wasn't fooled. Hunter had been looking for an excuse to move seats. Chris was sure of it.

Tom and Susan were introduced to those who didn't know them and they quickly became part of the group's tight circle.

During a lull in the conversation, Susan asked, "So why are all of you Immortals now?"

"We made the same deal you and the kid just made down at the harbor," Nick waved in Chris's direction.

"What deal?" Tom asked. Although his tone was quiet, a concerned look sparked in his eyes as he stared at Susan.

Susan avoided Tom's question and glanced around the room. "Everyone here made this deal...?" she scoffed.

Nick opened his mouth to speak but Chris beat him to it. "Everyone but Tay."

Nick took a breath and pointed his finger to say something but was cut short again.

Hunter looked worriedly at Taylor. "And that made her a target?"

Taylor trembled and wrapped her arms around herself as if a chill ran through her body. She pulled her knees up to her chest. Hunter gave her a worried look, but didn't say anything.

Nick shook his head and ran a hand through his hair. "How about Tom?" He finally blurted out. "He didn't make a deal but he's in danger now too."

"How?" Susan quickly inquired, taking Tom's hand in hers as if she already sensed what was coming.

Jean paused before speaking, choosing her words carefully. "Taylor found out about the deal and she's being targeted to die."

Nigel held a finger up and cleared his throat. "If I may..." He took a deep breath for effect and glanced around to be sure he had everyone's attention. "I've seen innocent people targeted when they get wrapped up with Immortals." He sighed and met Susan's expectant face. "The deal specifically said not to tell others." He cocked his head meaningfully at them. "It's been years but I still remember the deal and all the clauses as if it were yesterday."

"Tay guessed..." Chris interrupted loudly. "I never told her."

"Tom guessed most of it too. I let him in on the rest." Susan spoke up quickly.

Nigel exhaled deeply, "You let them in on it." He looked much like a lawyer defending a client, "You are in breach of contract."

Tom traded a glance with Susan and their hands linked together. "That accident at the funeral?" She asked, voice cracking. She wrung her hands. "It wasn't an accident?"

Chris's eyes fell on Hunter who had been very quiet. "Didn't Hunter's family knew too?"

"Yeah," Hunter nodded sadly. "I lost my whole family, the little girl died, Chris saved the mayor who lost his wife..." Hunter looked away. "My family suspected because I didn't age..." He didn't meet anybody's eye and it was clear he still blamed himself for their deaths.

Susan's mouth dropped open as she gaped at Nick then turned to the others in the room to confirm what her eyes were seeing. "You're the same rockstar from the 8o's?" Her hand fell slowly from her mouth and she shook her head in disbelief. "We really are immortal?"

"Seems so!" Nigel proclaimed, clapping his hands together. "Now it's up to us to make sure Tay and Tom don't get themselves murked."

Tom nodded and cleared his throat. "I can take care of myself."

"Lightning came for Tay," Hunter pointed out. "How can you take care of that? You should never be alone anymore."

Nigel shook his head in disagreement. "We have to find a way to fix it for them... for good." Opening his mouth and raising his hand, Nigel seemed about to say something when he thought better of it and dropped back down. He held back and Chris thought he looked uncertain.

Nick suggested, "Perhaps the answer is in Nigel's book?"

"You've already read everything there is to know in my book." Nigel sighed. "Plus we went to Marie and she claimed we were wrong and the book was wrong."

"Marie who?" Hunter asked quietly.

"Some hoochie momma." Tay exhaled and cast around her, grabbing a blanket from the chair's armrest. "We might need to find everyone a room."

Although the change in topic was abrupt, Chris yawned and realized how long they'd been fighting off sleepiness. "There's all the space in the family room or we can invade the guest rooms on the third floor."

Hunter shrugged. "I try not to sleep."

His face was drained of emotion and his eyes held the same state of shock from the explosion viewed earlier. Chris was anxious for Hunter as he had gone through the anguish of losing all his loved ones. How drastically could such a traumatic experience alter someone's life?

"Same," Susan, Nigel, Nick, and Jean all answered in unison.

Chris tried to suppress a yawn, worn out from the events of the day. They had been looking forward to curling up in their comfortable bed with silken sheets, not to tossing and turning in agony from their injuries. Such an idea was far from appealing.

Chris raised a single eyebrow as Tom stared, flabbergasted, when Susan agreed. Tom looked anxious yet was gradually understanding the impact of the situation.

Taylor spoke up, "I want to get some food."

Chris's head dropped and Nigel laughed, making Chris sit up straighter. They couldn't remember the last time they'd been this tired. The past few days' sleepless nights were taking a toll.

"What if we get it delivered?" Nigel suggested.

Tay giggled. "If you insist!"

Springing to her feet, Tay offered a smile. "I'll call for the food and see how long it will be."

Chris exhaled loudly, understanding that Tay must be trying to take her mind off of it all by doing one of her favorite things, sending out for food.

Jean followed her into the kitchen, despite the fact Tay shot the other woman an annoyed glare.

Nigel snickered at their departure, "I'm sure she thought Hunter would follow her!"

Hunter looked flustered before answering. "She's attractive, but..." Instead of finishing his sentence his cheeks flushed red, his eyes low to the ground, and his hands on his hips as he puffed his chest out.

Tom and Susan exchanged a look, then Tom pushed his glasses up his nose. "Would it be all right if Susan and I shared a room?"

Chris felt their head dropping, and they jolted it back up. They had nearly dozed off again. Chris sat up straighter and forced their eyes to stay wide open, hoping nobody noticed.

Nick shrugged. "It's Chris's house, after all."

Nigel straightened and determination settled on his features. "We'll all help keep Taylor safe."

Chris yawned, getting to their feet slowly.

The doorbell rang and everyone turned toward it. Chris jumped with a start and had to catch their breath. On the verge of sleep everything seemed a little scarier than normal. Yawning, Chris stretched and got to their feet, taking in the confused glances going round the group.

Nigel creased his brow. "Who did your sister call to get here that quickly?"

Chris furrowed their brow wondering if they had dozed off and were walking around in their sleep. Chris patted their pants for their phone and realized they must have left it in the kitchen or in the car.

Nick sprang from his seat and walked beside Chris, obediently keeping step with them like a well-trained canine.

Nigel got up too. "I want to check out the delivery boy as well."

With an eye roll, Chris checked their pants for their phone and followed the two to the door, phone in hand.

Susan held Chris back and gave them a meaningful look. "You're tired, so maybe let the others help out."

Chris gave a small nod hoping Susan's words weren't a warning. After saving Tom's life, they both surely looked like they had been in a boxing ring and taken on a champion. Chris was thankful Susan had held them back to spare him any possible embarrassment.

Nick shook his head, when a series of heavy knocks echoed from the solid wood front doors. "Yeah... how'd they get past the gates?"

Nigel's usually humorous expression turned serious as Nick jogged to the door .

Hunter stepped closer as Tay and Jean emerged from the

kitchen. Taylor still held her phone to her ear, an expression of fear in her eyes. She took a deep breath and focused on the conversation, giving out the address to the person at the other end of the line.

"Who could be at the door?" Jean asked, panic rising in her voice. She gave Taylor a gentle nudge toward the door. "Can you see out that window?"

Another knock sounded, and Jean jumped suddenly.

"Someone's at the door?" Tay asked incredulously.

Chris noticed how she seemed glued to the spot. Jean hesitated for a moment, but pushed into a run and grabbed the handle before Chris could reach it, one step behind her.

"Wait," Nick called. "Let's just check first."

Nick and Nigel rushed through the entrance, bringing up the rear. Releasing a deep sigh, Nick peered out the window beside the expansive double doors. "Well, the press is gone," he said just before a look of surprise washed over his features. He glanced fearfully at Chris when he muttered, "It's Marie."

Chris had been drowsy moments before but they were suddenly wide-eyed and alert. A memory of the voluptuous woman came into their mind's eye. Although, instead of thinking how stunningly beautiful she was, Chris remembered her rudeness and the accusations she had made. When Tay was almost killed, the elderly beauty shouted for them to hurry away, so as not to draw further attention. She hadn't shown any concern. Chris took a deep breath to prepare themself for more unpleasantness from the woman.

Nigel gazed out at their unexpected visitor with furrowed brows "How in the world did she find us? What is she doing here?" He added hopefully, "Maybe she brought beignets?"

Chris and Nick rolled their eyes while Jean tossed her hands up. "What gives?" She asked.

"I can hear all y'all!" Marie called through the heavy door. "Don't worry, the press is gone."

With a shrug, Chris took a step back and Jean opened the door. Nick pulled Chris behind him as the Cajun woman walked in with confidence, as if she owned the place, and drew something from her bag.

"What?" Jean exclaimed and backed up, but she was too slow.

A deafening bang echoed through the hall. Jean flew back and crumpled to the floor. The unnerving boom made Chris instinctively duck but Nick did the unthinkable. He sidled around behind Marie to grab her arm and wrestle the gun from her grip. She clung to the weapon like a leech. With a grunt, Nick heaved one arm back and struck Marie in the face.

Stunned, Marie's hands flew to her face and she lost her grip on the firearm. Nick caught the gun before it hit the ground and handed it to Nigel.

Disbelief coursed through Chris. Blinking away the shock, they slowly lowered onto the ground next to Jean. She lay still on the marble floor, a pool of blood seeping from her body. No breath escaped her lips. Her silence froze Chris and they tightly clasped her hand.

It was cold.

The unfathomable situation squeezed Chris's lungs and they gasped for breath. Their heart thudded wildly, echoing in their ears. Shock locked up their words. Chris strained until, finally, they strained. "Jean?"

Nigel snapped up the gun from Nick's outstretched hand and, like an old cowboy in a western, gestured with it toward a bench along the wall of the hall, commanding in a menacing tone, "Take a seat, luv!"

Marie followed the silent command, still clutching her nose, which streamed blood down her blouse.

"Thought you'd take us down, eh?" Nigel laughed at her. "Guess you didn't know that my boy Nick is a street ninja!"

"What you going on about?" Marie said as she stood again. She was statuesque to say the least and maintained her cool confidence even with her face and hand covered in blood. She shook her head. "You gone try to kill me?"

Taylor, Susan, and Tom rushed in, their eyes darting from Nick and Chris beside a bloodied Jean to Nigel who resembled a nervous sheriff.

"What the actual fuckity happened?" Taylor exclaimed. "We better get this cleaned before the delivery shows up!" She tossed her hands, ignoring Jean's condition. Chris wondered if she was compartmentalizing and trying not to think about the implications or if she hadn't noticed.

Jean groaned and her eyes flew open, wild and unfocused. Nick placed a calming hand on Jean's arm and when she was ready, helped her to stand.

Marie glared at Nigel and demanded, "Give me my gun back!" Her voice boomed and seethed with another voice echoing over her own. She held her hand out and Nigel meekly handed the weapon back to her. She took a breath and straightened her clothing as if she had a grand gown instead of clothes soaked in her own blood. "Now show me where I can clean up. Cause I'm not talkin' to y'all looking like this." She shook her head and her long braids danced, clinking like small wind chimes.

Nigel pointed to a door behind her and she opened it with a condescending, "Thank you."

Once she had vanished into the bathroom, Taylor shut the front door and the others began asking questions over each other.

"Why did you give her the gun?" Nick demanded.

"Who is this?", Susan gasped.

Taylor pointed to the bathroom door. "What's *she* doing here?"

Hunter, and Tom asked in unison, "What happened?"

Nigel had a far-away look in his eyes, but startled at the questions, and asked in a spooked tone, "I gave her the gun? Why did I give her the gun?" He lifted clenched fists towards the closed door. "Oh, she's a tricky shite!"

"She used her magic on you, Nigel..." Chris mumbled, wishing everyone would keep it down. Marie could hear them, after all.

At first, Nick supported Jean's weight, but she soon pushed off from him and stood on her own. "What happened?" she groaned.

Nigel shrugged. "I still have no idea."

The bathroom door creaked open at a snail's pace to reveal a much tidier Marie, although her blouse was beyond rescue. She stood, hands on her hips, looking at each in turn, like they owed her money. She didn't have the gun out but her stance still put Chris on edge.

Taylor pushed Marie against the wall and had her hand formed a gun, which she pointed at the older woman. "You've got the right to be quiet! You've got the right to some attorney or something! We can use your words for ummmm..." She looked at the others and shrugged. "A book? The news?"

Marie gave a trifling laugh. "Is she for real?" She nodded to Taylor. "You gone shoot me with those fingers chile?" She smiled and tossed her braids over her shoulder, turning her back on Taylor.

Nick's face contorted with rage and his eyes locked on Marie. His eyes narrowed and his pupils dilated. Chris took an involuntary step back, at this moment Nick was terrifying. He lunged at Marie and pinned her to the wall with his hands clamped around her throat.

Chris watched wide-eyed as Nick flew across the entrance to grab Marie by the throat. This situation was out of hand from the start, but it was spiraling. As the owner of the house, Chris felt obliged to step in and diffuse the situation, but before they could utter a word, Marie spoke up.

Marie laughed. "I'm immortal too, Cheri." She cooed. "Or maybe I like this..." She purred at the angry man, bestowing a wicked smile.

"There's more immortals here and they can make you leave!" Taylor scoffed.

Marie pushed Nick back until he let go of her neck. His eyes were still narrowed with pure hatred. Fury roared in his voice when he snapped, "Next time you better go for me first because if you touch her again I will rip your head off!"

Chris wondered if he meant Jean or Taylor. They shrugged off the thought. Nick was very protective of both.

Marie's unexpected arrival made Chris uneasy and they realized they'd already felt it back at the cafe when they first met her. There was something sinister about her very presence, which made Chris thankful for their loyal and strong friends.

Jean touched her chest where the bullet had hit and shivered like she had a chill. She looked at the bloody stain then peered at the place it had struck to see only had a scar "I have a scar shaped like a gun now." In shock, she looked at Marie, and her face reddened. "Why did you shoot me?"

Marie rolled her eyes and tossed her head back. "You were the first to answer the door and I wanted to make an impression."

The sound of another knock on the door followed her words, and Marie instinctively reached for the gun in her bag. Taylor stopped her, pushing back against Marie until Hunter intervened. Marie's eyebrows rose in surprise and she made a dismissive noise when she saw the way Hunter shielded Taylor.

"Yo, you this ain't the Wild West," Hunter said as he pushed himself between Taylor and the taller woman. "It's probably just a delivery."

"Really?" Marie strode and tossed the door open. A timid delivery boy stood there, eyes widening when he spotted the blood on Marie's shirt. With terror painted on his face, he looked around and Chris could see the boy's wild gaze taking in the bullet hole in the wall, and the dried pool of blood on the floor. Wordlessly, he held out a bag before backing away slowly.

"What? You never spilled the sauce before?" Marie scoffed and snapped up the bag. "What's this?" she asked to the assembly inside the house.

Chris made their way to the door and saw the delivery boy standing motionless, jaw agape. It was as if the young man was frozen in dread. Nick was by Chris's side in a second, his arms crossed and steel in his eyes. Waking from his stupor, the delivery boy bolted to his car and peeled wheels getting away. Chris agreed; Marie was scary.

"Omigod! I hope our cameras recorded that!" Taylor chimed from behind Hunter.

Marie shook the contents of the bag and Nick snatched it up quickly. "It isn't yours."

Chris kept a close eye on Marie, anxious to see what the voodoo queen would do next.

Jean stood unsteadily and Nick was right beside her. "You shot me?"

Tay eyed the bag and grinned. "Food's here!"

Chris took the bag pointedly. "That's ours!"

Marie seemed to see it as an invite and started to saunter

in. "Y'all got a fine house!" Marie ran her long fingers along everything she saw.

"Stop that!" Taylor pushed in front of Marie and flung her hand out like she was the police trying to stop a car.

"This chile got a death wish?" Marie laughed as Taylor kept sidestepping to block Marie off when she moved. Hunter stepped protectively in and nudged Taylor aside, at which Marie laughed. "Y'all best keep that one away from me."

"No," Taylor protested while Hunter tried to hold her still. "She's gonna put some kinda mojo or voodoo on us or our things or... something." Tay clenched her hands at her sides, exasperated. "Look what she did to Nigel!"

Hunter and the others traded a look and Hunter pushed Tay behind him. "You're a voodoo lady?"

Marie gave a short snort of a laugh and pushed her braids behind her. "Honey chile, I'm THE voodoo lady!"

"Then don't touch anything," Hunter ordered..

"Relax children," Marie cooed and she glided along the shining wood floors like a dancer. Her eyes roved over the house, her fingers twitching to touch everything she saw. "Mmmhmmm, this *is* a nice place."

As she made her way to the living room they all saw Tom and Susan getting up. Susan had a fireplace poker in her hand guarding Tom. Chris noticed that Susan was determined to keep Tom out of the altercation.

Tom locked eyes with Marie and grasped Susan's hand. He tugged Susan close while keeping his attention on the newcomer. Chris noticed Susan was about to step in front of Tom protectively, and was relieved to see her determined to keep Tom out of harm's way.

"What is it?" Susan asked quietly.

"I don't trust that woman," Tom replied. "Let's keep an eye on her to make sure she's not left unsupervised."

Marie eyed Hunter who still restrained Tay. "Shame, a fine man like you take up with that snooty chile." She sneered and went up to Nick. "What about you, handsome?"

Chris's eyes flew wide when Jean reacted, pushing her way between them. Marie just laughed in delight. Still she tossed Nick a suggestive smile. "You like that? Mmmmhmmm."

Throwing a hand up, Marie dismissed Nick and Jean like an afterthought. She moved closer to Hunter and ran one long nail over his chiseled jaw. "Immortal Olympian like you who can't die." Taylor slapped Marie's hand as the other woman moved closer to Hunter. "You really gone tempt me?" Her eyes still lingered on Nick and she smiled widely. "Now where is the chile I talked to in my cafe?"

Chris pushed forward but Nick stepped up right next to them, glaring at Marie, as though he dared her to harm Chris.

"You gone make me leave?" Marie challenged, crossing her arms in front of her chest. "Bunch of immortals fighting would be interesting." She smirked and waved her long fingers at Tay. "Except the collateral damage."

Jean stepped forward. "What do you want?"

"To talk to Chris!" She turned on her heel and looked at Chris, standing beside Susan and Tom. Marie eyed the two skeptically. "Movie stars?" She snapped her fingers at Chris. "Wake up chile!"

Marie prowled forward, as if she'd found her true prey. Chris took an involuntary step backward when she came too close, her brow furrowed. Her gaze fell on the bag Chris held and Marie gave a devilish grin. "Time to take your medicine, chile."

Tom stepped up beside Chris and they were surprised to see angry determination on the man's face. When Tom held up his hands, like a priest warding off the Devil, Marie leaped back and snarled before she examined him more closely from a safer distance. "Whole lot of good in this room?" Marie growled.

Afraid she might pull the same stunt she had on Jean, Chris dropped the bag and, without a second thought, bounded in front of Tom, declaring, "Hey! Don't." Her furious expression didn't intimidate Chris, who added, "He's a nice guy."

"I'm not here for him," she barked and jabbed her finger at Chris's face. "I don't like being anyone's Couyon and you really made somebody boudé, chile!" She lowered her voice until her breath sent chills down Chris's neck. "You're the one I want to talk to!"

Chris took a deep breath waiting for her to finish her tirade and cocked their head curiously. She was beautiful but she was dangerous and Chris couldn't relax until she was gone, no matter how exhausted they were. Since they made the deal with Deacon, their entire life had been on red alert. Each day the deal seemed less and less appealing, even more so now that Tay was suffering for it.

"This hero biz is causing a tracas!" Marie continued, hands on her hips. She glared at each of them in turn, undaunted by the room full of immortals. "Y'all need to stop drawing attention to yourselves and disappear, so people ain't seeing folks that should be geriatric acting like they teens."

Chris shrugged. "We didn't break the deal."

Nigel nodded vehemently but kept his distance. Since Marie bewitched him to get the gun he was more cautious and kept his distance. Nevertheless, the British know-it-all continued to prattle on with his endless stream of facts. "Technically they did keep the deal!" Nigel raised his pointer finger straight into the air. "When we signed, nobody mentioned the agreement in relation to this sort of thing. There were no instructions on how to behave or what one can or can't do once the deal is signed."

"Y'all playing with fire here. If I get another late night visit from some concerned party, then I won't be alone when I return. And it won't be an immortal that I'll target." She spoke through gritted teeth.

"So if we save someone like Tom again, then what? You'll be back?" Chris asked.

"OUI!" she growled.

"Looks like we'll be seeing a lot of you around here, Marie," Chris's gaze narrowed. "I can't sit by and let bad things happen to innocent people who aren't meant to die yet."

Nick stepped in and offered his support. "There's more of us than just you. Remember that."

"I got more going for me than meets the eye, too," Marie smiled mischievously with her eyes twinkling as if to issue a hidden challenge. Her expression twisted, contorting her face. "Remember that!" Once again, her voice layered and a deeper, more threatening, tone echoed over her usual timbre. With a huff she withdrew a small velvet bag from her pocket and threw it onto the pristine floorboards.

A blast of flames shot into the air and engulfed her. A moment later, the inferno winked out and only smoke remained.

"That stinks," Taylor waved a hand in front of her face in frustration. "She's pretty but I hope we kick her ass."

"Who was that?" Susan asked quickly.

"Marie, the voodoo queen," Chris muttered under their breath. "I think we made her mad."

CHAPTER 23

Dinners were always exciting at the Shepherds' home, but with their guests joining them Chris thought it turned into something truly special.

Tom and Susan regaled them with stories about the silver screen and acting. Tom described how he had worked with Susan to hone her craft.

They spoke of times before he met Susan, but it was apparent that his life began once he encountered her. Like many, Susan experienced depression and felt as if she merely existed until Tom came into her life. Susan was enthusiastic when she talked about the film and television industry. Her stories about blossoming on the screen as a child actor were captivating. Later, she'd worked together with Tom in an action movie and Susan described her journey to womanhood and her infatuation with Tom from afar.

Tom was humble and avoided eye contact, but his quiet stories about the movies were delivered with a big smile. He talked about how he had been in love with Susan since his childhood, and had tried to be part of any film she was involved in. With a rueful grin, he admitted that he had followed her around, close enough to smell her perfume. It wasn't an obsession, he said. He just wanted to keep an eye on her as she grew up. To him, saving her from the bus was non-negotiable – it became his life's mission, because he couldn't live in a world without her.

Hunter's stories jumped from place to place. His childhood had been devoted to winning gold, and so he was more familiar with the word victory than he was with his own name. He described his life pre-Olympics as an impenetrable fog, but everything changed when he reached the games. He likened it to a whirlwind of emotion and excitement, but knew that competing again was out of the question now. All he seemed to do was stay indoors, sleeping, eating and exercising.

Nigel waxed nostalgic about his idyllic upbringing in the British Isles. He was born with a silver spoon in his mouth and made it known that he was greatly favored by fortune. With this privilege came an expectation of excellence, one which Nigel found easy to meet but dreary in its everydayness. In his youth, he sought more attention-grabbing ways of expressing himself, such as skipping grades and enrolling directly in college.

His academic success earned him invitations from prestigious universities like Oxford, Cambridge, and Ivy League schools, followed soon after by job offers from abroad. His family's disapproval of his sexual orientation prompted them to tell him America could have him, instead of trying to make amends with their own son. But Nigel did not find relief in the fact that his life had been spared while his true love's had not.

Chris and Taylor sat side by side, bright eyes shining in the soft lamplight as they discussed their upbringing. "It wasn't easy growing up poor," Chris said. "We had to schedule our bills around when we could pay them or try to stretch what little money we had to cover all expenses. That's why it was such a surprise when the first app I released went viral and brought us sudden wealth. Every new app kept that momentum going and soon enough, we were doing pretty well for ourselves. We learned a lot, but it has definitely been one wild ride!"

Chris couldn't help but reflect on the difficult and isolated life they had before the success of their apps. Chris had been so depressed and lonely, with no friends or romantic prospects, and nights spent alone playing solitaire with a worn deck of cards. But now, seeing their friends' eyes sparkle while discussing their bright future, they were filled with hope.

Tay nodded in agreement when Chris spoke and shared snippets of the games they devised to pass time when their family was so poor that their electricity had been regularly cut off. King of the Hill (the game which the last person on the bed/hill won) had been a favorite and sometimes they'd build forts from construction leftovers. Taylor scoffed not missing the lack of funds but she did miss how close they all were before financial security came along. Chris, who always worked, and their parents' still taking care of each other. This time it was an easy choice instead of a necessity. When Taylor spoke, Chris could tell she longed for those days.

Nick had haphazard stories full of excitement from his life traveling and performing music, but his best recollections were from his early years. Constantly outdoors, creative and busy; he especially loved to share about his family taking him to places like circuses and concerts despite their limited finances. These special trips filled him with hope. It was obvious Nick felt something more than fondness in these memories as he kept stealing sideways glances at Jean.

Jean participated in the conversation, even though she didn't contribute much. She pushed her food around on her plate or shuffled it around on her fork. Sometimes she'd lift it to take a bite, but something always caused her to pause before anything crossed her lips.

She cut her food into smaller and smaller pieces until it was reduced to almost a paste. In reality, tiny mouthfuls did make it into her system – pieces so miniscule they could have been mistaken for pills.

When Jean spoke, she played with her fork and waved it around, emphasizing certain points as she spoke. She always took a plate but it seemed her fear prevented her from satisfying her appetite. For the most part, she just pretended to eat and focused on drinking, laughing, and listening to the stories. Whenever someone asked her about her past, she shrugged it off without mentioning the time she spent in the circus.

With a smile plastered onto her face, Jean just said, "I'm happy not to be in that life anymore." She offered no explanation of how she got away or why she became famous.

Chris met Jean's eye and then broke contact, sure she didn't want to speak about it but Nigel spoke up with a wave, his voice eager. "Oh, do tell them Ima!" He exclaimed as he used her Circus name even though it upset her.

It hurt Chris's heart when they saw a deep red blush grow on Jean's face when her old name was mentioned. Jean had said she loved her family in the circus, yet people considered it socially unacceptable. Everyone else had exciting histories with lots of attention, whereas Jean's past seemed to be the main target for jokes, much like Nigel's.

Nigel went on when nobody took the bait. "Our fair Jean here used to be a fat lady in the circus. She was so big she raked in all the money. But now she's literally half the woman she used to be."

Jean looked like a tomato now and shook her head lightly. "I'm not that person anymore," she said, struggling against the inquisitive looks all around her. When she looked down at her full plate, she tensed.

Chris opened their mouth, ready to jump in and defend their friend, but Nick had already begun speaking. His voice was strong and confident and left no room for dispute.

"Knock it off, Nigel!" Nick was on his feet and pointed his finger right in the other man's face. "You're not funny." Chris nodded in silent agreement, sick of seeing Jean tormented.

"I'm sure this is all for the benefit of the lovely Jean, but she's no damsel in distress here," Nigel taunted with a smirk. "After all, she did take a bullet directly to the chest and all she got was a nifty little scar!" He took a sip from his glass before sighing heavily. "Well, almost no mark... right?"

Nick whipped around and grabbed Nigel's collar in one hand. "I get it. You were bullied in school so now you're trying to bully Jean for revenge but that's done. It's over. You don't pick on her anymore."

Chris's expression changed as they came to a realization and spoke in a murmur, "You were bullied as well, so now you're taking it out on Jean." Chris gulped, understanding that few people had escaped torment from their peers and Nigel and Chris were likely targets because they belonged to the pride community. "Don't take your frustrations out on Jean... We've all gone through pain and we don't need to make others suffer to feel better," They motioned for Nick to release Nigel.

Letting go of Nigel's collar, Nick jabbed his finger into the seated man's chest, and said more sternly. "Nick-and-Jean, that's all one word," he emphasized before sinking back into his chair next to Jean and lifting his chin defiantly. "Got it?" His expression softened when Jean slipped her hand into his under the table, and Nick took a deep breath to calm himself down. Chris felt a lump form in their throat when Nigel made fun of Jean, but it got worse when Nick mentioned they were a couple and Jean didn't correct him.

Chris pulled their mind away from Jean and nodded, "I haven't really had many friends because of our financial situation and because I'm non-binary. The few friends I did have were in the same financial boat as us, but none of them understood that I was different like that. Some don't know how to talk to me or treat me so they avoid me, I felt like a new minority."

Chris looked down. "You keep trying to guess if I'm male or female. I don't identify as such and never really have. When I was little other children would refer to me as he or she because they didn't know if I was male or female. When they called me he or she, it would take me aback, it felt weird. When they didn't want to guess they said they/them and it felt better – right. What I began to realize is that I'm just Chris. Later I may see things differently but that's up to me and I'm in no rush." Chris looked at Nigel, "I've been attracted to boys and girls. I see who they are more than the faces. I'm not attracted to your soul, Nigel." Chris looked away, "I am thankful you all accept me and see me as Chris and that's all."

Looking around at the group, Chris went on, "I feel close to all of you now, even you, Nigel." They sighed heavily. "You guys aren't just my partners in crime. It seems like fate put us all together. Maybe it was our destiny to become friends; so, let's not take it for granted, right? We've seen some crazy stuff in the last few days and know better than to take every breath for granted."

Tom held up his glass full of soda and toasted, "Hear, hear!" The others raised their drinks and echoed Tom.

Tay sighed. "So all of you are connected for eternity but I don't fit in."

Hunter had an arm around Tay's shoulders. "No, you belong with us too." He gave her a kind smile.

Nigel looked as if he had been scolded and took a deep breath. "I wonder if we made the news again."

"I hope not," Jean murmured.

Chris stated quietly, "Marie was pretty mad. I get the feeling she's gonna be back."

Hunter scoffed, "Picking a fight with another immortal? We outnumber her!"

"Unless they find a way to get us, one at a time," Nigel joked.

"Lightning, a car, and bullets didn't work," Nick commented.

"A fire or a big branch from a tree?" Tom asked thoughtfully. "Why was Chris the only one injured?"

Tay looked at her sibling. "Chris, are you in pain from the injury? Do you need anything?"

Chris shook their head. They tried not to smile when Tay showed her sweet and caring side. It was easy to see her as a vapid and shallow trend maker who wanted social media attention. She didn't show her other side often but Chris was glad they had a glimpse of it today.

Susan sighed. "I'm pretty tired." She placed her napkin on her plate and Tom got up to help Chris clear the table.

Tay curled up into a ball and started tapping away at her phone.

Nigel rose and glanced at the others. "Would anybody fancy some wine or something a bit stiffer?"

Nick nodded. "Doesn't sound bad." He scanned the area for anything else he could do. Then he coughed as if it was a bad habit. He suddenly changed his mind with a groan, "I'll pass."

Hunter moved his chair closer to Tay to talk to her in a hush.

Tom trailed Chris into the kitchen, carrying some plates with him. He put them aside, next to where Chris had placed theirs. "Your sister seems very taken by Hunter."

Chris began scraping the plates and said, "Tay is quite selective when it comes to dating."

Tom nodded in agreement. "I haven't come across someone like her yet." He followed Chris's lead and started washing the other dishes. "I'd like to express my gratitude for what you did, whether you're immortal or not. It was very brave of you. Plus your hospitality."

Chris shrugged, "Anyone else would have done the same thing."

Tom sighed, "No. Not everyone would have done that, Nigel was right there and didn't lift a finger. It's not part of human nature to risk one's life for another person." He stared at his own hands while he spoke.

"Nick and Hunter did it, too," Chris said, nodding.

Tom's eyes lit up as he crossed his arms and leaned against the kitchen counter. "You are all quite extraordinary. Maybe that's why you got this deal." Then, as if on cue, Susan and Nigel burst in, both smiling from ear to ear. Susan touched Tom's arm as she asked Chris if they could find drinks downstairs.

Nigel waved towards the lower levels with a grin. "Let's partake!"

Tom chuckled and replied, "I'll just have coffee.". He smiled at them before turning to Chris. "coming?"

"In a few minutes," Chris answered with a smile.

The group had been having a great time playing truth or dare, and Taylor and Nigel kept upping the ante with their dares. That was until Nigel accepted Taylor's last challenge to run around the neighborhood in his birthday suit.

"I think Nigel had too much to drink," Hunter chuckled.

Chris glanced at Nick before they responded quietly, "Isn't he usually like this." Chris sighed while they stared down at their phone and felt the color drain from their face.

Taylor peered over Chris's shoulder to see their phone.

"Who is it?" she asked, scooting closer.

Chris frowned, "I missed that doctor's appointment, and now I have to schedule another." Chris shook their head and removed their phone from their pocket to check for a new time on the calendar.

Hunter shook his head and scoffed. "Yo, I think you're done with doctors."

Susan nodded, "I haven't even sneezed since I made the deal."

"Decon told me I had to get to a doctor and insist they find the cancer," Chris mumbled. "Don't I have to keep the appointments?"

Nick traded a look with Chris and Nick opened his mouth to speak but Nigel waved his hands to get everybody's attention.

Opening the book, Nigel narrated, "So, this is a demon," he pointed to the image, as if discussing it with kindergarteners. "This is the bloke who didn't fulfill his end of the bargain," and here," he indicated at the center of the page.

One picture displayed a man's face distorted in horror as he came face-to-face with a ghoul, depicting blazing crimson eyes. The next photo featured the same man, this time held down by the demon-like creature, and a gust of air blowing upwards from his body. "And this is when his soul leaves." Nigel snapped the book shut.

"Did everyone listen? You might be tested on this later!"

He waved an exasperated hand. "You must keep your part of the deal otherwise far worse than an immortal curse will get you. Still, Chris, we've seen you defy death many times so you should think over what, exactly, your deal entailed."

The rest of them shook their heads at Nigel, but Tom couldn't tear his eyes from the text. Chris hesitated, worried about the consequences of messing up the deal and frightened at the notion of the dreams. Chris started to ask more but Tom's glare at the book caught their attention.

"Where did you get that book?" Tom asked, studying its distressed cover.

"I work in a bookstore," Nigel said quickly.

"It's creepy." Tom muttered with a deadpan stare but looked like he could run at any given minute.

Chris agreed with a slight inclination of their head. "It's definitely creepy, but no more than the rest of this." Then again, Chris knew this was new to Tom and Susan too.

Jean took a breath before speaking, "Nigel has kept that book hidden away at the bookstore where he works."

"Can I hold it for a minute?" Hunter reached out expectantly. His eyebrows shot up his forehead when Nigel clutched onto it tightly, as if they'd requested a limb instead of just a book.

"This is my book and I keep it safe," Nigel said in an appalled tone. He glared at the looks his friends gave him and eventually held out the book towards Tom, waving it slightly.

Tom seemed frightened of the book and backed away from it. "I don't like that book..." he muttered.

Chris observed Taylor silently agree with Tom, but the others looked at Susan's husband like he was insane.

"See? All mine!" Nigel chuckled.

"Yo!" Hunter said fast. "Taylor? You take it?"

"Nah, it sucks," she muttered and pulled out her phone

trying to look like she was busy, but gave in a moment later. "Alright. I hate it." She finally admitted, setting down her phone.

Chris scrunched their nose in response to Tay's confession. She had said nothing about being scared of the book, so Chris felt a sense of betrayal that she kept it a secret. Why had she lied to Chris? She could have confided in them instead of keeping her fears locked up. Now they were bubbling to the surface, and Chris vowed to stay closer to Tay.

Nigel ran his hand along the binding of the book, as if petting a kitten. "Yes, that's right," he almost purred. "The book is very selective."

Chris noticed Nigel speaking of the book as if it was a faithful companion and exchanged a curious glance with Jean. Chris's heart raced, feeling the connection for a moment before she averted her eyes and the sensation of a link between them evaporated.

Jean sighed and leaned back in her seat, crossing her arms. "Just tell us what you're dancing around or we'll take it from you and read it ourselves."

"I did," Nigel replied quietly, settling back into his chair. "I'm not some tiresome think-bucket who recalls everything off the top of my head."

Jean scoffed. "Said the genius."

Nigel turned red and looked ready to banter before gripping the book tighter instead.

Nick stood up and said, "I think the rest of us should be able to read it too."

"It's always best to be open and honest with each other," Susan stated emphatically, squeezing Tom's hand.

Tom kissed her cheek in response. "Something bothering you?" he asked softly.

"I'm just impressed at how you're handling this," Susan

replied. He had taken in stride the news of her deal putting his life in danger.

Tom chuckled lightly. "We do come from Hollywood. We've seen a lot."

Chris nodded in agreement. "C'mon, let's get everyone to their rooms for the night."

Taylor pouted beside Hunter, obviously not ready to settle down yet. She perked up suddenly, "Is someone still sleeping in my room with me?"

Jean smiled as she looked over at Taylor. "I am... I was there last night. Where else would I sleep?"

Nick didn't say a word in response, but Nigel spoke up to fill the silence cheerfully. "Where else, indeed, Nick?" he said with a laugh.

Nick looked to Hunter in desperation, but the former Olympian seemed just as inattentive. Nigel was about to start another lengthy harangue when Tom stepped in.

"Is there a room big enough for Susan and myself?" he asked quietly.

Chris traded a look with Taylor and nodded. "They're all good sized rooms. Mom and Dad's room has the biggest bed." Chris stretched.

"Yeah," Taylor said. "Mom and Dad are really cool and won't mind unless you trash it or make a mess."

Susan smiled. "We won't."

Nigel cleared his throat. "Considering the circumstances at hand, perhaps we should all bunk down here like we did when we met? It would increase the chances of protecting the..." He paused dramatically and waved to Tom and Taylor, "mortals."

Taylor snapped her gum. "I didn't sleep down here and I can't sleep unless I'm in my bed." She paused. "Or unless I'm so exhausted that I drop."

Chris nodded. "We went camping a while ago and we had a

camper with beds but she couldn't sleep. We had to wear her down hiking and swimming until we could hardly keep our eyes open." Chris couldn't resist a smile at the simple, happy memories.

"Yeah and I'm all anxious," Taylor's eyes darted among them. "I feel like something is going to happen. Like it's Christmas, or the day before a vacation." She tucked her legs up against her body and pressed her lips together tightly.

"It doesn't feel like any holiday to me," Nick took a hard breath. "Whatever you decide with the sleeping arrangements is fine with me."

Susan stood to stretch her arms and Tom came to his feet dutifully beside her. He took Susan's hand and watched Chris heading to the stairs.

The rest of them began to rise and follow, but Taylor pouted. She frowned and rose excruciatingly slowly.

Nigel offered her a hand up. "I know, puddin'." He gave her a conspiratorial smile. "The party is over so soon."

A sound made them all tense up. Chris looked around, shaking their head, letting the others know they were unaware of the source. They motioned towards the family room for everyone to hide in.

As if fleeing a shark, the others flew down the steps and streamed back into the room. Chris turned off the lights. "Get down! Someone is up there!"

Tom pulled Susan down behind the loveseat and she chided him, "I'm supposed to protect you!"

"Shhhhh!" Taylor ordered from behind the computer desk waving her hand for them to get down. Hunter hunched next to her.

Tom followed and crouched between them while Nick, Jean and Chris stood to one side of the stairs. Chris was ashen. "How did they get past our security?"

"Where's Nigel?" Jean asked in a whisper, her head darting about.

The sound of footsteps grew louder, then stopped abruptly at the top of the staircase. A flash of light blinded them all when the shadow flicked the light on.

Chris could only see a shard of bright white light from under the door and the rest was darkness, that left them with heightened senses of sound. Chris's ears perked as they heard the creaking of the boards and the frantic breathing of the group in the darkness but they couldn't see anybody else. The door to the top of the stairs flew open and they could see a solitary slender silhouette.

Chris let out a long breath as they took in the person. After a moment, recognition sparked and Chris yelled out, "Jordan!" They rushed forward to greet him.

Taylor pushed Hunter away and glared up at him. "That's just Jordan!" She stood up and bolted up the stairs. She ran past Chris and jumped into her little brother's arms. "Thank you for being not creepy!"

Jordan disentangled from Taylor and scanned the room as everyone emerged from hiding. "Do Mom and Dad know about this party?"

Chris shook their head. "You're home early." The three siblings descended the stairs and Chris noticed everyone was staring at them. Not that Chris could blame them. Jordan had stunning eyes shared with Taylor and Chris. In contrast though, Jordan had a whimsical air about him and his hair was styled like someone in the latest fashion magazine, all one natural hue. His clothing consisted of the kind you'd see adver-tised on a high-end store commercial. His small smile made him look mischievous, while his soulful eyes slowly took in the view of everyone emerging from their hiding spots.

As the rest of the group gathered closer to the siblings,

Nigel whispered excitedly. "There's another one." He clapped his hands as if he had been given the Christmas goose early while he pranced toward the bottom of the stairs.

Chris nodded to the others behind the puppy-dog-eager Nigel. "This is Nigel." Chris stepped out and waved for everyone else to move closer. Chris pointed at each person as they called out their names for Jordan who returned a meager wave. "This is our younger brother Jordan," Chris concluded.

"Younger?" Nigel sighed deeply and rolled his eyes.

Taylor picked out some snacks and claimed the couch. She rolled her eyes and muttered, "He's straight Nigel."

Chris chuckled. "Jordan is 16."

Nigel flung his arm up as if he had been burned. "It was nice talking to you." He plopped on the couch next to Taylor, grabbed a handful of her cheesy snacks and muttered under his breath, "So close."

Jordan looked overwhelmed by the attention. "I just came in here for my inhaler; springtime is tough with my allergies." He held up the inhaler. "I tried to be quiet; I hope I didn't wake anybody."

Chris nodded. "We didn't hear you until we were halfway up the stairs on our way to bed."

"Okay..." Jordan seemed uncomfortable with all the new people around him. "Tell Mom and Dad I'm still at Morgan's house for spring break." He waved the inhaler with one hand as he moved toward the door. "Morgan's dad is waiting in the car, so I gotta go."

Chris nodded. "I'll walk you out."

Jean and Nick stood as well and strolled towards the stairs, Nick leading the way.

"I have lots to tell you later," Chris said quietly afterwards.

J ordan and Chris had slipped out of the front door and Nick and Jean followed, making sure they were not threatening.

Jean hurriedly pulled the door open before Chris could touch it.

"Thank you," Chris smiled at the kindness of their friends. When Nick popped from around the corner with the curtain still draped on his arm it was easy to see they had been looking out for them.

Nick doffed the curtain with an amused expression on his face, and then tactfully avoided mentioning that they'd been observing. "You look a lot like your brother and Taylor," he commented instead.

Chris smiled and gave a nod. "I guess so." Chris looked toward the kitchen and the doorway downstairs. "Is everyone still down there?"

Nick nodded in confirmation. "Should be." They descended the steps together and soon they heard loud voices.

"They should have never taken off Yo MTV raps," Hunter exclaimed. "That's dumb."

Nick looked intrigued. "They took off MTV? I liked that."

"No, just yo mtv raps," Hunter shook his head.

"I don't know it," Nick shrugged

Taylor glanced up. "Really? Even though MTV cribs was old, like you." It was evident that she either found Hunter's conversation intriguing or simply enjoyed having it with him.

Nigel never ceased to act bored and self-assured. "I know the mainstream rock tunes but I've never actually listened to them. If you want me to discuss music, let's talk classical... rock has a great rhythm but it tends to repeat itself."

Nick scoffed. "Classical repeats all the time too! They play the same bit again and again. It really depends on whether we're talking about symphonies, operas, sonatas, chamber music or concertos..."

The others stared at him, eyes popped out as if he had fish coming out of his ears, but Nick just shrugged. "I used to be a musician and studied at Juilliard."

Chris smiled in admiration. "You still are a musician."

Tom nodded and wiped his glasses with the corner of his shirt. "I guess it's like acting. You never forget your craft."

Susan concurred, "Especially if you've been doing it all your life."

Nick gave an indifferent look. "I know I was on the streets for a long time and everything changed. People had different phones and clothes, but I never felt like part of it. The '80s felt easy compared to the way things are now."

Taylor rolled her eyes and held up her phone. "You mean booooooooring."

Nick leaned over to her on the couch. "You don't get out as much as we did."

Taylor snorted in disbelief. "Ummm... you lived outside!"

Nigel chuckled but didn't seem amused by Nick's music comment. "Low blow from a millennial!"

Nick raised an eyebrow at him in puzzlement. "Millennial?" He nudged Taylor playfully. "I thought your last name was Shepherd?"

Taylor groaned loudly before standing up again. "Old people..."

She brought her wine glass to her lips, revealing that she had been drinking.

"Tay, are you sure that's wise?" Chris scolded her, feeling protective after her admission about the book scaring her. For her to turn to alcohol also felt self destructive – the last thing anybody needed right now.

"What? I'm the one marked for death," she almost spat at Chris. "I..." Taylor almost shouted, before attempting an awkward spin as if she were a dancer. "Am going to have fun!" She giggled. "While I can."

Hunter, who'd been sitting beside Taylor, looked up at Chris y. "It's all good. I'll keep an eye on her."

Taylor nearly lost her balance and Hunter was quick to steady her. She laughed at his closeness. "Okay! Bubble Buddy, play Tay's Awesome Mix," she bossed the AI.

Chris groaned hearing the music. This was turning into a party. Thankfully, Hunter took charge, keeping Taylor close to him as they talked quietly on the other side of the room.

"Bubble Buddy?" Susan said and giggled in a low breath.

Nick stared at Hunter and Taylor with an intensity so great that if either of them had said "boo" he would have jumped out of his skin. It was almost amusing to see how protective he was of Chris and Taylor, as if they were his real family. Chris was doing the same, carefully monitoring Taylor.

"I think he's in love with her." Tom smiled, gesturing to Taylor and Hunter. He held Susan's hand, and every so often ran his thumb over her fingers.

"Oh, he definitely fancies her, and she's over the moon for him," Nigel agreed quietly. "I think you'll have an immortal for an in-law." He joked weakly to Chris.

"Yeah, but he's a fifty-year-old in a twenty-year-old body," Chris shook their head. "I don't think he would ever..." They stopped short when Nick tapped Taylor's shoulder to capture her attention.

Chris took a few steps back, feeling the vibration of their phone in their pocket. With a nervous breath, they hoped it was a message from their parents, but the name on the screen made Chris's face fall.

"It's Jordan." Chris swiped open the message. "He had an asthma attack and is at the hospital." Chris stood. "Taylor and I need to go."

Nick spoke up, "But I thought he had an inhaler?"

"He didn't get it in time or it didn't work... I don't know. His friend doesn't say" Chris said quickly and moved closer to Taylor, only to hear her giggling and speaking under her breath.

Her next words stopped Chris in their tracks. "You're def my boyfriend," Taylor giggled.

Hunter chuckled and pressed his forehead to hers. "That's what you want?"

Before things could get out of hand, Chris cleared their throat and said, "Sorry to drop a bomb but we need to go, Tay. Jordan needs us."

Taylor wiggled until her feet hit the floor. "Let me ask my fiancé."

Chris blinked at Hunter, surprised. "How long have you been talking?"

Hunter shook his head. "We're not... She's still a bit tipsy."

"Tay, we need to go to the hospital for Jordan. He's had an asthma attack and it sounds bad." Chris said to help sober her up.

Taylor's eyes widened and she moved quickly. "I need to get my things and some juice or something to drink." She already seemed more with it. This left Chris wondering how much alcohol she had actually consumed. "I'm not drunk..." She rolled her eyes.

Hunter nodded. "I'll drive. You don't look okay to be behind the wheel, and..." He shifted his attention to Chris and nodded toward Taylor as he started walking. "I won't leave her alone."

Chris touched Hunter's shoulder gratefully. They both nearly jumped out of their skin when Susan and Tom cleared their throats loudly to get their attention.

"We're coming with you," Susan spoke for both of them.

Nigel had already sprung to his feet in excitement as he started to prepare for the trip. "Oh great! A jaunt to ICU Later Hospital!" He hadn't put down his book yet.

Tay watched from behind as Chris tried to protest. "We don't need everyone to come."

Hunter eyed the siblings gathering their things. "We are definitely going."

"You're really thick," Nigel griped. "You think you're going alone? Family stays together," he tossed the book into his bag and whispered to Nick with his eyes on Hunter, "Maybe he'll change his mind if you keep that up."

CHAPTER 24

Chris kept up with Tay running through the hospital's brightly lit halls like someone lit a fire under them and Taylor was right behind. Hunter trailed them, his eyes scanning vigilantly. Chris stumbled up to the nursing station, out of breath and regretting the mad dash from the car. Clutching their ribs and between labored breaths, Chris asked, "Jordan Shepherd?"

The nurse looked concerned and cocked her head. "Are you all right?"

The nurse seemed concerned and arched her head questioningly: "Are *you* alright?"

Chris nodded as Taylor marched up as if ready to bark orders for service at a drive-thru window. She snapped her fingers impatiently, prompting the nurse to look away from Chris. "Where's our brother, Jordan Shepherd? We got a message saying he was in the emergency room here."

The nurse smiled sweetly. "Ah! That's why you seem familiar. You have a strong family resemblance." She gestured toward the hallway. "He's the third door on the left."

They started off and Hunter followed, but the nurse held up a hand. "Only family!"

The others sat down, but Hunter waved off her concerns, his voice dripping with sarcasm. "I can't be family because I'm black?" He gave a scoff in challenge. "Don't be racist."

Taylor grabbed Hunter's hand and said, "This is my other brother." She shot the nurse a challenging look and added, "Family can be made up of more than blood relatives." Then she pulled Hunter along by his hand, following Chris up the bright hospital hallway.

Chris couldn't think. They needed to find Jordan. The trio came across Jordan in a bed with a pastel-and-paisley hospital gown on. He seemed worried but when he saw his siblings his expression lightened up.

Taylor pushed past and rushed onto his bed. "Are you okay? What happ..." She stopped short of hugging him and recoiled. "O.M.G.! What's that smell?" She pinched her nose.

Chris's head snapped up when a familiar stench of sulfur filled their nostrils.

Hunter, who had been silent until then, touched Chris's shoulder. "I'll be right back. I want to see where this smell is coming from." He slowly moved down the hall in search of the source of the stench.

Taylor ignored Hunter's departure and kept talking. "Did you mess yourself or did you just fart? Do you need me to get a nurse?"

Jordan rubbed his head and replied with a small chuckle, "I just woke up. I think I had some weird dream and I could smell this while I was still sleeping. That smell must have been what woke me up!"

Chris settled on the edge of the bed, ignoring Taylor's attempts to cover her face. "What was your dream about?"

Jordan seemed troubled. "There was this guy in a top hat.

He had a cane and red eyes. He said he'd be coming for me soon." Jordan looked spooked. "He had this voice..."

Chris sighed knowingly and felt a chill. Deacon. "Was it like multiple voices layered over one another, all speaking at different pitches?"

Chris was happy their parents weren't around to be targets for Deacon's dark magic. Exhaling, Chris wondered if Jordan had been a target and Deacon had just missed. Then again, Chris had spoken to Jordan that evening at dinner when Chris hinted to Tay about the deal.

"How did you know?" Jordan paled.

Taylor looked back and forth between them. "What is going on?"

Chris tried to act nonchalant in an effort not to frighten them. "It sounds familiar," Chris waited anxiously for Hunter's return. A shiver of apprehension ran down their spine. Why did they expect Hunter to bring back bad news?

Taylor sat beside Jordan on the bed now the stench had cleared away. She held onto his hand and looked pointedly at an IV bag.

Trading a look with Tay, Chris considered that usually when Jordan had the IV in after an asthma attack it meant he would be in hospital for a few days. Taylor bit her lip nervously. "Is it serious?"

Jordan exhaled slowly. "I only had one puff of my inhaler left when the attack came on. It's just allergy season..." He gave them a lopsided smile. "I need a new inhaler."

Taylor nodded. "So, are you coming home or what?"

Jordan shook his head. "They said I need to spend a few days on the wall hookah thing." He pointed to a mask and set of pipes attached to the wall.

"Nebulizer?" Chris raised an eyebrow. "You're being admitted?"

Jordan nodded. "I'm hoping the food is better this time." His voice became serious. "Did they get in touch with Mom and Dad?"

Tay rolled her eyes. "About that... they haven't responded to any of my messages. They must be on their second honeymoon at some spa/hotel combination."

Although Chris wanted to agree with Tay's explanation, a lingering doubt hovered in their mind. They hadn't heard from their parents at all. But this wasn't the time to raise the alarm unnecessarily. Hopefully Mom and Dad were okay. Chris wrinkled their nose unsure if they smelled that stench again and peered down the hall.

Jordan gave a wry chuckle. "Yuck." He directed his attention towards Chris. "What are you searching for?"

"Hunter," Chris replied, scanning the hallway. "He came here with us but he wandered off to see what the smell was."

"What?" Jordan asked.

"What that smell was." Chris glanced around warily. Their skin prickled and they thought their siblings were unconvinced by their response. Taylor shrugged and kept quizzing Jordan, letting Chris relax a little. Taking a deep breath, Chris hesitated. They wanted to find hunter but didn't want to leave Taylor and Jordan alone. Chris made a decision. The staff was close and Chris wouldn't wander far.

Hunter wasn't hard to find, but he shrugged and Chris's heart sank. Together, they walked down the corridor until they found the others in the waiting room. It was a relief for Chris to see all of them. They were family, no matter what the nurse said. Concerned expressions regarded Chris from all sides and they moved faster to update everyone.

Nick was the first one to react. "Shouldn't you be back there with your siblings?"

"I'm going back," Chris replied in a low voice. They

glanced around to make sure no one was eavesdropping. "We smelled brimstone." With a meaningful glance, Chris added, "Hunter wanted to see if it meant anything."

Tom narrowed his eyes suspiciously. "Do you often sense sulphur when that deal maker is here?"

Nigel shifted, a guarded look on his face. "You can't smell him often, but it's certain."

Jean wrinkled her nose. "How is Jordan doing?"

Chris shrugged. "It looks like a normal asthma attack. All seems legit, except for the smell of brimstone."

Nick nodded. "I'm coming back with you." He looked through the ER doors, worried. "You left them alone?"

Chris's eyes bulged with shock at the realization that they'd forgotten about Tay's vulnerability. How could they leave the two unsupervised? What would Chris do without Nick? He was a true guardian and didn't leave Tay alone – exposed and vulnerable. The realization only made Chris feel worse about how much better Nick treated Tay than they did.

Hunter glanced at the front desk. "Wait until the nurse is busy, then we can slip in unnoticed."

The phone rang and she started typing away at her computer while speaking into the receiver. Excited, Nick edged closer to the door. "This looks good," he said with a cocky smile.

Hunter motioned for the nurse to let him pass and they both snuck behind a giant ficus plant as she opened the doors. They returned inside without a reaction from the nurse.

Jean settled back and watched them go. "He's still protective of Taylor."

"Life debt?" Nigel cooed. "How sweet."

Chris faced them. "What about that incident on the news? Nick rescued her from the car."

"You think he fancies her?" Nigel gave a small taunt at Jean who bit her lip.

Chris sat down beside Jean on the seat Nick had sat earlier and took in Jean's worried look.

Narrowing their eyes at Nigel, Chris scoffed at the absurd notion. "Of course not! Nick seems to love her like an older brother would."

Jean looked dismal and stared at the door Nick had disappeared through.

Nigel bobbed his head. "We should review all media coverage of the events. I'm here because you found me but Hunter found you because of the accidents and they were all over the news. I wonder if that has something to do with it." Nigel gestured as he checked his phone.

Susan leaned forward, intrigued. "But we weren't there when the other incidents happened."

"I have a suspicion there is a connection between us immortals," Nigel suggested in a low voice. " We can look through pictures and see if anyone has similar markings."

"What scars?" Tom asked but nodded as he got out his phone. He made the most of the task. "It's something to keep us busy."

Each with a phone out, the group started sifting through the media coverage frame by frame. Nigel sat up straight and exclaimed, "Guv! Look at this!"

He pulled up the harbor rescue of the little girl; Jean was there as well as Nigel and their scars were visible to the camera lens. He went on to display the New Orleans crash footage with the vehicle behind Taylor and Nick. There was an old-time billboard featuring Susan's movie, still very much intact even though it had been faded over time by the sun.

"You were there... in a way!" Nigel pointed out. Then he looked at the footage of the fire-rescue by the harbor. Behind them was an old Olympics banner with Hunter on it. The state still boasted it had a local Olympian. There were other banners paying homage to other local athletes too.

Nigel tapped a finger on the screen. "He's harder to see but I think if we blew it up we could make out a scar." He pointed to a media storm behind the restaurant where Susan had taken promotional pictures. "I guess Susan and Tom were there the day we rescued the mayor."

"That was the same day?" Tom pushed his glasses up straining to look at each detail.

"Well, I'll be..." Susan whispered. "That was going on and we never saw the smoke or any of the fuss."

Nigel clicked his phone and expanded the display to reveal an image of a small woman with a delicate frame and light blonde hair. Chris narrowed their eyes at her and instantly compared her with Jean. They decided the woman on the phone couldn't touch their crush for Jean.

Nigel shook his head but continued on. "She's that dancer. I remember her from years ago because she was a shooting star... then gone." He met their eyes. "I don't remember her name."

Nigel seemed to love having their full attention. "Now..." He zoomed in on a clip of Taylor's rescue at the WTC and spotted a petite woman sporting sweats. She had her hair tied up behind her head and when he focused further, he noticed the scar on the back of her neck, a knife mark...

Chris shivered when Nigel announced triumphantly, "Another immortal!"

Jean cocked her head at the phone. "I think I remember her."

Nigel waved at her. "Hold onto your knickers we'll get to that." He searched for footage of Persephone's funeral and found one of the employees there who looked very familiar.

When he zoomed in on the man's arm, a lightning bolt scar became visible. "Who is this bloke?"

Susan tilted her head. "He looks like an athlete. Maybe Hunter knows him?"

"He could be another one of us." Nigel nodded. "Point made? In some way it shows who the other immortals are." He took a deep breath . "Each rescue seems to have an immortal lurking in the background." With his idea put forward, Nigel pulled his phone back.

Susan gave a nod. "We need to be more vigilant." She yawned and leaned on her husband. Chris took in the way she looked. Even though it was still early, it was obvious she was ready for bed.

Tom rubbed his wife's arm and looked at their companions. "How much longer do you think we'll be out?"

Nigel yawned. "We're in no rush to sleep, sir. It's when we sleep that bad things happen."

Susan fixed her gaze ahead and blinked away the tiredness.

Jean nodded. "I go all night if I can."

Glancing at the group before meeting Tom's eyes, Susan admitted, "I don't like those nightmares." Her voice was hollow and soft like an echo. She stared at the gleaming tiled floor of the hospital.

Chris took a deep breath, a little concerned after listening to Nigel. Sure much more was happening than they were aware of, Chris worried for Jordan and Taylor. The nightmares were sure to be blood-curdling, yet far worse was the dread filling Chris at the thought that Deacon might go after Chris's siblings. So many people had perished without explanation. Would Jordan and Tay become similar casualties of the deal?

"I'm going back..." Chris picked up their pace to catch up to Hunter and Nick who waited in the hall and leaned on the wall opposite Jordan's room with their eyes trained on the door. Chris smiled seeing the protective nature of the two and cocked their head to the side.

"I'll stay out here in case I'm needed," Nick mumbled.

Chris led the way in slowly and Hunter nodded before venturing further inside. To Chris's shock, a commotion was ongoing in the room. Taylor and Jordan gathered their belongings.

"Are we leaving?" Hunter asked, antsy to go.

Taylor inclined her head at Jordan. "They're taking Jordan to another room. He's not allowed visitors up there at night."

Chris couldn't hide their concern. "If you need anything, text or call us. If none of us answer, then keep calling the landline until someone does."

Jordan snorted. His gaze shifted to a group of people at the door who were trying to get past Hunter. "That's Morgan and his parents," he called out. They had bottles of juice and water as well as a large bag of snacks.

Tay popped her gum, looking at them with a blank expression. "The nurse said family only. So how did you get back here?"

Jordan pushed Tay slightly. "They brought me in, so they were my adult contacts."

Taylor shrugged and pouted a bit. "I'm an adult."

Morgan's mother, a glamorous blonde with porcelain skin, gave her a diplomatic smile. "We tried to call your family, but the cell service is terrible out here." She checked her watch, "We were going to try again on the landline now we're back with Jordan." She smiled at Morgan affectionately, "He was so insistent about getting all this extra food from the cafeteria because they couldn't read our texts." Her tall, athletic, dark-skinned husband held up the bag as if in proof of her words.

Chris noticed Hunter and Nick's glances at Morgan and his parents. At first it felt like they were spying to keep an eye on

Jordan and Tay but it was a look of curiosity more than protec-tiveness. Watching the two crane their necks to see the family better almost released a chuckle in Chris's throat. Morgan was a stunning sight with his good looks clearly coming from a perfect blend of his parents. Jordan's best friend had skin an even toffee color, which shone healthily. His eyes were light brown and hair a few shades lighter than his dad's. While his facial structure resembled his mother, Morgan had a body shape to mirror that of his father.

They glanced at Hunter curiously as if they felt the weight of the stares. Morgan's parents shrugged off the other man's curiosity and smiled warmly at Jordan.

"We brought you something to drink…" Morgan's mother said and handed him his backpack.

Tay loudly blew her bubble gum before declaring, "Get well soon, Jordan." She marched out the room without a backward glance.

Chris smiled knowingly. This kind of behavior wasn't strange to Morgan and his family.

"It smells like sick people and medicine…" Taylor whined to Hunter, just loud enough for Chris to hear.

Nick gave her a quick shake of his head and directed her to the waiting area. Hunter followed, his hands buried deep in his pockets as he shuffled out and Chris brought up the rear of their procession into the hall.

Tay fell back and looped her arm through Hunter's. When she leaned her head on his shoulder, Chris heard her ask, "What's wrong?"

Chris watched Taylor leech on Hunter's arm and sighed. She seemed determined to be as close to the former athlete as she could.

"That…" He nodded towards the room Jordan was in. "That'll keep happening."

Tay tilted her head in thought. "What happened?"

Chris raised their head catching on quickly and raised a brow. "People keep getting hurt, Taylor."

She smiled. "Nah, lots of people get sick or hurt all the time. This can't have anything to do with..."

A smile tugged at the corners of Hunter's mouth. Everyone seemed to love Tay's caferee nature. Hunter stared down at the choke hold she had on his arm. "Tay, you remember I should really look fifty, right?"

Confused, she asked, "So?"

Chris and Nick hastened their steps to give Tay and Hunter some privacy or else avoid a meltdown. Before long everyone else was filled in on the situation as Tay and Hunter lagged behind. With each step the two lovebirds took it seemed like another conversation passed between them.

"So, will your brother be okay?" Susan asked quietly even as she continued to stare at Tay and Hunter.

Chris nodded. "Jo gets this all the time. He just wasn't prepared and it went too far."

Nigel's eyes bounced from Chris to Susan, as if he watched a tennis match, before he cleared his throat. "We have news but should we wait until they catch up?"

Jean looked at Chris. "You look too tired to drive. Any of us can drive the van home."

Chrisrealized she referred to their home as hers and before they could ask about it she blushed as if realizing her mistake. All the immortals wanted were roots and family.

Gulping in air, Chris tried to act like they weren't exhausted. Despite their fatigue, there were a lot of other considerations to keep them occupied. Chris always felt a warmth from Jean's friendliness, though it seemed to cross the line into flirtation sometimes.

When Hunter and Tay joined the group, both were holding

hands. They moved slowly, speaking in whispers Chris couldn't make out.

Nigel took a hard breath and glared at them. "If you're done acting out a script from General Hospital, can we go?"

Chris thought Nigel seemed moody at the idea of Tay and Hunter still remaining a couple.

"Bite me, Brit," Taylor scoffed and narrowed her eyes. "Where's your green card?"

Nick chuckled, "Let's go."

Tom slouched in his chair, his head tipped to one side and Chris heard him snore lightly. Nudging him on the shoulder, Chris gestured to the exit when Tom startled awake.

They left the waiting room, still bustling despite the late hour. The harsh ER lights contrasted to the darkness that washed over the group and they all blinked away the moment of blindness.

In the darker atmosphere a set of flood lights drew the eye to a tall statue made of rocks. Each carefully placed stone seemed to accentuate the large, flat rock at the base that displayed a decorative gold plaque. The beautiful landscaping around the stone structure made it enticing – sight to behold.

Taylor moved towards it, entranced. She seemed elated, practically dancing in the open space around the statue. As Chris watched, she glanced back at them and grinned. Still worried Taylor's personality attracted trouble, Chris wondered at how she didn't seem to acknowledge how serious the situation was. Keeping an eye on Tay as she wandered off, Chris stayed with the group. Chris rolled their eyes when Taylor pulled out her phone and started posing with the statue behind her.

Nick leaned over to whisper in Hunter's ear and mumbled loudly enough for Chris to hear, "I love that kid like a sister, so you best not hurt Tay."

Hunter nodded, offense clouding his expression, and glanced back at Chris. "Never."

Chris hid a smile behind a hand listening to them. Even though Chris felt uncertain about the age difference, they felt secure about Hunter and didn't doubt him. Still, Taylor was an adult and Chris wasn't responsible for her. All Chris could do was worry about her possibly crying on their shoulder later.

Hunter pursed his lips together and admitted, "Every time I see her, my pulse quickens like I'm about to start a race. Don't worry, it's all good." Nick gave a nod and pulled ahead of them to catch up with Jean who was nearing the statue.

Chris couldn't help but smile at the ridiculous expression on Hunter's face as they strolled on toward the parking area

Taylor called exuberantly, "Selfies!" and beckoned Hunter to join her.

Watching Tay making silly faces while she leaned on the large flat rock was pretty normal to Chris. They crossed their arms, waiting for her to finish, and feeling like the responsible, older sibling.

Hunter hadn't taken more than two steps when a thunderous crack echoed and Chris watched in horror as the rock at the top of the sculpture teetered. A scream lodged in Chris's throat. Not a sound came out even as they tried to warn her, to get her out of harm's way.

All alone, Tay stood at the base of the structure, oblivious to the danger. More rocks moved and the whole statue tumbled toward the ground.

Without hesitation, Nick leapt onto her, stones raining down around the two of them. Taylor screamed and a moment later the rumbling rocks hit the floodlights. All went dark. Silence settled over the scene obscured by shadows and a thick cloud of dust.

"Tay!" Hunter screamed and raced to the jumble of fallen

rocks. Chris raced to Hunter's side while the former athlete threw huge boulders to the side, looking for signs of life under the rubble. The others arrived to help as well, but no one matched Hunter's frantic look as he dug for Taylor.

Chris saw something soft and pale peek out from under a shelf of stone. Taylor's hand!

They felt dampness against their arm and looked up to see tears course down Hunter's cheeks. The former Olympian made no effort to brush away the tears; his focus inspired the others to follow his lead.

The fingers on the ground twitched and Chris remembered to breathe. Hunter didn't stop digging though, calling Taylor's name over and over again. It wrenched Chris's heart to hear him. Hunter had already lost so much, Chris's chest squeezed over the thought of losing their sister.

"Tay?" Hunter almost begged.

A rock Hunter liberated and sent crashing down to one side sailed toward Tom, who leaped out of the way in time.

Susan pulled Tom back. "We're in the way..."

With a nod, Tom moved aside just as Hunter uncovered Nick's crumpled body. Jean gasped and Tom shook off Susan's hand to run forward and help get Nick out.

Nick's eyes flew open and he nodded at Taylor who lay sprawled beneath him. "I think I'm crushing her."

Hunter seized Nick's hand and pulled him up. Taylor lay curled in the space Nick had vacated. Nick was set free and Hunter pulled Tay from the rubble, but she lay motionless, her phone held close to her chest and her eyes shut tight.

"Tay?" Hunter cupped her face. "Open your eyes, baby."

Susan and Jean checked Nick but Chris ignored their fussing and focused on Tay. She couldn't be gone. She just... couldn't. Hunter's voice trembled in a plea for her to answer, making Chris fear the worst.

"Tay?" Chris sank down beside Hunter, fear stealing their strength. "Is she breathing? Can you feel her heart beating?" Chris reached for Tay's hand. Tears welled up and blurred the sight of Tay's prone body. Chris bit their lip, fighting the tears with hope. Maybe she could still live. They were at the hospital. Chris wanted to call for help, but their voice refused.

Hunter caressed her face and interlocked his fingers with hers. "Tay? Wake up baby..." He leaned down to her and kissed her cheek softly. His lip shook and his wide eyes were hyper focused on her face, waiting for any sign of life. He touched her throat, looking for a pulse, and put his head close to her body.

Something pulled Chris's attention to Taylor's face and they watched her eyes flutter. Her lips parted and air expanded her chest. It fell, rose then fell again. She coughed and moaned as she caught her breath.

After roaming around, disoriented, Taylor's eyes found Hunter's. "Did you call me baby?"

A security guard ran out from the hospital and eyed them over. "What's going on over there?"

Hunter ignored the man and chuckled through tears. "I guess I did..." He scooped Tay up in his arms and examined her for bruises. "Please, don't scare me like that again." He scowled at all the contusions blooming on her skin.

Chris took a deep breath and then shook their head in disbelief. Everything happened so fast. They locked eyes with the guard. "This statue collapsed."

More people craned their necks and looked out the hospital's glass walls. Chris was keen to avoid curious onlookers and feared the situation would not end well if hospital involvement was required. The helpless feeling of having no control over what happened next made Chris clench their hands.

Tom offered to help Taylor, but she refused to leave Hunter's embrace. "Don't let go, okay?" She bit her lip.

Chris considered how petrified she looked and touched her arm gently. "Tay...?"Chris swallowed hard. "Did you hurt anything?"

She scoffed as if she had come off a rollercoaster instead of living through a near death experience. "I'm fine. I just want to get home." She kept her eyes on Hunter.

Eyes drawn wide, Chris looked around and noticed hospital staff approaching with a wheelchair. Taylor's eyes fell on the white-clad newcomers and looked like she wanted to run.

"I don't want to be alone right now, please," she pleaded and gripped Hunter tighter.

He lifted her in his arms and cradled her to him, keeping his worried gaze on her face.

Chris saw her wince and gestured for Hunter to give her up. "You're hurt, Tay. They'll need to check you."

Although the ER staff wanted to take Taylor away in the chair, Chris smiled to see their friends refuse to leave her side. Her friends. Chris relaxed, watching the others with Tay.

Like Chris, Taylor never had many romances or close friends. She had a few friends, but never anyone who would jump in to save her from being crushed by rocks. Watching Hunter's hand on Taylor's and the way they looked at each other meant everything. Hunter had saved her from lightning, and dug her out of the rubble in record time. Nick had saved her twice, too. Despite all the bad luck, these new friends made Chris's heart swell. For what it was worth, they felt extremely lucky.

"It's just policy," the nurse explained sternly.

Tom pushed his glasses up by the bridge and indicated to the number of people around them now. It was getting light out and the traffic in the ER began to increase. "Let's..." He cleared his throat. "Elsewhere?"

Susan stayed close to Tom and kept her head down. Chris wondered why until they remembered Susan had an unmistakably famous face. Tom too for that matter.

Nick ducked under his hoodie and signaled for the rest of the group to do the same.

Although Jean whispered, "Nobody knows me," she still tried to blend in with the crowd.

CHAPTER 25

On the way back home, the group had much to discuss. Chris listened but, unlike the rest,, Chris and Tay fought to stay awake on the ride. Chris attributed the others' wakefulness to the fact the nightmares gave them insomnia. Or was it because they had not slept the night before?

Taylor had been so determined to be discharged from the hospital that Chris figured the staff must've been ready for her to go. She was adamant about leaving despite all the tests they wanted to run on her. Eventually, she convinced them by pledging to come back immediately if any symptoms presented themselves. They found nothing wrong and readily agreed.

"So, Deacon's got her in his sights, huh?" Susan pondered. "What about Tom? And your brother at the hospital, Chris?"

Nick nodded. "We need to figure this out soon, or more people are going to die."

"Not my husband!" Susan exclaimed so loudly Chris thought she might wake the dead.

Jean drove but it was clear she was listening as she offered small nods when her name was mentioned. Nick kept half an eye on Taylor, his gaze preoccupied, and Nigel still looked like a cat that ate a canary.

Suddenly, Jean stopped the van and held a faraway look as she stared out the window. They should have been pulling up the driveway right about then, but she stopped on the street to stare blankly ahead.

Chris had their phone out to open the gates but paused, watching Jean.

"What is it?" Nick asked worriedly and jumped out of his seat to peek ahead.

"Uh oh," Jean murmured.

"What now?" Susan sighed in exasperation.

"We're home and there's someone waiting for us," Jean nodded and pointed at a person standing by the gate to the house.

Nigel squinted at the short woman. "This early? She's barking mad to be here waiting for us!"

Chris peered at the figure and recognized a ballerina they'd seen in pictures. She was very pretty, her hair piled on top of her head with strands framing her face. She wore jeans that hung loosely off her frame and a cami tucked into them paired with a shrug tucked around her arms. It was clear she knew how to dress for Baltimore's precocious weather, and that did impress Chris.

Tom stirred, opening his eyes from his sleepy state and looking around. Tom grasped Susan's hand in his and planted a kiss on it.

Taylor intertwined her fingers with Hunter's as the alluring dancer came into view. Tay narrowed her eyes at the other girl as they approached.

"What does she want?" Nick groaned.

Taylor scoffed at the petite girl who looked about her age. "By the look of it? Boobs."

Chris sighed, "Tay... don't be mean."

Hunter laughed softly, still holding onto Taylor's hand before lifting their interlocked digits up to show their bond. "Remember? These stay together."

Nigel pretended to vomit. "Just go get hitched already."

Hunter rolled his eyes as the van crept forward and Chris opened the gates to let them inside.

Nick watched the ballerina trail behind them. "Looks like she's coming inside

too."

Chris took a hard breath and debated whether it was really fine to let another stranger in after everything that had happened with Marie. The voodoo woman had been rude but seemed fine... at first. Now they knew she was capable of anything. Chris squinted into the morning light, trying to keep an eye on the newcomer.

"Do you think it's safe?" Jean asked when she came to a stop.

"Safe from what?" asked the girl, peering in through the window.

Nick chuckled and stepped out of the vehicle, followed by the rest. Hunter held on to Taylor to help keep her steady.

The young woman rocked from toes to heels and put her hands on her hips. "So you're the immortals?" She studied each of them carefully. "Most of you are famous."

Taylor scoffed. "They're all famous."

The girl turned to Taylor and said firmly, "No, you're not!" She moved toward Hunter and remarked, "But he is. You're an athlete like me."

Hunter turned, flustered at the sudden attention. He looked to Taylor, as if seeking her approval to speak to this girl, as the dancer locked eyes with him. "Yeah, I was. I was in the Olympics."

The newcomer stepped forward and thrust her hand out in front of Hunter. "I'm Olivia Kempt. I was a dancer," she said before Taylor shoved Olivia's hand away from Hunter. She scoffed loudly at Taylor. Turning toward the rest of them, she gave a dazzling smile. "Most of you are actors?"

Nick nodded and pulled out a cigarette. "I'm a musician. And I need a smoke."

Jean jumped up to stop him. "Nobody is alone now!"

Olivia stared at them wide-eyed. "You have nightmares too? Is that why you can't be alone?"

Nick watched despondently as he moved to exit the room. "Pretty much," he muttered under his breath. Jean stood with crossed arms in the doorway and shook her head at Nick. Her eyes narrowed at him but relaxed when he moved back to the rest of the group.

Chris shifted their weight from foot to foot but relaxed and stifled a smile at the silent debate between Jean and Nick. Olivia glared at Jean, and Chris swallowed. This was trouble.

"You're the rockstar, aren't you?" Olivia asked Nick with a grin.

"Not anymore." Nick mumbled and avoided her gaze.

She laughed heartily. "Cool! I'm not my daughter! I had to pretend to be my own child so I could go back to work," Olivia revealed.

Nick bobbed his head. "You must be about forty then?"

She rolled her eyes. "Try fifty-five! I know I look like a teen; I made the deal when I was eighteen."

Nigel sighed. "All these daft younglings tossing their lives away," he waved his hand at her. "You're still a child compared to the rest of us." He looked at Nick, "especially him."

Nick nodded and shifted closer to Jean. "I am old enough to be a grandfather."

Olivia eyed Hunter and Nick appreciatively. "But you're not."

Tay held up a hand and jumped to Nick's defense. "Don't come into my house to flirt with my friends or my boyfriend!" She took a step toward Olivia, but Hunter stopped her.

"Tay, if you do that, it'll make this worse," Hunter advised her. Lowering his voice, he added, "You're only going to get hurt again."

"Wait... You've been hurt?" Olivia looked at Taylor and narrowed her eyes, weighing her worth. "Do your injuries take a long time to heal?"

Hunter shrugged, "Taylor isn't immortal."

Olivia nodded. "I had a regular boyfriend when I first made the deal, but he died..."

"Did you kill him with that rapier's wit?" Tay cocked her head and crossed her arms at Olivia.

Nigel screeched like a cat and imitated claws scraping against something. "Cat fight!" he exclaimed, his gaze trained on the two young women as if relishing the entertainment.

Jean wrinkled her nose in disapproval. "What are you thinking?"

Olivia replied sarcastically, "Well, I'm sure you know Regulars die quickly. I'll let this one run its course." She waved a dismissive hand at Taylor.

"Like die?" Hunter knitted his brow. "That's just wrong, and even if something happened to Tay, I still wouldn't have anything to do with you." He shook his head. "I've been alone since the deal... It took Taylor to..." His voice trailed off before he muttered, "Yeah, no." He glared at Olivia. "Don't you come near Taylor."

Chris stood closer to Taylor and Hunter feeling a little worried about this new person. Olivia gave Taylor a challenging look, but continued to smile at Hunter between glances.

Olivia pulled her knapsack off her back and drew out a knife. "And I'm immortal."

Hunter gaped at Olivia. "I'm not going to fight you. You're a girl."

Taylor shook her head frantically. "Hunter, no!"

Chris moved closer, a scowl dominating their usually soft features.

Olivia laughed, but suddenly Jean snagged her from behind by the hair. The dancer twisted and when Olivia broke free, she stood face to face with Jean, eyes ablaze with anger.

"I'm a girl and I'm immortal. Still want to fight?" Jean stared Olivia down. "Last time I fought, I took a gunshot to the chest and healed right away. What about you?"

Olivia was at a loss for words.

"Oh..." Jean pursed her lips. "I see."

Nick caught up to the conversation and found a place next to Chris. He looked at Jean with admiration and whispered, "God, I love her."

Olivia heard Nick and snarled at him, "You have nothing to do with this."

Jean stepped closer, her voice dripping with venom as she spat out her words. "Tay is like my little sister. These people are my family, and you are messing with them. Now apologize or get out of here."

"I was going to show how fast I would heal from the knife..." Olivia lowered her eyes timidly. But then she lunged forward, slashing Jean across the face with her knife. The cut dripped blood but the injury diminished fast, leaving fresh skin and a red stain on Jean's shirt.

Taylor leapt after Olivia, but Hunter pulled her back.

Jean grabbed a tire iron from the table and asked Olivia smugly, "Okay?"

Olivia looked doubtful and confidence leached out of her when her eyes settled on Jean's healed cheek. "You're a lot bigger than I am."

"But you would fight Hunter?" Jean scoffed.

"He's hot." Olivia turned up the corner of her mouth as she glanced over her shoulder to look at Hunter. "Mr & Mrs Smith fight."

A tire flew out of nowhere and hit Olivia in the head. Stunned, the dancer crumpled to the ground. Chris turned to see Susan relax her stance and let her arms fall to her sides. With a huff, Susan said, "That's enough from the little boneyard! I'm immortal too... I just don't want to leave Tom unguarded." She turned back to her husband and smiled.

Turning their attention back to Olivia, Chris saw she was splayed on the ground, out cold.

Nick shook his head as he picked her up, and said, "Let's not be too quick to judge her. Not all of us had it easy after the deal."

Tom agreed, "I can imagine she may have been lonely and misguided."

Tay huffed, but Susan warned, "Misguided or not... if she tries to attach herself to one of you again, I'll do worse next time."

Chris shook their head at Tay. "Be nice..."

Taylor ignored Chris and wrinkled her nose. She looked from Susan to Jean, and mumbled, "An immortal battle? You can have big battles?"

"Let's get inside." Chris pulled off their shoes, tired of standing around the garage.

Taylor sighed, following Chris, and dragged Hunter by the hand. Nick kicked his shoes off and walked barefoot into the living room where he placed Olivia on the couch. Taylor kept her gaze firmly on the newcomer, as if she expected the ballerina to attack at any moment.

Tom, ever the peacemaker, looked at Olivia with sympathy, and spoke up, "Maybe we should offer her some hospitality?" Her diminutive frame was swallowed up by the couch cushions, and her expression in sleep would make even the toughest soul melt. "Why don't we give her something to eat and drink?"

Chris heard Taylor mutter under her breath, "She's probably dieting."

She looked over her shoulder and saw the others glaring at the rude comment, matching Chris's expression. Considering their friends were backing them up, Chris decided to let it go. Taylor was usually cut and dry and not very charitable with her actions or words. Chris knew Taylor was probably jealous, and hoped the others would dismiss her rudeness as well.

Tom let out a sigh and placed a hand on Taylor's arm. "Sometimes people change their behavior in different situations. Maybe if she sees that we're friendly, then she will also change how she acts."

Tom's kindness brought a smile to Chris's lips and they caught Taylor's eyes meaningfully. She dropped her gaze, and Chris was satisfied the silent reprimand had been understood. Chris sighed. Taylor was unlikely to change, even though they wished she would stop popping off without thinking when she was upset.

Jean grabbed Olivia's bag before anyone had time to object. She dug through it, then met their looks of disapproval. "I just don't feel like getting shot again, or stabbed. So, I wanted to make sure she didn't have any other weapons." She set the bag aside.

Remembering Tom's suggestion, Chris ran to the kitchen

and brought back a tray with juice and snacks. "Anybody else hungry?" Chris asked as they offered it around. With tensions high, it seemed a good idea to distract everybody. Olivia's unexpected arrival had ruined the harmony among the others.

Taylor took a glass from the tray and groaned when Hunter sat down beside her. "I'm exhausted," she said with a sigh. "Can we tie her up with zip ties so we can all get some rest?"

"Tay," Chris reprimanded. "Let's give Olivia a chance."

Nick grabbed a blanket and covered Olivia. "I agree with Tom and the kid," he said and sat down. "But if she gets violent again, I won't be so forgiving."

Chris nodded, and watched as the others grabbed cereal bars and juice.

"Maybe we should all get some sleep," Jean suggested, glancing at Taylor.

"What about Sleeping Beauty?" Nigel inquired, gesturing toward Olivia.

"We could lock her up outside or in the garage... or shed?" Taylor suggested.

"We can take turns watching her," Nick proclaimed. "I'll take the first shift."

Jean shook her head. "I'm bunking with Taylor today."

Nigel shrugged. "I hardly sleep. I'll take a shift."

"Tom's tired. I'm staying with him," Susan said with a shake of her head.

Nigel squinted past his trendy framed glasses. "Next shift it is!"

Hunter sighed and pretended not to notice Taylor's side eye at him. "I can help out."

"No," Taylor said quickly.

"I'm not going anywhere," Hunter kissed her head. "You need to rest."

Nick traded a look withNigel.. "We can each watch her for four hours."

"I could do six to eight hours," Nigel smiled.

"It looks like none of us want to sleep," Jean sighed.

"I do!" Nigel whined.

Satisfied everything was taken care of, Chris stretched and led the way upstairs, making sure everyone who'd said they'd be going to bed was following.

Once they were upstairs Hunter went with Taylor to her bedroom. Jean followed them inside. Chris sighed and also stepped into Tay's room, honor-bound to be the sane sibling.

"Nice room," Hunter commented, glancing at the bed adorned with lights spelling out Taylor's name.

Tay groaned, "It's so annoying having to go to bed at this time. It throws off my entire schedule."

Hunter settled into a chair beside the bed. "Just take a little nap now, and go to bed early tonight."

She stuck her lip out when Chris cleared their throat at the doorway. The siblings traded a look and she tossed her hands up. "Fine... Make everybody go nini!" Then she stuck her tongue out at Chris.

Chris waved at Hunter. "Come on, let me show you where you can crash."

Jean moved next to Taylor and pulled up the covers for her. "Do you need any help getting ready?"

"No, I'm just going to get some shut-eye." She winked at Hunter.

"Wake me up when you get up," Hunter threw over his shoulder when he walked out the room with Chris to meet Susan, Tom, and Nigel in the hall.

Closing the door lightly behind them, Chris pointed to a spacious bedroom along the hall, and commented, "Susan and Tom, this is our parents' room."

Susan nodded in exhaustion. "Much obliged." She opened the double doors to peek inside and looked impressed. "Why, I'll be..."

Tom pushed his glasses up the bridge of his nose. "Thank you. It's really nice."

Chris directed Hunter to another room near Taylor's. "This one has two beds so Nigel and Hunter can sleep here while Nick stays here permanently." Chris watched as Nigel stumbled into the room he had been in before, a crooked smile on his lips.

Chris gestured to the door and Hunter stepped forward to take a look. The room had a view of the garage and street; sunshine streamed in through an open window.

Hunter remarked, "Nice," He took small steps and let his bare feet sink into the plush carpet. "Yknow..." Hunter looked sheepish. "If it's about Taylor... I won't hurt her. I tried to resist her, but I'm hooked."

"You saved her life," Chris tried to say, but a yawn distorted their words.

"Seriously, I will back off if you want me to."

Chris shook their head. "You saved her life, and she's over the moon." Chris patted Hunter's back before they exited the room. "If you need anything, my room is right there." Chris indicated which door.

"I should check on Nick before I sleep," Chris added with a grin.

"Night, chum," muttered Nigel.

Chris crept down the stairs, hoping not to disturb anybody who might already be asleep. Remembering how everyone had behaved when Jordan fetched his inhaler, Chris also considered being quiet to keep people from jumping at noises. Chris could hear voices as soon as their foot hit the bottom step, and they quickly recognized that Olivia was speaking.

Olivia whispered, "They're gone now."

"You're awake?" Nick's voice skipped in surprised.

Chris crept closer and peered around the corner, half wishing Nick would fall for Olivia and straighten her out. The image of Jean came to mind, and Chris's heart skipped at the idea of her being single after all. Chris sighed. Jean had genuinely grown to care about Nick and Chris felt a twinge of sorrow at the thought of her breaking down in tears, or the very real option of her not being able to love Chris back.

"You know, I didn't recognize you at first," Olivia rose and sat on the piano bench beside Nick. "If you play classical music, I'll dance for you."

Chris sighed and leaned against the wall watching and waiting to see how this would unfold. It sounded like she was baiting Nick, and Chris could only stare from the dark. Should they step in and stop this... whatever it was? Or would it better to keep waiting and see.

Nick shrugged, "I'm not that good on piano. I was in a rock band."

Chris tried not to laugh. Nick was amazing on the piano. Had it only been two days ago that Nick had proved it on the very same piano? Chris smiled at the memory of the wonderful music they'd woken to.

Their smile widened when they saw Nick hadn't taken the bait. The former rockstar displayed zero interest in Olivia.

The rightness of that settled in Chris's stomach even though a twinge of disappointment surfaced. Chris's intuition said Olivia wasn't trustworthy... not at all.

"Then I'll keep you company." Olivia put her hand on Nick's thigh and smiled, oblivious to everything Chris could tell from Nick's stand-offish behavior.

Nick's eyes moved to her hand as she glided it further up his thigh. He jumped back and hit the piano hard enough to bring forth discordant notes.

"Whoa!" He exclaimed scooting away from Olivia. "Listen, kid, I'm not interested."

"I'm not a kid," she challenged him as he stood and tried to move away. Olivia countered each of his steps with her own, and seemed unconvinced. "You may appear older than me, but I'd bet my life that I have more energy than you do. So why run?"

Chris shifted closer but was careful to stay out of sight. They watched intently, debating if they should try to let the two in the room know Chris could hear them, or if it would be better to let Nick handle this battle.

"Look, you threatened Jean, and I'm not good with that... and you look 15. I'm not cool with that either," Nick stopped, and Olivia nearly collided with him. "Stop, or I'll figure out where the ties are."

Olivia's smile was rather forced. "Alright then, let's do something fun to kill the time."

"Depends on what your idea of fun is," Nick replied hesitantly and crossed his arms.

"Well... That weird guy left the cool book over there." She pointed at the coffee table.

Chris's eyes shot open seeing Nigel's sacred tome just lying around. How had he left it behind?

Nick followed the line of her outstretched finger. "Nigel

must have been really tired."

"It's early," Olivia pointed out.

"Yeah. We were up all night," Nick said before approaching the book. Nick picked it up and turned it over in his hands.

"I'm actually here because of the book," Olivia admitted. "I saw him carrying it on the news and thought it might help me figure this out." When Nick didn't seem too keen on her proposal, she sighed heavily. "Unless you'd rather kiss me?"

"I wanted to get my hands on this book, but he never lets us go near it." Nick said simply, and ignored her flirting.

Chris smiled, Nick had once again proved what a great guy he was. With a quiet yawn, they settled back on the stair. Olivia was persistent and maybe Nick would wear down and give her a chance. The thought was unlikely but Chris could still hold out hope. Then again, Olivia didn't sound like she deserved someone like Nick.

Shifting to see better, Chris watched Nick open the book, and slowly turn a page.

Olivia scurried next to him. "It was my idea," she said proudly.

Nick had wrinkled his brow. "It's pretty weird."

Olivia nodded. "It gives me a creepy vibe, but I have to read it."

Nick inhaled sharply. He rolled the tome until it closed and placed his hand on the book's cover. "I feel like I'm touching something that's plugged in... it's fuzzy... like it's electric."

Reconsidering the situation, Chris crouched down, thinking it might be the right time to make their presence known without being too obvious about having been eavesdropping up to this point.

Olivia put her hand on the book too, and jumped back in surprise. "Why does it feel like that?"

Nick flipped through the pages as if the answer would be

found in the book. "No clue..." He set it down on the table and sank to the floor beside it. "I should get Jean."

"Ah," Olivia giggled, "You're pretty whipped by her, huh?" The young woman tried to take the book, but Nick jerked it back.

Chris rolled their eyes at how shallow Olivia seemed to be, and made a face. This was fun. Nobody was looking and that made Chris feel at ease. Was this how Tay felt?

Chris realized they could see Nick and Olivia even better if they looked in the mirror. The two were sitting in the light from the window whereas Chris sat in the shadows by the stairs.

Nick let out a deep sigh. "This is a strange book," he muttered so low Chris could hardly make out the words. "It's like one big story without any breaks."

Olivia peered over his shoulder as he turned each page, her eyes darting back and forth across the text. Suddenly, she grabbed Nick's hand and he jumped in surprise. "Did you see that?" Olivia whispered urgently.

Nick shook his head, confused. "See what?"

"The words," Olivia replied, shakily. "They're moving."

Nick stared at the page for a moment longer. Nick stared at it with his mouth agape. "What the..."

Chris was on their feet trying to see but didn't interrupt, for fear of breaking some enchantment.

"It must be our eyes," Nick said, taking a deep breath. "Like when you'd get those 3D cups in the '80s with the moving pictures?" he reasoned.

"Sure, you believe in immortal beings but not magic?" Olivia gave a small giggle.

"Baby steps, you know?" Nick affirmed. He inhaled deeply. "I just need to get used to everything."

"Okay, let's read faster and not be afraid of the book." The corners of her mouth turned up in a faint smirk.

Nick cleared his throat and turned the page. "It doesn't make any sense."

The book glowed with dazzling light and Chris watched, mouth open slightly, as the letters rose to hover above its pages. Words formed one by one. The shining text emitted a misty vapor. The steam curled from every letter.

"I make perfect sense!" it declared.

Chris stumbled back in shock and fell back on the stairs and had to catch themself on the railing. They hadn't even noticed how they got to their feet and were drawn closer by the strange things happening in the other room. The book was bright – so bright now that Chris didn't even need to strain their eyes.

Olivia tripped over the rug while Nick shot up from the ground. "Did you hear that?" Her eyes were locked on the ancient book. "So is it supernatural or is it alive?" she asked and dropped to her knees to observe the shimmering pages.

"We should probably get the others," Nick suggested.

Chris started to make themself known, but Olivia made a noise in her throat, and Chris stopped in their tracks.

"No!" Olivia stared at the papers and exclaimed, "Look!"

Nick gazed at the volume, which glowed with a dimmer, eerie light. Inhaling deeply, Nick agreed, "Okay, so I knew this book was creepy but..."

Mesmerized, Chris stared at the words hovering above the book like a 3D hologram. When the book started reading them out loud in its signature voice, Chris swallowed hard. It was hard to remember they were supposed to be hiding when the book did this.

Olivia stared in fascination as the book told its own story. "It seems to know what we're looking for," she rasped.

Nick nodded, repeating, "All agreements are binding once they have been made. If any aspect of the deal is not respected, punishment becomes imminent."

Olivia sighed, "That's not what I was looking for."

"It's what I was," Nick looked at the book, but before he could reach out to grab it Olivia did.

"Then it's my turn," she spoke arrogantly. "Besides, we can't break these deals." She flipped the page and the book stopped glowing. The words dissipated.

"Did you break it?" Nick asked, eyeing her suspiciously.

"I think the book has to reset, like a web page," she laughed.

Nick nervously chuckled, "Yeah, like that."

Chris felt a pang of sympathy for Nick. Computers were quite foreign to him. Technology had advanced rapidly around him while he was homeless, and Chris had seen now Nick struggled just to keep up with the cell phones.

"You don't know what I'm talking about, do you?" Olivia turned a page, but nothing happened and sighed dejectedly.

"What are you trying to find?" Nick asked, eyeing the pages she was flipping through.

She turned the next page and let a breath go. "It's clear we exist, which means other things must too. I think this book is some kind of magic or something else I'd like to know more about. I heard there was a woman who made a deal like ours."

"You made the same deal? With the guy with the cane?"

She gave a single nod. "Duh. He took all I had, and I was grateful to be living with my folks, who were already incredibly wealthy. They were my agents. In return, they looked after me for a long time. Now my lifestyle is comfortable, but there are times when I cannot work. I've already had to fake my identity once to become my own daughter. I won't be able to keep this round up for long, so I am going to need some help."

Her lips curled into a smile as she glanced at Nick. "I'm sure you know what it's like, being out there on the streets." She emphasized the word 'there' tauntingly, and raised an eyebrow with a wicked gleam in her eye.

"Okay, it's obvious you know I was homeless." Nick showed a hint of frustration with this bratty woman.

"I suspected as much," she replied coolly. "Unlike Susan, the movie star, I don't have a sugar momma taking care of me, so I need to find something."

"So, now you want to be like Marie?" Nick shook his head in disbelief

Chris sighed. The more they saw of Olivia, the more they realized she acted like Marie: cocky and vain.

Olivia smiled, looking pleased with the information she'd managed to extract. "Marie?" She kept turning pages.

Nick slammed the book shut, just barely missing Olivia's fingers. "Marie is not a nice person, and she's dangerous. Is that what you want to be?" His voice was low and serious as he looked at the dancer.

Chris groaned at the idea of two people like Marie running around. Olivia only seemed to care about herself, like the voodoo queen did. Marie's beautiful face was a farce and her vile nature had proven to be something to contend with.

Olivia turned to Nick with her eyes narrowing. "What I want is to maintain my lifestyle. I'm not here to stay cooped up in some superhero's lair. If you, Hunter, or even that snack... Tom wants to come home with me later, then that's fine." She reached her hand to run a finger over Nick's face but he batted it away.

Chris tried not to laugh. Clasping a hand over their mouth, they muffled the sound enough so Nick and Olivia didn't hear anything.

"I'm with Jean," Nick said tersely.

"Oh yeah, the fat lady? She cleans up nicely, but underneath all that... she's still just a fat lady."

Olivia opened the book again, but he slammed it shut fast.

"Jean has grown from who she was." He shook his head in disapproval. "Marie is evil. Is that how you want to be?"

Olivia brushed a tendril of hair from her face. "No, I won't be evil. I'm cleverer than that. I do want the answers." She opened the book again.

Chris had to stifle a laugh when Olivia declared she wouldn't be evil. She'd been nothing but impolite, and concerned only with her own welfare the entire time. It was difficult to envision someone so egocentric doing anything good for anyone else.

"Look, I think Marie made a different deal. She was sent here to deliver a message earlier... To put it mildly, it wasn't very nice." Nick held Olivia's gaze and added, "Think about it carefully before you make your own decision. Just like with the deal we all made, there are a lot of things you find out after."

Olivia paused as if to consider the possibility of Nick's suggestion. "I'd like to meet this Marie for myself and make my own judgment," she said simply.

Nick gave her a disbelieving glance and arched his brow sarcastically. "Go to New Orleans, then. That's where she is. We found her at her Cafe. I didn't see information on her in the book."

"Was that so difficult?" Olivia cooed. "So, I guess that's where I'm heading to, then."

"You're not gonna help out?" He looked let down.

"To be a media freak? How long until the press turns against you? It always does." She scoffed and glanced at her watch, before taking out her phone.

"What are you doing?"

"This... is a smart phone." She said, as if speaking to a

toddler, and gestured toward the device. "It's like a palm sized computer, and with it, I'm buying plane tickets go see this Marie lady." She pouted as she looked at her phone display. "But I have to wait a few more hours."

Turning to Nick, she asked, "Want to give me a lift to the airport?"

He closed his book and rose from his seat. "No," he said firmly.

"Guess it's a taxi or Uber," she replied, and promptly resumed tapping on her phone.

Nick sighed but Chris was proud. Nick had risen to the challenge and Chris was immensely satisfied that they had provided this good person with another opportunity to prove himself.

Olivia flashed Nick a small smile. "What shall we do until my ride arrives?" She took out lip gloss from her bag and applied it with an even bigger smile.

"Forget it," Nick scoffed loudly. "Maybe you're trying to get with the wrong people? If you pick someone who likes you back, you won't be alone."

She rolled her eyes. "I did. They died." She paused and watched his response. "I guess you haven't tried to hook up yet." She muttered, putting her lip gloss away.

"Died? I thought you were younger than that."

She shook her head. "You think they died of old age?" She shook her head. "I know you're not new to this deal but you act oblivious." She tossed her bag on her back. "Each one of them died due to accidents and sudden illnesses." With that, Olivia adjusted her bag on her back.

"Are you saying that any non-immortal will die quickly if they're with an immortal?"

"Wow!" She said, her voice dripping with sarcasm. The expression on her face became more serious. "One had a heart attack at thirty, another suffered from cancer in his twenties, one died in a car accident, another perished due to a house fire – he was the only one inside – and yet another person was struck by a bus..." Her gaze shifted elsewhere. "That list is just part of it."

Nick stared at her with empathetic eyes. "No wonder you're so angry."

"I thought you knew this already because you kept rescuing that girl," she sneered.

"We thought it was because we were saving people, or because she knows about the deal. He shook his head. "I don't think you're right."

She rolled her eyes. "Sure."

"How old are you?" Nick wrinkled his brow.

"About your age," she replied while tapping away at her phone. "My Uber will arrive shortly." Olivia stood tall and poised with perfect dancer posture, placing her hands on her hips. "You have two choices: let me out or I'll set off the alarms."

It was time for Chris to reveal they had been there. Chris coughed loudly to alert them, and stepped out of the shadows as they pulled out their phone. "I'll let you out."

She twirled around and gave a quick nod. "Thanks."

"You're a piece of work," Nick complained. "The kid didn't have to be that polite to you, but you got what you wanted and you're running. You're still fresh as paint."

Olivia turned and chuckled. "Paint? Geez, you're still living in the '70s and '80s! Nobody talks like that anymore." She tilted her head to the side, looking like she would laugh.

Chris was already on the phone and deactivated the alarm. Just in time to watch Olivia skip out of the door, right as a car pulled up outside.

"Gotta say, I'm not gonna miss her," Nick muttered. He

glanced at Chris, who stared at their cellphone as they re-entered the alarm codes.

"So what did you hear?" Nick asked, pushing his hands into his pockets.

"Everything? I came down to see if you wanted anything, but at first it seemed like a personal conversation," Chris said with a shrug. "Then all that weirdness happened and she was leaving and I didn't really need to say goodbye, but letting her wake everyone..." Chris tucked away their phone.

"You heard about all her exes dying suddenly?"

Chris nodded gravely. "And about her wanting to meet Marie." Chris shook their head, and the idea of Nick being gone made Chris's heart cinch. "Were you trying to break the deal, Nick? A sacrifice? You can't leave this world yet," Chris said firmly. "You have so much more to offer. Your music, your art... don't deprive us of that."

Nick chucked Chris in the shoulder. "That's really kind of you to say, but if I could find a way to make others stop suffering, then I would break the deal." He looked sheepish. "Don't get me wrong, Deacon scares the crap outta me, but if I can find a loophole I will."

"I think Jean is in love with you... " Chris admitted and considered they really had no idea about Jean's heart, but it was obvious Nick was nuts about her. Maybe it was true, or a fib, but Chris realized they would say anything to keep Nick from doing something dumb. He was their first real friend. More important than anything or anyone. "If one of you changed back into a regular person, it might complicate things," they added.

Nick followed Chris back to the living room and said, "You should check this book out..."

"I want to read it, but I'm already so tired," Chris said with another yawn. "I struggled to stay awake while Olivia kept talking."

"I'm going to stay up and check it out a little more," Nick nodded in the book's direction. "I don't feel we can trust everything Olivia said."

Chris gave him a small chin dip of acknowledgement. "You're living here now, so help yourself to whatever you need." Chris gave Nick a humble wave before moving back towards the stairs. "See you later."

CHAPTER 26

Chris and Tay were busy by the stove, and Chris looked over to the door when they heard Hunter come in. The former Olympian sniffed, eyes wide and overwhelmed from the aromas drifting from the food. Bacon, coffee, and pastries. There was more than enough to make mouths water.

Tay signaled to the countertop. "Help yourself."

Susan excitedly held a juice-filled glass aloft and exclaimed, "They have juice at the table!"

Hunter looked around. "Where are Olivia and Nigel?" He located the coffee maker and filled a cup.

"Nigel is snoozing, and Olivia..." Chris searched for the right words.

"Doesn't play or work well with others?" Hunter laughed.

"See? He knows what she's about," Nick guffawed. "She hightailed it last night."

"She's gone?" Hunter asked, his brow furrowed in confusion.

"She had a talk with Nick before she left." Chris returned to their cereal bowl, not looking up.

"What was it about?" Hunter pinned Nick with his gaze.

"She persuaded me to take a peek into Nigel's book, gave me some details about what she knows," Nick answered and shrugged, keeping his eyes on the countertop.

Hunter picked up the cup Tay passed to him, took a sip, and nodded his head. "And?" he prompted, eyes narrowed.

Jean sighed and crossed her arms, a sour look on her face. "She hit on Nick and pushed him to do things."

Hunter plopped down next to Taylor and smirked. "Snap!"

Nick looked around the room at their anxious faces. "Yeah, she did tell me something. All of her past boyfriends have been mortals; each of them died from unexpected health complications or accidents."

Chris swallowed their cereal, looked up at Taylor, and watched her gaze drift down toward the floor. Her shoulders slumped and a cloud passed over her eyes. Knowing her well, Chris recognized the signs of impending tears and felt a wave of sadness.

Hunter eyed Taylor and took in the silent convo between the siblings, which he interrupted when he asked, "How many boyfriends?"

"I have no idea how many, honestly, man. It makes me a little nervous." Nick shook his head and his face hardened in determination. "We won't let anything happen to her!"

"Do you think Olivia lied?" Chris still wasn't convinced she had told the whole truth.

To avoid eye contact with everyone at the table, they glanced down at their phone. There was no call, not even a text message from Mom or Dad.

Nick shook his head. "I don't think so. Olivia wanted information about Marie. It sounds like she wants to learn magic or something. She said since we exist and so does magic, she aims to learn how to do it like Marie."

Tay raised her eyebrows in what looked to Chris like disbelief. "So if you all exist, then so do witch academies or schools? And what about vampires and werewolves?" She smiled, but at this point she looked more unsure than anything else.

Nick shrugged his shoulders. "Something else definitely exists." He gave them all a playful grin and nodded to the living room door. "We could check the book out while Nigel is sleeping." He looked at Chris and meaningfully bobbed his head again.

Chris tried not to laugh at Nick's not too subtle hint and pushed the spoon around the cereal a little more. The chatter about magic made Chris anxious. There were unknown implications with this situation. Jordan had ended up in hospital, and people were continually passing away. Was it all witchcraft? At least Mom and Dad were out of harm's way.

Tom shook his head looking spooked once again. "I think we should stay away from that book."

Hunter looked like he was anxious to read it. "We need to get information from somewhere."

Chris swallowed their cereal. Hunter was probably right. They needed to know more and the book might provide the answers. Chris was eager to get a look at it without Nigel snatching it away.

Taylor slouched in her seat, her face grim. "So, now I know that if I'm with Hunter I'll die?"

Susan sighed and patted her hand. "It doesn't matter. Deacon's already after you."

Chris rolled their eyes and scoffed at Susan's comment. "That's not very encouraging." They pivoted toward the others. "Maybe we should take a look at the book. We need some kind of guide. Nick is the only one who has really seen it so far, and maybe if all of us examine it, then things might make more sense."

Tay still seemed in a funk about Hunter, but he clasped her hand in his.

Jean got to her feet and murmured, "It beats sitting around."

Nick stood up next to her.

A sound from the hallway drew everyone's attention and a moment later Nigel stepped into view. His eyes settled on their grim faces and the few already standing and asked, "What did I walk into?" His sleepy curiosity turned into a glare. "Where's the book?" His gaze darted around, looking for the well-loved volume.

Worry transformed into a sharper glare and Nigel reiterated, "Where is it?"

Jean stood her ground. "It doesn't belong to you. Do you have proof of purchase?"

Nigel snarled at her and stormed off to the living room.

Chris shook their head sadly as they tidied up the mess in the kitchen. "He hogs the cappuccino maker, and gets mad when he can't find something immediately."

"I'm with Jean, he never paid for that book. It's not his or ours." Nick said, watching Nigel search in the room adjacent to the kitchen.

"Guess we'll have to either go downtown or phone the store and pay for it," Chris sighed.

Jean smiled slyly. "That would mean the book won't be Nigel's."

Tay shook her head looking frustrated and ready to scream. "Don't we have enough to worry about without worrying about who owns what?"

A high pitched scream emanated from the living room and interrupted the conversation. Everyone jumped. Well, Chris noted, not everyone.

Nick turned slowly and peered into the living room. "The book was on the rug and he's freaking..."

Before Nick could finish, Nigel pushed his way in. He pointed his finger at them. "Who touched it?"

Tom paced nervously and muttered, "That book gives me the chills."

Nigel's eyes were wide as he gasped, "Someone touched it!"

Nick chuckled under his breath, "Olivia did right before she left."

Nigel scanned the room in disbelief. "She left?"

"Olivia was only seeking answers for herself, she did not want to be part of a group," Chris said quickly. They hoped to lessen Nick's humiliation from being hit on by Olivia.

"So, she violated my book?" Nigel sat down with a huff. "We're better off without Miss Thoroughbred."

Nigel sighed and looked up, picking up on everyone staring at the book. "What?"

Hunter cleared his throat. "We were talking about the book before you came in."

Nigel rolled his eyes and moved to the coffee. "Like any of you sods would understand it."

Nick took a seat next to the book. "Olivia seemed to." He ignored Nigel's icy glare. "It did some cool things I hadn't seen before," He raised a brow and went on, "She opened it to find out about Marie, and how to get another demon to take her deal..." Nick shrugged. "It looks like it's partly electronic."

Nigel rushed over with his coffee. "What did she do?" He snapped the book up in his free arm quickly. "Did it..." Nigel lowered his voice, "Speak?"

Chris cocked an eyebrow. It was clear Nigel knew much more than he had told them.

Nick shook his head. "It had some fancy floating text like a hologram as it was read."

"What did you do?!" Nigel slammed his cup of coffee onto the table, showering brown droplets in an arc onto the surface of the table.

"Fess up. You know more about this book than you're saying!" Jean shouted, barely containing her frustration. "It's clear you're hiding something from us. We're supposed to be friends here. No more games." She sucked in a deep breath and continued, "Be honest with us."

"We're not friends!" Nigel said in what could be classified as a growl. His eyes darted around to gauge the reaction of the others. "We are all working together towards a common goal. That doesn't make us BFFs. Think of us as schoolyard mates, and not even friends on social media. Trapped in the same fate. Once we achieve our goal, I doubt we will ever speak again."

"Speak for yourself," Hunter snarled at Nigel.

Nick folded his arms and looked at the others. "For me, this is my family now. I don't know about the rest of you, but I won't be leaving anytime soon unless I'm asked to."

Chris nearly scoffed at the idea. Despite being an obstacle in Chris's chances with Jean, Nick was family to them. They had a soft spot for the former rockstar.

"That's precious, but I have other plans," Nigel said, rolling his eyes as the others nodded in agreement with Nick.

Chris retrieved their phone and opened the bookstore's site. "If you're not part of our family or even a friend, then you can go. I'll buy the book so it stays with us... you know, our family." Everyone stared at Chris in surprise.

Nigel settled into his chair and sighed heavily. "I love it here but I'm so lonely," he said, taking his hands off the book in front of him. "I don't want to have close relationships with friends, because they get ripped away." He sighted, "I am fond of Jeremy, but he is mortal..."

Tom nodded. "We're not going anywhere, and we're here for

you too." Tom squeezed his shoulder reassuringly. At the gesture, Nigel's expression seemed to change, as if something had just dawned on him. Chris thought his eyes displayed a wisdom men would go to great lengths to search for, but often never attained.

"Just consider us family, like we do you," Nick nodded.

"I was in the closet with my family, so this is a bit new," Nigel breathed. "I'll try not to worry about the book so much."

"Will you tell us more about it?" Tom asked in an almost-whisper.

"It's not any ordinary book..." Nigel started. "Think of it more as an advisor. If it likes you, it will do a lot more than just let you read it."

Nick wrinkled his forehead in curiosity. "Floating letters?"

"It must really like you if it did that," Nigel said with a dreary expression. "I waited years before it ever showed me any sign of attention."

At this, Chris snickered. "You mean the book likes Nick?"

"It's not just a book!" Nigel countered.

"Olivia believed that if we exist, then so does other magic," Nick began. "She wasn't too shocked when she discovered what the book can do, or about Marie."

"Marie?" Nigel looked worried. "We don't need another one like her running around."

"Nigel, why don't you demonstrate what the book can do?" Chris said, pushing the volume closer to Nigel.

"It might not work for me," Nigel responded in a low voice. "Maybe Nick can get it going."

Nick grabbed the book and, remarkably, Nigel didn't try to snatch it back. Opening it gently, Nick revealed the words come alive on its pages. They radiated an array of colors. In a flash, the light assembled into the shape of letters that glowed in a neon blaze. "Help me!"

"What in the wide world of sports..." Nigel's face scrunched up as if he had drunk something sour. Nigel clapped a hand over his mouth. "Well, it likes you, Nick, but it never asked me for help before."

Nick looked around the bookbinding, as if to find a way to help it. "How do we help you?"

A shriek escaped the book and Tom hastily shut it. "I'm sorry, I can't stand that thing. It gives me the creeps." Tom's hands trembled as he pushed his eyeglasses further up the bridge of his nose. "I'm sorry," he whispered, his voice strained and quiet.

Susan took his hand. "Maybe we should go in the other room while they read."

Tom shook his head firmly. "I won't do it again." He pursed his lips. "If it's open, I have to stay here. We're a family, after all."

Nigel laughed gruffly. "The motley crew of a family that we are."

"Good band!" Nick said quickly and looked impressed at Nigel. Nick looked around the group for their consent. "Are we all ready?"

Everyone nodded, gazes fixed on the book in anticipation. Nick slowly and carefully opened it this time, and as soon as it was wide enough to see the inside, the same words appeared. "Help me."

"How?" Nick repeated, as the book started to screech. Tom brought his hands to his ears. Chris noticed an array of voices within the scream.

"Who are you, and why do you need help? Are you like a cursed soul?" Nick inquired and gestured to the others to look at the pages. They were blank.

"No, you moron..." one voice bellowed as it became

distinct among the others. Once again, the same words appeared above the page as this one voice stood out.

"Olivia?" Chris asked incredulously.

"This is bad." Nick whistled low.

"Thank you, Captain Obvious!" Nigel sneered.

"Get me out of here!" Olivia whined from the pages.

"How did you get in there?" Tay exclaimed as she aimed her mobile phone at the book. Her eyes were pulled wide, and she took it all in through her camera lens.

Chris grabbed the phone and demanded, "What are you doing? You were trying to record this?" Tay snapped her hand toward the phone but Chris snatched away the device before Taylor had a chance to reclaim it. "Why would you record that?"

Taylor simply shrugged. "Social media. Nobody is going to believe it, otherwise."

Chris's mouth dropped open at the thought of anybody outside their group seeing this. The media already stalked them. Things could get so much worse if all they had to do was find Tay's social media pages. Chris took a few deep breaths in hopes that perhaps she was joking. To Chris's relief, Hunter stepped in.

"We don't need that kind of attention."

Olivia's voice cut into the argument, "STOP SQUABBLING!"

Chris glanced at the book then back to their friends in confusion.

Nick lowered his head to it as if listening intently, only for Nigel to laugh out loud. He straightened and cleared his throat. "How did you end up here?"

Olivia's voice drifted in like a whisper, "Is that you, Nick?"

Jean sighed in exasperation and crossed her arms. "He asked you a question!"

"I found that voodoo lady and she did something. I'm in this library," Olivia spoke rapidly and as clearly as if she were next to them.

"Marie?" Nigel exclaimed with a hint of disbelief in his voice. "This was Marie's doing?"

Susan raised an eyebrow. "You're going to act surprised? I saw the news with your miracle rescue in New Orleans and Marie didn't seem like she was pleased to see you there." Susan placed a hand on her curvaceous hip, "Then she came here with a gun!"

Chis rolled their eyes at her because they all knew that already, and Susan wasn't being very helpful.

Tom still looked scared silly and did not move, but kept his gaze on the book. Tom hushed them all with an index finger on his lips, yet still kept a frightened gaze on the book.

"Stop arguing and help me!" Olivia demanded from within the book.

Jean rolled her eyes and responded with disdain, "We don't owe you anything." She snapped the book closed.

Chris turned hard to stare in response to Jean's curt tone.

"Someone is jealous," Nigel said with a low whistle and held a bent hand to resemble cat claws.

Chris heaved a sigh. "Maybe we should help Olivia."

Jean pulled her shoulders back. "You mean that tiny little girl got all she wanted in normal life, then had to get more in her immortal life? No, that wasn't enough because she came at us for more, but we couldn't deliver, so she went to that witch woman?" Jean stood tall and folded her arms on her chest. "I'm not jealous of that, but I'm not being used again. She got what she deserved."

Tay raised a brow. "Don't hold it in..."

Chris sighed looking sadly at the book.

Hunter managed to let out a quiet laugh, but Jean's intimidating stare silenced him.

Nick shrugged his shoulders and said, "I agree with you, because Olivia got what she wanted in the end."

"She's truly immortal now," Nigel piped in. "Good, now that's all sorted."

Chris shook their head. They couldn't stop the heavy sadness from welling up inside them. What happened to Olivia could easily happen to any of them. They were all searching for answers. Maybe she'd not gone about it the right way, but did she really deserve to be trapped in a book for all eternity? Their heart said she shouldn't.

"This isn't right. We should help her." Chris felt obligated to help the ballerina, because she had been their guest, and the information for her damnation had come straight from this book. Chris could understand the others wanted to write it all off, probably because they were scared of what would happen if they helped, or they were just scared of Olivia.

In the back of their mind, Chris could hear Taylor once again saying that people used Chris, abused their kindness. Now it felt like maybe Chris was letting people take advantage of them again. They stopped the train of thought. No, this was different. Everyone in this room was cursed because of Deacon's deal. Chris stared at the book, glad Olivia wasn't with them... but nobody deserved this far worse curse.

Nigel nodded. "Even if we could, I wouldn't help her. We can't, so why entertain it?" He waved his hand at the book dismissively.

Nick eyed Taylor with suspicion and asked, "Why were you recording that?"

They all looked to see Taylor with her phone still aimed at the book. They watched in amazement as she fumbled with the screen and fingers dancing across the touch screen. When their gaze met hers, her expression changed as she realized she'd been caught.

Taylor gave a small shrug and responded, "For social media." She took a sip from her drink. "I post everything, but nobody believes it... they all think it's CGI. It's hilarious actually."

"What?" Chris yelled and was next to her in an instant. Chris felt their face flush with anger. Dimly, they considered how rare it was for them to get so mad, but Taylor's stupidity pushed them to the brink. They might, quite literally, boil over.

"Tay, delete it all right now!" Chris fumed. How could Taylor to do something so ridiculous? Had she lost her mind to the thrill of a few strangers on the internet giving her attention? Chris ran their hands through their short hair and pointed a finger at her. "Delete it now!"

Tay giggled, "Nobody believes it! There's nothing to worry about."

"Yet? We have mutual friends and family there, and if they see this... Not to mention all the news about it going around already..." Chris took her phone and started swiping rapidly. "You posted pictures of the blood from the hallway when Marie shot Jean? And lots of photos of Hunter too?" Chris spun back to Tay sharply. "Delete it all!" Chris had their finger in her face again. "Your life has been in danger all this time and you've been adding fuel to the fire. Did you see what happened to Olivia? You could be risking getting us all killed... even Jordan!"

She snapped her phone back. "No! I have millions of followers now!"

"What if Mom or Dad saw this? Or Jordan?" Chris countered in an angry tone. "Remember that people who find out about the deal have died and you had how many close calls?

What happens if these people figure it out? They might be in jeopardy too!"

Nick crossed his arms. "You have to delete it before it gets too big."

Jean sat down and tossed her head in her hands. "Millions of followers? I'm sure the government will be knocking with questions next."

Tay glared at Nick then Hunter, eyebrows raised. "Really?"

"Are you that thick?" Nigel asked with wide eyes. "What do you think will happen when all of your followers catch on? It could endanger them too. Don't you think drawing additional attention on us will get us all slaughtered?"

"Everyone will start putting the ages together and see it... or they'll start to figure out that some of the injuries should have been worse... or caused death." Chris touched Tay's hand as she pouted. "You need to take it down, Tay. Please." Chris crossed their arms and locked eyes with Taylor. "Take it down Tay, before millions figure it out and all end up breaking that little clause of the deal. If something bad happens to that many people... I know you won't be okay with it."

Taylor gave a big sigh and reluctantly agreed. "Okay." She took out her phone and started swiping the screen. "It's not like anybody cares..." She said under her breath.

Nigel heard her and shook his head. "Just millions of followers! Who might all die because they know too much now."

"Do you think we should be concerned?" Jean glanced around the group.

"If something's going to happen, it already would have," Nigel replied nonchalantly and gestured dismissively. He yawned as he raised his arms above his head to stretch it, and then looked at them with a grin.

"Anybody hungry?" Nick looked around at them, curious,

and pointed to the food, still out from breakfast. Jean turned away.

Nigel watched Jean. "Not anxious to sup? Anybody?"

Chris ignored him and looked at the book. "I feel we should help Olivia." Chris met their eyes. "I keep thinking if it was one of you..."

Tay looked up from her phone and shook her head. "It's not! She's a bitch, and she went to Marie and landed *there* after hitting on our men!" Tay stood up and pulled Hunter up with her.

Jean rolled her eyes. "Our men? You think that's why she ended up in that book?"

Nigel shook his head, looked at the others, and gave a comical smile. "Now, that was an interesting idea! Punishment for nicking a man.

Chris watched Tay start to 'clean' and rolled their eyes as Hunter joined her. He was simply following her lead, but it was clear they weren't getting much cleaning done on the kitchen counters. Hunter leaned over, but it wasn't to hear what Tay was saying. Chris did a double take. It looked like they were stealing kisses here and there.

Tay leaned to pick up a napkin off the floor and tumbled down, but Chris wasn't fooled. She wanted Hunter to help her up. Another Taylor game. Chris rolled their eyes. Hunter chuckled lightly and offered Taylor his hand, shaking his head.

Taylor accepted Hunter's hand, but when he tugged her up, she was pulled toward him like a rag doll. Chris stared open mouthed as Taylor bounced off Hunter's chest and Hunter had to scramble to hold on to her elbow, steadying her. Taylor dusted off her clothes as if nothing strange had happened.

Chris went to help Tay clean up, but she pushed them away, embarrassed, and Chris shrugged at her.

"Hunter, have you been working out? You seem stronger," Nigel asked, eyes burning with curiosity.

"I just pulled her up," Hunter explained as he gently touched her face. "Are you alright?"

Chris craned their neck to see that Tay was okay, but was amused at the situation. Taylor was never caught in something that looked clumsy or like she was out of control. Now, Chris made a mental note to tease her about it later.

Tay nodded in response, but the others remained skeptical.

"Are you stronger, man?" Nick asked and raised a brow.

Chris nodded trying to back Nick up a little. "For a second there, it did look like you would put her through the roof."

"No..." Hunter stammered. "Yes? I don't know?" He glanced between them in confusion. "How do we figure out if I am?"

Tay blew a bubble of gum and grinned up at him. "Go outside and try to break concrete, like those vampires in the movies..." she joked, but Hunter seemed to take it as a challenge.

Chris chuckled at that, because Tay had seen way too many vampire movies.

Hunter seemed ready to take up the challenge. He stepped outside onto the patio and spotted a large, odd-looking stone near the side.

Chris hurried to explain. "That's for the koi pond we're building..." But before they could finish, Hunter clenched his fist and slammed it against the rock with force, creating an intense *boom*, like thunder.

Tay looked excited and proud, while the others wore worried expressions.

Hunter stared in awe at the shattered rock. "What the..." he murmured.

When he came back inside, Hunter stared at his hands as

he clenched and relaxed them. The others began to fill the room and seats quietly with unspoken questions.

Nick sauntered up to the bar to get a drink. However, Jean had beaten him to it and Nick became slightly flustered when he noticed. Nick kept his gaze lowered, acknowledging that all eyes were now on him. "After all, he was an Olympian," Nick said under his breath.

Chris looked over and sighed heavily as Nick and Jean moved in harmony. Chris's gaze followed them around the room as they listened to the conversations of others. Chris sighed, feeling out of their element. Nick and Jean were clearly crazy about each other, but weren't admitting it. Still there was a nagging feeling that they might never get together, and in some far off alternative universe, Jean might choose Chris over the handsome rockstar. Watching them now, it did not seem likely. Chris fumbled with their watch, trying not to look at what a nice couple they made.

Jean blushed as Nick reached for the ice and she smiled. He whispered something in her ear that made her throw her head back with laughter. As always, Nick was enthralled by Jean, and he inched closer until his hair brushed against her forehead. She slowly lifted her head up, and he caught her chin. Neither seemed to remember there were other people in the room.

Chris couldn't take their eyes off of Nick and Jean. The two had become Chris's closest friends, and seeing them together made Chris feel happy for them. At the same time, the sight of the two together broke Chris's heart in two.

It was as if Jean and Nick were pulled together by an invisible force, lips dangerously close. Chris sighed and, even though they wanted to, couldn't tear their eyes away. Despite Chris's love for them both, and the desire to see them happy, their crush persisted. It left Chris feeling as if they were being pulled in two different directions.

Chris watched Nick brush the hair from Jean's eyes, and Chris's heart sped up. They found themself not staring at Jean but, instead, staring at Nick made their heart pound. Chris never cared what gender a person was, as long as they had a good heart. In Chris's mind, anything physical that wasn't working for a person could be changed, but not hearts. Those were special.

As if waking up to the fact they were having an intimate moment with an audience, Nick and Jean looked up at everyone watching them without remorse and the two seemed... guilty. In an instant, the two of them leaped apart as if struck by lightning.

Jean glanced at the marble countertop, while Nick tilted his head to the side and raised one eyebrow at the gathered friends, all staring at him. "Nothing better to do?" he challenged.

Tay peered upward and flashed him a dazzling grin before giggling. "Nope."

Nick chuckled. But when Jean pushed past him to rejoin the others, Nick exhaled deeply and locked eyes with each one in turn in an attempt to stare them down.

Jean settled into the couch and tucked her knees close to her body.

Hunter shifted his position from an embrace with Tay. He flashed a smile at Jean and lightly nudged her leg with his foot that was clad in a sock. "Mhmmm," Hunter alluded with a nod at Nick to tease her lightly.

Jean pushed his foot back then glanced at Chris. She furrowed her brow and quietly asked, "Are you all right?"

Chris merely nodded in response. Suddenly, the sound of the door opening grabbed their attention, and they whirled around to find Nick with the open door in hand. He looked like a deer caught in headlights as all eyes turned to him.

"I need a smoke," he said sheepishly, while pointing to the door with his drink in one hand and cigarette pack in the other.

Nigel scoffed loudly as he flipped through the book without looking at the pages. "We shouldn't be alone, Luv," he muttered, eyes glued to Jean's face. The corner of Nigel's mouth curled up in amusement when Jean became flustered.

"We can see Nick through the glass..." Jean said.

Chris nodded, relieved when Nick seemed to think better of it and decided not to leave. Chris's attitude lightened up with the two of them apart, and they felt like a traitor for it. They couldn't help but be jealous of the attention Nick received from Jean. Nick was also starting to feel like a brother to Chris. Except of course for that strange moment...

Shaking their head, Chris brushed away the thought.

Tay smiled brightly. "Let's get something to eat!" She jumped up quickly, knocking the book off the table in her haste. She grabbed it and placed it back on the surface. "Why does every page look blank to me?"

Nigel whipped his head around. "Are you mad?" Nigel nearly shouted and met her eye. "Do you see blank pages?"

Tay nodded. "Why don't you? Isn't that why it talked?" She shrugged. "I saw something when it was talking, but nothing on the pages."

"Tay, I see writing," Hunter took her hand. He gave her a concerned look and sighed.

"It must be just Tay," Chris reasoned.

The rest of the group nodded in agreement, but their eyes were focused on Tom, the only other mortal among them.

"Do you see anything written?" Chris asked him.

Tom hesitated. "I've stayed away from it, but I haven't

been able to out any words," he said, his voice low and wavering slightly. He pushed his glasses up by the bridge of the nose with one finger, and Susan clasped his hand more tightly. "Maybe we should go get something to drink from the kitchen?"

Susan agreed and they marched upstairs as Nigel began pacing with his hands behind his back.

Jean wrinkled her brow. "Why are you pacing?"

"I think better when I walk," Nigel mumbled, and turned his head. Nigel shot a hostile look in Nick's direction when Nick interrupted his thoughts .

Nick tossed his hands up in resignation. "Dude, I needed a cigarette. I'm immortal, smoking won't kill me!" He felt challenged as the others began to scowl. "Okay, fine..." He shut the door and stayed in.

"We knew this, Luv," Nigel teased. Then he stopped and snapped his fingers. "It's an age thing. Tay is the youngest so she can't read it."

"What?" Nick seemed baffled and stepped in closer to the discussion. "What's wrong with Tay?"

Chris stood up and exhaled. "I don't think it's not a matter of age."

"Weird," Nick mumbled, before grabbing a soda off the bar. He started chugging it directly from the bottle.

"Do you want some ice to go with that?" Chris offered, making their way toward the counter to help out.

Nick dismissed the suggestion with a shake of his head, saying, "Nah, I can drink it any old way."

Chris frowned, wondering if that came from Nick living on the streets. Maybe he was just used to food and drink not the right temperature, stale or even rotten. It was depressing.

Tay suddenly appeared from upstairs, laughing with Hunter

following behind her. "We ordered lunch!" she exclaimed between fits of laughter.

"What did you order?" Chris asked warily. There had been a lot of takeout already and Chris knew that she liked to order plates of sushi shaped like animals. So far, she hadn't embarrassed them with that one yet.

Tay pointed with her finger at Chris and gave the best imitation of their mother. "It's best to eat sooner rather than later!"

Nick grabbed a seat next to Jean, dropping into it noisily and holding the drink in his hand.

Tay tilted to her tip toes until Hunter pecked her lips, and a few of the others groaned.

"I know you're probably going to be my in-law, but could you not..." Chris grumbled waving hands as if to wash the view away. "At least not in front of me."

Susan and Tom descended the stairs, carrying bags of snacks and a tray of various finger foods. All the way down the stairs he doted on her, and was careful she didn't slip.

Susan stopped at the bottom step, and placed the tray down on a nearby surface. She looked up with a questioning glance. "What is it?"

Tay smiled at the couple and batted her eyes. With a silly voice, she chimed, "Old people can be so cute!"

Susan put her hands on her hips and jabbed a finger in the air toward Taylor. "Now, look here, missy..." But before Susan could continue, her words were cut off by a loud noise.

CHAPTER 27

A ll eyes turned to the top of the staircase where the unexpected sound was coming from.

Chris had their cell phone in hand, and rapidly scrolled through the surveillance camera feed. There were no signs of anyone entering the building. "Nothing out there. No unfamiliar vehicles, no open gates..." they murmured to themself.

But then the sound came again. The usual creak of floorboards was accompanied by an occasional rattling.

"That's not nothing," Nick squared his shoulders, stepping in front of Jean as if he were ready to fight.

"I took a bullet to the chest and nothing happened," Jean rolled her eyes at him. "You don't have to protect me."

Nick's gaze met Jean's and he shook his head. "Yes," he murmured. "If something happened to you... a part of me..." He vigorously shook his head, and looked at her with such warmth it could have melted the stoniest of hearts. It sure melted Chris's. They shook their head, trying to dispel the distraction and focus on the strange sound, but Nick's next words cut through them.

"You're everything to me and I can't be without you, all right?" He nervously gulped and averted his gaze to focus on the noises coming from above.

The sounds Chris couldn't place echoed in the utter stillness of the living room where no one seemed to dare to breathe.

Jean leaned closer to Nick and uttered in a harsh whisper, "I was shot in the chest and yet here I am, healed up as if nothing had happened. You don't have to be my knight in shining armor." She waved off his words, but Chris saw her eyes and detected another story there. She stared at Nick with such intensity, her eyes seemed to take over her face, and they expressed undeniable adoration.

Chris choked up, looking at their hands and pretending they never heard the whispered conversation. Chris had to brush it off, because coming to terms with the Jean and Nick situation couldn't happen now. That didn't stop it leaving a knot in Chris's throat. They swallowed it down and tried to figure out what the noise above them was.

At the top of the stairs, a door squeaked open and sent Chris into a frenzy to find anything they could use as a weapon. Several of the others seemed to have the same idea.

Tay leaned forward to get a better view of what was ahead but Hunter stepped in front of her holding his fists up like a boxer. Nick stepped up next to him and Nigel grabbed [something that's not the book], holding it like a bat. Relief washed over Chris at the sight of all their friends standing between Tay and Tom, ready to protect the two mortals from whatever had breached the security system. Everyone was prepared to fight off the intruder.

"Chris!" A voice called from the top of the staircase. "Tay?" The two looked up to see an old-school fish-head shoe, then a face that looked much like Tay and Chris's.

Everyone let out a collective sigh of relief as Taylor rushed to greet Jordan.

"Jordan, what are you doing here?" Chris questioned.

Tay groaned. "He got us again."

Chris tilted their head at Jordan. "They just sent you home?"

"After you left, it was like the asthma attack never happened. I got an inhaler, and was told to come back if things got worse," he confessed. "Besides, I can't sleep in hospitals."

Tay grabbed Jordan's arm and, in her enthusiasm, nearly dragged him over to the others. "We have so much news to share!" She announced quickly.

"No," Chris said firmly, and cut her off.

Hunter and the others snickered as Jordan's eyes shifted back and forth between the siblings, mouth slightly agape in anticipation.

"Are you having a party?" Jordan asked, and stepped up to Hunter. "You were at the hospital earlier."

Taylor beamed as she announced, "He's my boyfriend." She couldn't contain her excitement, bouncing up and down and interlacing her fingers with Hunter's.

Hunter nodded at Taylor, giving a bashful reply, "Yeah, we're working on that." He smiled and held his hand out to Jordan, introducing himself. "I'm Hunter."

Jordan gave a slight nod and smiled in response. "Yeah." His voice softened as he observed them interact and he reached out and grasped Hunter's hand, shaking it firmly while introducing himself. "I'm Jordan."

A thump startled them, and they looked to see Jordan had knocked the book off the table onto the floor. Jordan grabbed it, then surveyed the startled group with a raised eyebrow. He chuckled. "It's all good..." After examining the book for a few moments, he asked in puzzlement, "Why is this old book completely empty?" Then, giving a slight shrug of dismissal, he put it back on the table.

Chris stepped nearer to examine it. "Blank?"

Jordan scoffed and spread the book open. "Yeah, blank page," he repeated, then glanced over at Taylor. "Fancy new diary?" He laughed.

Tay rolled her eyes and threw up her hands. "Don't ask me," she groaned. "I don't get that book either."

Jordan shook his head and shot a glance at Chris and Tay. "What's up with the early party?"

They began to relax and take seats, with Chris plopping down beside Jordan on the floor. "Same people you met before," Chris replied. "We're just chatting."

Jordan glanced from one person to the next. "About empty books?" He shook his head. "Okay, so don't tell me."

"We were just talking," Chris insisted. "We bumped into each other at the harbor, that's all..." Chris looked away, attempting to stick to the truth without stretching it too far. It was well known that Chris wasn't a good liar, so rather than try to fib their way out of this, they decided to stay quiet or answer only what they could. They didn't want to get Jordan in the same kind of danger Taylor was in.

"We met in my bookstore at the harbor," Nigel cut in. "We all shared the same interests and we got along famously!" He beamed and patted a hand over his heart. "Chris offered up this humble abode but if it's an inconvenience..." He glanced to the side. "Tom and Susan graciously offered to host our small yet geeky get-together at their posh home."

Susan and Tom gazed into each other's eyes as if to determine if either of them had said such a thing. Tom gave her a small nod and she finally understood, exclaiming, "Oh yeah! We said we could muddle through at our house, since it's the maid's holiday." He nodded his head again in agreement.

Jean added, "I don't mind, but Taylor insisted that her bed is here."

Jordan raised an eyebrow as everyone else agreed.

Letting out a yawn, Jordan chuckled, "It's all good. But our parents might grill you with questions, Chris." He pointed to the stairs. "I'm gonna crash. Hospitals are the worst."

Chris and Taylor embraced Jordan, taking turns to give him a heartfelt hug. When it was all finished, Jordan made his way up the stairs with another yawn.

When Jordan reached the top step, Chris shouted after him, "If you need us for anything at all, don't hesitate to text or call us; we'll be right here."

Jordan just raised his thumb at them to acknowledge the thought, and continued on his way.

Tay shook her head. "We really aren't doing anything wrong. Why don't we tell him?"

Hunter replied quietly, "He'll be in the same danger as you are."

Tay's lips curled into a pout as she crossed her arms.

Jean nodded in agreement. "Everyone who knows and who isn't an immortal seems to be targeted to die..."

Chris stepped toward the book, opened it, and mused, "I can make out what's written here, but Jordan couldn't even see writing. It must be an immortal thing, right?"

"Glad that's all sorted, chap!" Nigel exclaimed, dropping down into the armchair.

"If you need a place to stay, our house is still available," Tom offered from the couch.

"I'm comfortable here!" Tay exclaimed.

Taylor was snuggled up to Hunter's shoulder, nearly dozing off when she wrinkled her nose and peered up at him. "Did you just pass gas?" She asked with a giggle, clamping her fingers over her nose.

Hunter looked alarmed. "That's not me," he insisted and glanced over his shoulder to see Nigel craning his neck, nose twitching.

Nick jumped up and Chris followed suit. "It smells like Deacon," Chris muttered as they looked around urgently. "It has to be..."

The sudden flare of lightning made everyone in the house jump, and a loud clap of thunder followed close afterwards, alerting them to the storm's arrival. The sky was pitch black, and they could see the gleam of the rain slashing through it. The downpour outside their french doors was almost deafening and seemed to bounce off the ground like hail.

"Did they forecast rain for today?" Susan spoke in a soft tone as she walked to the door to observe the pouring rain.

"It's quite the deluge," Nigel remarked, his eyes widening as he stayed close with the book in his hands. Lightning struck, a white-hot blade flaming through the sky. The earth trembled the moment it struck the ground. Like a beacon, the bright shard of light blazed through the room and revealed everyone's scared faces for a mere moment. The blinding darkness gave way to a deep rumble of the thunder, like the report of a bass cannon, that throbbed and shook the earth for miles. It even made Nigel flinch. "That was close." He stood up straight.

Chris shook their head and rubbed their arm. Hairs were standing up on the back of Chris's arms and they kept pushing them back down. "Something doesn't feel right."

Taylor's eyes grew large and Chris saw fear in her expression. "Jordan!" She leaped off the couch and ran upstairs.

"Tay!" Hunter shouted and raced after her, with Chris close behind.

Chris stopped beside Tay at the top of the stairs by the doorway to the kitchen and scanned the tiled area. "Jordan?" They said in unison.

Hunter came to a standstill just behind them, and soon enough Chris heard the thud of footsteps climbing up to meet them. Their friends were with them, ready to investigate.

Tay pointed to the open fridge, and asked, "He left it like this?"

Chris responded with a nod of their head, "That's not like him." When they got closer to the kitchen, they could see that more than just the refrigerator had been opened. Pickles lay scattered among shards of glass and liquid pooled onto the floor.

"Jordan?" Chris called as they made their way to the staircase leading up to the next floor. Chris pulled out their phone and tapped out a text message.

With the skittering sound of something plastic hitting the ground, Hunter held up a bag from the floor at the entrance between the kitchen and dining room. "Is this Jordan's?"

"Ohmygod!" Tay exclaimed, her hand covering her mouth. "He wouldn't leave his stuff behind like this."

Chris heaved a sigh and bent over to pick what had fallen out of the bag. "And he definitely wouldn't abandon his inhaler," Chris declared, holding it up for Taylor to see. The sulfurous odor hit Chris's nostrils. "The same smokey smell from Deacon is coming from the inhaler..."

Hunter brought the bag close to his face and flinched. "It's coming from the bag, too."

"He got him?" Taylor whimpered in shock through her fingers covering her mouth. She sank to her knees and tears poured down her face. "Ohmygod!"

Hunter hurried to her side, kneeling and folding her in his arms; all he could do was hold her.

"What's going on?" Chris looked at the discarded inhaler sadly. "Nobody's heard from Mom or Dad since they left, and now Jordan is missing?" Chris said angrily as they placed the inhaler down. "This deal keeps getting worse..."

Tay cast her gaze down to the floor. "I haven't heard anything from Mom and Dad, and they haven't returned my messages."

Nigel stood by the door to the stairs, shaking his head. "One need not be a chamber to be haunted..." He looked at their questioning stares, before rolling eyes and adding, "Emily Dickinson said that."

Everyone returned to the family room and were seated in the center on the oversized couches. Taylor absently gripped a warm mug of tea Jean had thrust into her hands. Hunter draped a soft throw blanket over her shoulders before taking a spot next to her, yet she still appeared lost in her thoughts, so very different from how Chris had observed her earlier.

Taylor glanced up at the group and bit back tears. "Is he really out there? Did he get our parents and Jordan, and am I going to be next?" She pressed her temples with her fingers and shut her eyes.

Nick waved his hands. "But we didn't find any evidence of a body. If he killed your brother, wouldn't there be proof?"

"Sometimes they do forget about their phones..." Tay rolled her eyes. "They're old."

"Yeah, but..." Chris trailed off, not wanting to frighten Tay into further tears. They were certain that if Jordan had gone to the hospital, they would have received a call. Everything felt off and it was alarming.

Nigel sat with the book in his hands and paid no attention to the bustle around him.

A thorough search of the house for Jordan had turned up nothing more than the bag, inhaler, and broken condiment containers beside the refrigerator. It was proof Jordan had been there, but there was no indication of what had happened. Jordan had vanished – swallowed into thin air.

Chris tried to explain it away in their mind, saying that Jordan probably just went to get a bite to eat. In the hopes of proving that desperate wish true, Chris reviewed the camera footage. They needed to pinpoint when Jordan had left the house.

Taylor cuddled into the blanket and finally sipped her tea.

Nigel scoffed and looked up. "It's all a bit dodgy." he said, as if this was a conclusion he had come to on his own. He raised an accusing finger at the others. "It almost seems like he's warning us?" Nigel lifted the finger higher. "I think Deacon's scared."

Jean muttered, "Coming from the guy who hides behind Nick."

Tom chimed in loudly. "It is odd. In the movies, threats are made when people are trying to get a point across before something important happens."

"Or when they're too close to the truth," Susan said quickly. "I think you're right. He's scared of us."

Fear lined Taylor's voice when she asked, "So he'll get rid of everyone he can?"

"There's no proof anybody is dead," Nigel countered, his nose back in the the book.

Chris kept flipping through the phone's screens until footage of Jordan came into view. "I've got it!"

Tay sprinted over to get a better view and the others gathered around Chris, all eager to see the small screen. Chris took a deep breath and projected the feed to the larger TV. Chris gestured toward it and said, "Look…"

Jordan entered the garage, his face exhausted and cautious. He stepped carefully toward the stairwell, as if he had heard something.

"I guess he noticed us down here," Chris said in a low voice, leaning their head on their hand

Chris sped up the footage gradually, and soon they noticed Jordan laughing as he resurfaced from downstairs. He shook his head and wandered over to the refrigerator, rummaging around before stopping suddenly, lifting his head up, and spinning around.

"I think he heard us or someone else?" Taylor asked from the corner of her seat

He wrinkled his nose and glanced around as if he expected to find someone in the room. Suddenly, the image morphed into a fuzzy mess of electronic interference.

Taylor nearly shouted in frustration, "You can't be serious! The video was cut off?"

Chris skipped ahead to where the static ended, and the next scene they saw was an abandoned kitchen with the same disarray they had witnessed beside the refrigerator.

Tay sank into her seat. S Her shoulders slumped, her eyes brimmed with tears, and her bottom lip quivered. Hunter gently placed his hand on her back, offering silent support as she tried to hold back the flood of emotions.

Nick looked at Chris. "We should make sure the house is locked up and the grounds are clear."

Nigel appeared as if he was about to raise his index finger and wave it around like a foam finger, but instead, he let his head slump down again, eyes on the book. Chris wondered at how Nigel had, on several occasions, been acting as though he wanted to say something, but kept silent instead.

Chris agreed with Nick, Jean quickly rose to her feet and

nodded in response to the idea. "I'm going too!" She looked over to Chris. "You do have cameras outside right?"

Chris nodded in response, still looking at their phone. "Yes," they replied. "But there are blank spots so we should stay together..."

Nick reached for Jean's hand. "We should be safe."

Jean and Nick hurried away while the rest shifted around the coffee table. Nigel resumed poring over the book once more.

Nigel inhaled deeply and nodded before he spoke. "Listen, you lot... There is a bit about someone who made an enormous sacrifice for another." He opened up the book and pointed to a picture of a young girl. "Emily had a twin brother called Emile: he had made a pact, and Emily discovered it. Both were terrified and, ultimately, Emily gave her life to save Emile. He eventually stopped having nightmares and realized he could still communicate with her even after she passed away."

Taylor glanced at Tom, then the others. She said in a small voice, "So, if Tom or I offered ourselves as a sacrifice, the rest of you would be able to live in peace?" Her expression was filled with fear, but she seemed to be considering the idea.

Chris shook their head with a sharp jerk, and shouted, "No way, Tay!"

Hunter gently squeezed her hand and met Chris's gaze. "She won't," he confirmed. "I plan to stay with her forever."

Taylor stared at him in astonishment and stammered, "Wait...are you asking me to marry you?"

He chuckled softly and said, "When I do, it'll be a special moment between us two, not something that involves a crowd." He smirked looking at the prying eyes and added, "Not that you all aren't great, but I have my own plans for it." And with that he gave her a quick wink.

Taylor squealed and hugged Hunter, pressing a kiss on his

cheek. "Are you serious?" she asked in disbelief. For once she seemed at a loss for words.

Hunter grinned bashfully and wrapped the blanket snugly around Taylor. "It's going to take a lot to keep me away from you."

Chris exhaled with relief, and then joined Nigel to read the story he had been talking about. "Nobody is going to sacrifice themselves."

Susan chuckled and nudged Tom gently as they found seats near the book too.

Taylor grumpily complained, "I don't like this book."

Tom gave Taylor a gentle and reassuring smile with a nod. "Jordan is probably fine," he said in a calm voice. "If something had happened," he placed his hand on his chest, indicating his heart, "I think you would know."

Taylor offered a hint of a smile, but the worry was still evident in her eyes. She snuggled close to Hunter, yawning widely. Whether it was Tom's calming voice or all the stress she'd been under lately, she soon drifted off into slumber.

Chris noticed Taylor sleeping and glanced at Hunter's face, which held an amused yet satisfied expression. "I'm glad she's finally getting some rest. I haven't seen her this worked up in a long time. She's usually really cheerful and never frowns, even when times were tough for us." Chris spoke quietly so as not to disturb Taylor's sleep.

Susan shook her head in disbelief. "I could never be that consistently joyful." She smirked with a smile tugging at the corner of her lips. When compared to people like Tom and Taylor, who carried themselves with an air of carefreeness, Susan seemed to be a world away from their state of happiness. It could have been due to her level-headed attitude or the fact that she appeared older than most of them. Whatever it was, everyone paid attention when she spoke.

Chris took a deep breath and swallowed nervously. "Should we check on Jean and Nick?"

Hunter's eyebrow rose as the others seemed to pick up on Chris's envy. He quietly muttered, "Do you think Tay is comfortable?"

Chris frowned seeing her head on Hunter's shoulder. "I assume so... but maybe you should help her down to the couch. It looks like she'll have a stiff neck if she stays like that."

Tom stood and, seeing Hunter having trouble lowering Taylor, Tom helped lay her down without disturbing her.

Hunter smiled at Tom, speaking in a whisper. "Thanks. You're pretty quiet, huh?"

Tom adjusted his glasses and gave a noncommittal shrug, not meeting Hunter's eyes. He tucked the blanket around Taylor before answering, "I guess you could say that. Being an actor, I'm used to adjusting to different personalities."

"Modest, too!" Hunter remarked, glancing past Tom toward Susan.

Chris found themself reading and rereading as Nigel played with his phone. It was clear to both of them that Chris's mind was not completely on the reading and each time Chris sighed it confirmed it.

Glancing up, Chris exhaled heavily as they watched Tom and Susan converse quietly. It was amusing to watch Hunter peer over Tom's shoulder while trying not to wake Tay, who was sleeping by his side. This sight had Chris looking away because they were so content with each other. Even the coldest heart would be moved by their happiness, let alone somebody in their position who had no one.

With a heavy feeling in their chest, Chris turned away from the loving pairs.

They had grown accustomed to being on their own. Academically, Chris had always been gifted, and this tended to isolate them from their peers. Others felt jealous of the ease with which Chris obtained answers. Socializing was a thing of the past for Chris, and they hadn't had any close friends or crushes, until now.

Seeing Jean and Nick together caused a twinge of pain to come over Chris. A heavy sigh escaped their lips as they ruminated on the current situation; although it was tough not having someone to talk to, Chris wouldn't trade their new friends for anything. They finally smiled, coming to peace with the fact Nick and Jean were a couple. As peace settled inside Chris, they hoped to have a love like that one day.

When Chris glanced up, they saw the others watching them closely, and cleared their throat in response. "What is it?" Chris whispered.

Nigel scoffed and took the lead, giving his own little sigh as he began. "Well... you've been over there sighing away for a bit now." He leaned his head on his hand and stared at him expectantly. "Spill the tea?"

Chris raised an eyebrow at Nigel. Had they really been sighing? They couldn't deny they felt like sighing now.

Susan wrinkled her forehead. "What does that mean? Spill the tea?"

Hunter chuckled. "It means tell the gossip... Spill the beans! That's how my parents used to say it," he finally exclaimed.

Tay stirred. She blinked when she noticed she rested on Hunter's lap and then grinned. "What tea?" she asked sleepily and stretched her arms up above her head. Her smile grew even wider as she stared up at Hunter and then shifted her eyes to take in the rest of the group.

"They think Chris has some thoughts," Tom said with a slight grin.

Chris shook their head. "No," they replied quickly. Even

though it felt like fibbing, Chris deflected. "I was just thinking of the people who have been lost... Jordan... and I can't help but worry that Mom and Dad are among them," Chris murmured softly.

There was no way they were going to go into details on their other thoughts or add further explanation. Trying to force themself not to think of Nick and Jean, and their realization, Chris became hyper aware of Susan and Tom's hands joined together.

Tay's face drooped as she looked at Chris. "Do you think they're gone?"

But Tom quickly interjected, "No, if they were gone, you would feel it here," he added, pressing a palm to his heart.

"I guess..." Tay muttered as she held up her phone to show the display. It revealed she had been texting Jordan, but hadn't received any response.

Chris let out a sigh and drew out their own mobile device from their pocket. "I found his cell in the bag." As Chris watched Tay worrying about the situation, they attempted to comfort her, despite their doubts. "I'm sure they're okay."

"By Jove! I think I've got it!" Nigel exclaimed with his finger pointing in the air.

Hunter rolled his eyes and said sarcastically, "You keep saying that."

Tay sat up straighter. "Is it catching?" she giggled.

Nigel dismissed their comments with a wave of his hand. "I'm serious, you lot!" He turned the book so they would all be able to see the writing. "If you read the book enough, then you notice the writing changes. It's like the book has its own mind."

Tom's voice was soft as he inquired, "Or its own soul?"

Chris straightened in his chair and glanced at the book. "Like Olivia?"

Susan stared at them in surprise. "Are you suggesting that... what are you

saying?"

"Well," Nigel paused for effect and made sure they were all paying attention. "I have a theory that the book is created from the spirits of condemned souls. They're unable to speak in harmony, so the words continually fluctuate."

"An infinite book..." Chris whispered, overwhelmed by the idea.

"A cursed tome," Tom said, eyes wide with fear.

"I had my doubts, but I'm certain now that these are Olivia's words," Nigel pointed out. "She's a snarky lass..." He raised the corner of his mouth and stared at the book as if it were a cheat sheet.

"You shall be eternally lonesome, unless you accept those who are ageless..." He began to recite from the book. "Every mortal that loves you will only bring themselves closer to the grave." He took a hard breath and shrugged his shoulders, "That minx must have found a dictionary..." They exchanged worn glances, not convinced by his words.

"That's why she wanted Nick?" Tay inquired, popping a stick of gum in her mouth.

"She was quite determined to be with either Nick or Hunter," Chris answered, tapping their fingertips together gently.

Nick, and Jean returned to the room and everyone's eyes followed them. Nigel threw his arms up in despair. "I guess this means we have to start at the beginning," he groaned, waving his hands in the air for emphasis.

Chris chuckled. "Nigel has a theory..." Chris tried not to look at Nick and Jean too closely but it was hard to ignore that there seemed to be no change between them.

Nick put his hand on the lower part of Jean's back, as if to guide her toward the group sitting on the couch. When they took their spots next to Hunter and Tay, they looked like any other couple in love.

Nigel didn't seem to pay attention, but he showed them the new writing anyway. "It sounds like it could have been written by someone we know... or used to know."

Hunter yawned and leaned in to get a better look, while Nick's eyes widened in surprise. "That's exactly what Olivia said," he breathed.

Jean's eyes widened as she scanned the group, but everyone else turned their attention to Nigel.

"Now," Nigel started. "The book is in constant motion, so I think it's made up of souls who have been lost to it. Olivia went to discover the mysterious and never-aging Marie. Considering we heard Olivia's voice from the book, we assume she's trapped in it, and that's most likely Marie's doing. I had seen somewhere that breaking a deal like what we have with Deacon can lead you to become locked between two worlds." Nigel took a breath. "Plus the book responded to Nick with Olivia's voice asking for help, and Olivia was over the moon for Nick."

Nigel looked pointedly at Nick and then Jean, as if expecting jealousy from them. However, when neither of them responded, he groaned and shoved his hair to smooth it before continuing. "I think there's someone else in the book who could help us... Olivia might help Nick," Nigel showed his doubt with a stunned expression.

Chris wondered if Nigel was simply drawing at straws now, and took a deep breath. They traded a look with Nick and sat back a little.

Nick looked dubious. "I don't think she'd be able to do it. She looked so afraid and lost."

Nigel enlarged his eyes and handed Nick the book. "Let's find out," he said, with a hint of challenge in his words.

Nick glanced at the others, who all seemed rather uninterested. Sighing, he accepted the book. "All right... but if she starts flirting, then I'm hanging up."

Tay erupted in a fit of laughter, took out her phone, and started tapping on it without making any sound.

Nick opened the book and browsed through its pages, eventually coming to a halt when he noticed something. "My name is here?" he pointed out.

At once, the book emitted an eerie gurgling noise. Nick stumbled backward as letters formed in mid-air and a holographic image of Olivia's face appeared above them. Her expression was fierce as she stared Nick down with a furrowed brow.

"You call me but you're with HER?" Olivia's voice accused.

"I called you?" Nick managed to get out.

Tom squirmed in his seat. "I don't like this."

Olivia kept her focus on Nick. "Yes, you called me!" As she spoke, the words appeared in text beneath the apparition of her head. "I don't want to help... her," Olivia spat out the last word as she turned her ethereal head in Jean's direction.

"You must lend a hand," Nigel said in a gentle tone while propping two fingers on the table as if scheming. The see-through head spun in his direction and sneered, "You have no choice – isn't that right, love?"

Olivia spun to face Nick. With a stern expression, she asked him sharply, "What do you want?"

Nick gave her a sorrowful glance, tilting his head curiously. "What happened to you?"

"That woman you sent me to killed me with some demon!" Olivia said through gritted teeth.

"I thought Marie couldn't take out an immortal..." Nick mused.

"No, she didn't," Olivia said sharply. "She got someone else to do her dirty work.

Some demon guy she knew."

They exchanged a knowing glance, realizing that there was a way for them to end their suffering. Ending up trapped in a book was not a desired outcome to end the deal, but it was an end to the nightmares.

Chris recalled what they heard Nick and Olivia talking about. Nick was ready to break their agreement, and sacrifice himself in order to protect everyone else. It seemed like Olivia had figured out how to kill an Immortal, even if it was herself.

"What do we have to do to break the curse?" Nick inquired urgently.

"I just want these nightmares to go away." Nigel cut in. "How can I make them

stop?"

"You can't!" Olivia hissed. "They're a part of the curse."

"Anyone who learns about the curse and isn't immortal... dies?" Nick cut in hastily.

Olivia, who appeared weary, even as a disembodied head, answered, "Yes, everyone who finds out does and everyone who means something to us eventually dies of some horrible fate." She laughed. "That's why I needed an immortal mate."

Susan questioned, "Will Tom and Taylor be killed?"

"Unless you can shield them continuously," Olivia replied in a mirthful tone. "I've been there and you can't be with them all the time... so yes, eventually an accident will find them."

Taylor clung to Hunter's arm as she shared a panicked glance with Chris.

"What happened to Jordan?" Chris demanded.

"What about our parents?" Taylor demanded.

Olivia sighed in boredom. "Are they dead? No. Are they here? No. They're being held by the same guy that gave me immortal life..."

"Deacon? Why?" Chris asked scooting forward as if to hear better.

"I don't know why. I don't know how I know, but I know," Olivia's temper started to show. She hissed, "What I do know is this: they'll be dead in a few weeks."

Nick lifted his eyebrows in surprise. "A few weeks?" He looked at the others. "We have a time limit?"

Chris glanced at Tay and was expecting to see her clenching her teeth, but instead she appeared close to tears. "Tay..." Chris murmured.

"Oh come on!" Olivia scoffed. "Ask me what you want now, because I don't have to stay here talking to you."

"Is there a way to bring them back?" Nick asked quickly.

"Yes," Olivia replied shortly.

"What do we have to do?" Tay interjected hastily.

"You'll need to break an agreement," Olivia said, sounding unenthused. They detected a sigh from her direction.

"But we can't break the deal," Hunter added.

Olivia had a mischievous smile on her face. "I found a way out. If anyone here wants to save their family, then you need to visit that Cajun witch!"

The group gave each other an apprehensive look as Olivia gazed around.

"You know they'll go after the other mortals, just like they did with everyone I care about," Olivia seemed to be challenging them.

"You're in limbo, love!" Nigel chirped with an eager point of his finger.

"I'm in a book!" Olivia shouted. "I don't have to help you!" She looked directly at Nigel.

"Mortals like the mayor's wife or Persephone?" Chris asked quickly. The feeling they had got those innocents killed somehow stuck with Chris even when they tried to convince themself otherwise.

Suddenly the book shut itself, and Olivia was gone.

"Great..." Hunter sank back into the couch. "You pissed her off!"

Chris cocked their head, "Not me..."

"She was on about nothing," Nigel adjusted his thick frames and held a hand out. "So, to bring the missing people back we need to go to Marie, and get her demon friend to kill one of us." Nigel sighed and crossed his legs slowly. "Not it! There must be another way."

Tay playfully threw Hunter's hand up with hers, shouting. "Not it!"

Chris exhaled noisily and looked around at the others. Tay always seemed to enjoy the humor in any situation. It was clear she was confident nothing bad would ever happen to her, and that she would continue to live her charmed life.

Nick had a more serious expression and suggested, "Maybe we should draw straws?"

"I'm not offering this fine bod up for sacrifice!" Nigel waved his hand in front of his body like a game show hostess. "I'm not quite through with this life."

Jean sighed. "How much of a difference will I really make here?"

Nick's face fell at the thought. "There are people who care about you here, Jean."

"Ima might have a point there, rockstar," Nigel winked.

With an expression of determination, Tom shook his head and told Susan and the rest, "Susan, no way it's gonna be you. Remember that it's a sin."

"The way I live my life is a sin according to some people.

Some things are subject to opinion." Chris sighed heavily. "It's not going to be any of us. We have to find a better solution."

Hunter gave a nod. "We should take turns reading that book and see who else it answers. Maybe if we get another soul, they might help more than Olivia could." He sighed. "She's not very nice."

Chris chuckled. "You think?"

Tay firmly shook her head in disagreement. "Nobody should sacrifice themselves! Let me make the deal too!" She glanced at Chris. "You have plenty of money. It keeps coming in..."

Susan sat upright. "We could do that!"

Tom shrugged. "This Deacon fellow has to pick us for the agreement, doesn't he?" He squeezed Susan's hand as he looked down thoughtfully. "I don't want that deal. I could never stomach those dreams – especially not for eternity."

Susan was about to say something in response, but something flashed in her eyes as she changed her mind. No one wanted those kinds of nightmares.

Tay laughed, "I do all I can to have bad dreams! I eat spicy food before bedtime and watch all the horror flicks. I also read plenty of spooky stories, and I have a 3D makeup collection that could turn anyone into something truly lifelike and disturbing."

Chris laughed, "Tay has a real fixation with horror. She knows all the movies and classic scary tales."

Tay nodded proudly. "Even the black and white shows on TV."

Hunter shook his head and held Taylor's hand. "It's not the same, Tay," he said softly. "Imagine being conscious when you get blown up over and over..."

"...on a crashing airplane," Nigel added.

Jean swallowed hard as she added, "Your throat is

constricted with bad food or your heart feels like it's about to burst from your chest?"

Tom and Susan just nodded with the same dazed expressions on their faces. Susan trembled and Tom tucked her close to his side.

Tay raised her hands up in the air. "I could manage it." She turned her gaze toward Chris. "What kind of nightmares do you have?""

Chris shook their head as if to shrug off the topic. "I haven't really had one yet." Chris took a hard breath. "I have a recurring nightmare but it's not too bad."

"Mine are the same nightmares I had before the deal. They're the same thing, but now... they're like living death over and over again." Nick nodded in understanding. "When you have them, we'll be here for you."

Tay rolled her eyes at the concern in the room. "I could handle it." She muttered something else under her breath that included "wussies" before sharing a teasing smile with them.

Nigel pointed a finger at her. "That's not funny." He pulled the book to him and began to read.

Tay shoved the book into Hunter's hands with a cheerful, "Let Hunter read!" With a wink she commented, "It looks like guys like you and Nick are the ones getting attention from the book."

"From Olivia?" Hunter chuckled, but still accepted the book.

They handed the book over to Jean, who rolled her eyes in displeasure. "I feel like you're my pimp," Jean muttered quietly.

"Well, if we could make money off of it..." Nigel teased.

Jean opened the book, and started flipping through its pages. "What am I looking for?" she asked.

As soon as Jean spoke, the pages of the book shuffled until

they settled on one page. One paragraph stood out above the rest, glowing brighter than the others.

Jean squinted her eyes to read it and slowly recited, "The power of blessing and faith can ward off many perilous things. In the distant past, a man worked to safeguard his lover from harm by confining her within the safety of their dwelling. Whenever she ventured outside, her life was in danger, but the blessings kept her safe inside. The Undying must shield the ones they love if they are to survive."

Nick sat upright, his eyes wide with surprise. "Is that book talking about Us?"

"That's right," Tom confirmed, nodding his head. "I had our home blessed after Susan and I got married." His hands fidgeted in his pockets as he looked down at the floor with an awkward expression. "She had just cheated death, and I wanted to make sure that it wouldn't come back for us."

"He's right," Susan said with a smile. "We also have a cross hanging on the wall now."

Chris gave the pair a perplexed glance. "Are you very religious?"

Tom responded with a grin, "I do think that there is something more than us in this world. I believe it's worth exploring and finding out more about."

"Luv, you've got a point," Nigel jumped in. "We already know the baddies exist so why not the good guys?"

Taylor's eyes widened at the suggestion. "We're going to church?" she asked hesitantly.

Chris laughed softly. "Yes, Tay. We're going to church. I promise you won't burst into flames or anything."

"I could go." Tom offered, slowly stretching out his limbs to try and get rid of the knots. "Do we need any particular denomination?"

"Why is he speaking in math?" Taylor yawned.

"We go to a Catholic Church?" Chris questioned in a low tone.

"I'm going to grab my slippers," Tay interjected, clearly bored in the discussion at hand.

"You know everything scary happens in Churches?" Hunter released a long sigh and followed Taylor as she started up the stairs to get her warmer shirt and some slippers.

Chris frowned at the idea of the church because they had been avoiding going there. All they kept hearing since they came out as part of the pride community was how unaccepting the church was of people like Chris. Although they felt bad for avoiding it, Chris did not do well with confrontations.

Chris smiled watching Hunter's bewildered stare at Tay's pumpkin slippers.

Finally Taylor turned and demanded, "What?"

"Aren't those a bit out of season? I didn't think you were into Halloween yet," he chuckled.

She swatted at him, lightly tapping his arm. "I like pumpkins!"

"Alright, alright! I give up!" Hunter shrugged as he chuckled. "It's just you're normally so trendy and elegant."

Taylor stuck her tongue out at him and declared, "I don't wear them in public."

"Why does your family have so much stuff?" His gaze traveled over her.

Chris frowned but remained quiet as Taylor had clearly taken their brother's things without asking. Had she asked, it wouldn't have been an issue, however now it seemed like a betrayal, which stung more because Jordan was missing. Her looking constantly at the door in expectation of him coming back showed that she missed him.

Chris knew it wasn't Taylor's intention to write Jordan off, just her self-absorbed behavior making her think she could take what she wanted. Chris looked away from her so as not to scowl and instead tried to give Hunter an explanation. "A few different sets of pajamas... some for different seasons... gifts..." But Hunter was far too amused about Taylor and Chris trailed off.

"Each day of the week?" Hunter laughed

"Mmmhmmm," Tay confirmed and dared him to argue it. She looked to Chris for help, but when they didn't say anything, she finally added, "Hunter, you just don't understand."

Hunter frowned in disbelief. "What are you talking about?"

"We weren't born rich," she admitted, her lips pursing together. "For a long time, we struggled for money to even buy bread. We were unfazed by the cold winter weather. It was too cold for them to turn off our power. But when temperatures rose, we kept a close eye on the door, dreading someone would show up and take away what little we had." She looked up at him before taking a deep breath. Then she met Chris's eyes with a sad smile.

"Y'all changed all that," Hunter nodded in agreement. "It's all in the past now."

"You never forget it," Tay admitted with her face tinted red. "Once I had the means to do so, I was buying all of the name brands and things I always wanted." She smiled fondly at Chris. "Chris helped us to become spoiled, and Chris takes good care of Mom and Dad too."

"When I was growing up in the city center, it felt like my star was rising. I was the Chris of my family. We had nothing, and the fame of being in the Olympics changed that, but the tragedy of 9/11 was a blow for me. We were poor and dependent on food stamps to get by again." Hunter glanced down sadly. "I lost all of my family in the last explosion." Hunter avoided eye contact, and Chris noticed unshed tears glistening under his eyes. Losing his whole family must still be a difficult reality for him to accept.

Chris silently agreed with Hunter, feeling a sense of humility as he reminded them of how poor they had once been. Chris was the only one who truly understood the pressure of being in that situation; not only had they struggled financially, but their family depended on them for the life they lived now. Chris wanted to be able to express their sorrow, but they could tell by the way Hunter was avoiding eye contact that there was nothing Chris could say to make it better.

Tay stepped forward and embraced Hunter. "Now do you get why we have to keep up with this house?" She grinned at them all now. "Every Easter and Christmas time, our family tidies the spare rooms and hosts a big get-together for our relatives. And when someone from out of town visits, they can stay here!" She took a breath. "That's why we need all these bedrooms and all the extra clothes too – everyone uses them when they come over." She laughed, shaking her hair back. "So much better than when we were poor and only had one pair of shoes each!"

Hunter glanced at his footwear. Despite being of good quality, they were worn and tattered. His shoes were clean, but evidence of scuff marks and tears was still visible on them. The soles were thinning from constant wear. "I know the feeling," Hunter mumbled.

Tay looked around sadly. "I don't think having everything matters that much if I die tomorrow…"

Chris was surprised as Jean kept flipping through the book with ease, her eyes barely registering the words on the pages. It was almost like she was reading a book meant for summer leisure instead of one filled with information.

Nigel smiled from his perch behind the computer screen.

Chris turned their head, in wonder at how Nigel seemed to gravitate to the tech, and how easily it appeased him.

Nigel gave a slight nod and motioned for Susan and Tom to take a look at the computer as well.

Tom and Susan joined Nigel but Chris tried to stare over their shoulders at the screen.

Chris glanced over at Jean, drinking in the subtle scent of her perfume and memorizing every line on her face. Suddenly, a loud noise from upstairs broke the spell, causing Chris to lurch forward off their seat and crash into Jean. In an attempt to steady Chris's fall, Jean reached out but instead fell with them to the ground.

"Sorry, I lost my balance," Chris apologized as they got up from on top of Jean with a small smile.

Taylor rolled her eyes. "You are soooo obvious," Taylor said through a giggle and popped her chewing gum.

Hunter and jogged over to help Chris off the ground with a single pull, sending them crashing into his chest. Chris felt limp and lifeless in Hunter's arms, staring up at him with confusion. "Hunter," they started slowly, narrowing their eyes. "You barely touched me and

yet..."

Hunter reached down to help Jean but Chris stopped him. Chris shook their head and said, "Maybe I should help Jean up. You're much stronger than you realize." Chris gave Jean a hand to get on her feet again and she rose slowly.

Hunter pulled his hand back but too fast and the marble ashtray went flying. He caught it roughly and it crumbled in his desperate grasp. "Sorry," he said, already reaching to pick up the broken pieces of jasper.

"It's alright," Chris assured him. "Alex! Run vacuum!" Chris called out in a clear voice, summoning the A.I.

The grinding and scraping of wheels was heard and a small robot showed up, running in straight paths.

Tay popped her gum as she said, "That ashtray wasn't all that."

Tom glanced down at his wristwatch, a look of worry on his face. "We should get someone to bless the house," he mumbled and edged his glasses up his nose again. "I'll feel better when the house is blessed." He offered a weak smile before suggesting tentatively, "We could do it ourselves."

Taylor stared with a look of astonishment. No words came out of her mouth as it hung open in shock. Her eyes widened like two saucers and her eyebrows shot up in surprise. She slowly shook her head and cracked a sarcastic laugh.

Chris rolled their eyes at Taylor's response then turned to Tom. "Do you think it would even work if we don't have strong faith in our religion?"

Tom folded his arms in front of his chest. "Don't you have faith?" It seemed like a challenge coming from the timid man.

Chris replied hesitantly, "Yes, but not nearly as much as someone like a monk or priest."

Tom smiled encouragingly and replied, "I believe that if we are faithful then we can do it."

Nigel scoffed and waved his hand in a dismissive gesture. "I haven't been on good terms with my Church for quite some time."

Jean shook her head sadly. "It seems wrong to try and talk to God after all these years."

Nick chimed in, "I'm with Jean, I don't request favors from someone who I haven't spoken to in a long time."

Susan stepped forward. "I think it's a wonderful idea. I still talk to the Almighty every night and ask God for strength and that the nightmares will go away." With enthusiasm in her voice, she added, "We can do it instead of asking a priest to bless it!" She beamed at Tom. "I think Tom can do it. When we go to church he seems to know more than the priest does."

Tom sighed and blushed. "I am not all that." Chris watched as Tom seemed to fight the embarrassment from his wife gushing all over him. He was definitely a peacemaker like Chris and his actions even with Olivia were kind.

Hunter nodded. "I might have been raised poor, but I was raised with God." He looked at Taylor expectantly. "You go to church?"

Taylor rolled her eyes. "Yes, but I didn't think we'd be doing it on a weekday."

"We can still do a brief prayer together here at the house." Tom interjected with a smile.

"Do we need any incense, a smudge stick, or something?" Taylor asked skeptically.

"You got something?" Tom asked, his face lighting up.

"Yes, we've got a gong too," Taylor explained in a monotone voice.

Tom grinned and waved for them to follow him. "I think it's just a matter of believing in ourselves," he said.

Taylor threw her hands up in frustration. "Why are we going through all this?"

Susan dramatically sighed and pushed Hunter and Tay away. "We might as well go, at least you can show us what we missed on the house tour."

Tom's lips curved up in a half-smile as he said, "A little faith never hurt anyone."

Chris stood up, gazing at Nigel, Jean and Nick. "Will you join us?"

"I would burst into flames if I went," Nigel joked. "I'm better off searching for a way out of our sitch on the net."

Jean glanced up from the book, "I'm going to keep searching for more answers too." She turned a page frowning at it with her eyes running over it. "It's like the words keep changing."

Nick sat next to her. "If we get desperate, I can try Olivia again."

Chris paused, half hoping that the theories weren't true, and that the book wasn't really trapping lost souls. It would explain why the book was never consistent and constantly changing. It would also explain why Nigel was on the computer for answers, rather than arguing about the cursed tome for once.

Jean, Nigel and Nick exchanged amused glances.

Nick sucked on an unlit cigarette. When Jean glared at him he held it out for inspection. "Not lit! See?" Once appeased he pointed to the book. "Find anything?"

"Just what we already knew," she exhaled heavily. "It looks like one of us will have to figure out how to break the deal."

Nigel whipped around in the chair. "Would it break the deal for all of us?"

Jean nodded. "It says if they break the deal they can request terms."

Nick wrinkled his brow. "Sounds sketchy."

Jean looked skeptical. "We don't know who's giving us what advice."

Nigel exhaled unhappily. "So we have to goad Marie into picking which one of us will die."

Nick nodded in agreement. "Marie should decide who it is."

Jean groaned in disbelief. "this sounds like a bad game show."

CHAPTER 28

C hris took the lead as they walked through the house, anxious to be the first in case something happened. The smell of coffee and toasted bread that had emanated from the kitchen faded away as they moved into the living room. Taking its place was the unmistakable scent of roses.

The sound of the scent sprayer made Susan jump, and Chris couldn't help but smile. They had all kinds of scent containers in the house – some that sprayed, some that were flameless lanterns, diffusers, plug-ins, and even ones that would dissolve after 30 days.

Chris wouldn't admit it, but they enjoyed the various smells that wafted through their home. The change of season or simply feeling more at home was always comforting.

Susan finally caught the scent and smiled. "I like the smell of roses."

Chris shrugged. "Mom's always been obsessed with pleasing scents," they said. "We have sprays, candles, and stuff all around the house."

Tay rolled her eyes. "She doesn't think about allergies," Tay complained. "She just thinks everyone can take Claritin now."

Tom nodded. "Your family is very welcoming. She can't please everyone."

"Tom is usually the peacemaker, and that could be because of his religious background. He was raised very strict, and still holds firm in his beliefs." Susan laughed lightly. "If you'd like, Tom can take over and lead us in a prayer."

"Group chanting hour." Taylor rolled her eyes.

Chris stepped forward. "She's not much for religion outside of church."

"I do pray…" Taylor pouted.

They all walked around the rest of the home at Tom's direction and when they finished Tay had her phone out.

"I want to order food for everyone." Tay said as they slowed down a little. "I'm hungry and others might be…"

Chris shook their head, "let's make something. We haven't had much luck with delivery people lately."

Tay looked like she would argue but sighed, "Oooookaaaaaaaay."

Once they cooked, they all carried it down to join the others. It was a welcomed distraction, aside from Jean.

Chris watched Jean again worriedly because she barely touched her plate. She put a few bites into her mouth from the salad, and mostly stuck to drinking water. All the while, she avoided eye contact with the others as they enjoyed their meal.

Hunter devoured his food so quickly it was almost hard to watch; even though it wasn't particularly gross.

Nick ate his food sloppily and stuffed bread in between swallows of his drink. Chris attributed the way Nick ate to him being homeless for so long.

Nigel held a small sandwich and kept flipping through the book as he ate.

Susan doted over her husband, who ate, but did not seem very interested in his soup. Susan's soup was long gone, and she pulled apart the small salad.

Taylor had demolished her food, and didn't seem to care about talking with her mouth full as she kept up a running conversation with Hunter.

Chris watched Jean observe the others, with eyes darting to and fro. It was easy to see how anyone could lose an appetite. Chris enjoyed soup and salad, but ate slowly. Surprisingly, the light meal filled them up and the salad became too much for them. Chris realized how little everybody had really been eating.

Hunter glanced at an untouched plate of sushi and questioned. "You gonna eat that?"

Chris pushed it across the table towards Hunter, saying, "No, you can have it."

"This was like a lunch?" Hunter asked and gestured to the people still eating.

The rest of them stared at him in disbelief — except for Tay. She had a brilliant smile for every quirk and peculiarity he made.

Tay flashed her grins towards him and grabbed a piece of sushi. "We could order more food if you're still hungry." She pulled out her phone and started tapping it rapidly.

Chris put a hand on Tay's phone, and shook their head.

Jean tidied wrappers, and Susan leapt to her side to lend a hand.

Taylor jumped in response, also wanting to help. "I wish you would've asked for help."

Chris softly uttered their thanks for Jean and Susan's help.

Tom stared at the patio door with wide eyes and Chris whipped their head around to see what had caught Tom's attention, and saw a mysterious figure making its way up the slope of the backyard, like a lion stalking prey.

The ebony beauty glided past the pool, her strides sly and graceful and her weight shifting from foot to foot with such finesse that it seemed more like she was dancing than simply walking. Her footsteps were light, yet measured, as she balanced her body's movements perfectly.

"Marie?" Chris stammered in confusion. All they could do was observe as she continued to approach but when she reached the back door, they noticed she was completely drenched and her garments clung to her curves.

Tom Kept his eyes wide and unmoving with surprise as Marie came closer, "What is this?"

Nigel muttered gloomily, "Trouble."

Tom seemed absolutely terrified by her presence, stammering, "She's... evil."

Nigel offered a slight assurance, "Just a pain, Tom."

Susan snorted cynically, "I agree with Tom."

Marie stood by the glass of the door now and simply stared at them with her head turning from side to side. She raised a lithe hand to the glass and tapped on it with a single fingernail. Looking back at them with eyes that pierced each of their souls, she asked, "Ain't y'all gonna let me in?"

"How about NO!" Tay nearly shouted to make her point.

Marie rolled her eyes and carefully turned the doorknob but no alarms sounded when it turned and she stepped in slowly. Inching her way in, Marie's eyes darted about until her gaze fixed on Susan and Tom. Marie cocked her head looking right at Tom. "I didn't get to play with y'all last time."

Tom stood by Susan and scoffed but he looked spooked. Chris watched Tom seem very uneasy about Marie, but noticed the man didn't back down or run away. As a matter of fact, Tom seemed ready to protect his wife, which was amusing considering he wasn't immortal.

"Do I scare him?" Marie let out a chuckle and placed her hands on her hips before she tossed her head back. She seemed very aware of the practiced motions she was going through as she let out a hearty burst of laughter. IHer head tossed forward and back again, and her bosom shook ever so slightly in what Chris interpreted was supposed to be an enticing way.

Nick cleared his throat and, a moment later, shook his head as if he needed to clear that too. The strange action made Chris worry that Marie was using some spell like she had on Nigel.

Tom blurted out, "She's evil! Evil incarnate!" Tom stood firmly next to Susan and narrowed his eyes at the newcomer.

Marie smiled like a predator. "Well, he's flattering," she cooed, moving forward.

As she edged closer, Tom backed up closer to the steps, but strangely enough, he didn't seem willing to back down. Chris watched Tom counter her, trying not to be too close to the wicked woman, but his eyes were locked on hers, as if anticipating her next move. Tom and Susan kept their hands clasped tightly together too.

"What do you want, Marie?" Nick demanded stepping forward and placing himself in front of Jean.

Chris was taken aback when they saw Nick's gesture of devotion for Jean. It was unmistakable that he would go to the ends of the earth for her. Chris gulped, regretting that they never had a passionate love like this. Chris took a breath seeing the same with the others. Tay and Hunter, Tom and Susan, and even Nigel had his new boyfriend but Chris had nobody.

In a moment of clarity, Chris thought back and realized this situation was their fault. Taylor wouldn't be in danger and

Jordan wouldn't be missing if they hadn't made the deal. Then again, this group of people wouldn't have come together and Chris wouldn't have gotten to know all of them either.

"I need help," Marie shifted her weight as if to try to coerce Nick with her feminine wiles.

"You shot me!" Jean stepped around Nick and shoved the woman with enough force to make Marie stumble backward a few steps. "Why would we ever trust you enough to help you?"

Marie didn't strike back but watched. "I might be sorry if you stop pushing me." She locked eyes with Jean as if she hoped to bring her around. "We're two immortals that can't die! You really wanna fight cause all we gonna do is leave a mess."

"Not if I take you apart piece by piece," Jean threatened and snatched one of Marie's long braids. Chris loosened Jean's grip and gave her an empathetic stare.

"Let's hear her out." Chris waved at Jean and the others to calm them for a moment. Chris stood with a measured look on their face. They wondered about the timing of Marie showing up so soon after Jordan disappeared.

"I don't feel safe around my family because your *friend* is after me now. That chile y'all sent down to me has him sniffing around." She folded both hands across her chest.

"Olivia?" Chris asked quietly.

"That little blonde chile came to find me and demons," Marie started, but then feigned a chill. "Think you could get me something dry?"

"Did you swim here?" Nigel asked sharply. "You tried to take one of us out last time." He took a step forward, prepared to defend himself. "What doesn't kill us..." He paused, then yelled, "ONLY PISSES US OFF!" He tried to hit the stunning woman, but she gracefully dodged his attack. Nigel was clearly not one for physical confrontation.

"I can help!" Marie snapped. "I'm an immortal like y'all and we could help each other." She tossed her head up, sending her braids dancing past her shoulder. "But I guess y'all wanna stay enemies."

"You think we should trust you after you killed Olivia?" Chris exhaled heavily through their nose. They took in the way Marie was still dripping on the floor, and hoped she might give them insight about their missing family's whereabouts. "We can get something for you to wear that will keep you warm."

As if anticipating Chris's thoughts, Nick handed Marie a glass of red wine. "This should help raise your temperature." He narrowed his eyes as he spoke. "Any false movement, and we won't hesitate to do away with you."

Tom shook his head in disbelief, saying, "I usually try to be understanding, but this woman just..." He cast a glance at Susan and suggested, "My vote is we give her some clothes and send her on her way."

Chris nodded, "I agree with Tom. Even though we can't fully trust you, we're not going to be cruel." Chris gave a slight smile to the always kind Tom. Chris began to see Tom as a role model and a mentor. He was very kind and tried to see the best in everybody but was still fair.

Marie lifted her chin and asked, "How 'bout some food? I fed y'all free at my cafe!" She gave them a sad face. "C'mon, be a sport."

Jean exhaled hard. "Fine, but then you're gone." She headed to the stairs. "I'll get you something to wear."

Marie took a sip of the wine and, although Chris saw her pull a face, she didn't comment on it. She appeared to keep her snarky remarks to herself. Marie watched them scramble a bit, taking in the dynamics slowly. Tom had half an eye on Jean with the same look Nick did. The corners of Marie's mouth turned up at the corners at the sight of them.

Chris headed for the bathroom door and came back with a towel, saying, "You can dry off here. Jean has gone to fetch you a dress."

As Marie moved into the bathroom, she brushed her damp body against Chris temptingly and gave them a smile. "Thanks. You're a peach."

"She's bad news, luv," Nigel cautioned, settling himself on the couch with his gaze still fixed on the door. "Plus she's powerful."

Chris acknowledged the warning, yet didn't really need Nigel to tell them again. Chris had no intention of heeding the voodoo queen's words after she had shot Jean. Still, Chris hoped she would give them some insight.

Jean ran down the steps with an old dress balled up in her hand and went to the bathroom door. She opened it without warning and threw the clothing in a direction only she could see. "Put this on," she commanded gruffly.

When confronted with wary eyes from everyone else, she dismissed them with a scoff. Marie reached a bare arm out of the door holding a damp towel. Jean scoffed, taking it from her roughly. She blushed as she turned to her friends and Nick. It was clear Jean just got an eyeful by being so rude. Nick's mouth hung open slightly as he watched Jean shut the door fast.

"You're not missing out on anything," she muttered before stalking away.

Nick widened his eyes in surprise. "I didn't even ask!"

Tay glared at Hunter, who looked indifferent, then popped her gum at him waiting for his response.

"I don't want some old voodoo woman..." Hunter gulped, but still remained by Taylor's side. "I don't want to see some two hundred year old..."

Jean groaned, cutting Hunter off when she looked at Nick. "Why do you and Nick have to swipe away the drool?"

Hunter shrugged. "That wasn't me."

When Marie emerged from the restroom wearing Jean's dress, she had it slip off one shoulder wearing it very differently than Jean would have. She had hoisted up the bottom of the garment and tucked it into the belt that she'd arrived in, making it much shorter. She rested her arm on the doorframe, trying to appear delicate and submissive. She took a long deep breath.

"I feel better now..." she said coyly.

Nick swallowed hard and moved to see her better. Jean intertwined her arm with his and lifted their clasped hands. Nick's eyes met hers, and he smiled. Having longed for Jean's attention and now that she had given it, Nick completely forgot about Marie.

Jean pulled Nick's arm. "Let's get her something warm to drink so she can be on her way."

Nick followed her up the stairs but not before tossing an angry look at Marie.

Susan nodded at Tom, amused. She wrinkled her nose at Marie. "You don't like her?"

Tom shook his head. "All I can feel from her is that evil smile." He pecked Susan on the cheek. "Remember I have the perfect person already."

Susan smiled, and doted on the man who had saved her from the bus. She interlocked their fingers and nodded. "I won't let her harm you. None of us will."

Marie glanced at Nigel and edged nearer but was met with a scoff. "Luv, you're trying to turn the wrong doorknob." Nigel nearly spat the words with an arched brow.

"That's not what I want," she purred in his ear. "How would you like to shake the curses, then get back your money an' fame?" She spoke in a soft whisper only for him to hear. "I can do it, for a fee."

Nigel raised an eyebrow at her. "You can really do that for us?" His eyes were wide in surprise and his brows raised up. He looked at her with a far away glint playing in his eyes now.

She cracked a wicked grin. "For you, cheri." She waved her fingers enticingly at his face and he moved a bit closer now, as a lover would.

They could all see Marie's behavior toward Nigel, suddenly she seemed to take a keen interest in a man that she hadn't said two words to before.

Taylor sighed hard and rushed over to push the calculating woman away. "I have no idea what she's telling you, but it's a lie!" Taylor moved her feet back and forth, as if preparing for a physical confrontation. Taylor pulled off her earrings and stuffed them into her pocket.

Nigel narrowed his eyes. "Your fabrications don't sway me." He pushed Marie back a bit, breaking the spell she seemed to have cast.

Chris rushed forward for Tay, but looked at Marie. "What can you do? What do you know about our missing family?"

Marie looked amused at them and slinked closer to Tay as Taylor countered by stepping back. "You're the human... the mortal." Marie sneered the words then gave a look of mock sympathy. "The one who *can* die?"

Chris jumped between them in an attempt to be a barrier and Hunter pulled Taylor's hand to bring her closer to him. Marie simply side stepped Chris and tossed her hand on her hip before shifting her weight.

She locked eyes with Hunter and scoffed, "What is a fine man like you doing with this girl?" She cocked her head and clicked her tongue, looking Hunter up and down.

Hunter scowled. "I love Tay."

Marie laughed so hard she tossed her head back. "Boy, this girl is too young for you. You're definitely not the same." She touched her ebony skin, then waved her hand at him. "We're the same."

Hunter shook his head at her, trying to get her meaning then he seemed to register it. "Because we're the same color, or because we're both immortal?" He barked back at her, looking offended.

Marie said sharply, "Both!" and tilted her chin in defiance.

Hunter shook his head. "My family is gone. This is my family now." He glanced around the room and everyone nodded to confirm it.

Chris moved closer between them and glared at Marie. "You look pretty dry now…"

"Yeah! Bye!" Tay chimed in with a mock wave.

"You gone toss me out?" Marie looked to Chris's usually sympathetic eyes.

"My husband doesn't want you either!" Susan interjected hastily, grabbing onto Tom's hand possessively.

Marie laughed. "I didn't do nothing wrong." She brought her arms closer around her body, as if she was trying to keep warm. "I'm still cold…"

Tay sighed. "You're full of…"

"Hot cocoa!" Jean shouted from the stairwell, followed shortly by Nick. When they reached the bottom step, Nick's eyes studied the scene with visible tension in the air. "Now what?"

Chris held a hand up to them, as if to pause them from handing out drinks.

Jean looked at them from behind Nick and bit her lip. She was still on the stairs and could only watch with Nick blocking her path, but that might have been his plan to keep her out of the fray.

Marie popped her lips and chuckled, "I was speaking to this fine man…" she gestured to Hunter. "…because he's too old for this girl and he belongs with someone more..." She paused with a smile, and shifted her weight suggestively towards him... "suitable."

She moved closer to the group with a smile and sighed. "Now if y'all were smart, you'd join me, because I know more than you do..." She swaggered forward to Hunter and touched the collar of his shirt with her fingers, letting the material slide between her digits.

Tay batted her hand away with an angry look, and Marie gave her a Cheshire grin at her annoyed look.

Chris moved closer to Tay, worried she would lose her temper with this woman and get hurt.

"I can help you get rid of those nightmares..." Marie swayed over to the large couch and sat down in a fluid motion with her arms over the back of the headrest, laying claim to the space on the couch and lowering her chin. "Y'all need me."

Nick stepped aside for Jean to pass, before handing a cup of cocoa to Marie. She took it slowly and watched him over the brim as she took a sip.

Chris cocked their head. "Can you tell us what happened to our brother and parents?"

Nigel looked into her eyes at the same time, asking, "Can you really make the nightmares go away? Can you help us?"

"Of course!" Marie scoffed and leaned closer to Nick, her gaze unyielding. "Whatcha gone do for me?" To Chris, her tone sounded deadly but the look in her eyes as she spoke to Nick seemed inviting. The corner of her mouth upturned ever so slightly, and just like that, it was gone. She darted her head to each of them and gave a slight bob of her head. "Y'all been rude since I got here."

"Rude?" Susan echoed and narrowed her eyes at Marie.

"At least we didn't shoot you!" Tay crossed her arms. "We gave you clothing and let you come in!"

Chris held their hand up, hoping to stifle Taylor in hopes they might learn something from Marie, and to keep Tay safe.

Tom still stood far from them, even as Susan inched a bit closer.

Jean glanced at Nick, who was clearly still entranced by Marie's presence. "Nick?" When Hunter nudged him, he finally realized he was being addressed.

"What did you say?" Nick's cheeks flushed as he looked up.

"Ain't that sweet..." Marie chuckled and watched them with a practiced eye.

Jean kept her gaze on Marie and hardly moved a muscle.

Nick tapped his pant pockets then stood, checking his back pockets.

Jean gave him a sidelong glance. "Missing something?"

Nick answered with a nod, "My lighter. I've had it since my first time on stage." He gave a nod to the ceiling. "It's probably in my room."

Marie chuckled condescendingly. "Sentiment."

"Sentiment is good..." Chris countered fast, in a defensive tone. "Don't you have family and mementos that you treasure?" Chris took a deep breath, losing their patience with Marie and looking down on their friends.

Nick made his way up the stairs, but Jean followed him. He stopped and turned, looking at her in surprise.

"We can't be alone," Jean reminded him with a frustrated sigh and a slight toss of her hand. She motioned for him to continue up the stairs and followed him slowly.

Marie cackled, "I guess that man is taken..."

Chris and Taylor backed away with Hunter in tow. "I think it's about time you were leaving, Marie," Chris asserted as they stepped forward. "Once again you haven't really given us any answers and you're just causing trouble."

Chris was growing very weary of Marie. It was becoming all

too clear she wasn't there for any other reason than to try to start fights between them. From the flirting with everybody but the ladies, to the false promises, to being able to end the curse, it all kept Chris on edge. Olivia had stopped the curse because Marie killed her, and now her soul resided in that book. Chris sighed. Nothing had been easy since they made their deal with Deacon.

CHAPTER 29

"What did we miss?" Jean shouted from the foot of the stairs with Nick standing beside her.

"They want me to go!" Marie cried out dejectedly.

"Duh!" Tay scoffed. She turned to the floor length mirror only to pop her gum in the reflection.

Marie shot a look of disapproval at Nick for his lack of response, then glanced in Jean's direction. The latter stood near Nick as if to mark her territory.

"She got her nails in you?" Her words seethed with anger, and rang in Chris's ears.

Marie looked at Chris. "You in love with the fat lady? He's ruined it, so toss him out." She waved a hand scoffing at the couple.

Chris glanced over at Jean and Nick with a puzzled look. "What does she mean?"

Nick shrugged, "I haven't made it a secret I'm in love with Jean."

"Yeah, but you a couple now!" Marie hissed and turned to Chris. "Toss him out. He stole your girl."

Chris watched as Jean grabbed onto Nick's hand and her gaze fell to the floor. It was suddenly obvious something happened. Before, Jean seemed a little angry at Nick. Now, she made a mad grab for Nick's hand. Chris's face flushed, and they took a deep breath. The look on Nick's face was joy and guilt. Chris thought back to the almost-kiss on the plane, and realized now why she couldn't meet their eyes. Chris took a hard breath and nodded.

"Kid, it's nothing against you," Nick said quietly and looked at Chris with tender eyes. Then he took a deep breath for emphasis, and glared at Marie. ""You're not going to split us up. Nick and Jean... is one word!"

Chris nodded seeing their hands and the unity it represented. Chris smiled at them, then looked at Marie. "They're my best friends and I'm happy for them." Chris shrugged. "Anybody could see it was going to happen and I'm glad."

Tom gave a huge smile in agreement. He reached out and drew Hunter and Tay closer into the group, nestled between Susan and himself. "This vile woman isn't separating any of us." He looked between them and smiled.

Marie gnashed her teeth in response, but before she could take a step toward Nigel or Hunter, Chris confronted her.

"If they are truly in love, then I'm happy for them both," Chris quickly added. "Just like how we all love each other... like a family."

Marie snarled as Chris pushed her toward the door. "You thought you could come here and divide us?" Chris said, and pointed an accusing finger at her. "Well, you failed! You didn't tell us anything or help us at all. We helped you. We're done. Leave!"

Their will to argue abruptly ceased when the putrid smell of sulfur filled the air. The lights flickered and, a moment later, everything went dark.

Chris fought to see as shadows fell across them, and a cold chill sent shivers up through their body.

It took everyone a few moments to register a green glow emanating from the corner of the room. Bit-by-bit, Deacon emerged from the shadows, and drew ever so close to Chris. Every step was accompanied with a loud clicking sound, like tap dancing shoes on pavement and, as Deacon came nearer, the pungent smell intensified.

The circumference of darkness plunged into the center of that light from where Deacon stood was a blackness that had no walls, but was infinite and looming, a chasm so immense that even the darkest soul might never find solace.

As Deacon emerged, a dark looming chuckle filled the air, and he took languishing steps toward Chris. He straightened to his full, intimidating height and exhaled menacingly once he had. Deacon's spindly fingers were adorned with razor-sharp nails that stabbed his lit cigar. He brought it to his lips, taking a leisurely puff, and gave Chris a ghost of a smile as his mouth bent around the cigar. The acrid stench of the stogie blended into a noxious combination with Deacon's sulphuric odor.

Chris and the others stepped back in shock. The hollow sockets of Deacon's eyes were sunken into his head, and his skin seemed to be stretched taut over bone. His hair was matted and disheveled, but despite the drastic alteration in appearance, there was no mistaking who it was.

A sinister cackle escaped from Deacon's lips while he tipped his top hat, the brim still covering his eyes. "Miss me, minions?" Deacon roared with laughter, his voice a chorus of twisted vocalizations.

Chris recognized the cruel smile from their last encounter, and it was unnerving. It was one of the first things Chris had noticed when they saw him in person. Now, Chris noticed

Deacon's smile seemed forced – if he tried to stretch it any further, his skin would likely crack off his pale face.

Fear radiated from everyone in the room, and Marie's became as still as a board. Her eyes darted left and right like a cornered animal, her breathing was shallow and rapid. She looked like she wanted to run but was frozen in place by an invisible force. Her eyes were wide and her mouth slack, her chin quivered. Chris saw fear in her eyes as she stepped backward. With a determined expression on their face, Chris stepped into Deacon's path and spread out their arms.

Chris held no love for the witchy woman but, at the same time, Chris considered she might be as much a pawn to Deacon as they were. The expression on Marie's face confirmed Chris's suspicions and they turned their attention back to Deacon. Chris inhaled slowly and contemplated if Deacon intended to dispose of the immortals he had created. Deacon held all the cards... or did he? The wheels spun in Chris's head. How could all of them walk out alive and in one piece?

"You gone protect Marie?" Deacon's lips curled and the corners of his mouth tilted up slightly. "I can't kill her. I don't have her contract." He smiled and pointed toward her, shifting to the side so he could catch a glimpse of her behind Chris.

He brandished his arm with such speed it cut the air and created a gust of wind. Narrowing his now yellow eyes, he began to mumble in a cacophony of voices. Marie's eyes filled with terror as a verdant fog circled her feet. She spun around in a vortex, gradually increasing her speed until she flung her arms out, as if frantically reaching for assistance. She dissolved into green incandescence, her mouth twisted in a wordless cry.

Transfixed in helplessness, Chris watched Marie wink out and vanish. She was gone.

"Don't you fret 'bout her none. She gone be back up to no

good by the bayou." Deacon swiveled around so that he was facing the others, a playful glint in his eye. With a long exhale, he pondered, "What to do with the immortals, eh?"

He looked down at them like a parent disappointed with defiant children. "You gone and found a way to make the agreement... interesting?" He shook his head.

"We didn't do anything!" Taylor shot at him, but his quick look at her made her recoil.

"You are not even immortal," Deacon cackled loudly.

His hand rose languidly, and they all watched as Taylor was lifted off the ground. He clenched his hand into a tight fist and, for each motion it gave, her helpless body corresponded. He waggled his fist in her direction and she was sent flying toward him. She hung there watching him, silent as a mouse. Her usual quick wit, bouncy steps, and popping gum had vanished, replaced only with a piercing stare and an unspoken plea.

"What to do?" Deacon tapped his long fingernails against the handle of his cane thoughtfully.

"No!" Hunter yelled, his voice full of anguish as a tear rolled down his face. Hunter moved toward Taylor and groaned with the strain, sweat pooling on his forehead as he pushed against an invisible force. His body quivered, and he inched closer to her, every inch a massive effort.

Chris and Nick crept closer. Deacon nonchalantly raised a hand, and the small gesture effortlessly halted their advancement as well. Relishing the moment when the three were unable to move, Deacon teased, "Don't do something you'll regret."

He shifted Taylor so she was looking towards him and sighed. "I think my point is not made..." He moved her closer to his face until there was scarcely any space between them, and a faint gasp of surprise escaped Taylor's lips and echoed in the quiet room.

"Get off!" Hunter pushed against the intangible power, managing to draw closer painstakingly slowly. By some miracle, Hunter reached Deacon and threw a punch at the entity. He was flung back against the mirror on the wall like a ragdoll.

With a groan, Hunter stood and dusted off his clothes. A cloud of fine dust hung in the air around him and Chris stared at the impression Hunter had left in the cracked and crumbling wall. Hunter took a step and mirror shards crunched under his feet.

"The girl in the harbor not enough? The parents not enough?" Deacon met Chris's eyes. "The ballerina not enough? The little brother not enough?" He paused, inhaling a deep breath as though he was gathering the courage to continue. Chris wondered if it was a sign this was not an easy task for Deacon. "The younger sister not enough?"

Chris gawked at the strength and determination radiating from Hunter as the former Olympian struggled once again to move against Deacon's paralyzing barrier. They wondered if perhaps this brave warrior could be the one to finally vanquish the malevolent menace. Chris paused with a mixture of awe and a growing glimmer of hope.

Maybe this was why Hunter had suddenly become so strong. Conscious of their own weakness, Chris was unable to act. They could do nothing to comfort Taylor as she suffered through Deacon's sadistic enjoyment.

Deacon raised his arm, and Taylor flew upwards toward the ceiling, her head arching severely backward so she looked right at Hunter behind her. Chris thought she might be trying to say something with just a glance, but the demon's influence nipped that attempt in the bud.

Wrenching his hand back, Deacon twisted Taylor's arms

back around themselves and she emitted a horrible shriek when they snapped. Her legs did the same, bending back over themselves until there was an awful, sickening crunch.

Slowly, her head turned and Taylor shot a terrified look at Hunter, asking for help without saying a word... but it was all for naught.

Their eyes met in a goodbye. Taylor's mouth moved but no words passed her trembling lips. Deacon delivered the final blow with a crack of his fist. A loud snap followed and Taylor whimpered one last time before silence descended on the room. Taylor's huge moon eyes stared blindly into nothingness – lifeless.

Air rushed out of Chris. Taylor. How? Why? After everything they'd done to keep her safe... They couldn't breathe as Deacon ripped Taylor apart. The demon's glee was like two children fighting over the same poppet.

Chris's chest jolted and they sucked in a sharp breath, but their throat constricted and they fought back tears. Their hands started to shake and their heart pounded faster than ever.

Deacon slowly lowered his arm, cruelly releasing Taylor's body so it fell in a heap on the ground. Her limbs flew out in all directions and Hunter let out an agonizing cry as he rushed to her side.

"Tay?" Hunter pulled her limp body against him and looked at her. To Chris's shock, her eyes moved and her mouth opened slightly. Chris raised their eyes to meet Hunter's, and a spark of hope glimmered. Could it be possible she was still alive?

Chris swept away the tears that had pooled on their cheeks, and croaked, "What do we do?" They dropped to their knees, fists clenched tightly in a mix of grief and desperation as they joined Hunter beside Tay's motionless body. Pleading silently for some miracle that just wasn't there.

Chris felt a sharp pain in their chest at the sight of their sister. It all seemed for naught. Watching over her, all the worry and isolation to keep her safe was for nothing now.

Deacon sneered, "Say your goodbyes…"

Tay shuddered uncontrollably. Her lips trembled as she tried to form words, but all that came out was a moan. The corner of her mouth quivered and her eyes glistened with unshed tears. She looked at Hunter and then Chris as if she could see right into their souls, speaking to them without saying a word. Her love was palpable and engulfed her fright.

Her body spasmed and jolted as tears finally streamed down her face. Her whole frame trembled violently. Her arm dropped while her eyes looked upward, leaving her with an emotionless face.

"Tay!" Hunter screamed. "Tay?" His voice was desperate and he reached for her shoulder.

Feeling the blood drain from them, Chris watched as the light dimmed in Taylor's eyes. The last of their family was now gone. Fun-loving, snarky Tay was no more and Chris felt utterly alone. They looked to Hunter, then the others, for help but everyone in the room looked as helpless as Chris felt.

Chris was cold. Nothing made sense. How could Tay be gone? Something wet hit Chris's arm and they blinked.

Hunter sobbed, "Tay… I love you."

Chris sat in wide-eyed shock, looking between Taylor and Hunter. Taylor would never again sit at the breakfast table. She wouldn't chide Chris about taking all the rides at the amusement parks, or opening gifts at holidays and birthdays. Too many memories flashed before their eyes. Chris's heart squeezed. It was all gone and done.

"No..." Chris could hardly feel their legs but that seemed insignificant. "Tay?"

Taylor glowed, bright light shimmering from her form. Chris blinked. They couldn't believe what they were seeing. Taylor's body seemed to be turning into pure light, getting brighter as the seconds passed. She started to blur around the edges until her body disintegrated. The light dimmed, slowly dispersing like ashes in the wind. Chris reeled back, their eyes wide. What was going on? Where was Taylor? Underneath the shock, a deep sorrow grew. It was like a storm cloud, inevitable and heavy. How had Taylor disappeared? Chris was left without even a body.

Chris went over it again. All they could do was watch in their mind's eye as Taylor dissipated piece by piece until she was gone. Hunter's embrace was empty and Chris let out an anguished wail.

"Now..." Deacon said joyfully and did all but skip as he loomed over Tom. "The other mortal."

"Enough!" Chris stood and grabbed a jagged piece of the broken mirror Hunter had destroyed and stepped threateningly toward Deacon. They felt their throat tighten with rage as they took another step forward and narrowed their eyes threateningly.

"This ends now!" Chris took a deep breath, mustering the courage they needed to keep going despite the overwhelming wave of grief they felt in the face of Tay's death.

Deacon tossed his head back in a symphony of laughter and gave a rakish grin. "You can't hurt me, child!" Like a clap of thunder, Deacon's laughter filled the room, and his eyes gleamed with malevolence. The darkness intensified with the laughter, which reverberated through the room and sent opalescent waves rippling through the air. The only light was the flicker of yellow and orange flames in Deacon's eyes. They rose higher until they engulfed his irises, leaving only that pair of blazing eyes to light up the dark.

Chris took a deep breath and mustered the courage to stand their ground. "No, but I can hurt me!" Chris's brow furrowed as adrenaline surged through their veins. "Our deal isn't finished yet. It's not complete. I'm not a full immortal, am I?"

Deacon averted his gaze, confirming Chris's suspicion. The ominous specter of a man tilted his head and nudged his top hat upward a bit as he considered Chris's words. They watched Deacon, whose brows furrowed and arms crossed, while his gaze traveled from Chris to their friends and back again. Deacon's demonic presence lessened and he did not lift a finger against Chris while he deliberated the possibilities.

Chris stared at the spot where Tay had stood mere seconds before. The empty space seemed to stare back at them. All of the pain and anguish of their losses rose up in Chris's throat and they clenched their jaw, determination replacing the fear that had been there earlier. Taking a deep breath, they steeled themself, ready to take on Deacon.

"If someone cancels your deal, then everything else is canceled." Chris remembered what Nigel had found in the book and exhaled deeply. If that was true,Deacon wouldn't risk harming Chris and canceling the deal. Thinking about the others, Chris felt certain it was the entire reason they couldn't kill themselves. Deacon needed them alive. They were his toys.

Deacon raised a brow, intrigued. "What you gone do?"

Deacon squared up as if he was preparing himself, expecting Chris to lunge toward him. Standing tall, head held high, Deacon's gaze met Chris's in a challenge. He had the composure of a hammer looking down at a nail, confident in its ability to overpower and control.

Nigel seemed to catch on to what Chris meant and held his

head up. "Get him, Chris!" Nigel snarled. "Maybe you can't die but Chris can tick you off and you can't touch them!"

"That's not quite it," Chris whispered as they sliced a glass shard across their wrists. It cut through the skin like butter, and the flash of pain was followed by the drip of blood as it ran down their hand and soaked their shirtsleeves. The vivid red liquid oozed from the wound, pouring and splashing into an expanding pool. "I'm breaking our deal," Chris said. "If somebody finds a way to cancel the deal, the rest are released." Their face screwed up in anger as they shifted the shard from one hand to the other and dropped to their knees.

The others inched closer, apart from Tom. Chris repeated the slicing movement on their other wrist – their gesture of sacrifice. Chris looked up at Tom, and their eyes met. The two stared at each other for a long time. Chris opened their lips to speak, but no sound came out.

After they took a deep breath, they found their voice and said quietly, "You should be safe now. You're all safe..."

Tom released Susan's grasp. "If Chris dies, it will be clear that the Shepherd guided them." He grinned and removed his thick rimmed spectacles. He stepped forward until he was near Deacon, whose gaze was now locked onto Tom.

Chris swallowed hard, feeling weak, and expecting their life to ebb out of them, but for some reason they seemed to have a front row seat to watch Tom confront Deacon. Every word seemed like a hammer strike. Chris inhaled. They hoped Tom wouldn't ruin the offering they had just given to keep everyone safe.

The metallic smell of blood hung heavy in the air, and Chris lay motionless, surrounded by an ever-growing pool of crimson liquid. Chris blinked. It was strange how the expected sleep of death did not come. They remained very much alive.

Deacon slowly tilted his head to the side, unable to contain a smile that tugged at the corners of his lips. "What are you doing?" He tossed his head back tauntingly, clearly enjoying their little challenges. "Let de child die in peace, non?"

"Are you nuts?" Susan hurried after Tom, and clasped his hand. "He just tore up Tay!" After a moment of looking into Tom's face, Susan released him. The man's eyes shone with an effervescent luminescence that seemed to come from within. "What on earth..." Susan exclaimed, perplexed at the sight of him.

"Deacon," Tom spoke in a soft, calming voice but turned his back on the adversary and reached out his hands toward Chris. As his skin touched Chris's, the gash on their right wrist glowed with a faint purple light that slowly extended further up their arm before disappearing altogether, followed by the same process on their left. "You may not have this human. They have proved they are pure of heart, and would give themselves for another." He gave Nigel a sideways glance. "Even Nigel..."

Deacon stepped forward, hissing as he scrutinized Tom. "What are you?" He gritted his teeth, and a deep rumble rose from his throat. "You have no power over me." Deacon's gaze pierced through him as he stood in silence for what seemed like an eternity. Finally, Deacon stepped back and narrowed his eyes, keeping a close watch on Tom's every motion.

"I am an angel," Tom said quietly.

Deacon laughed and loomed over Tom. He sneered, "Says he's an angel!" He raised his arm yet, when he struck out at Tom, nothing happened. Baffled, Deacon tried again with his other arm with the same result. He swiped at Tom with ferocity, but it was as if he swung into the wind.

"Chris defeated you, Deacon," Tom smiled. "They put the needs of others before their own and they acted selflessly. I have witnessed them time and again helping others, no matter the pain they felt."

Deacon stood, amused. "An angel?" A hearty laugh tore from him, as if he were trying to pass the situation off as a joke. Deacon tossed his hand upward and it looked like he was trying to release a bird. He chuckled, and Chris thought Deacon shrank. He still tried to intimidate them with his malice, certain his plan had been foolproof, and acting so confident. Although Deacon still looked like he believed no one would be able to beat him, doubt crept into his eyes and overshadowed his reluctance to accept a thing this angel said.

Chris's throat felt tight and they could feel their heart thudding in their chest. Tom was an angel? Their brain raced with the information, and for a moment it felt like time had stopped as they tried to process everything. Chris managed to look up, blinking away the blurriness of their vision.

I am alive, they realized and sat up.

In amazement, Chris watched as mild-mannered Tom faced Deacon, chin held high and determination blazing in his eyes. He spoke with intensity and conviction, gesturing to punctuate his words as he argued against the injustice that Deacon sought to impose.

Briefly, Chris's gaze met Tom's, and they could see the recognition in his eyes. A second later, Tom drew in a large breath unfurling enormous, downy wings from his back like a blanket of starlight.

"You cannot have them!" Tom said, his voice powerful but gentle. He raised his hand, palm up, and golden light emanated from the floor around Deacon, slowly radiating outward and encircling the demon. "And you will not torture them any longer."

At that moment, something seemed to awaken in Tom. His

face softened, and he lowered his arm. The light around Deacon grew brighter, until the whole room was illuminated.

For the first time, Chris saw Tom for what he truly was: a messenger of peace, a guardian of the oppressed, and a protector of the innocent. Tom swiftly lifted his other arm, and Deacon stumbled backward as the ground split open beneath him. The space filled with frightening voices echoing in the air and sinister laughter cascading down from above.

Tom stepped forward and roared. "They are not yours, Deacon!" He pulled his arms down hard, and Deacon was plunged into the abyss. No shrieks sounded as he faded away. There was no scrambling for safety. Deacon was just gone, and the floor returned to its former state. All that remained of Deacon was a vague scent of sulfur, which slowly dissipated.

Chris sat still. They glanced around the room, fearful something – or someone – would suddenly appear. Their mouth hung open and they barely dared believe what had just happened. Running a hand up and down their face, Chris was surprised to find nothing had changed; the situation remained the same.

Tom turned to look at the others with a smile. He spread his billowy wings out and then he gracefully tucked them away until they were invisible. His eyes continued to glow as bright as star-filled emptiness. He smiled and the room warmed in the glow of his joy.

Chris touched their sore wrists and was surprised to see only faint pink lines on their skin. "Is Deacon…"

Tom shifted in place. "Dead? No. But he won't bother you any longer. I couldn't help until the pact was shattered."

Susan gaped, fingers lightly grazing her collarbone. "So I married an angel?"

"No, you married Tom, but his soul is a pure vessel, so I inhabited him," Tom's lips curled into a smile that was so warm and genuine, even the most hardened of people could feel their hearts melting. His usual kind demeanor had been replaced with something more meaningful as he beamed benevolence upon them.

Nigel, looking confused, spoke up. "So, wait, if you're an angel, does that mean that Christianity is the one true religion?"

"Actually, they're all equally true," Tom said calmly. "Christianity, Buddhism, Islam... By holding genuine faith in a higher power, you make it real, even if you can't see it."

"So, what does this mean for us?" Chris asked, shaking their head in confusion.

"You never completed the deal you were given. You never went to see your doctor..." Tom lamented. "You were the only one who could break the deal. By doing that, you freed the others and gave me an opportunity to intervene."

"No more nightmares?" Nigel asked, his voice almost a whisper. "Son of a dogma..." Then he wrinkled his brow. "What about the rest?"

"The book tried to explain it all... the damned souls, the gifts." Tom placed his hand on the cover of the ancient tome, tracing the letters carved into its leather. He slowly looked up at them, his face filled with regret. "I'm sorry I wasn't able to help earlier. But now, this can be your light in the dark."

"Are we still going to be immortal?" Susan inquired in a hushed voice.

"You fulfilled his stipulations, you suffered his torment and performed selfless acts. So yes, you should have immortality," Tom replied. Then he narrowed his eyes at Chris. "But... *you* didn't follow through with the entire agreement, so you won't be able to reap that benefit. Except that..." Tom grinned softly. "You are completely healed now. Your gesture of good will has been seen and you are immune to cancer."

"So we get to stay immortal?" Hunter said sadly. "I'd rather have Tay…"

Tom waved a hand as if to stifle his sadness.Fixing his gaze on each in turn, Tom said, "You discovered a way to turn Deacon's cursed deal around for something beneficial – helping others. Every time you saved someone, you were upsetting the demon's plans."

The Angel began to pace and Chris stared at his heavenly glow. As enthralled as Chris was, they were impatient to bombard Tom with questions. However, the angel was not done, and cocked his head.

"Olivia was determined to find Marie and have her alter or revoke the agreement made, so the two visited Papa Legba, the trickster who Marie knows. But Papa Legba and Deacon agreed. Papa took Olivia's deal and canceled it by taking her life."

Chris looked at him curiously, but Tom carried on. "Yes, there is a way for the unfortunate souls tricked by demons to break their contracts; they become guides dwelling inside of the book forever."

Chris nodded, "And Jordan and my parents…"

Tom simply gave a slight nod in Chris's direction, almost as though he was trying to avoid the question until the conversation had run its course. "You used the power of the curse to do good deeds and keep an eye out for one another. You took this curse and turned it into something helpful for those around you. You are truly blessed."

Hunter looked up suddenly, a hint of surprise in his expression. Chris considered all the losses the former Olympian had experienced and the knowledge of it sank into them like a stone.

A small muscle in Hunter's jaw twitched as he asked, "So that's why I'm so strong now?" His shoulders sagged. Chris thought about Hunter's posture and they understood; despite the newfound strength, Hunter's loss still weighed heavily on him.

Tom nodded. "If you had a deal before, you were blessed with a gift such as Hunter's newfound strength. Everyone else will have to find out what that gift is, just like Hunter did. Chris's gift is uncomplicated. They'll have good health for the rest of their life."

Susan's voice cut in. "Where is my husband?"

Tom turned to her with a smile on his face. "Don't worry, he's safe and sound right now," he said reassuringly. "He's very proud of you." The angel lifted his arm, and said, "First..." Blinding light spread outward from Tom's raised hand and engulfed the small group in a bright glow.

Chris's vision blurred, and the world spun out of control. They squeezed their eyes shut, hoping to regain their balance and orientation. For a moment, they were suspended in time and space, lost in the dizzying void.

Chris stirred in their bed, feeling the soft sheets beneath them and hearing the cries of seabirds from outside their bedroom windows. The memories of last night came flooding back. Chris ripped the covers off their bed in a single motion and sprinted to Nick's room. With a loud bang, Chris burst through the door and stood breathless as they surveyed the dimly lit space. Nick wriggled out from beneath the covers, sleepily blinking as Chris's eyes adjusted to the faint light.

"Nick?" Chris asked excitedly, their voice trembling with hope.

The former rockstar sat upright and turned toward Chris, still shaking off the cobwebs of dreamland. A wide smile spread across Chris's face and they watched Nick's lips silently mouth the same question, "Was it real?"

Bewildered, Nick said out loud, "I was just having a dream about an angel..." His eyes widened and he leapt out of bed. "Where is Taylor?"

Chris's eyes became wild with panic, and they both raced to Taylor's door, yelling her name. Nick and Chris burst through the door, their faces ashen with worry. Jean stood frozen next to Taylor's bed, her eyes wide in shock. Finger pressed against her lips, Jean's gaze tilted meaningfully to Taylor's sleeping form. Chris's sister inhaled and they all let out a slow breath of relief.

"She's alright?" Nick asked before Chris had a chance.

Jean simply nodded.

Tay groaned and sat up. "What's so wrong about sleeping in?" she croaked, rubbing her weary eyes. "Old people... not everyone wants to get up at 5 am."

Nick reached out and ruffled Tay's hair, his smile stretching from one ear to the other. He nodded in Chris's direction and gestured toward the doorway. "Come on, let's see how everyone else is doing."

Chris tiptoed through the dimly lit hallway with Nick and they were careful not to wake anyone else. The scent of lavender and chamomile floated from Hunter's room, where soft snores could be heard. The grand room Nigel had claimed was marked by a deep silence; the only sound being that of his steady breathing. Chris took a deep breath and moved on to the next few rooms, preparing for whatever awaited them.

A piercing shriek cut through the air like a razor and echoed off the walls. Startled, Chris and Nick stopped, turning toward Chris's parents' grand bedroom.

Susan stood in the doorway and looked into the room. "What do you mean you don't remember?

As Chris and Nick reached her, Tom settled his glasses in place and chided her, "Dear, you woke the entire house..."

"We were already up," Chris replied with a smile, their eyes darting to Tom. Despite the large frames of his glasses obscuring part of his face, they could finally make out Tom's features and see how blue his eyes were. They still couldn't believe Tom had been an angel.

Susan gestured for them to come into the room and asked in a hushed voice, "Did what I think happened last night... happen?"

"If you mean there was an angel who saved us?" Nick asked skeptically.

"Tom did," Chris said with a sly grin as he looked at Tom. Tom's eyebrows raised in confusion, and it was clear he had no idea what Chris was referring to.

"I don't really recall," Tom murmured as he stood up.

Nigel let out a yawn as he entered the room. "No more nightmares, and I finally got some real sleep for the first time in two decades. Thanks, luv."

Susan grinned. "He has no recollection of any of it."

"Any of what, dear?" Tom said in a gentle voice. He reached up to adjust his glasses, which had slipped down to the bridge of his nose.

Hunter flung open the door with a bang, wild eyed, and scanning the room desperately. He seemed to not even notice he was in the house as he gasped out, "Was it all just a dream?" before quickly taking off down the hallway, shouting, "Tay!"

The sound of the door squeaking open made everyone jump. Jordan stepped into the hallway, eyes heavy and unfocused. He wore the same clothes he had on when he vanished the day before. "Any sign of Mom and Dad?" he asked, his voice barely a whisper.

Chris's jaw fell open and their eyes bulged. The surprise was too great. They couldn't say anything. Tyalor and Hunter came into the hallway only for Tay to stand there with her mouth hanging open. Coming to her senses, Taylor bolted over to Jordan and embraced him before Chris could. Chris followed suit, but both stumbled back a bit from the force of their reunion hug.

Chris held their siblings tightly, fighting back tears and a lump in their throat. As they embraced, Chris scanned the room with wide eyes, taking in the joyous reunion of friends and family. The warmth of the moment was overwhelming and Chris closed their eyes, exhaling deeply in relief at this moment of happiness. Chris made a mental note to let Tay order out all she wanted this week.

Jordan stepped away from Chris and looked over at the others. A sudden ding from a text rang out and he yawned. He swiped the message open and read. "Mom and Dad want to know if they should get breakfast on their way home."

Chris snatched up Jordan's phone and looked at it. "They're okay?"

Jordan eyed him incredulously before he said, "Alright... I'm gonna take a shower, you can answer that text for me."

Jordan's eyes widened in surprise as he turned to find Taylor and Hunter standing side by side. He scoffed loudly, and a snort of laughter followed. "I never saw you with a boy at home, Tay," he quipped before hurrying back to his own room.

Tay put her hands on her hips and pouted before she called to Jordan's closed door, "I had an old woman in my room, not a man!"

"Are we still immortal?" Nick asked softly.

"I guess we'll have to test it," Nigel sighed.

Jean glanced at Nick before finally asking, "So the part with my pic was true too?"

Nick gave an affirming grin and interlaced his fingers with hers. Jean shook her hand free and threw her arms around him, and Nick lifted her up off the ground. He held her up like an angel hovering above him. He lowered her gradually, cradling her until their lips touched. Chris smiled as the two kissed again lightly despite all the catcalls and whistles from Nigel.

Chris marveled at the change they felt. This time instead of cringing or wishing away the notion, Chris smiled. They knew there was somebody out there who could love them as much as Nick and Jean loved each other. Fate was fate, and Nick said he'd loved her for decades.

Chris felt Taylor grab them in a hug, and Hunter quickly joined in, laughing. Chris ignored Tom and Susan, and he continued to tell her he didn't know. Taylor whispered in Chris's ear that there would be somebody for them and Chris nodded.

Right now it didn't matter to Chris because immortal or not, tomorrow would come for each of them. Chris smiled as Taylor's phone showed another text from their parents. As she started to answer, Chris pulled out their own phone, texting the doctor for an appointment to confirm they were indeed cancer free.

The folks at the portside cafe downtown were enthralled as they watched the leaves float on the breeze and meander across the boat hulls. They sipped on coffee and savored meals while surrounded by peacefulness. Most appreciated the calm and privacy the waterfront had to offer.

A man stretched back in his chair and gave the impression that he was at two tables simultaneously. His gaze focused on a young woman reading a book. He cleared his throat to capture her attention.

"Tell me, Chérie," he crooned. "What would you do if you knew when you were going to die," his hands spread wide in a dramatic gesture, "and I could save you?" He smiled at her with a charm none could rival.

ACKNOWLEDGMENTS

Special thanks to my incredible ARC team: I am at a loss for words to convey how grateful I am for each and every one of you. Did you all give me glowing 5-star reviews? No, and that means everything to me. Were you all honest with your feedback? Absolutely, and I cannot thank you enough for that. ARC readers hold a special power in helping authors improve and succeed. Every writer should be thankful for the support and guidance they provide. You have truly made me a better writer.

Tanesha, Aubrey, Frey, Brooke, Miranda, Jamesworld, Alison, Hannah, Kayla, Jordan, Liz, Arliegh, Hailee, April. Laura, Natasha, Terri, Dedra, Daneille, Josie, Kiki, Jarriel, Beegers, Treefflower, Iisha, Stephanie, Natasha, Samantha, RS, BookDragon, Michaela, Carah, Yesenia, Alex, Nazaria, Milenia, Hilary, Rain, Chastity, Korinna, Kodi, Khalessi, Kaela, Jessa, escapethrouhabook, Kristin, Ridley, Kelsreads, Rhiannon, Carah, Missallinicole, Diana, Anna Marie, Mkbook, Breanna, Stephanie, Jessa, Hrreads, Jaycruzin, and Frey.

A special thank you to Astrid for being an amazing editor and friend.

My siblings - Tom, Ken, Brian and Tracy. All the years of playing together helped make our stories.

My children - You are the four chambers of my heart.

My husband - who always encourages and has supported every journey.

My parents - who shaped me in ways they could never imagine.

My in laws - who taught me that even we can fix anything except death but even death can't divide us.

CUT SCENES
OLIVIA'S CANCELED DEAL

As Nigel said, New Orleans was a sexy town. Not because it was full of sex or bad behavior, but because it had fun and flair. New Orleans had zest for life, and that was what made it so captivating.

Mardi Gras put them on the map when fans from around the world watched the creative antics with both admiration and amusement. The streets were a mix of traditional conservatism and wild abandon. Some streets were quiet and some were just off the hook.

Marie lived and worked where it was off the hook. There were a plethora of activities, and everyone seemed to have something to laugh at. Her cafe's silent motto was, 'Eat, drink and be merry,' since one never knew what might happen the following day. Marie prided herself on being a good hostess and reveled in the attention, not to mention the money that came with it.

The music from the jazz band filled her heart with joy. It transported her mind to another place. Whenever she had a few moments of peace, she'd take her cappuccino and savor every sip, eyes closed, and let the melody take her away.

As her eyes opened, Marie noticed a petite, blonde woman walking in her direction. The stranger wore a tiny bun and moved gracefully. When they made eye contact, the smaller woman walked faster as if she was been beckoned. They both stared intently at each other, but neither of them showed any sign of friendliness. It didn't sway the little blonde from closing in on her.

Marie breathed in deeply and settled onto an unoccupied chair. When the tiny girl drew near, she waved lazy fingers to indicate to the empty seat across from her.

Instead, Olivia held out her hand to shake, only for it to be ignored. "Hello there. I'm Olivia. I'm looking for Marie."

"Come here acting like you selling Girl Scouts cookies?" Marie laughed and enjoyed the surprise she saw flicker over Olivia's gaze. Marie'slaugh echoed with another underlying voice, the two overlapping each other. Eyes narrowing to slits, Marie grinned when the girl withdrew her hand in silence.

"What you want, chile?"

"Are you Marie?" The girl asked and stared at Marie with wide, fragile eyes that didn't mask distinct egotism beneath. Although her lips trembled ever so slightly as she spoke, the girl's words were confident.

She was a predator in sheep's clothing, and Marie knew it. There was no fooling her. She was the master of this art after all. Marie curled her lips in a sneer and lifted her cup in salute; she wouldn't let this charade go any further.

"Don't do that? Don't you pretend you're not as wicked as I am." Marie cocked her head in a mock challenge. "Yeah, I see that scar you got. It's right pretty on you." She took a long sip of her cappuccino before setting it down with a clink. She leaned forward, her expression fierce. "Now, don't be rude. Tell me what another one of you cornbread children want with me!"

Olivia raised her eyebrows and drew in a sharp breath. She crossed her arms. "I think it's quite clear who's being rude here." Her voice was honey sweet, but her eyes flashed with anger. A saccharine smile twisted her lips, and she added, "Rest assured that I'll be giving a review of your establishment. Isn't the atmosphere here just fantastic?"

Marie wasn't daunted. "You haven't said what you want. You've found me. Now, spit it out."

Olivia sat down. "I want to be like you!"

Marie's throaty laughter echoed off the walls, followed by a deeper voice, which synced with her own. Slamming her hand down hard on the table, she felt a wave of satisfaction when Olivia jumped in her seat.

A sly smile tugged at Marie's mouth as she leaned over and sneered in the young woman's face. "There's only one Marie, chile!"

Olivia's cheeks flushed through various shades of pink and white. Marie settled down into her seat and gave a chuckle. "Your face... it's like a mood ring... always changing!"

"What I mean to say is, I would like you to train me. I want to learn your magic." Olivia leaned in conspiratorially. "I want you to renegotiate the deal for me. I want to be like you with the deal maker."

Marie stilled. She stared at the woman who treated Marie as if they were BFFs. She blinked, and then she laughed so hard spit flew in a wide arc.

"You gotta be born with this magic, girl!" Marie said pointedly but quietly. "What makes you think you can get me to go against your deal?" She watched Olivia take a napkin to wipe away the sweat that ran down her own face and when the other woman stayed silent, Marie added, "Papa? You think Papa can help?"

"He might." Olivia said quietly, "I thought you could ask

him." She turned up the corners of her mouth and sent a dazzling smile at Marie as if on pure reflex. "We're alike!"

Marie let out a high-pitched cackle. as she wiped tears of amusement from her eyes. "Oh, I see that!" Marie said between breaths, lifting her chin in a pointing gesture. "I thought I was looking in a mirror when I saw you." She twisted her lips in contempt, drawing her chestnut brows together. "We ain't nothing alike!" She brought her face within inches of the blonde's.

"I mean in spirit," Olivia said quietly.

"Sure," Marie mocked her tone. "I can show you how to talk to them. That's all I can do."

"Yes!" Olivia exclaimed quickly. "I mean, please."

Marie rose from her seat. Grim determination burned inside her when she motioned for Olivia to follow. She weaved her way through the tables of customers who sat sipping cappuccinos or typing on laptops. When they came to a windowed door that read "Employees Only" in bold black lettering, Marie slid open the door and ushered Olivia into the back of the cafe.

The air was filled with a buzz of activity. The kitchen was full of people working with quick precision across various stations. Saucepans clanged as one stirred vigorously and, nearby, knives whisked away scraps from cutting boards.

Marie ignored it all and led Olivia to a beaded curtain that hung from the frame of a doorway. The colored glass clinked as she stepped through and the sound of tiny bells rang out from the end of each strand.

Olivia rushed after Marie who noticed how the other woman skirted the mayhem in the kitchen and glided through the beaded curtain without rustling it. Not a single strand managed to touch her lithe body. Marie became conscious of Olivia's superhuman speed and agility, and spun around.

"You something special? Papa might like that..." Marie cackled as she led her past the kitchen and into their personal space of their home.

Olivia paused and took in the floral wallpaper and ornate café curtains, before slowly making her way past an overstuffed couch, upholstered in paisley print. As she approached the hallway door, Marie could see a younger version of herself reflected standing in the doorway, wearing familiar pink slippers. With a satisfied grin, Marie continued on her way. "I'm taking her to the wine cellar. I won't be long."

The woman across from her shifted in her seat and a barely perceptible arch formed between her eyes. Her lips pursed as she looked away, refusing to meet the other woman's gaze. An uncomfortable silence stretched on, heavy with the unspoken truth that seemed to hover just beneath the surface.

Olivia's lips were pressed together so tightly they formed a tiny white line. Her eyes darted around the room. She stood up straight, her chin lifted in determination, but her jaw was clenched tight to keep her fear at bay. Taking a deep breath, she stepped forward

Marie glided down the stairs, her hips swaying in a mesmerizing rhythm. As she descended, Oliviat gazed upon her beauty with admiration, taking note of how each step gracefully curved to match her curves and how her bemused smile lit up every corner of the foyer. She watched Marie's every move as if transfixed, admiring the way she carried herself with such elegant confidence.

Marie and Olivia stepped cautiously through the doorway into the cool, damp cellar. A few steps in and the darkness enveloped them, only broken by the shimmer of moonlight refracted from the thick glass of wine bottles stacked on shelves with uneven lengths of wood. Marie shuffled to a small bench near the entrance, her feet dragging on the earthen floor. She exhaled heavily, her breath curling in the air as she spoke in a low voice.

"To call papa you have to offer him something just to get his attention.I can provide something suitable but you have to pay me first/up front." She planted her hand firmly on her hip, waiting expectantly for an answer.

Olivia nodded. "How much?"

"Five thousand dollars. In cash. Now." She towered over Olivia, her shoulders stiff and her lips curled in contempt. Her nostrils flared as she tried to intimidate the much shorter woman with her height advantage.

"Okay," Olivia nodded quickly and made quick movements to grab the backpack from off the floor.

"You always carry that much cash?"

"I knew it would cost a lot so I brought a lot."

"How much you bring? Maybe I can sweeten the deal for you to get him here faster." Marie cooed.

"15." Olivia was lying and Marie knew it a mile away.

Marie retrieved a knotted, wooden cane that had been leaning in the corner. She lumbered to the center of the room and drove the end of the cane into the dirt, creating a perfect circle around her feet. "Sit here," she said through gritted teeth, her mouth barely curling into a thin smile as Olivia quickly followed orders.

Marie watched as Olivia lowered herself onto the packed dirt floor, her spine looked stiff at the cold, grainy touch of the earth. She shifted her legs under her, trying to find a comfortable position, but the ground seemed to press up against her with malicious intent. The scent of dust and decay hung heavily in the air .

Marie gingerly lifted the bottle from its perch on a high shelf, its age-worn glass encasing mysterious amber liquid. She cradled it carefully with both hands as if it were a fragile gem, and a few beams of light danced off the glass's green tint. A faint whiskey aroma greeted her as she set it down on the table.

"Do I drink this?" Olivia's hand trembled as she hovered it over the dusty bottle of wine, its label faded. Before her fingers could wrap around the neck of the bottle, Marie's sharp voice broke through the air. "You don't touch that! That's Papa's!" She hissed, her eyes narrowed and her lips pursed in a tight line. Olivia quickly drew back, shrinking away and pressing her back straight until she had perfect posture. "You shut up and stay still."

Marie glided over, carrying a silver tray with a long wooden pipe and pouch of tobacco resting on top. She lowered the tray next to Olivia, then sank to her knees as soft chanting spilled from her lips. Olivia closed her eyes and smiled, until the faint sound of breathing could be heard. Olivia's eyes opened so suddenly, Marie seemed to stifle a chuckle.

"Marie..." came a gruff voice, low and muffled by a cacophony of voices around it. Marie peered over and saw a tall figure with his face illuminated by the dim light of the basement. His lips were tightly pursed into a scowl as he glowered at Olivia. Marie's body tensed as her breath hitched.

Marie saw the color drain from Olivia's face as she recognized the man standing in front of her. He had a wide-brimmed hat with jagged teeth and bones around the edge. The abhorrent sight was accompanied by the man's own array of yellowed, rotten teeth, visible through his curled lips. Even under the tattered clothing he wore, Marie felt a chill emanating from him. His underlying gruesomeness was incomparable to the other man whose flawless complexion and alluring eyes seemed to charm the Yanks into signing some kind of deal.

"Why you call me here?" He stepped around Olivia, and his

eyes widened when he spotted the bottle of whiskey on the mahogany desk. A satisfied smile curved his lips as he took in the pipe next to it, a masterpiece of fine Italian craftsmanship. His gaze shifted back to Olivia. "A rare vintage. This must be serious." He pouted slightly and raised an eyebrow at Marie. "I don't see any rum."

"Papa, do I need to want something to see that handsome face of yours? For me, I want the pleasure of your company," she ap[eared to feign innocence. "But this chile wants you for something else."

Papa's eyes rarely left Olivia, tracing the faded scar on her face with his gaze. His fingers tightened around the tumbler of whiskey, and he grunted as he took a seat. He poured some whiskey slowly, studying it almost tenderly before finally taking a long sip. The alcohol seemed to quell some of his emotion as he let out a satisfied sigh. He breathed out again, his voice barely more than a whisper: "She don't want me... she wants someone else." His finger shook slightly as he pointed at the scar.

"No, I want to make a deal!" Olivia's hands shook as she presented the tray of tobacco to him, along with the pipe. Her voice cracked as she spoke, her eyes pleading. "Can you take my deal and make me like Marie?"

He widened his eyes in disbelief and waved his hand towards Marie's scar. "You want me to go against...?" He snickered, cutting off the thought as he glanced up at Marie and then back down to Olivia. His lips curved into a cruel smirk. "You best be talking to him," he added, and glanced up at Marie, snickering. He pointed at Olivia. "This little Jolie here so you get your laughs, eh?" His tone was condescending and his gaze mocked her.

Olivia met his eyes. "Can't you buy my deal? So, can I deal with just you?"

He leaned back in his chair, a smirk playing on his lips. He slowly packed the tobacco into the bowl of the wooden pipe with a turn of his wrist, the smell of cherry and almonds drifting up from the table. "Do you know what he wants?" Papa lit it and watched as smoke curled above him.

Olivia shook her head as she watched him lean in with the pipe in his hand. She exhaled but seemed frightened.

Papa thrust forward, a grim flash of steel glinting off the mouthpiece of his pipe. Olivia staggered back, her hands groping at her throat as she tried to stem a rivulet of wetness cascading from her. Her eyes were wide with shock as she gasped for air, she looked as if she would scream but producing only strangled choking noises.

Papa slowly exhaled, his shoulders sinking as he leaned back in his chair. He brought the blood laden pipe between his lips, and with a few strikes of a match, lit dry tobacco. His brow furrowed as the smoke rolled from his mouth, a thick fog filling the space between them. "He wants to break your contract too," he said softly, each exhale of smoke carrying his disappointment.

Olivia's pale hand shot out pleadingly towards Marie, her fingers clawing at the air. But Marie gripped the sides of her long skirt and stepped back, her lips curled into a cruel smirk. "We are alike now aren't we? We both bleed red!" she spat as Olivia's knees buckled beneath her.

Marie and Papa both cackled as Olivia's struggles came to a violent end and in doing so she canceled her deal.

CUT SCENES
NICK AND JEAN (WITH A FEW EXTRAS)

Nick's Lament

Nick stood listening to the sound of the twilight as it fell over the beach front home. He exhaled a slow smoke ring and listened to the distant sound of the sea and a bird in the trees. It was so serene that he actually began to relax and leaned on the house.

He could hear muted conversation from within until it was nothing more than a lingering echo, and he knew his new friends had to be inside by now. He smiled at the idea of calling someone his friend again. It felt good to not feel alone and to care for somebody else. Nick closed his eyes thinking back to the events because it all happened so quickly.He didn't deny that he had long wanted to meet Jean, and Chris had made it possible. He grinned as he remembered meeting Nigel, and he had to admit he liked the snobbish Brit. Still he was curious about what Nigel really knew.

Nick opened his eyes when he noticed the birds had ceased making noise. The darkness struck him next and stamped out his cigarette. How strangely calm it was now that neither the breezes nor the waves could be heard. All he could hear were footsteps, so he turned to see whether it was Nigel or Chris who had come searching for him.

Instead, he saw Deacon's flaming eyes and his ominous chuckle. Deacon curled his lips over yellow teeth and moved within a breath of Nick. Deacon's stench immediately overpowered the nasty odor of Nick's cigarette – brimstone.

"Mon Cherie, why you all alone?" The tall, elegant figure drawled softly, allowing his breath to mix with Nick's. "I think you abandoned already, non?" Deacon made a tiny wave with his palm, causing smoke to trail behind his fingers like a vapor trail. The smoke weaved a cloud and revealed the three friends, but suddenly only Jean and Chris. Chris and Jean danced in the hazy crystal ball, and Chris drew Jean into a desirous kiss. Nick swatted at the smoke filled vision until it faded away.

Nick balled his fists at his sides and forced out a shallow breath. He raised his chin ever so slightly and said, "Good for the kid."

Deacon's laughter filled the air and his eyes narrowed into slits as he leaned in with a cocky grin. "Is that really how you feel?" he challenged.

Nick shrugged, not caring about much with the demon of a man this close. "What do you want? What do I need to do for you to leave me alone?"

"What I want?" Deacon chuckled, his eyes momentarily twinkling with amusement. But then his face quickly contorted, as if a predator was taking over and his features had been replaced by something sinister. His mouth hung open in an angry snarl, baring sharp teeth that glistened beneath the dim light like daggers. His hands clenched into fists and seemed to grow longer, knotty skin stretching from each knuckle like claws tipped with razor-sharp nails. "Your soul!"

Nick stood rooted to the spot, his body tense and his

breath heavy. The oppressive heat seemed to be pressing against him from all sides, leaving a sheen of sweat on his skin. He could feel Deacon's ice-cold eyes boring into him and he tried again to pull away, his feet like lead weights in the ground. When Deacon stepped closer and licked a drop of sweat from his forehead, Nick saw a forked tongue flick out from between his lips - sending chills of fear down his spine.

His gaze held Nick in a vice. "I love the taste of fear," he hissed in Nick's ear then pulled away. With a venomous grin that stretched the corners of his mouth into an evil sneer, he extended his arm towards Nick with fingernails sharpened to deadly points. He lunged for Nick, and with a power that felt greater than gravity and time itself, his fingers pierced through Nick's chest and wrenched out his heart. "Tell them, I always win," he sneered.

Nick attempted to move, flee, or scream, but he was paralyzed. He saw Deacon tear his heart from his body and bite it with fangs sinking in almost perversely. He swirled it around in his mouth, chewing loudly as blood trickled from his razor-sharp teeth and down his chin. Nick gasped loudly and the noise seemed to appease the demon-like man who stepped back. Nick could move but instead of running he dropped to his knees with his hands grasping his chest. He noticed no blood or mark to show Deacon had ever touched him but the ground was so cold that it seemed to freeze beneath his feet . A dark hand sprang up from the ice, grasping Nick, and he felt something grab him from behind. He couldn't tell how many hands held him and dragged him to the dark ice.

He heard repeated over and over, "I always win..." Deacon couldn't be seen but his voice floated on the air. It was then Nick heard a scream before everything went dark.

Nick & Jean at the cafe

Nick lit a cigarette and looked at Jean, "Nigel is crushing on Chris so he's gonna help us." Nigel stole a glance at Jean now that nobody else was around.

"Is Chris a man?" She asked quickly.

"No idea," he chuckled. "haven't had the guts to ask them. Since I met them they have helped me out. They brought me to their home and fed me. They offered to let me stay as long as I liked." He butted the ashes off his cig, "I'm not about to insult them by asking." He chuckled, "Besides, if they're a chick, they're not my type." His eyes locked onto Jean's and his lips curled into a knowing smile. He leaned in, willing her to come closer.

"You mean they're not big enough up top?" She groaned.

"Nah, I'm not that shallow. I dated flat chicks but it's the personality." He was clearly enjoying the banter but he was worried about what she thought of him. " I'm used to women that have more passion and fire in them."

Jean chuckled, "it's the breasts."

Nick's gaze fell to the conservative neckline of her dress, noting the distinct lack of cleavage. He moved closer, feeling a sense of challenge and excitement rise within him. It had been at least twenty years since he had pursued a woman, but he was confident in his charming ways from back in the 80s. He hoped they would still work on this lady who caught his interest.

Nick noticed Jean's pupils dilated as she looked up at him. He leaned in, his lips grazing her earlobe, causing a shiver to run down her spine. She inched closer, but Nick abruptly pulled away, leaving her wanting more.

"No, it's not," He leaned in close, his voice barely above a whisper but his grin wide and confident. Nick noticed her confusion, her eyebrows furrowed and lips slightly parted as she tried to understand his cryptic words. He couldn't help but recall how shy and timid she used to be. But now, in this moment, they both knew that they would have to put aside any past differences and work together for the greater good.

She cleared her throat, "you're saying I'm your type?"

"I didn't say that." He tinted red and shrugged the notion off, "I've seen you before Jean. I saw you at the circus in Baltimore."

"When I was still fat?"

He nodded, "yeah, your hair shined and you had really light eyes." He took a drag from his cig, "that was me being shallow. I couldn't talk to you then because ...." he reminisced. But then, he let out a long sigh, realizing that his shallow flirtations back then had paled in comparison to the depth of her poetic soul.

Jean's lips tightened, and she folded her arms tightly across her chest., "nobody was interested in the fat lady. Instead, I lived in dreams." she muttered bitterly. She shuddered a little lost in her thoughts. "But I convinced myself I was happy," she said with a hollow laugh, tears forming in her eyes.

Nick sat back with his cigarette and nodded. "Are you happy now?"

"I guess, but it's different. I have an active life and I'm not hidden away. I don't disgust people but I fit in."

Nick's jaw dropped, his eyebrows raised in surprise. "I never thought you were disgusting," he said with a hint of shock in his voice. "You looked bigger, but definitely not disgusting.

"Definitely not shallow," she groaned.

Nick took a big gulp of his steaming coffee, avoiding eye contact as he spoke. "Once we gather the rest, we need to have a solid plan in place," he said. His hands gripped his mug tightly, "I felt Nigel overpowered us and we weren't ready."

387

Jean nodded, "then we need to prove ourselves and do something people will take notice of?"

Nick flicked open his old lighter and brought the flame to the tip of his cigarette. He inhaled deeply, letting the smoke linger in his lungs before exhaling with a slow sigh, "that's a start."

"We could help at shelters or a soup kitchen."

"Nah, I hate to say it but Nigel was on track. We can't die so let's pretend to be heroes." He slumped back in his chair, avoiding Jean's piercing gaze. She remained silent, but he could feel her eyes on him, searching for something deeper than his casual nonchalance. Despite his efforts to appear unaffected, the tension between them was palpable. "Jean...." It was shattered too soon by their friends' return, breaking the spell that had briefly held them captive..

Jean's Nightmare

Jean slumbered so intensely that her subconscious was no match for the disturbing dreams that usually came with it. She was oblivious to the noise and chatter that surrounded her at first. But when everyone had gone and she was alone, Jean's sleep reached a new level of unconsciousness. That's when she saw Deacon. He paced around her in a void of darkness while his laugh reverberated through the emptiness.

"Think you figure this out?" He spun to meet her face. His intense gaze bore into her as she fought to control her emotions.

"It's just a dream." She kept her eyes shut, refusing to look at him.

His cackling laugh was resonating and shaking her to her very core.

"You're not real." She refused to accept what he was saying.

"Non?" He laughed but this time his laughter was accompanied by a chorus of other voices, chanting, "Then what are you?" He nicked her hand with the tip of his cane, and she stepped back with her eyes wide in shock. "Then what's that? You supposed to be dead fat lady!" His words stung until she felt her knees weaken. Once again, she felt the heaviness of her old body and she was surrounded by food.

"So, This your time to die, ma Cherie?" He taunted her, his deformed hand with razor-like nails inches from her face. "Want the life in the deal?" He sneered and leaned closer, his forked tongue flickering against her skin. She tried to move, but his weight kept her pinned down. She was held frozen by his body weight on her stomach. His features contorted with rage,, "Then keep your part!!"

Jean felt her throat constricting and gasped for breath, to no avail. All the while, Deacon's booming laughter filled the silence. She clasped her neck in desperation, begging for whatever air she could get.

"Jean!!!" Chris shouted, eyes wide as watched her gasp and clutch her throat. Nigel was now awake and on his feet. Nigel's bleary eyed gaze was unfocused as he watched. Before he could say anything, they heard running footsteps coming down the stairs. Nick was jumping the stairs two at a time to get down faster.

Nigel's plane ride

Nigel held his book close as he observed the sunset from his airplane window. Although the other passengers were quite chatty, he was lost in his own thoughts. Spending time with Chris or Nick would have been entertaining but instead, he was alone. Nigel had wanted to take a road trip, but the siblings were determined to travel quickly. He sighed, feeling anxious about the flight. All around him, twilight was settling in. Now, he sat in the plane seat buckled in and only staring at the twilight outside.

He yawned and tried to find a comfortable position when he noticed a flicker of light outside the plane. He blinked and squinted, wondering what it was. The sparkles were growing bigger, and he soon realized the wing was on fire. He leapt from his seat and shouted to the others, but they were too preoccupied to hear him. Finally, he screamed out "Get me off this bloody plane!" In mere moments, a loud explosion erupted and fire started to spread across the cabin. He could hear Chris and Taylor scream and Jean's soft whispering.

"I said give it back!" Taylor screamed when Chris snatched her phone back.

Nigel jolted awake and remembered that it was only a nightmare, yet his skin still felt stiflingly warm and he could have sworn he was smelling burnt flesh.

Taylor and Hunter

Taylor inched her way forward to Hunter as if she were approaching an injured animal, straining not to make a wrong move. When she finally reached him, she offered the wine glass with a hesitant smile and draped the blanket over his legs before seating herself beside him. "I'm here for you, whatever you need," she told Hunter softly.

"Are you old enough for wine?" His light brown eyes met hers and he held back a smirk.

She took another sip from her glass and adjusted the blanket. With her face only inches away from his own. "I'm over 21." She pointed out with another sip but it was clear she was hiding a smile. She was attracted to Hunter and she wasn't shy about it. "You don't have to be alone..." She trailed off as she tried to close the gap between their lips.

Hunter pulled away and looked down at his glass with a smile. "I can't." He looked out to the birds on the lake. He glanced back at her with a meaningful gaze. "It's not that I'm not attracted to you - because I am - but I'm too old for you," Hunter sighed heavily. "As much as I'd like to...I just can't."

"How old were you when you made the deal?"

"21." He put his glass to his lips and let the liquid swirl around before taking a drink.

"So, you're like stuck at 21 forever?" She shrugged, "I'm 22."

He took another sip and gave her a sad grin, "It's been two decades since I was 21. Can you imagine buying something with your ID when you're 50 or older?" His head shook slightly.

Taylor nodded and gulped down some wine, "I dunno" she smiled at him, "women mature faster than men right?" She found his empty hand and locked fingers with his.

He shook his head, chuckling. Taylor's mission to cheer him up worked but he looked to the water knowing it couldn't be.

A Love of a Lifetime

Jean trailed Nick to a space she hadn't realized existed. It was more spacious than the area Hunter stayed in, but not quite as big as Taylor's room.

Nick immediately went to the bed and located an aged backpack. The bag was so tattered it appeared almost like a well-traveled suitcase, yet Nick handled it as if it were just another object. He upended it on the bed and started rummaging through its articles in a rush.

Jean saw a photo drift onto the ground, and when she got

close enough to recognize it, her heart sank. It was an old picture of herself, taken during her time at the circus. The image was bent until it appeared distorted, but there she was —smiling and looking content in a way she hadn't felt in years. She bore no resemblance to who she had been then.

Nick shifted uncomfortably and uttered, "I took that pic years ago." He moved closer to her and pointed to her face in the photo. "Your eyes captivated me. They always have."

Jean studied the portrait and then glanced at him, speechless. She extended the picture towards him in a feeble gesture.

Nick let out a heavy sigh. "I wasn't stalking you..."

She shook her head wearily, as if trying to shake away a fog, "I know..."

Nick held up a lighter that shone golden with his initials imprinted on it. "I thought I had this with me." He mumbled and put the cig in his mouth but did not lit yet. He tucked the lighter away and kept the cig between his teeth without lighting it.

Jean's arms crossed her chest as she spoke. "So it's all true about ...before the deal...you..." She stumbled over her words, trying to express what she was feeling.

Nick glanced up from collecting his items on the bed. He stared at her with a confused look and his clueless face searched hers slowly. "You didn't believe me?" As he rose to his feet and held the photograph, he then flipped it over in his hand. "I've carried this since the 80's."

Jean kept her head bowed as she nodded, still looking at the picture in Nick's hands. "I had no idea," she murmured quietly. She held the photograph and wondered what could have been if Nick had approached her during that time. Would she have responded to him positively? They both might have wasted years instead of spending them together. She felt the air catch in her lungs as Nick's words settled in her mind and she began to realize that he had loved her all along. Her eyes welled with tears, her heart pounding in her chest.erienced true love and now she knew it had been following her around since the 80's. She lost her breath overwhelmed with the notion.

Nick heaved a sigh and then took her hand. With gentle pressure, he drew her closer. "I told you the truth," he said softly. Tilting her chin until she met his gaze, Nick looked over as her eyes were glistening with unshed tears. She touched his heart and when he brushed his thumb over her cheek the droplets slowly cascaded over his fingertips.

He inhaled deeply as he said, "I've been in love with you for a long time, Jean." Without another second's thought, Jean seemed to surrender as they met in a soft and tender kiss, both giving themselves over to the moment.

ABOUT THE AUTHOR

Pamela has been cultivating her skills in writing and drawing since she was able to grasp a pencil. Born in Massachusetts, she then relocated to the Baltimore/DC area when she was four years old. Her family is highly supportive of her interests and passions, being involved in theatre, art, writing, and wildlife conservation. Together, they live in a quaint town in Maryland where they dedicate their time to rescuing cats and helping local animal rescue foundations.

Mary Stewart, Tolkien, Poe, Laura Ingalls Wilder and Shakespeare - all the literary greats had her enamored with reading from a young age. She and her siblings would spend hours immersed in bookstores, reading each books. It came as no surprise when she began writing her own short stories as early as elementary school. Her talent for storytelling was further confirmed when one of her enemies admitted to being addicted to her work and wanted to know what she'd write next

Writing page turning stories has always come naturally and she tuned her skill through college and writing with other authors.

Currently featured to write with the extraordinary talents such as Astrid V.J. with the *Children of War* Anthology for charity.

She is currently spearheading a project to support the victims of unprovoked attacks on schools.

Her highly-anticipated novel contains an extremely diverse

crew of characters all faced with the same quandary. Its release is set for this summer, and you can read a summary on her social media accounts.

She gives special thanks to both her husband and late parents.

If you can dream it, you can do it.

You can follow Pam's work here:
TikTok

Printed in Great Britain
by Amazon